PRAISE FOR REN

"Move over, Inspectors Alleyn, Dalgliesh, and Morse, and make room for John Madden in the pantheon of great, civilized English sleuths." —*The New Yorker*

"Madden is seamlessly admirable. . . . In an era when our real-life heroes tend to have feet of thick, grubby clay, it can be bracing to spend time with a man who is naturally but not implausibly noble." —*The Washington Post Book World*

"One of the best mysteries in years." —*The Boston Globe*

"Airth writes with arresting authority and compassion . . . a major talent." —*Chicago Tribune*

"It's the tactics and the terrain, the morale and the characters that make the difference between an average thriller and one as good as this." —*The New York Times Book Review*

"Up there with the works of P. D. James and Ruth Rendell. High praise indeed." —*The Cleveland Plain Dealer*

"I have been a huge fan of Rennie Airth's novels featuring John Madden since first reading *River of Darkness*. . . . Airth is at the top of his game."

—Jacqueline Winspear, author of the Maisie Dobbs series

A PENGUIN MYSTERY

THE DECENT INN OF DEATH

RENNIE AIRTH was born in South Africa and worked as a foreign correspondent for Reuters news service for many years. The first novel in his John Madden mystery series, *River of Darkness*, won the Grand Prix de Littérature Policière for best international crime novel of 2000 and was nominated for Edgar, Anthony, and Macavity awards.

THE JOHN MADDEN MYSTERY SERIES

RENNIE AIRTH

THE DECENT INN OF DEATH

PENGUIN BOOKS

PENGUIN BOOKS
An imprint of Penguin Random House LLC
penguinrandomhouse.com

LIBRARY OF CONGRESS CATALOGING-IN-PUBLICATION DATA
Names: Airth, Rennie, 1935– author.
Title: The decent inn of death / Rennie Airth.
Description: New York: Penguin Books, [2020]
Identifiers: LCCN 2019013183 (print) | LCCN 2019015245 (ebook) |
ISBN 9780525506065 (ebook) | ISBN 9780143134299 (paperback)
Subjects: LCSH: Murder—Investigation—Fiction. | GSAFD: Mystery fiction.
Classification: LCC PR9369.3.A47 (ebook) |
LCC PR9369.3.A47 D44 2020 (print) | DDC 823/.914—dc23
LC record available at https://lccn.loc.gov/2019013183

Printed in the United States of America
3   5   7   9   10   8   6   4   2

Set in Stempel Garamond
Designed by Gretchen Achilles

My friends we will not come again or ape an ancient rage,
Or stretch the folly of our youth to be the shame of age,
But walk with clearer eyes and ears this path that wandereth
And see undrugged in evening light the decent inn of death.

G. K. CHESTERTON

THE
DECENT INN
OF DEATH

PROLOGUE

'O God, our help in ages past,
our hope for years to come.'

Luckily the choir was in good voice that morning. The hymns chosen were among their favourites and with the lusty support of the congregation they were drowning out the small mistakes that Greta Hartmann made as her fingers stumbled over the organ keys.

'Our shelter from the stormy blast
and our eternal home.'

She played in a daze, the same thought running through her head over and over, the self-same words. *It can't be him.* Yet she knew she was not mistaken. Although he had aged—the hair, once so thick and lustrous, was thinner now—his face was not one she would forget. Their eyes had met outside for a moment, and she had frozen on the spot, unable to move. Luckily he had given no sign of having recognized her. At that moment he had yawned, and then looked down to say something to the boy who was crouched in front of him. But was his reaction, or lack of one, genuine? She couldn't be sure. The appearance he had always presented to the world made it difficult to guess what his true feelings were, or indeed if he had any. It was his glance that she remembered best. Although at pains to make himself agreeable, there had been moments in the past, most memorably when he believed himself to be unobserved, when his gaze had changed, turning flat and cold, as though there was something quite different going on inside his head.

But what was he doing *here*, in this country of all places?

*'Time like an ever-rolling stream
bears all its sons away . . .'*

Time indeed . . . so many years had passed since that night, so many had died. Why not him?

But who would listen to her after all this time . . . after all the dead? Even then the police had had their doubts. She had not struck them as a reliable witness. An overexcited woman, one under great stress furthermore—she had seen it in their faces.

Who would believe her now?

Still, she could not ignore the brief glimpse she had just had of him. She could not turn away, pass by on the other side. What would Manfred say? She smiled for a moment as the image of her husband's face, dead these past twelve years, broke like a beam of light through the clouds of doubt that beset her. What would he think?

But although she prayed for Manfred's immortal soul every night on her knees beside her bed, she must look for other help now, other advice.

*'Be thou our God while life shall last
and our eternal home.'*

At last the service was over, or nearly so.

'The grace of our Lord Jesus Christ, and the love of God, and the fellowship of the Holy Ghost, be with us all evermore. Amen.'

The closing prayer was one that Greta usually murmured to herself along with the vicar, Father Beale, as he intoned the well-loved words. But that morning she could barely control her impatience as she played the organ voluntary that always followed the end of a service, glancing over her shoulder to watch as the congregation made their slow way out of the church, waiting only until the last of them had disappeared through the arched doorway before bringing the recital to a swift end. Switching off the organ she hurried to the vestry, where she paused only to shed her white surplice and don her coat and gloves before slipping out through the side door. The gravelled path outside led around the church to the front where Father Beale would be chatting with members of his flock. Not wishing to delay her departure, Greta picked her way through the gravestones to a gate in the low stone wall surrounding the churchyard which led to a path outside that took her down to the road. There she paused.

To her left she could see the village pub—it was called the Horse and Hounds—and the forecourt, which was empty. Opening time was still an hour or so off. Nevertheless, she hesitated a moment longer to scan the small paved patio at the side of the pub where wooden tables lined with benches, much favoured by the patrons in summer, but little used at this time of year, stood. She was relieved to find that it too was deserted and for the first time she began to breathe more easily.

Now her problem was of a different order. Earlier she had

dreaded coming face-to-face with him. He must know what she had told the police all those years ago. He would not have forgotten. But since he had disappeared so quickly, what was there left that she could do? Who could she warn? She knew he was dangerous—she had always known it, even if she had kept silent—but now any story she had to tell would seem even less believable than it had in the past.

Who? What man? Where is he?

She could imagine the questions that would be fired at her like so many bullets, questions to which she had no good answers. He had appeared suddenly like a ghost from her past and vanished just as quickly. In the end it might be best if she simply held her tongue. There was a saying for it in English which she had heard others use: let the dead bury the dead.

But something in her rebelled against the thought and as she hurried to cross the road she resolved, at the very least, to relate the whole story to Vera, who was certain to come up with a good, sensible solution to her dilemma. Dear Vera: it was she who at the outbreak of war, when the mere fact of being German had made Greta an object of suspicion and dislike in the village, had boldly and publicly stepped forward to invite her to move in with her and share her home; she who had dared anyone to challenge her decision. Although Greta had opened her heart to her new friend and spoken freely about her life, this one thing she had kept to herself, mainly because it would have been so hard for anyone to believe; but also because it was something she had wanted to forget.

The path she was following skirted the pub and after passing an apple orchard entered a small wood on the other side of which was a row of cottages, one of which belonged to Vera Cruickshank. Although there was no rush now, no need to hurry, Greta continued to walk quickly, looking forward to the thought of the fire her friend would have lit in the sitting-room and to the cup of tea that undoubtedly awaited her. Once they had sat down together she would finally unburden herself; she would tell Vera all.

Busy enough during the week, the path was deserted that morning, it being a Sunday, and in the silence of the wood Greta could hear the dead leaves that covered the path rustling beneath her feet. Ahead of her was a stream that could be crossed via a set of stepping-stones. Something of a hazard in wet weather, when the water often rose to the height of the stones and even lapped over them, they presented no obstacle now apart from one small anomaly well known to all who used the crossing. One of the stones—the third from the direction in which Greta was coming—wasn't altogether steady on its base. It had a tendency to rock if you put any weight on it, and was best avoided, which was easy enough.

'Provided you know it's there,' Vera had pointed out in her sensible way. 'Someone ought to put it right—reset the stone—but who? I should have thought one of the farmers around here would have gone to the trouble. Their workers come this way often enough on their way to the pub. Mark my words, one of these days someone's going to forget about that stone—or else come back from the pub tiddly—and take a purler.'

Tiddly? Purler? Greta had needed to have the meaning of the two words explained to her and then happily tucked them away in her memory for possible future use.

No such danger threatened her. She had come this way so many times she could have crossed the stream blindfolded. But still, being cautious by nature, she kept her eyes down and having taken two careful steps skipped lightly over the third stone onto the one beyond it.

Only then did she look up.

I

'ARE YOU SURE, ANGUS?'

'Quite sure, thank you.'

'You haven't forgotten anything?'

Angus Sinclair considered the question with furrowed brow.

'If I had, I probably wouldn't remember it, would I?' He stole a sideways glance at his companion.

Lucy Madden frowned. The raw December day had been sharpened by a cold wind that had got up overnight and she was showing a pair of cheeks that must be as red as his own.

'You're being defensive now,' she said finally, 'but there's really no need. We all get forgetful as we grow older. You mustn't think you're to blame; it's your hippocampus that's at fault.'

'I beg your pardon.'

'I was reading about it only the other day, in the *Encyclopaedia Britannica*, as a matter of fact.'

'Am I to take it that's your bedtime reading?'

The chief inspector—for so he was still called by many despite having long since retired from his job at Scotland Yard—was enjoying the moment. They were walking arm in arm along the path beside the stream that led to the Maddens' house, Lucy having come down to his cottage to 'collect him', as she put it, making him feel for a moment like a parcel, albeit a well-contented one. Pleasures were hard enough to come by at his age, he reflected, and there were few to compare with the satisfaction of being fussed over by a lovely young woman, one moreover whom he had known since childhood and had a deep affection for.

'Now you're being facetious,' she accused him.

'Not at all. Tell me about this hippocampus.'

'It's a neural structure shaped like a seahorse located in the medial temporal lobe of your brain, and its job is, or was, to process short-term memories and then dispatch them to the appropriate part of your cerebrum where they wait ready to be summoned up.' Lucy spoke like a child reciting her homework. 'Unfortunately, as we get older it tends to atrophy and stops doing its job. Hence your ability to recall something that happened twenty years ago as though it were yesterday, but not something that might or might not have happened this morning, like forgetting to bring your pills, for example. That's what I'm here for,' she added kindly. 'Just think of me as your hippocampus.'

They had reached a stone bridge that spanned the stream and Sinclair paused in the middle of it to gaze down at the running water below. Lucy eyed him.

'You're trying to think up a suitable riposte, aren't you?'

'I was just picturing tomorrow's headline in the *Daily Mirror*.' He mused. '*Hippocampus found strangled in stream. Police at a loss.*'

'That's very unkind.' She giggled. 'And not at all appreciative. You haven't answered my question.'

'What question might that be? It seems to have slipped my mind.'

'Have you remembered to bring your pills?'

By way of an answer Sinclair reached into his coat pocket

and with a flourish fished out a small bottle filled with white tablets.

'I'm sorry.' She was contrite. 'But Mummy said I was to make sure you didn't go off anywhere without them.'

Lucy's mother, Helen Madden, was the village doctor and, since Angus Sinclair's decision on his retirement from the Metropolitan Police at the end of the war to make his home in Highfield, his physician as well.

'And to remind you that you had to take one in the morning and one in the evening . . .'

'. . . and at any other time of the day if I happen to feel dizzy or breathless. Thank you, my dear. I haven't forgotten that.'

The chief inspector was not unaware of the worry that lurked behind his companion's lighthearted tone. He realized that Lucy's mother had probably revealed her own concern for his health before going off on holiday. She had made no secret of it to him.

'It's your blood pressure, Angus,' Helen had told him at their last meeting. 'It's starting to worry me. Not enough blood is reaching your heart. It's caused by a hardening of the arteries and since that's a symptom of age it's not a problem that will go away. These tablets I've given you will help, they'll thin your blood, but you must promise to take them as prescribed. If not, you may start to feel a shortness of breath and very possibly a pain in your chest that could spread to your arms and neck, and then you must take a pill at once and rest for at least ten minutes. Otherwise . . .'

'. . . otherwise I shall probably keel over on the spot.' He had smiled. 'There! I've said it for you.'

They had known each other for the better part of thirty years and Sinclair was perfectly prepared to admit—to himself if to no one else—that his feelings for her went well beyond friendship. They were best described by the French word *tendresse*, a deep if unexpressed emotion that had grown to embrace her daughter, whose resemblance to her mother, not only in looks, but in word and gesture, was so marked that there were times when he felt he had been transported back decades to the day when he first cast eyes on the young woman who was to become the wife of his friend and then colleague, John Madden.

'You're looking very thoughtful,' Lucy observed.

They had entered the garden by way of a wooden gate and having passed through the orchard, now bare of both fruit and foliage, reached the long lawn that led up to the half-timbered house where the Maddens lived.

'I was wondering if you'd heard from your parents,' Sinclair said.

'I had a letter from Mummy two days ago. She said Venice was enchanting.'

The Maddens had departed for Italy three weeks earlier to stay with an old school friend of Helen's who had married a Venetian nobleman of all things and lived in a palazzo on the Grand Canal.

'He's a count,' Helen had explained before their departure. 'That sounds very grand, I know, but according to Angela they're ten a penny in Italy. But he does have a palazzo, so John and I are looking forward to a taste of the high life.'

'They had just been to a ball the night before in some other palazzo,' Lucy revealed now. 'Mummy said it was lovely, but rather cold, so she danced all night to keep warm.'

'But not with your father, I imagine.'

They shared a conspiratorial chuckle. Madden's rare

forays onto the dance floor were a source of mirth to his family and friends.

'They'll be back on Wednesday. They're coming straight home from the station, so you'll see them before I do.'

Lucy lived in London and by all accounts (mainly her brother Rob's, who shared a flat with her) enjoyed a social life that would long since have left most other mortals, himself included, prostrate. A rising star in the salon of a well-known dress designer, she had recently been named head of a department, though Sinclair didn't know which since Lucy had made nothing of her promotion, being possessed of that peculiarly English vice—in the chief inspector's stern Scottish eyes at least—of never wanting to appear to be trying too hard. Knowing how busy her days were, he was all the more touched that she should have found the time to come down to Highfield to see how he was managing.

'You will be back on Monday, won't you?' she asked anxiously.

'That's certainly my intention.'

'I'm not sure Mummy would have approved of you dashing off like this.'

'Dashing off?'

'It seems to have been very much a last-minute invitation. I do think Sir Wilfred might have been more considerate.'

'I don't know what you mean. The explanation's really quite simple. They've got a guest staying with them who wants to meet me. But she only revealed that after she arrived. She's apparently a well-known neurologist called Ann Waites who has also practised as a psychiatrist and has a particular interest in criminal psychopaths.'

'And you couldn't resist the temptation, of course,' Lucy scoffed.

'Why ever should I?' Sinclair refused to rise to the bait. 'Anyway, Sir Wilfred decided to ring me on the off-chance that I could come over.'

'I just hope he realizes you're not to exert yourself.'

'Now, Lucy, that's enough.' The chief inspector stopped in his tracks. 'I'm not an invalid. And if it comes to that, Bennett is no spring chicken himself. As like as not we'll probably spend most of the weekend sitting by the fire mulling over old times.'

'Old crimes, you mean.' Lucy Madden's smile was the mirror image of her mother's. 'Actually, it's a pity Daddy won't be there too. The three of you always have a wonderful time when you get together, raking up the past.'

Formerly an assistant commissioner at Scotland Yard, the man they were speaking of, Sir Wilfred Bennett, had been in overall charge of the CID when Sinclair and Madden had worked together as detectives. Retired for some years now, he had settled in the neighbouring county of Hampshire, but the three of them had kept in touch and Bennett and his wife had visited Highfield more than once as guests of the Maddens.

'I'm not sure your father enjoys it that much.' Sinclair was judicious. 'One of the things you have to learn as a detective is how to distance yourself from violent crime, particularly murder. You mustn't let it get to you, as the Americans say. Your father never quite managed that, even though he was so good at the job. It affected him.'

'Is that why he gave up being a detective?'

'Partly.' The chief inspector caught her eye. 'Though I suspect meeting your mother had more than a little to do with it.'

They shared a knowing smile.

'Then again, John always wanted to live in the country and work the land. He grew up on a farm . . . but you know that.'

They had climbed the steps from the lawn up to the terrace and Lucy led the way around the house to the garage, where her mother's Morris Minor was parked. In a matter of minutes she had settled Sinclair in the passenger seat and stowed his light suitcase, which she had insisted on carrying, on the backseat behind them.

'I won't be here when you get back,' she warned him as they started down the drive. 'I have to be at work on Monday. But Will has promised to be at the station to meet you.' She meant the Highfield bobby, Will Stackpole, an old friend of Sinclair's. 'He'll see you safely back to your cottage.'

'In case I can't remember the way?'

'Now stop that, Angus,' she scolded.

He studied her profile.

'I know I've mentioned it before,' he said, 'but you really ought to get married. It will give you someone else to badger.'

'That's what Rob says. Mind you, he just wants the flat for himself. But I've told him I'm not ready yet to dwindle into a wife. In fact, I may never be.'

'Dwindle . . .' Sinclair savoured the word.

'The trouble is I can't see myself tied to any one man.' She sighed. 'The shine wears off so quickly. What I'd really like is to be one of those sultans who had scores of wives and kept them in a harem. I could probably manage with four or five—husbands, I mean. It would be so nice to be able to say, I'll have you today . . . No, not you . . . *you*.'

'You're joking of course?'

'Am I?' She sent a sly glance his way.

The chief inspector shook his head in despair.

'Somewhere there's a young man who even as we speak is all unknowing and I can't help pitying him. He's got absolutely no idea of what's lying in wait for him.'

'You and Rob should compare notes. He says if I ever acquire an actual fiancé he'll advise him to flee the country at once.'

She had slowed the car as they entered the village and she turned to look at him.

'You were married years ago, Angus. It's sad your wife died so young. But I can't help noticing that you never took the plunge again.'

'True enough,' Sinclair admitted. He had been a widower for the better part of twenty years.

'So tell me honestly: what's your opinion of marriage—as an institution, I mean?'

'Why, I believe it's an honourable estate, just as the Book of Common Prayer says.'

'That's hardly an answer.'

'And not one to be taken in hand wantonly to satisfy carnal lusts and appetites, nor lightly as you seem to be doing, but reverently and soberly in the fear of God.'

'Thank you. I should have known better than to ask.'

Lucy spun the steering wheel and came to a halt in front of the station entrance. She turned to him.

'Dear Angus, please take care.' She spoke in a different voice. 'Don't overdo things, and don't forget your pills. Do as Mummy says, please.'

'But of course.' He was caught off guard by the sudden change in her manner.

'I never knew my grandparents, you see.' She took hold of his hands. 'They died before I was born. I've only got you.'

'Meaning . . . what? That I'm better than nothing?' He tried to keep up the teasing tone.

'No . . . better than anything.'

She kissed him on the cheek and then hugged him for a long moment.

'My dear child . . .' He was overcome in spite of himself. 'I'm only going away for the weekend, and only as far as Hampshire.'

2

'ANN'S A COUSIN OF MARGARET'S,' Sir Wilfred said. 'A distant cousin; we don't see much of her. She lives in Oxford. In fact, she's attached to one of the women's colleges— Somerville, I believe. She's part of the medical faculty and lectures on neurology. But she was a practicing psychiatrist at some stage earlier in her career and she's writing a book about psychopaths.'

He paused to negotiate the narrow lane they were driving along, which was partly occupied by a slow-moving tractor. The Bennetts lived a few miles outside Winchester in a village called Fernley and Sir Wilfred had driven into the city to collect Sinclair at the station.

'You won't meet her till later,' he said. 'Margaret's taken her to Stockbridge to spend the day with a friend of theirs. I do hope you don't mind being dragged over here at such short notice. I'm afraid it's my fault.'

'How so?'

Despite the impromptu nature of his visit, the chief inspector was already enjoying the sense of liberation it gave him. In truth his life had become somewhat constricted of late. Repeated attacks of gout, mercifully in abeyance at present, had kept him chained to his cottage for long periods and now this new problem with his blood pressure had put a further cramp on his movements. He was looking forward to the change of scenery—and company—that the next few days would offer.

'I'm afraid I dropped your name, and Ann pounced on it at once.'

Sir Wilfred shot a guilt-ridden glance at his passenger. A year or two younger than Sinclair—and now quite bald and starting to put on weight—he had not aged particularly well, or so the chief inspector thought. The sharp and at times challenging intelligence that he remembered from their years together at the Yard seemed to have dissolved with passing time and been replaced by a hesitancy that tended to show itself in the worried expression that Bennett habitually wore now. He looked like a man who knew there was something he ought to be doing, but wasn't sure what that was. *Does he see me the same way?* Sinclair wondered. *Is this old age? Are we just a pair of old buffers dwelling on past glories?*

'Pounced, you say?'

'She was telling us about this book she's working on and asked me if I could offer her any insight into the minds of psychopaths. After all, I must have come across a good many of them during my time at the Yard, she said.' Bennett shook his head ruefully. 'I was obliged to tell her that she was barking up the wrong tree, that I had always worked at one remove from actual malefactors, psychopathic or otherwise. She ought to talk to the detectives who had dealt with those sorts of individuals, I said. "Now if Angus Sinclair was here," I began, and got no further. Your name was . . . I was going to say like catnip to her, but that doesn't sound quite right. But you get my drift.' He peered anxiously at his passenger.

'If I were her I'd try talking to the forensic psychologists the police use now.' The chief inspector mused. 'We didn't have the benefit of them in our day. In fact, we were lucky if we were even allowed to talk to a psychiatrist. There was a prejudice against them, if you remember. Trick-cyclists they were called then.'

'Be that as it may, it was your name that got her going, Angus. You forget it was often in the newspapers in your heyday. She knows who you are . . . or were.'

'Were . . .' Sinclair echoed the word with a growl. It hadn't occurred to him to think of himself in the past tense.

'I doubt they'll be back from Stockbridge before this evening. But you and Ann will have a chance to talk at dinner. There'll only be one other guest. Margaret's invited the vicar, Father Beale. The poor fellow's in low spirits at the moment and she thought he needed cheering up.'

'Has something happened to upset him?'

'He's lost his organist, a German lady called Greta Hartmann. She tripped and fell crossing a stream on some stepping-stones. Hit her head on a rock and ended up lying facedown in the water.'

'Do you mean she drowned?'

Sir Wilfred nodded. 'It was very sad. She was a wonderful organist. Harry Beale has been quite disconsolate, and to add to his woes the lady Mrs Hartmann shared a cottage with— she's called Vera Cruickshank—has taken to pestering him, and me, I might add, saying there was something fishy about her death and that we ought to take it up with the police.'

'How extraordinary!'

'I've tried to explain to her there was really nothing we could do.' Bennett wore a hunted look. 'I had a word with our village bobby. He's a sensible fellow, been with us for years. He heard about it very soon after it happened and went to the spot. Her body was still lying in the stream and there was a rock near her head with blood on it. He said it was obvious she had tripped and fallen. One of the stepping-stones is unstable.'

'So why did this friend . . . what was her name?'

'Miss Cruickshank.'

'Why did she think there was more to it than that?' The chief inspector's curiosity was piqued.

'She just kept saying it couldn't have happened that way.' Sir Wilfred shook his head unhappily. 'That Greta would never have been so careless. I tried to say that she must have lost her footing, that it could happen to anyone. But Vera wouldn't listen . . . ah, here we are.'

They had reached the outskirts of the village. Bennett drove slowly past the line of shops.

'You'll remember the church . . .' He pointed. 'We're rather proud of it. It dates back to Norman times.'

Sinclair studied the handsome edifice. He noticed there was a woman in the churchyard; she was bending over a grave.

'That's her. That's Vera.' Bennett spoke up. 'She comes here every day, I'm told. She's actually been seen praying by the grave. They were very close, she and Greta.'

'It happened recently, did it?'

'A fortnight ago. It was a Sunday. Greta had been playing the organ as usual for the morning service. Margaret and I were there, but we didn't see her afterwards. Normally she would come out by the front after she'd finished playing and join Father Beale, who'd be chatting to members of the congregation. She was very well liked in the village. But that day she must have slipped out through the vestry.' He shrugged.

'The pub's just across the road.' He brought the car to a halt and pointed again. 'We could stop for a drink and a sandwich, if you like. Margaret left some stuff out for our lunch. But there's usually a good fire going inside. We could sit there and talk.'

'Why not?' The idea appealed to the chief inspector.

'And besides, it will give me a chance to think up an excuse.' Sir Wilfred winced. 'I was supposed to return some books Margaret borrowed from the Winchester library. They're all overdue. But I clean forgot. They're still sitting there on the backseat.' He nodded without looking round. 'Do you have that problem, Angus?'

'Do I not?' Sinclair chuckled. 'But take courage. I have a ready-made excuse for you which I'm sure will elicit Margaret's sympathy once you've explained it to her. You can tell her you're not to blame; it's all the fault of your hippocampus.'

Just as Bennett had predicted, the two ladies were late getting back from Stockbridge and it wasn't until shortly before dinner was served that they made their appearance in the drawing-room downstairs. Sinclair had already been there for some time talking to the Bennetts' other guest, Father Beale, while Sir Wilfred busied himself in the cellar downstairs digging out, as he put it, a suitable wine for them to drink at dinner. Elderly—and, like the chief inspector, a widower—the vicar had made no secret of his distress at the loss of his organist, nor shown any hesitation in talking about her after Sinclair had raised the subject with him.

'Her life had already taken a tragic turn,' he said. 'She was the widow of a Lutheran pastor called Manfred Hartmann, one of those brave men like Dietrich Bonhoeffer who stood up to the Nazis, and one of the first to be arrested and sent to a concentration camp, where he died only a few months afterwards, of typhus apparently.'

White-haired, and with fingers that were red and swollen with arthritis, Father Beale had stared into the fire. He was silent for some moments.

'That was in 1938. Prior to that he'd been a pastor at one of the German-speaking Protestant churches in London—there are two, you know—and after he died Greta decided to return to England. She couldn't stand to watch what the Nazis were doing and she had friends in England. Then, at some point—it was shortly before the war started—someone told her we were looking for an organist here in Fernley and she came down to talk to me about it. I liked her immediately, and once I'd heard her play, the issue was settled as far as I was concerned. She was like a gift from heaven. I say as far as I was concerned . . .'

His face showed pain.

'I'm sorry to have to tell you that when the war started soon afterwards the village turned against her. She was the enemy in their eyes and she was all but ostracised. People can be so mean-spirited. But I stuck by her, even though attendance at church diminished for a while.'

'Wasn't she interned?' Sinclair asked.

'Yes, briefly, but very soon released when her background and sympathies were determined. But that wasn't enough for my parishioners. They continued to be hostile towards her . . . that is, until Vera Cruickshank stepped in.'

'Sir Wilfred told me about her.' Sinclair was paying attention.

'She's a lady of very strong opinions and has no hesitation in expressing them. I've had some run-ins with her myself in the past.' Father Beale smiled ruefully. 'But I can't speak too highly about the way she acted in this instance. To begin with she invited Greta to move in with her, not as a lodger, but to share her cottage with her. Greta had been renting a room from one of the shop owners but had been given notice to leave—another example of petty spite. Vera not only took Greta in, she let it be known to the world that she would not stand by and listen to any more derogatory remarks about her. That may not seem like much to you, but there aren't many people in Fernley who would care to get on the wrong side of Vera Cruickshank, I can tell you.' He chuckled.

'Sir Wilfred told me she'd become well liked.'

'Greta, you mean? Oh, yes. Well loved, I would say. She was the soul of kindness and generosity, a truly Christian lady. She took over the Sunday school after my wife died in '43. The children adored her. Poor Vera—they were very close, you know, and she just can't come to terms with what has happened.'

'Sir Wilfred said she had some doubts about the way Mrs Hartmann died.'

'More than that, I'm afraid.' The vicar bit his lip. 'She positively refuses to believe it was an accident, but with absolutely no evidence to back that up, it must be said.'

'What does she think happened, then?' The chief inspector was baffled. 'Surely she doesn't imagine that someone from the village . . . ?'

'No, of course not.' Father Beale shook his head vigorously. 'The idea's absurd. She hadn't an enemy in the world here . . . not any longer. No, I believe it's just a manifestation of grief. Vera can't bring herself to believe it was a simple mishap, and I'm afraid I'm one of those who has had to suffer her recriminations, her accusations that we've let the matter go without trying to discover the truth. The fact is I miss

Greta as much as she does. The village isn't the same without her.'

He paused once more to gaze into the flames. Sinclair searched his memory.

'I seem to recall Sir Wilfred saying something about her leaving the church after the service that day without speaking to anyone. Was that unusual?'

Father Beale stared at him, blinking.

'Well, yes, as a matter of fact,' he replied after a moment. 'Normally when she'd finished playing she would come out to the front to join me and to chat with members of the congregation. And to be honest she didn't seem quite herself that day. She even made one or two mistakes at the organ, which wasn't like her at all. Why? What are you suggesting?'

'Nothing really.' The chief inspector brushed the question aside. 'It just occurs to me she might have been upset about something, or distracted.'

'And wasn't really paying attention when she came to the stream, you mean?' Father Beale nodded to himself. 'Yes, I suppose it could have happened that way.'

Sinclair drew the curtains of his bedroom window back. The sky had been clear all day and with the moon riding high the handsome beeches framing the lawn in front of the Bennetts' house cast dark shadows on the silvery turf. Given the unchanging tenor of the life he led now in retirement, it had seemed a day unusually full of incident, starting with the enjoyable exchanges he had shared with Lucy Madden that morning and ending with his talk with Professor Waites. It was this last conversation that he was turning over in his mind now.

Earlier, as if by unspoken agreement, they had avoided the topic which the chief inspector already knew his fellow guest wished to explore. She had probably felt, like him, that it was best not discussed in front of Father Beale, who surely had enough on his mind to upset him.

But once the vicar had departed—the following day, being a Sunday, was a busy one for him—along with Sir Wilfred, who was to drive him home, and after Margaret Bennett, a busy presence as always, had excused herself on the pretext of having to attend to some domestic matter, the two of them had settled down by the fire with the fresh pot of coffee their hostess had left them.

The chief inspector had been wondering what it was exactly Professor Waites wanted to talk to him about, and not surprisingly he quickly discovered that his old chief at the Yard had got hold of the wrong end of the stick. It wasn't his opinion on psychopaths in general that the professor wanted to explore, but rather his reaction to an idea of her own that formed the basis of the book she was working on.

'It's along the lines of some work that's been done on this question in America in recent years,' she had told him. 'Briefly, there's a feeling in the profession now that we ought to expand our notion of what constitutes a psychopath. Previously, it's rather tended to focus on men—and a few women—who suffer from the kind of severe mental disorders that lead frequently to violent acts for which they feel no guilt or responsibility. Now we're beginning to see that this lack of affect can be extended to cover other individuals far more difficult to detect, but who are equally antisocial in the broadest sense: people emotionally disconnected from those around them, but nevertheless quite able to convince doctors and even psychiatrists that they're perfectly sane.'

Sinclair had listened with interest.

'Yes, but by that yardstick you could include most of the criminal population of any country,' he said. 'I mean those who choose crime as a profession. They prey on their fellow men without giving a thought to the suffering they cause, at least none that I've ever been aware of.'

'That's true.' Ann Waites frowned. Unmarried, or so it appeared, and in her early forties, she was slightly built, and together with her closely cropped hair, to which clearly she gave no thought, and the nondescript skirt and blouse that she was wearing, little concerned with her appearance. 'But they're not necessarily dead to feeling, are they? I'm sure quite a lot of them have families, wives and children who they probably care for. They're not psychopaths in the accepted sense.'

'What about the politicians, then?' The chief inspector was in the mood to be mischievous. He wondered if some of what he was saying might end up one day in the book Professor Waites was set on writing. 'These leaders who behave with little or no concern for the effect their actions might have on other human beings. Hitler could certainly be said to have instituted a murderous state; and whatever our communist friends might say, I believe Joseph Stalin has much to answer for.'

'You have a point,' the professor conceded. It seemed she was taking what he said seriously.

'And let's not forget businessmen, the great moguls of commerce. Most of them seem quite capable of taking decisions in the name of the great god Capitalism that lead to untold misery for thousands, jobs lost, lives ruined; and do they ever turn a hair? Do they actually feel anything? If so I must have missed it.'

At that point Ann Waites had produced a smile. Up till then her rather severe features and sharp, birdlike glance had projected an image of solemn attention.

'Are you by any chance pulling my leg?' she asked.

'Heaven forbid.' He chuckled. 'I wouldn't dare. But you're right to question what I've said. In fact, I think we should approach the whole matter with caution. We can't be sure that people feel nothing, no matter how badly they behave. In my experience most human beings are able to rationalise their actions to an extraordinary degree, to tell themselves that whatever they have done was necessary, however regrettable. As I understand it your true psychopath feels no such qualms.'

There was a pause while Professor Waites refilled her coffee cup. When she glanced up she saw that Sinclair was staring into the fire, frowning.

'You look like a man who has just had an unpleasant thought,' she said.

The chief inspector grunted. 'I was remembering something a wise friend of mine once said to me. He was a Viennese psychiatrist called Franz Weiss. Does the name mean anything to you?'

'I should say so.' She put her cup down. 'He was a wonderful man—one of Sigmund Freud's first pupils. I've read both his books and I once had the privilege of hearing him lecture in London. It was before the war. I do envy you. I would have given anything to have known him personally.'

'As you probably know he spent the last months of his life in England. He had been living in Berlin but left when the Nazi persecution of the Jews became intolerable. At the time I was occupied with a terrible case, one of the worst I ever had to deal with. We were trying to track down a man who had murdered a number of children and I asked Franz if he could give me some clue to the kind of criminal we were seeking. I should add that we had reason to believe that the killer had been active for some time and I wondered how such a man could have managed to carry on a seemingly normal life and hide his true nature for so long without being unmasked.'

'Yes . . . and?' Ann Waites pressed him to go on.

'I'm afraid Franz's reply was not encouraging. He said the man we were seeking was clearly an exceptional case and that to call him a psychopath was merely to touch on the challenge that such people presented to your profession. That despite their best efforts, psychiatrists had yet to achieve any great understanding of them. Would you say that was still the case?'

'I would.' She didn't hesitate.

'And then he said something I've never forgotten.' The chief inspector bit his lip. 'He said where the darkness of the soul was complete, where all sense of right or wrong was lacking, even the most sophisticated clinical approaches were ineffectual.'

Silence followed. Ann Waites sat with eyes downcast.

'The darkness of the soul . . .' When she spoke finally, it was to echo his words. 'I can't think of a better way to describe the condition: it's perfect . . . and chilling.'

She shivered. 'But you've hit the nail on the head, Mr Sinclair. These are the sort of individuals I'm thinking of: people who operate under the radar of public perception, seemingly respectable members of society who pursue their goals, which can be violent and destructive, with complete disregard for those around them—monsters in all but name.'

At that moment the door opened and Margaret Bennett stuck her head in.

'How are you two getting on?' she asked.

'Very well.' Professor Waites was first to reply. 'And I only wish we could continue. But I fear I'm keeping Mr Sinclair from his bed.'

She had just caught sight of the chief inspector stifling a yawn, and he acknowledged the fact with a rueful smile.

'This has been a long day for me,' he admitted. 'But I'd be very happy to continue with our talk tomorrow if you like.'

'Alas, I have to leave immediately after breakfast.' She was clearly regretful. 'I've got an old friend coming to stay for a few days. She's driving down from London in the morning, so I must get back. But I do hope we can keep in touch, Mr Sinclair.' She smiled. 'And if by any chance you find yourself in Oxford, please let me know. I've many more questions to ask you.'

3

AT BREAKFAST THE FOLLOWING day the Bennetts invited Sinclair to accompany them to church later that morning.

'Margaret and I usually attend the service,' Bennett said. 'And we feel more than ever that we ought to show support for poor Harry Beale just now. He'll have to manage with no organist. He told me last night he hadn't found a replacement for Greta Hartmann as yet.'

Though raised a Presbyterian, the chief inspector had grown accustomed during his years of retirement to the Anglican services conducted at the Highfield village church and he replied that he would be happy to join them, but that he would like to walk into the village ahead of time.

'It's for the exercise,' he explained. 'Helen insists on it— within moderation, of course.'

'You're very lucky to have her.' Sir Wilfred looked morose. 'Dr Maddox, our local quack, is quite hopeless. He's only a step or two away from the grave himself if you ask me. Margaret and I have taken to consulting a doctor in Winchester.'

Soon afterwards the chief inspector set off down the lane that led to the village and found when he reached it that he had arrived a good ten minutes before the service was due to begin. Having peered inside the church and found the pews empty and the building all but deserted apart from one of the vicar's acolytes, dressed in a white surplice, who was busy inserting the numbers of the hymns to be sung into a slotted board above the pulpit, he retreated to the churchyard and wandered among the graves.

Spying one that was freshly dug—the mound above it was still bare of grass—he made his way over to the spot. There was no headstone as yet to indicate who lay there and he wondered if it might be the remains of the late Mrs Hartmann.

'Would you mind?'

The voice came from behind him and the tone was sharp. Turning, the chief inspector found himself facing a middle-aged woman who had a bunch of flowers in her arms. Dressed in a military-type greatcoat, her greying curls were all but hidden under a felt hat of ancient design that was pulled down low, almost reaching her eyes, which rather than meeting his seemed to look right through him.

'I beg your pardon.'

He stepped aside politely, allowing her to pass. She moved closer to the grave and began distributing the flowers on top of it. The chief inspector watched her in silence for some moments. Then he spoke:

'Miss Cruickshank, I believe?'

She gave no sign that she had heard him, but continued with her self-appointed task.

'We haven't met. But I was told your name by Sir Wilfred Bennett. I'm very sorry for your loss.'

'Indeed?' Laying the last of the blooms down on the ground, she turned to him. 'I can't think why.' Her voice was cold, her glance hostile. 'As you say, we've never met. Nor can I say I'm pleased to hear that my name is being bandied about, particularly by the likes of Sir Wilfred Bennett.'

'He seemed more than sympathetic when he told me about Mrs Hartmann's accident.'

'Her *accident*? I see. That's now the accepted truth, is it?' Her eyes bored into his.

'He also said you disagreed with that finding. You thought it unlikely that she could have tripped and fallen.'

Her lips twitched momentarily.

'I would have thought that a former assistant commissioner at Scotland Yard might have taken the trouble to look into the matter more carefully.'

'It was hardly his place to do so.' Sinclair saw that she was determined to be difficult.

'And what is your place, then, Mr . . . I don't even know your name.'

'Sinclair.'

'What brings you here to Greta's graveside? Not idle curiosity, I hope.'

Sinclair paused. He had addressed her by name on an impulse—one he now regretted. It was probably the moment to apologize for intruding on her grief and withdraw. But he felt compelled to go on.

'I should tell you I was a policeman myself before I retired a few years ago, a chief inspector at Scotland Yard. That's how I know Sir Wilfred.'

'Should I be impressed?' Her gaze was unflinching.

'According to Sir Wilfred you felt something wasn't right about the way your friend died. Is that correct?' He was copying the same flat tone that she was employing and he kept his gaze neutral.

Miss Cruickshank was silent. But he thought he detected a slight change in her expression, a flicker of interest in her leaden gaze.

'It may interest you to know that I was a detective for the better part of thirty years and one of the things I learned over time was that when people feel something is "not right" about a situation, there's generally a good reason for it—which is not to say that the explanation necessarily accords with their suspicions.'

He added the last words quickly. He had sensed she was about to speak.

'I . . . I'm not sure I understand.' For the first time she sounded uncertain.

'If I'm not mistaken, you think foul play might have been involved in Mrs Hartmann's death. I'm saying that even if there was more to it than met the eye, that's not necessarily the case.'

Vera Cruickshank shook her head in annoyance. 'Are you playing games with me, Mr Sinclair? What are you suggesting?'

The chief inspector hesitated. He was searching for the right words with which to frame his reply.

'Before I answer that, can you tell me why you believe her death was no accident? I mean your specific reasons.'

'I should have thought they were obvious.' She glared at him. 'The idea that Greta should have tripped on a set of stepping-stones she must have crossed a thousand times in her life is simply ridiculous. She was not a careless person—quite the opposite, in fact. If anything, she was overcautious, and I used to tease her about it. And what exactly do you mean by saying there might be "more to it than met the eye"?'

'What if she had an altercation with someone at the stream and either fell or was pushed off the stones? What if whoever else was involved panicked when they saw her lying there facedown in the stream and ran off?'

'That's a ridiculous idea,' Vera Cruickshank scoffed.

'Is it? I can assure you that during my time as a detective I came across even more unlikely ways of losing one's life than that. I take it you don't believe there's anyone in the village who would have wanted to do her harm.'

'It's out of the question.'

'Then if it wasn't an ordinary accident, something unexpected may have occurred while she was crossing the stream, something that might, just *might*, have involved encountering another person there—with fatal results. But blaming the police won't help. It would be next to impossible to prove it was other than accident without some evidence to support that. Have you any?'

She stared at him, blinking.

'I have a suggestion,' he said. 'Why don't you show me the place where Mrs Hartmann died? I can't promise it will lead to anything. I'm no magician, and it's years since I did any police work. But after what you've just said I'm curious to see the spot. It's for you to decide, though.' He waited.

While they were talking the congregation had begun to arrive and when he glanced over his shoulder Sinclair saw that the Bennetts had just come into the churchyard from the road and were walking up the path to the church entrance arm in arm. It seemed they hadn't caught sight of him yet.

'Do you mean now?' Miss Cruickshank had finally replied to his question. 'Aren't you going to the service?'

'I'd just as soon not.' The chief inspector hazarded a smile. 'I was raised a Presbyterian, you know. We tend to look askance at you Anglicans.'

'And you're quite sure of that, are you?' Sinclair peered at her. 'She was in good spirits when she left the house?'

'Absolutely certain. Why should you think otherwise?'

Miss Cruickshank had made no attempt to alter her manner: the aggressive note in her voice made it clear that even if a truce had been declared between them it was an armed one. They had walked through the scattered graves in the churchyard to the gate and out onto the road. Looking back, Sinclair had caught a brief glimpse of Sir Wilfred. He was standing in the doorway of the church looking back, and the chief inspector had waved to him but carried on without stopping.

'Because apparently she wasn't quite herself at the service that morning. According to Father Beale she made some mistakes at the organ, which he said was most unusual, and when the service ended, instead of joining him outside to chat with the congregation she slipped out through the vestry and wasn't seen by anyone.'

'That's the first I've heard of it.' Miss Cruickshank was clearly put out. 'And I wouldn't take it as gospel if it comes from Father Beale. All I can tell you is that when Greta left the house she was behaving quite normally and not bothered by anything.'

They had crossed the road and walked past the forecourt of the pub to a path that ran alongside it. Presently they came to an apple orchard and Sinclair saw that there was a small wood ahead of them.

'You didn't go to church yourself that day. Was there any reason for that?'

'Yes, a perfectly ordinary one.' Miss Cruickshank kept

her gaze on the path ahead. 'I'd recently had an attack of bronchitis and was still coughing a lot. I didn't want to sit there in the church, which is freezing anyway, and disrupt the service.'

'So Mrs Hartmann walked there alone?'

'As a matter of fact she didn't.' This time she accorded him a brief glance. 'Edna Harris, who lives in the cottage nearest to mine, happened to be passing by as Greta left and they walked into the village together. I spoke to her later. She said when they got to the road they parted. She had to walk a little way down it to collect an old lady who needs help getting about. Greta always made sure she got to the church early so as to begin playing before the congregation arrived.'

'So she walked the rest of the way on her own?'

'For God's sake, man!' Vera Cruickshank stopped in her stride to glare at him in exasperation. 'It's barely fifty yards from where she and Edna Harris parted company. I tell you nothing could have happened to Greta before she reached the church. Father Beale's an old fool—and your friend Sir Wilfred Bennett isn't much better.' She strode on.

They had entered the wood, their footsteps cushioned by the carpet of dead leaves covering the path, and in a matter of minutes they reached the stream. There Miss Cruickshank paused. She pointed at the stepping-stones in front of them.

'The third one from this side is unstable. Here, I'll show you.' She walked ahead of him and stopped on the stone in question. 'See?' She rocked to and fro. The chief inspector noted that the movement was slight. 'No one who isn't either blind drunk or playing the fool could possibly lose his or her balance on it, yet there are people who are trying to say that's what happened to Greta. And I'll tell you something else.' She faced him. 'Dear Greta was such a cautious soul she always stepped across it. She didn't want to take a chance. I told you I used to tease her . . .' She turned away angrily and Sinclair saw her put a hand to her face. He gave her a moment to compose herself.

'I take your point,' he said gently. 'But if she was distracted that day it's possible she was careless for once. Is that where she struck her head?'

He indicated a rock no bigger than an orange that was lying in the streambed close to the stepping-stones. It was the only one showing above the level of the running water, which looked to be no more than a few inches deep. Miss Cruickshank nodded.

'There was blood on it. Greta had a cut on her forehead. She was lying facedown in the water.'

Her gaze remained fixed on Sinclair, who said nothing for the moment. He was thinking.

'Well?' She couldn't contain herself for long. 'You say you're a detective. What do you make of it?' Giving him no chance to reply she went on: 'You're going to tell me it was probably just one of those things, aren't you? That accidents happen.' Her voice dripped scorn.

The chief inspector shook his head. 'As a matter of fact, I was going to say something quite different.'

Edging closer to the bank, he glanced upstream where a dense tangle of bushes overhung the water, and then down, in the other direction, where part of the bank had been washed away by floodwater and a small bay of dried mud had been left in its wake. He spotted an empty beer bottle stuck into the surface of the mud. Bits of orange peel were scattered about beside it.

'Yes . . . ?' She urged him on.

He turned to her. 'What would you do if *you* fell headfirst into the stream?'

'I beg your pardon?'

'Now, this moment . . . what would your first reaction be?' She stared at him for a second.

'I'd try to break my fall.'

'Exactly . . . you'd put your arms out. Of course, you might sprain a wrist, or even break it . . .'

'. . . but I wouldn't fall flat on my face onto a rock.' Her eyes came to life for the first time. 'Is that what you're suggesting?'

'More or less. Were there any injuries to her hands, cuts or bruises?'

'I don't know. Her body was examined by old Maddox, our village doctor, but I wouldn't put much faith in his opinion. He should have retired years ago. He's in his dotage.'

'It wasn't seen by a pathologist?'

'Not to my knowledge.' She wet her lips. 'Do you think . . . ?'

'I don't think anything, Miss Cruickshank.' He cut her off quickly. 'It's just an observation. I'll be honest with you. I'm far from coming to any conclusion. But you're right about one thing . . . something unusual seems to have happened to your friend when she was crossing these stones. I can't say more than that at this stage.'

'At this stage?' She clutched at the hope his words seemed to offer.

'I'm going to think about this. I promise you that.' He met her gaze.

'But . . . isn't there anything you can do about it?'

'I don't know,' he replied honestly. 'It wouldn't be easy.

As I say, I retired from the force some years ago. They won't take kindly to my interfering.' He saw she was struggling to say something, and he waited.

'She wasn't a nobody, Mr Sinclair.' At last she found the words she was seeking. 'I want you to know that. She was a rare soul, and dearer to me than anyone.'

'I understand.' He nodded solemnly.

'And whatever conclusion you come to, I want to be informed. Don't leave me in the dark.'

'I won't,' he promised her.

4

SINCLAIR WATCHED HER RETREATING figure until it had disappeared around a bend in the path on the other side of the stream. Then he walked across on the stepping-stones and made his way carefully downstream through the bushes until he came to the small bay at the side of the stream that he'd spotted earlier.

Something there had caught his eye, but he had waited on purpose for Miss Cruickshank to leave him before setting out to examine it. The bay was a good three feet lower than the bank, but once the chief inspector had made his way to it through the bushes he found he had a close view of the patch of mud and what he saw there brought a grunt of satisfaction from his lips.

He saw he would have to lower himself onto it, and, having removed his shoes and socks and rolled up his trousers, he sat down and carefully levered himself over the edge and down onto the muddy ground below. It was the sort of activity his creaking joints no longer took kindly to, but having managed the manoeuvre without mishap he bent down to examine a small indentation in the mud that had caught his eye earlier.

'Well, well . . .'

Murmuring the words to himself, he walked around it to the edge of the stream and stepped in.

'My God!' The water was freezing.

Gasping from the shock—he had felt a sharp stab of pain in his chest—he made his way slowly upstream, feeling for any sharp pebbles underfoot, until he reached the rock beside the stepping-stones, the one which Vera Cruickshank told him had borne traces of blood. There were none to be seen now on the smooth surface of the object and the chief inspector lost no time in bending down to pick it up. He found he was able to lift it quite easily—it was lying on the surface of the streambed, not embedded in it—and he estimated its weight at no more than a few pounds. Turning, he retraced his steps to the patch of mud.

The imprint he had noticed was less than a foot from the water's edge and it was the work of a moment to bend down again and carefully place the rock he was carrying into the cavity. It fitted perfectly.

'If only I had a camera!' Sir Wilfred's voice shattered the chief inspector's quiet moment of triumph.

When he looked round he saw his old chief was standing by the stepping-stones regarding him with an expression of disbelief.

'What on earth are you doing, Angus?'

'Something your village bobby should have done if he'd had his wits about him.' Miffed as any schoolboy at being caught off guard, the chief inspector hastened to plod his way back onto dry land. 'My God, that water's cold.'

'I should think it is. But what *are* you doing?'

'Trying to set Miss Cruickshank's mind at rest. Mind you, now that I think about it I doubt I can do that either way.'

'*Either* way?'

'If I tell her it was an accident after all, she'll think I'm part of a conspiracy to ignore the facts, and if I say it wasn't, she won't rest until she discovers the truth.'

'Are you saying it's possible it *wasn't* an accident?' Bennett scowled.

'I'll explain in a moment.' Sinclair shifted unhappily on his cold feet. 'But let me put my shoes on first.'

A few minutes later, shod once again, and feeling at least some warmth coming back into his extremities, the chief inspector made his way back through the bushes to where Sir Wilfred awaited him by the stepping-stones.

'What you saw me doing was putting back the rock that the unfortunate Mrs Hartmann struck her head on into the hole in the mud from which it originally came.'

'How do you know that?' Bennett flushed angrily.

'Well, I don't for certain.' Sinclair blew on his hands. 'But it fits like a jigsaw piece and I'll wager it was lying there once.'

'Just what do you mean?'

'I mean before someone plucked it out.'

'And placed it in the stream? Is that what you're implying?'

The chief inspector's wordless grunt seemed to suggest there might be even more to the matter than that.

'I really can't see what you're getting at.' Bennett was still red in the face. He was clearly unhappy.

Not convinced that the circulation had returned to them yet, Sinclair stamped his feet.

'One might be tempted to wonder why,' he suggested mildly. 'I mean, who would want to pick up a rock lying over there'—he pointed—'and bring it over here? Can you think of a reason?'

'I could probably think of several.' Bennett was growing

flustered. 'What if . . . what if some boys were fooling around and one of them picked up that rock and threw it into the water here so as to splash the others.'

The chief inspector tugged an ear thoughtfully. 'Ingenious,' he conceded. His old chief's failing wits seemed suddenly to have sharpened.

'What I mean is, there doesn't need to have been a *reason*.' Sir Wilfred paused to let his words sink in. Then another thought struck him. 'You're not going to cause trouble, are you? Start some . . . some . . .'

'. . . hare running?' The chief inspector completed the sentence. 'Perish the thought. It's odds on this was an accident, just as everyone thinks. But there are one or two points I'd like to clear up first, simply to set my mind at rest.'

'Damn your mind,' Bennett spluttered. 'Now see here, Angus, this is a small community and I don't want you upsetting people. Unless you show me absolutely cast-iron proof that this was no accident—and I don't believe you can—I would rather you dropped the whole matter here and now. I mean that.'

'Oh, I agree, sir. I wouldn't dream of stirring up things for no reason.' Sinclair's tone was conciliatory. 'However, I would like to have a word with the landlord of the Horse and Hounds if that's possible. He's the one person who might be able to clear this up.'

Bennett rapped on the door.

'I can't think why I let you talk me into this,' he muttered. He knocked again.

'We've no business disturbing Hooper at this time of the

morning, especially on a Sunday. I just hope you have a good reason for doing so.'

Sinclair looked about him. They were standing in the forecourt of the pub. It was still a good hour and more to opening time and thus far Sir Wilfred's attempts to rouse the landlord had gone unanswered. Glancing back across the road, he saw Margaret Bennett sitting in their car. She waved to him. Bennett had told his wife firmly that she was not to accompany them when they went to talk to Ted Hooper, the landlord. This after Lady Bennett had shown more interest in Sinclair's quest than her husband thought fit.

'An investigation! How wonderful! I could never get Wilfred to tell me anything about his work when he was at the Yard. Now I can observe you both at close hand.'

Lady Bennett had adopted a teasing manner after her husband revealed to her what their guest had been up to while they were in church; possibly she did so in response to his attitude, which was disapproving. Sharp-witted, and with a mischievous air, she had shown a lively spirit on the rare occasions when they had spent time together, and Sinclair was not surprised when she had quickly begun pumping him for information.

'But what do you hope to learn from Ted? Surely you don't think he could be involved in poor Greta's death.'

'Not for a moment,' Sinclair had assured her. 'But it's too complicated to explain in a few words. It all depends on what he may or may not have seen that day. You'll understand better when you hear what I have to say to him.'

Margaret Bennett's evident delight at the prospect of being allowed to witness this interrogation had quickly been quashed by her husband, who had declared that on no account was she to accompany them when they descended on the unsuspecting Mr Hooper.

'I want to get this over as quickly as possible,' he had said sternly. 'And I don't want him facing a deputation. I'll tell you all about it afterwards.'

Lady Bennett had accepted this decree with surprising meekness. But catching a glint in her eye, the chief inspector wondered whether his erstwhile superior might not find himself in hot water with his spouse later on.

As Sir Wilfred raised his hand to knock for a third time, the door opened. A middle-aged man with red cheeks and curly fair hair stood before them. Dressed informally in tattered trousers and a sweater that had seen better days, he sported a dishcloth draped over one shoulder.

'Ted! I'm so sorry to disturb you, but could we trespass on your time for a minute?' Bennett made no attempt to hide his embarrassment. 'My friend here—he's an old colleague, actually—wants a word with you. Do you mind?'

'An old colleague?' The landlord's face lit up. He turned to Sinclair. 'You came in with Sir Wilfred yesterday for a sandwich, if I recall, sir. I wouldn't have taken you for a police officer.'

'Long retired, Mr Hooper.' The chief inspector grasped the outstretched hand offered him. 'Sinclair is my name. Sir Wilfred and I worked together at Scotland Yard for years and thanks to his wise leadership many was the villain we laid by the heels.'

'Oh, for heaven's sake, Angus!' Bennett had gone red in the face again. 'Will you stop that? Do be serious. I apologize for this intrusion, Ted. We won't delay you for long, I promise.'

'Don't worry about that, sir. I've got young Fred setting

the place to rights.' He jerked his head backwards and Sinclair spied the figure of a young lad at the rear of the bar who was busy wiping the tables clean. 'Come inside, both of you.'

They followed him into the interior, where they were greeted by the rich, mingled odours of stale beer and cigarette smoke.

'Would you like something to drink?' Hooper asked as he seated them at a table in the corner.

'Goodness me, no. Not out of hours.' Bennett was scandalised.

'Oh, it wouldn't be illegal, sir. It's not as though I'd be charging you for it.' The landlord grinned. He appeared to be enjoying the occasion.

'Thank you, but no. Angus?' Sir Wilfred turned to his companion.

Sinclair cleared his throat. 'Could you cast your mind back to the day Mrs Hartmann died?' he said. 'It was a Sunday.'

Hooper's eyebrows shot up in surprise. Although there was an empty chair beside him he had remained standing.

'Is that what this is about, sir?' He looked from one to the other. 'But surely it was just an accident.'

'Ted . . . please . . .' Bennett broke in. 'Just answer Mr Sinclair's question.'

'Well, I remember the day all right.' Ted Hooper scratched his head. 'Though we didn't hear what had happened to the poor lady until later that evening.'

'What I want to know is whether anything unusual occurred earlier, anything out of the ordinary,' the chief inspector resumed. 'If it happened at all, it would have been here—right in front of the pub, most likely—and just before the church service began.'

'What are you driving at, Angus?' Bennett couldn't restrain himself. His discomfort was evident. 'I can tell you myself that nothing untoward occurred. Margaret and I were present at the service. We were just across the road.'

'I was also wondering whether you saw Mrs Hartmann arrive at the church.' Ignoring the interruption, Sinclair continued to address the landlord.

'Did I see her *arrive*?' Hooper seemed more puzzled than ever. 'No, I can't say I did.'

'She would have come by the path that joins the road right next to your forecourt. I thought you might have seen her.'

'I'm sorry, sir.' He shook his head. 'Most likely I was inside, maybe in the kitchen at the back. It would have been well before opening time. So even if something did happen in front I wouldn't have seen it.'

A loud cough was heard. Glancing up, Sinclair saw that the boy who was busy at the other end of the pub was looking their way.

'Yes?' he called out to him. 'What is it?'

'There was that bloke who stopped, Dad.' The boy addressed his father. 'The one with the flat tyre . . .'

Ted Hooper slapped his forehead. 'Of course!' he exclaimed. 'I'd clean forgotten. This chap pulled up in the forecourt. I never set eyes on him myself, but Fred here— he was clearing the tables—came to the kitchen to tell me the fellow was asking if I had a jack I could lend him.'

'A *jack*?' Bennett repeated the word with a scowl.

'It seems he didn't have one in the car,' Hooper explained. 'Fred, come over here . . .' He beckoned to his son. 'You're the one who talked to him. Tell us what happened.'

Apparently eager to join in the conversation, the boy hastily made his way through the tables to where they had gathered in the corner. A skinny lad with straw-coloured hair like his father's, he looked to be no more than fifteen; but he had an open face and a bright eye in which the chief inspector fancied he saw the gleam of intelligence.

'I saw the car pull up through the window and I was about to go out to see what the driver wanted when he opened the pub door and stuck his head in.' Pleased with the role he'd been cast in, the boy launched into his story at once. 'He asked if we had a jack we could lend him and I told him to wait while I went back into the kitchen where Mum and Dad were having breakfast. Dad said to get the jack out of our car and give the bloke a hand with his tyre, which is what I did.' He shrugged.

'Yes, but wait a moment.' Sinclair held up a hand. 'Let's take it slowly. While you were changing the tyre did you happen to notice Mrs Hartmann passing by?'

'Yes, I did.' The boy nodded vigorously. 'I saw her on the path with Mrs Harris while I was jacking up the car. When they got to the road Mrs Harris went off the other way to collect old Miss Potter. She does that every Sunday.'

'So Mrs Hartmann walked the rest of the way to the church on her own.' Satisfied, Sinclair grunted. 'Did anything happen then?'

Fred shook his head. 'Not really, sir . . .'

'Not *really*?'

'Well, just as she came opposite to us she stopped for a moment and looked this way.'

'She looked at *you*?'

The sudden sharp note in Sinclair's voice made the boy blink. For the first time he seemed to hesitate. 'I'm not sure.' He was frowning now. 'See, I was down on my knees unscrewing the bolts on the wheel when I happened to look up and saw she had stopped and was facing our way.'

The chief inspector was silent for a few seconds. Then he leaned forward as though to lend emphasis to his next question.

'This is very important, Fred. Was Mrs Hartmann looking at *you*, or was she looking at the *man*? Think hard. Take your time.'

The boy swallowed. He glanced at his father, who reached out a hand to pat him on the shoulder.

'Go ahead, son. See if you can remember.'

Fred sucked in his breath with a whistling sound. His brow was furrowed in concentration. Finally he produced his answer.

'It was him, not me.'

'Are you *sure* of that?'

Transfixed by the look in Sinclair's eyes, the boy swallowed a second time. Then he nodded.

'I remember now,' he said. 'The bloke was standing behind me, and when I glanced up, I realized it wasn't me she was looking at. It was him.'

The chief inspector took a long moment to consider what he'd heard. His glance remained fixed on the boy's face.

'And did *he* look at her?' he asked.

'I can't say.' This time Fred was prompt with his reply. 'He was behind me, like I said.'

'And how long did that go on for—her looking at him, I mean?'

'Just a few seconds. Then she walked on . . . to the church, I suppose.'

'Did she look back?'

'I don't know.' The boy shook his head. 'I went back to working on the wheel.'

Sinclair was silent. Bennett stirred restlessly in his chair.

'Well, if that's all, Angus . . .' he began. But the chief inspector cut him off.

'Can you describe this man?' he asked.

'I don't think so, not really.' Fred made a face. 'I hardly looked at him.'

'Do your best.'

'Well, I'd say he was in his forties.' The boy shrugged. 'And he had brown hair. But there was nothing about him you'd notice especially.'

'What about his eyes? What colour were they?'

'I'm sorry, sir, I don't remember.' Fred bit his lip.

'Don't worry about that.' The chief inspector's tone was soothing. 'You're doing very well. Tell me, did you talk to him at all?'

'Oh, yes.' The boy's face brightened. 'We had a bit of a chat while I was changing the tyre. He was friendly enough— and he gave me five bob for doing the job.'

'That was kind of him. What did you talk about?'

'His jack, mostly—the one he didn't have.' Fred grinned. 'He said that was the trouble with these car-hire firms. You couldn't trust them to check on something like that. But he blamed himself, said he ought to have had a look in the boot to make sure there was one before he set off.'

'So it was a hired car he was driving?' The chief inspector's gaze had sharpened.

'Didn't I say, sir?' Realizing he'd presented his inquisitor with a valuable piece of information, Fred's voice took on a new note. 'It was an old prewar Hillman.'

'Did he happen to say where he was going?'

The boy shook his head. 'But it could have been Oxford.'

The chief inspector cocked his head to one side.

'I dare say you had good reason for thinking that,' he said.

The boy's grin widened. 'It was on the car-hire sign that was stuck to the windshield. It had an Oxford address and a phone number on it.'

'And also the name of the firm, I would guess.' Sinclair kept the faint pulse of excitement he was starting to feel out of his voice. 'Do you know, Fred, you're one of the most observant witnesses I've ever had the pleasure of questioning. Would it be too much to hope that you remember that as well?'

The lad suppressed a giggle.

'As a matter of fact I do, sir,' he said.

'Now, now . . .' Spellbound listening to his son's replies to the chief inspector's questions, Ted Hooper seemed to feel the moment had come for him to intervene. 'Don't go making up something just to please Mr Sinclair. I don't see how you could have remembered it, son.'

'But I did, Dad, and that's a fact.' He turned to his parent. 'You see, it was a name I wouldn't forget: Hutton.'

'Hutton?' His father blinked.

'Same as *Len* Hutton.' Thinking perhaps that the chief inspector, with his Scottish accent, might actually be unaware of the existence of England's stellar opening batsman whose name he'd just uttered, Fred turned to him. 'He holds the world record for the number of runs scored in a single test match innings: three hundred and sixty-four.'

'I believe I've heard of the gentleman.' Sinclair smiled. 'But are you sure that was the name?'

'Absolutely, sir.' Fred was in no doubt. 'It was there on the windshield: Hutton's Car Hire.'

Sinclair sat down on his bed with a groan. It had been a long day and one far more taxing than he was used to. The first hint that he might be overdoing things had come at the stream when he'd felt that stab of pain in his chest. It had passed, fortunately, and while he and Sir Wilfred had been walking back to the village he had surreptitiously slipped one of his tablets into his mouth and held it under his tongue until it dissolved. Thereafter he had felt better, but later he'd suffered a sudden second attack while sitting quietly in the drawing-room downstairs with Margaret Bennett after dinner. The spasm had lasted only a few seconds, but Lady Bennett's eagle eye had not missed her guest's momentary discomfort and she had suggested it might be best if both of them had an early night.

The episode had followed on the heels of a conversation they'd been having during which Sinclair had given her a detailed account of the sequence of events on the day Greta Hartmann died as reported to him by Ted Hooper's son. He had felt it was the least she was owed, given that her husband had succumbed to a fit of pique following their interview in the Horse and Hounds and refused to discuss the matter further. Lady Bennett had simply bided her time and after dinner, when Sir Wilfred had disappeared into his study on some pretext, leaving them alone, she had pressed the chief inspector to tell her what had happened earlier.

'It all boils down to one puzzling question,' he had concluded. 'What disturbed Mrs Hartmann that day?'

'Wilfred said he found you at the stream after the service today.' Margaret Bennett had been paying close attention.

'He said you were "fooling about" in it. Did Vera take you there? We saw you two together in the churchyard.'

'She was hostile initially.' Sinclair frowned. 'But when she discovered I'd once been a police detective she offered to show me where Mrs Hartmann had died and when we got to the place I couldn't help wondering how it was her friend had managed to fall in such a way as to crack her head on the only rock that was visible there in the streambed. At that point I'm afraid I became rather overenthusiastic and took off my shoes and socks to examine the spot more closely. Sir Wilfred caught me paddling.'

'The water must have been freezing.' Lady Bennett made no attempt to hide her amusement at the picture.

'It was.' The chief inspector grimaced. 'But to cut a long story short, I did feel that the manner of Mrs Hartmann's death was unusual and could bear further examination. It was then that I decided to have a talk with the landlord of the Horse and Hounds.'

'Because whatever upset poor Greta that day must have occurred when she walked past the pub on her way to the church?'

'Precisely.'

'And . . . ?'

'Something did happen . . . something very minor. A car had stopped in the forecourt of the pub with a flat tyre and young Fred Hooper was helping the driver to change his wheel. There's a suggestion—and it's no more than that—that Mrs Hartmann might have recognized the man. At all events she stared at him for several seconds—or so Fred says—before going on.'

'Only now she was in a different frame of mind.' Lady

Bennett had grasped the essence of the problem at once. 'Yes, I see what you mean. She *must* have recognized him.'

'Not necessarily.' Sinclair raised a warning finger. 'I'm afraid one of the more painful lessons one learns as a policeman is not to jump to conclusions. That way disaster lies—or at least it can, and only too often. Yes, she might have recognized him. But equally he might have reminded her of something or someone; awakened a painful memory. From what I've learned of Mrs Hartmann's past that does seem all too plausible . . .'

'You're thinking of her time in Germany . . . what happened to her husband?'

'That could easily have played a part in her sudden change of mood,' Sinclair agreed. 'There must have been things in her life she wanted to forget. It might even have led to her crossing those stepping-stones without due care.'

'But what if *he* recognized *her* as well?' Lady Bennett had let her words speak for themselves and the chief inspector had grunted in acknowledgement.

'That would change everything.'

Realizing then that he had gone rather further with his hostess than he meant to, he had quickly appended a cautionary note to what he had said.

'But all this is pure supposition and I do beg you not to repeat it to anyone. If it gets about, the whole village will start talking and the person who will suffer most from that is Vera Cruickshank. I've promised to let her know if I discover anything of interest or importance about her friend's death. Can we leave it at that for now?'

'Yes, of course,' Lady Bennett had reassured him at once. 'But is there anything you can do?'

'I'm not sure. As things stand, I doubt the police could be persuaded to open an inquiry. There are no hard facts I can put to them. As I say, it's all supposition. I shall have to think about it.'

It was then that the chief inspector had felt a renewed stab of pain in his chest and found his breathing grown short. Lady Bennett's eye was on him.

'I don't know about you,' she had said. 'But I'm quite exhausted. Shall we call it a day?'

More than ready for bed, in fact, the chief inspector still had a chore to attend to, and before retiring he retrieved a small leather-bound notebook from his suitcase. Aware of his failing memory, he had taken to leaving notes for himself in a book bought for that purpose—reminders to buy this or that for the house or attend to other small business matters—and was in the habit of consulting it every morning to see what he might have forgotten. He had already noted Ann Waites's name and phone number together with a reminder to order some flowers for Lady Bennett from the florist he had spotted outside Winchester station when he'd arrived.

But now for the first time in many months he had something of real importance to relate, and, having settled at a writing-table beside the window, he spent the next ten minutes jotting down a concise account of what he had learned from both Vera Cruickshank and Fred Hooper.

Even then his day was not quite over yet. In telling Margaret Bennett there was nothing to be done for the moment, he had not been entirely truthful. Ever since hearing the boy's account of how Greta Hartmann had reacted to the sight of the man whose tyre he was changing, he had been considering a course of action.

While there were all sorts of reasons why she might suddenly have felt unsettled that morning, one in particular had occurred to him almost at once, and as luck would have it, he was in a position to seek an answer to the question it posed without stirring things up.

Having completed his notes, he settled down to compose a carefully worded letter.

5

'LET ME GET THIS STRAIGHT, sir.' Billy Styles took a cautious sip of his wine. 'You're not suggesting we should do anything about it, at least not yet?'

'That's correct.' Angus Sinclair sounded positive. 'There's nothing to be gained by throwing a cat among the pigeons, not at this stage. There may be nothing to it. And since no postmortem was carried out, at least as far as I know, we can't hope to learn anything from the medical evidence. But I wouldn't rule out foul play, and I thought the Yard ought to know that.'

Billy stirred uncomfortably in his chair.

'I'm sorry, sir, but I have to ask you this . . .' The man he was speaking to had been his superior for many years, and Billy knew he wouldn't be where he was today—a detective inspector at Scotland Yard—if it wasn't for the interest Sinclair had taken in his career. 'Please tell me you're not planning to pursue inquiries on your own.'

'Heaven forbid!' The chief inspector brushed the suggestion aside with a grin. 'No, there was only one step I decided to take, and there's no need for you to worry about that. I won't be treading on anyone's toes.' He smiled benignly. 'How's the lamb?'

'Excellent, sir. You really shouldn't have . . .'

The telephone call Billy had received from his host that morning had come out of the blue—but it was nothing to the surprise that had followed. Sinclair had casually invited him to lunch at the Savoy Hotel, which, in spite of the fact that it was only a short step from the Yard, was a spot Billy had rarely set foot in, and never for such a spread as he was now enjoying at his old chief's expense.

'Don't mention it.' Sinclair replenished their glasses from the decanter of claret that stood on the table between them. 'It's years since I've been here and it occurred to me that since I wanted a word with you, what better place than this for us to meet?'

He turned his gaze towards the window and watched as a slow-moving tug ploughed its way up the muddy river below. The view of the Thames and the tree-lined Embankment beside it was one he knew well, albeit from the window of his old office at the Yard, and the glance he bestowed on it now was accompanied by a stab of nostalgia. The fruits of retirement that had seemed so enticing half a dozen years earlier when he quit his job had long since lost their appeal and he had come to the disheartening conclusion that whether he liked it or not, idleness didn't suit him. He had relished listing the various unanswered questions relating to Greta Hartmann's death to his erstwhile junior while they settled down to their roast lamb, which had been carved off the bone in front of them, and heartened to find that he still possessed the gift he had tried to encourage in others during his time at the Yard of presenting the facts of any case as concisely as possible. Nor had his guest failed to grasp the argument he was making.

'If this bloke she saw in the forecourt was someone she

knew from the past, and if he remembered her too, maybe he felt he had to do something about it.' Billy had nodded wisely. 'Maybe her death wasn't an accident after all.'

But the chief inspector had raised a fresh point now, one that was causing Billy more immediate concern.

'You say you've already taken some action, sir?' He asked the question hesitantly.

'Quite so.' Sinclair's smile was one of pure innocence. 'Does the name Hans-Joachim Probst mean anything to you?'

'Hands who . . . I'm sorry?'

'He was that German detective who came over from Berlin to help us with the Lang case. It was before the war.'

'Oh, that bloke!' Billy's face cleared. 'The *Kriminalinspektor* . . . it was all one word, I remember. You thought a lot of him as I recall.'

'So I did. He was a first-rate detective. And a good man too—he resigned from the police as soon as the Nazis came into power. He refused to work for a government he regarded as criminal. I'm happy to say he survived the war. He's back with the Berlin CID now and he's not just an inspector any longer; he's a *Kriminalkommissar* . . . that's detective superintendent to you.' Sinclair grinned.

'You kept in touch with him, then, did you?'

'Not at first—I lost sight of him for a while. But after the war I received a letter from him telling me he was back in his old job and since then we've corresponded. In fact, I posted a letter by express mail to him only this morning.'

'Was it about this business?' Billy couldn't hide his unease.

'It was. But don't be alarmed. I simply asked him for a favour. I gave him Greta Hartmann's name and asked him to check and see if the German police had any record of it—in particular, whether she'd ever testified in a court case or been questioned as a witness. And something else too . . .'

'Something *else*?' Billy's discomfort was growing by leaps and bounds.

'I asked him whether he could discover any link in the past between her and some man who might now be regarded as a war criminal. I mean, someone she would recognize as such. As I told you, her husband died in a concentration camp. It's possible she came into contact with some individual in the Nazi setup who later became notorious.'

'And the man she saw that day in front of the pub could be the same bloke?'

'It's just a guess.' The chief inspector shrugged. 'A long shot, I'll admit.'

'I know they're looking for these people.' Billy reflected. 'But as I understand it, most of them are thought to have gone to South America. Surely Britain's the last place a chap like that would risk showing his face.'

'You would think so,' Sinclair agreed. 'Although that could be a reason for his coming here. But you're right: it's highly unlikely.' He swallowed the last of his wine.

Billy sat pondering.

'Does Mr Madden know about this?' he asked.

'Certainly not.' The chief inspector's brow darkened. 'He and Helen are in Venice at the moment. Why do you ask?'

'I was wondering what his reaction would be.' Billy stood his ground.

'You mean, wouldn't he in all likelihood counsel me to stop all this nonsense and go back to tending my roses?'

'I wouldn't put it that way, sir.'

'I don't imagine you would.' A twinkle had appeared in Sinclair's flint-grey eyes. 'But if it's any consolation, I'm sure that's exactly what John would say. Helen would be even more forthright. Fortunately, they're not around to confirm my diagnosis. You might say I'm on the loose and fancy-free.'

'Sir . . . please . . .'

'Calm yourself, Billy. I'm pulling your leg.' The chief inspector chuckled. 'I was going to return home this morning. But I changed my mind and came up to London instead. I thought you people at the Yard ought to know what I've been up to in Hampshire. But enough is enough. I shall simply get back to Highfield this evening a little later than planned. If I learn anything interesting from Herr Probst you can be sure I'll pass it on to you. Does that ease your mind?'

'It does, sir.' Billy took a deep breath. 'Just as long as you're not planning to go off on your own and . . .'

'William Styles!' Sinclair affected a stern look. 'In all the years we've been acquainted have you ever known me to do anything so rash?'

'Smoked salmon! Saddle of lamb! A bottle of claret! No wonder you're looking so pleased with yourself.'

Detective Chief Superintendent Chubb glared at Billy.

'And now you've dropped into my office to rub my nose in it, have you?'

'No, I'm here on business, sir.' Billy grinned. Like most of his colleagues at the Yard he had a soft spot for the chief super, whose drooping jowls and generally lugubrious appearance had caused him, even in his younger days, to be compared to a bloodhound. 'Mr Sinclair reckons this German lady might have been murdered. He thought we ought to know about it.'

Billy had indeed dropped into his superior's office uninvited on his return from the Savoy and had been unable to resist enumerating the gourmet delights he'd been treated to. The fact that Charlie Chubb had suffered more than a little under the lash of Angus Sinclair's sometimes sharp tongue in the years they had worked together only added to Billy's enjoyment as he recalled what the chief inspector had told him.

'Why'd he invite you?' Chubb's glare remained fixed. 'Why not me?'

'Well, he doesn't want to make too much of it, sir.' Billy adopted a more conciliatory tone. 'He probably didn't want to bother you. It's not as though he's suggesting we step in, or anything of that sort.'

'I should hope not.' Chubb scowled. 'And correct me if I'm wrong—but isn't this the business of the Hampshire constabulary? What are they doing about it?'

'Nothing, so far as I can gather.' Billy pursed his lips. 'The local bobby put it down to an accident.'

'Well, there you are!' Charlie was in no mood to relent. 'And you say Mr Sinclair was spending the weekend with Bennett?'

'That's right.'

'How strange that our esteemed old assistant commissioner saw nothing amiss about this lady's demise. Doesn't that tell you something?'

Billy coughed. 'According to Mr Sinclair, Sir Wilfred has slowed down a bit since he was with us. That's how he put it. It seems he's not keen on stirring up things in the village.'

'I'll bet he's not.' Chubb brought his fist down on the desk in front of him with a thump. 'And neither am I.'

He swivelled round in his chair and stared out of the window. Billy waited.

'How serious is Sinclair about this?' The chief super spoke over his shoulder. 'He's not just bored with retirement, out to make trouble for someone—me, for example?'

'He wouldn't do that, sir. He really thinks there's something to it. Or there could be.' Billy corrected himself.

'Could be . . .' Chubb snorted.

'The thing is there's really nothing we need do for the moment.' Billy sought to pacify his chief. 'Mr Sinclair has written to this copper in Berlin like I said and depending on what *he* says we'll know whether it's something we ought to look into.'

'And you're quite sure that's all he's going to do.'

Chubb swing round in his chair. He fixed Billy with a penetrating stare.

'Mr Sinclair, you mean?' Billy sucked his teeth. 'I hope so, sir. He's not all that well, you know.'

'It's the first I've heard of it.'

'I spent a weekend down in Highfield with Elsie and the kids not long ago.' Billy was proud of his status as an old family friend of the Maddens. 'Helen told me she was worried about him. It's his heart . . . blood pressure . . . that sort of thing. She's told him to take it easy.'

'And this is how he behaves the minute she's out of sight?' Chubb shook his head in disgust.

'Well, I wouldn't worry, sir, not for the moment anyway.'

'What makes you say that?'

'I happen to know he's on his way back to Highfield.' Billy grinned. 'I put him in a cab myself and told the driver to take him to Waterloo.'

'Not Waterloo, cabby.' Sinclair leaned forward. 'I've changed my mind. Make it Paddington.'

Even as he rapped out the order the chief inspector felt a twinge of guilt. He was aware he'd misled Billy Styles, even if he hadn't meant to; he'd had every intention of going back to Highfield when they parted. But the thought of returning to a cold, empty cottage struck him now as a feeble response to the slow-growing suspicion he harboured that he had perhaps stumbled on a crime as yet unrecognized by the Hampshire police. After a career spent enforcing the law, much of it as a senior detective, he was in no mood to turn his back on a situation that cried out for further investigation, one with so many questions still unanswered.

A day or two spent in Oxford would do no harm, he reasoned. Even if the man whose identity he was hoping to pin down didn't live there, he had certainly rented a car in the city. It was the natural place to begin his inquiries. A name and if possible an address was all he was seeking. After that—and depending on what he heard from Hans Probst—he'd be happy to hand over the matter to the competent authorities.

As for his health, it was true he had suffered slight spasms of the kind Helen Madden had warned him about while he was in Fernley. But there had been no recurrence of them. The Maddens themselves would not return from their holiday until later in the week, by which time he expected to be safely back in Highfield and prepared to deal with any reproaches that might come his way. He couldn't deny that he was disobeying doctor's orders—something Helen was bound to remind him of when she learned what he had been up to—but as his taxi neared Paddington station, where he could board a train for Oxford, it occurred to him that, all things considered, he hadn't felt so well or in better spirits for months.

6

SINCLAIR PICKED UP THE OBJECT lying on the desk in front of him and examined it closely. Shaped like a small mushroom, it had a stem, which he was holding delicately between finger and thumb, topped by a black lacquered disc the size of a shilling, or perhaps a little smaller. On top of the disc and welded to it was a design worked in gold and it was this last feature that the chief inspector was peering at.

'It looks like a snake,' he said.

'That's what I thought,' Alf Hutton replied. 'Nasty-looking creature, isn't it? Who'd want to put a thing like that on his cuff link, I ask myself.'

The reptile, shown in profile, had its mouth agape. Its single eye glowed red, and the body behind the head was fixed to the metal disc beneath it in the shape of the letter W.

'A cuff link! Yes, I think you're right, Mr Hutton,' Sinclair concurred. 'This is part of one. The stud at the opposite end of the stem is missing. You can see where it broke off. That must be how the larger piece slipped out of his cuff.' He laid the object back on the desk. 'And you're quite sure this wasn't in the car when the customer took possession of it.'

'Quite sure, sir.' Hutton nodded briskly. Middle-aged, with a balding head and a cheerful salesman's manner, he had seemingly set out to be as agreeable as possible, even going so far as to offer his visitor a cup of tea, which the chief inspector had declined. 'I always see to it the cars are cleaned properly inside and out before we hand them over. You'd be surprised what can get left behind in the glove compartments. This thing must have slipped down between the driver's seat and the door. It was found there by one of the staff when he was checking the car over. Like I say, I've written to the bloke who hired it, but so far I haven't heard back from him.'

'But you have his name and address?' The chief inspector sensed he might be closing in on his quarry.

'It'll be in my book.'

Opening a drawer in his desk, Hutton pulled out a black ledger. He began to riffle through the pages. Sinclair waited patiently. He'd had no difficulty locating the firm, which was listed in the Oxford telephone directory. Situated in a narrow street in the Cowley area, it consisted of a front office with garage space behind it. Apart from the receptionist—a young woman—the only other member of staff to be seen was sitting behind a desk at the back of the room. Hearing Sinclair ask if he could speak to the proprietor, he had risen to his feet and introduced himself as Alfred Hutton. 'Though most people call me Alf,' he had added with a grin as he invited his visitor to come around the counter where the girl was seated and take a chair in front of his desk.

Having earlier given some thought as to how to approach the interview, the chief inspector had opted for a bold strategy.

'I used to be a police officer, Mr Hutton,' he'd announced as they shook hands. 'At Scotland Yard, as it happens. But since retiring I've been keeping my hand in working as a private investigator.'

'Sort of like Bulldog Drummond?' Hutton had said helpfully.

'Very like that gentleman; but not quite so dashing.' The

chief inspector had thought it best to play along. 'The inquiries I make are discreet and, without going into details, I can tell you that money is quite often at the heart of them: as it is in this case.'

'I see . . .' Alf Hutton had looked wise.

'The gentleman I'm trying to trace is the subject of a court order that my client obtained some months ago. Since then I'm sorry to say that he's made himself scarce, to the extent of moving out of the flat where he was staying in Winchester without leaving any forwarding address. As far as we know, he is living under a false name.' Sinclair had showed his disapproval with a scowl. 'He owes my client a substantial sum of money, but as long as he escapes detection he thinks he can avoid repaying it. We have been searching for him for some time. But now, thanks to a stroke of good fortune, I have been able to link him to a car he hired from you not long ago. And while, as I say, I don't know the name he's living under, we do know that the car he returned to you had a flat tyre—the spare, I believe.'

'Stone the crows! Would you believe it?' Alf Hutton was openmouthed. 'I know the fellow you mean. It was only a couple of weeks ago that he returned the car. He said he'd had a puncture on the way back to Oxford and had to change the tyre. What's more, he found there was no jack in the boot, which should never have happened. But he was quite decent about it. He didn't make a fuss.'

It was at that point that Hutton had produced the broken cuff link from another drawer in his desk and shown it to Sinclair. 'He left this behind in the car by mistake,' he said. 'I've been wondering what to do with it.'

Now he paused at an open page in his ledger and pointed with his finger.

'There he is. A Mr Beck, initials J. H. He gave his address as 15 Meadow Close, Chipping Norton. That's up in the Cotswolds. Is that his real name?'

'I'm afraid not, Mr Hutton.' Sinclair looked regretful.

'Well, I can tell you he had a driving licence to back it up.' Hutton scratched his head. 'How did you manage to link him with my car?'

'It was pure luck. A close friend of my client who lives in a village in Hampshire called Fernley saw him. He was standing beside the car while the tyre was being changed by a young lad who had offered to help. This friend of my client— a lady who happens to live there—was well aware of the situation I've described and didn't want him to know he'd been recognized. She waited until he had gone into a tobacconist's and then crossed the road to where the car was parked. She was intending to take down the registration, reasoning that his new home address could be traced that way, when she spotted your sign stuck to the windshield—Hutton's Car Hire—and saw that your firm was based in Oxford. Hence my appearance here today.' The chief inspector spread his hands in explanation.

'That's what I call a smart piece of detective work.' Alf Hutton was clearly impressed by what he'd heard. 'And now you're going to have a word with him, I suppose, this Mr Beck, or whatever his name is?'

'I may well do so.' Sinclair stroked his chin. 'Mind you, first I'll have to check and make sure he really is residing at this address in Chipping Norton.'

'You'll be wanting a car, then.' Hutton's face brightened.

'Thank you.' The chief inspector coughed to hide his embarrassment. He was getting in deeper than he had planned.

'But I fear my driving days are over. I was hoping there might be a bus I could take.'

'I understand.' Hutton tried to hide his disappointment. 'There's a regular service to Chipping Norton, as it happens.'

'Thank you again.' About to rise, Sinclair's eye fell on the broken cuff link lying on the desk before him. Though he would have been hard put to say why, it continued to fascinate him and he picked it up.

'I wonder where this was made.' He peered at the gold-wrought design. 'It looks foreign to me . . . and that figure seems pagan.'

'Pagan?' Hutton's eyes lit up.

'The snake, I mean. Could it have some religious significance, do you think?'

Alf Hutton looked nonplussed. Then a thought occurred to him.

'You wouldn't like to take it with you, would you, sir?'

'I'm sorry?' The chief inspector glanced up.

'You could show it to this fellow you're going to see, and if he says it's his you can give it to him . . . with my compliments.' He grinned.

'I don't know . . .' Sinclair hesitated. He could hardly say so now, but as things stood he had no intention of actually confronting the mysterious Mr Beck. It was enough that he had a name and an address. That was what he'd been after. Any future action would be up to the police and would probably depend on what Hans Probst had to tell him about Greta Hartmann's past.

'Oh, go on, sir. You'd be doing me a favour. If it isn't his, you could always send it back to me. Just pop it in an envelope.'

He waited hopefully. Caught in his own web now, Sinclair

decided it would be best to go along with the suggestion, or at least pretend to.

'Very well, if you insist.' Slipping the cuff link into his pocket, he rose.

'And if you're set on going to Chipping Norton, I wouldn't hang about, sir.' Hutton got to his feet too. He held out a hand for his visitor to shake. 'There's snow on the way—a heavy fall, according to the forecast. I should get up there sharpish if I were you.'

Faced with something of a dilemma now, the chief inspector returned to his hotel in the centre of Oxford. Was there any further step he could take?

He had asked the clerk at the reception desk to see if he could find out from directory enquiries whether they had a phone number for a J. H. Beck at the address he'd been given in Chipping Norton. He was toying with the idea of ringing the man and, if he answered, say he'd got a wrong number and apologize. That way at least he would hear his voice, something the chief inspector thought might be important. If Beck had a German background it would surely show, no matter how hard he might try to disguise it. The name "Beck" was interesting in itself. It was of no particular ethnic origin as far as Sinclair knew—it could be either English or German—and would explain his accent, if he had one.

But his hopes of acquiring a quick answer to the question had been dashed. Directory enquiries had no record of such a man living at the address given, though of course this didn't mean he wasn't there. Number 15 Meadow Close could well be the address of a residential hotel or a boardinghouse. It seemed to the chief inspector the only solution to the problem he faced was to go up to Chipping Norton and find out for himself if a man called Beck was living there.

But it was a step he was reluctant to take. He felt he had already gone beyond the bounds of what was acceptable—if he were still in his old job at Scotland Yard he would be more than a little peeved to learn that some retired detective long since put out to pasture was meddling in what was purely a police matter (if it was anything at all). His wisest course of action would be to return to Highfield at the earliest possible moment and await developments.

'Mr Sinclair! I thought it was you.'

Glancing up, he saw the figure of Ann Waites standing before him. She was dressed as she had been before, simply, in a skirt and plain blouse. The only difference was that now she had a handbag hanging by a strap from her shoulder. The chief inspector rose to his feet.

'No, please . . .' She gestured to him to sit and without waiting for an invitation drew up a chair and joined him at the table. 'I was having lunch with a friend over there'—she nodded behind her—'a colleague from America. I spotted you a moment ago, only I wasn't sure at first it was you. You didn't say a word about coming to Oxford when we talked. And you did promise to get in touch with me if you did.' Her glance was accusing.

'So I did. Please forgive me.' Sinclair had got over his surprise at seeing her. 'I travelled down from London yesterday on the spur of the moment, quite literally. I was on my way to Waterloo station intending to return to Highfield when I changed my mind and came here instead. I'm afraid it didn't occur to me to call you. There was something important I had to do in Oxford and I was rather fixated on it.'

'That sounds very mysterious.' Her tone was teasing now.

'But since I've cornered you I'm going to insist that you have dinner with me this evening. I have my friend staying with me—the one I told you about—and I've invited another guest as well. Please say you'll come.' She smiled.

'Of course, I'd be delighted to.'

Cornered, as she had said, Sinclair was more than happy to accept the invitation. Apart from anything else, it resolved the question that was troubling him. Now he had no choice but to remain in Oxford overnight. He could postpone deciding what to do about Mr J. H. Beck and Chipping Norton until the following day.

7

'THANK YOU, MR SINCLAIR. That was most enlightening. If I seem to have been picking your brains, I'm afraid that's just what I was doing.' Ann Waites smiled. She rose from her chair to place another log on the fire.

The chief inspector had taken a taxi from his hotel to her house off the Woodstock Road, arriving early at his hostess's insistence so that they could continue the conversation they had begun at Fernley before the other dinner guests arrived, and they had been talking in her sitting-room for close to an hour. She had wanted to know about his former association with Franz Weiss and Sinclair had spoken at length about the two occasions when the Viennese psychiatrist had been of help to the police, beginning with a murderous attack on a house in Highfield called Melling Lodge more than a quarter of a century earlier, when he and John Madden, then a detective inspector, had worked together to track down the deranged killer.

'In fact, it was John who first made contact with Weiss,' he told Professor Waites. 'And that was through Helen, who had known Franz for years.'

'She was the village doctor Madden later married.' Ann Waites had resumed her seat. 'I've heard the story. It may surprise you to learn that both you and John Madden are household names to many in my profession, particularly those of us with an interest in forensic psychiatry. The Melling Lodge case is still regarded as a classic of its kind.'

'A classic?' Sinclair smiled wryly. 'I must say I've never thought of it that way. But I became close to both John and Helen after it was over and it's a friendship I've always treasured. In fact, it's why I chose Highfield as a place to retire to.'

Ann Waites glanced at her watch.

'And now I'd better fill you in quickly before Julia appears. I told her I wanted to talk to you alone, but she should be along presently.'

'Is she the friend you mentioned before?' Sinclair asked. 'I thought she was staying with you.'

'She is. She's been resting.' Professor Waites hesitated. 'What I didn't tell you is that poor Julia has been in a wheelchair for years. She was a wonderful skier in her youth: she won the British Ladies' Downhill Championship two years running before the war. Julia Drake she was then. Perhaps you remember it. But later she had a terrible skiing accident and broke her back. She's never walked again.'

'How sad.'

'Before that happened, though, she had married a Swiss businessman called Andre Lesage and he was wonderful in the way he cared for her. There wasn't a doctor in Europe they didn't consult and he even took her to America to be examined by surgeons there in the hope of finding some way of repairing the damage to her spinal cord. But it was no use, and in the end they had to accept that she'd be confined to a wheelchair for life.'

Ann Waites rubbed her forehead.

'At first they travelled a good deal, looking for doctors, as I said, but when they realized their search was fruitless and it was clear that war was about to break out they settled down in Switzerland. Then, about a year before the war ended, something truly awful happened. Andre was killed in a motor accident. It meant Julia hadn't simply lost a husband whom she loved, but the person who had been at her side all these years taking care of her. On top of that, too, she was stranded in Switzerland. There was nothing she could do but wait until the war ended. Only then was she able to come home to England.

'We've been friends since school days, so I was one of the people Julia got in touch with when she returned and we've been close ever since.' Professor Waites ran her fingers through her hair. 'She's managed to make a life for herself between here and London: I say "here" but in fact her house—it's called Wickham Manor—is in the Cotswolds, though she comes to Oxford a lot. And she has plenty of support, thank goodness. She's got a secretary who's not only a great help with business matters but also a trained masseuse—something Julia needs— and a rather wonderful chauffeur called Baxter, Hieronymus Baxter.' She laughed. 'Don't ask how he came by "Hierony- mus", but if I tell you he's the salt of the earth you'll know what I mean. Julia hired him three years after she returned to England and he's turned out to be a tower of strength. He's quite devoted to her. And now someone else has appeared in her life and I'm wondering what will come of it.'

She paused to catch her guest's eye. Sinclair smiled. 'I'm on tenterhooks to hear what you're going to say next.'

'About a year ago Julia got to know a very interesting gentleman by the name of Philip Gonzales. I can't tell you where he comes from exactly, though I believe his father was Spanish. The name suggests it. But apparently he passed at least some of his youth in this country and he sounds

English. But he's travelled widely and according to Julia he speaks several languages. All in all, he's something of a mystery, to me at least.'

'How did your friend come to meet him?'

'It was at some party in London. He introduced himself and told her he had actually witnessed one of her victories in the women's downhill championship years before and had never forgotten her. They got talking, and from that moment on their friendship blossomed. I will say this for Mr Gonzales. He knows how to make himself agreeable—and useful, as far as Julia is concerned. Indeed, he's proved hard to resist.'

'I take it you don't altogether approve of him.' The chief inspector eyed her curiously.

Professor Waites weighed her reply. 'Well, it's really not up to me, is it, but I do fear for Julia. To tell the truth I don't know what to make of him. He seems straightforward enough on the surface and he can be quite charming. But so were a lot of the people I treated when I was practicing as a psychiatrist and I must tell you there are times when he reminds me of some of them. There's a glibness about him that I don't altogether trust. I might add that he recently asked Julia to marry him.'

The chief inspector's eyebrows rose in response to her words.

'I don't think it came entirely as a surprise to her; Philip has been very attentive. And I think it's true to say she feels flattered by his proposal. She's been quite transformed since she met him, a new person. Being in a wheelchair has tended to make her think all that was behind her, which was ridiculous, of course. Julia's an extremely attractive woman, as you'll see in a moment, and, in spite of what happened to her, still full of life. I think any man would be lucky to have her.'

Her tone bore a note of challenge and Sinclair bowed his head in acceptance of her judgement.

'But there is one further element in the situation that I haven't mentioned. I wonder if you can guess what it is.' She waited for his reply.

'Is she by any chance rich?' The chief inspector spoke after a moment's pause.

'Very. Her family had money, and she was an only child. Plus Andre left her his fortune, which was considerable.'

'And that makes you question just what Mr Gonzales's true feelings are towards her?'

The professor shrugged. 'He does seem genuinely fond of Julia,' she conceded.

'Would it be so bad if her wealth was one reason he was attracted to her?' Sinclair mused. 'Whatever the poets may say, marriages are not made in heaven. Often they have very earthly roots and aren't necessarily the worse for that. There's an exchange involved, after all, isn't there? Each partner offers something to the other.'

'My dear Mr Sinclair—you were wasted as a detective. You should have been a diplomat.'

She paused to cock an ear.

'Ah! That sounds like Julia now.'

At that moment the chief inspector heard the sound of squeaking wheels behind him and when he looked round he saw that a woman in a wheelchair was just entering the sitting-room through the open doorway.

'I *must* get Baxter to oil these wheels. They make a dreadful noise.'

The occupant of the chair was already stretching out a hand to greet him as he rose to his feet. Striking to look at,

Julia Lesage's red hair, cut simply to shoulder length, framed a face whose pale skin was lit by a gaze as direct as any the chief inspector had encountered. It took him a moment to register that her eyes, which at first he'd taken to be brown or hazel, were in fact dark green.

'How do you do, Mr Sinclair?' She continued without a pause. 'I'm so pleased to meet you. Did Ann tell you—I'm quite *addicted* to detective stories. But you're the first real sleuth I've met. This is so exciting.'

'Hang on, Julia. Give me a chance to introduce you at least.' Ann Waites had risen, laughing, to her feet. 'This is Julia Lesage, as you must have gathered, Mr Sinclair. And it's perfectly true—she has been longing to meet you ever since I mentioned your name.'

'Then I hope you won't be too disappointed.' The chief inspector addressed Professor Waites's friend gravely. 'I expect you were referring to private eyes—gumshoes, as I believed they are termed in certain circles. I'm afraid we policemen will seem like a dull lot after those glamorous gentlemen and that applies particularly to retired ones.'

'Oh, I'm sure that's not true.' The green eyes shone with laughter. 'And I'm never wrong about people.'

As Sinclair paid off the taxi that had brought him back to his hotel from Professor Waites's house he felt the kiss of a snowflake on his cheek. Looking up, he saw others spiralling down in the lamplight.

'And this is just the start of it.' The cabby had caught the direction of his gaze. 'You wait till tomorrow, sir.'

The words were not without importance for the chief

inspector. He had a decision to make, and on returning to his room a few minutes later he sat down on his bed to review the situation.

He had spent an enjoyable evening with the professor and her friends and much of the pleasure he'd derived had come from the presence of Julia Lesage—or plain Julia as she was to him now. She had insisted that he address her by her given name.

'I've a feeling we're going to be friends,' she had told him.

'Extremely attractive' were the words Ann Waites had chosen to describe her guest, but Sinclair thought this was an understatement. Even setting aside her dark red hair and piercing gaze, she would have been a striking presence, he thought. There was a sense of urgency about her, a reaching out to grasp what she could of life, wheelchair-bound as she was, that had touched him deeply. If this was what had captivated her new admirer—the one Professor Waites had told him about—the chief inspector could well understand it. And if the feeling was returned, then Philip Gonzales was a lucky man indeed.

But agreeable though the dinner had been, it was not of Julia Lesage's green eyes that he was thinking now, but rather of some information that had been imparted to him towards the end of the evening by Professor Waites's other dinner guest, an anthropologist by the name of Andrew Fielding. Attached to the famous Pitt Rivers Museum in Oxford, he had seemed diffident at first, with little to say, though he appeared to enjoy the company he found himself in, taking particular pleasure from an exchange between Julia and the chief inspector that had occurred near the end of their meal. Having earlier introduced the subject of fictional detectives into their conversation, she had quickly discovered that her own knowledge of the personages involved far outweighed that of Sinclair, who had felt obliged to defend his relative ignorance.

'Please don't think I despise them,' he had said. 'But their ability to solve all puzzles does border on the miraculous, not to mention their capacity to dazzle the reader by gathering all possible suspects together at the conclusion of each of their investigations and then pointing the finger of guilt at the one least likely to be a murderer. If only I had been granted such insight . . .'

'Are you by any chance referring to Miss Christie?' Julia's bright gaze had carried a challenge.

'Perish the thought. I've enjoyed several of her tales. Mind you, that Belgian detective she favours does have an appalling taste in sickening liqueurs. It's enough to turn any self-respecting Scotsman's stomach.'

'But you must admit her puzzles are ingenious.' Julia had seemed to take pleasure in their sparring.

'Breathtakingly so.' The chief inspector had grinned. 'Indeed, in all my years at the Yard I never came across one to compare with them.'

'And speaking of puzzles . . .' Professor Waites had interrupted at that point. 'What I'm dying to know is what you're doing in Oxford, Mr Sinclair.' She turned to the others. 'Mr Sinclair and I only met for the first time a few days ago. We were staying with some mutual friends in Hampshire over the weekend and as I understood it he had every intention of returning home afterwards. He lives in Surrey. Instead I came on him quite by chance in the Randolph Hotel this morning. He told me he had changed his plans at the last moment, but not why. However, he intimated that a matter of some importance was involved, and I've a feeling there's a mystery behind it. Admit it, Mr Sinclair. Isn't that so?'

'Do tell us,' Julia had begged him. 'I love mysteries. And you never know—one of us may be able to help you with it.'

Cornered once again, the chief inspector had thought quickly. He didn't wish to disappoint this new and charming acquaintance he'd made with a flat refusal to discuss the matter. It would have been a poor return for the warmth she had shown him.

'I can't tell you exactly what it involves,' he had begun. 'I'm afraid it's confidential. But there is one puzzle associated with it I've been trying to solve, so far without success. It fell into my hands quite recently and anything I can find out about it would be most welcome.'

With a flourish he had taken the cuff link out of his jacket pocket and placed it in the middle of the table.

'It's the design that interests me,' he said. 'It's most unusual. Does it mean anything to any of you?'

Ann Waites had been the first to react. Picking up the cuff link, she had held it to the light.

'You're right: it's bizarre . . . and rather creepy.'

'Let me see it,' Julia Lesage pleaded. She took the cuff link from their hostess's hand and peered at it. 'Is it a snake?' she asked.

'I think it must be,' Sinclair agreed.

'May I?' Andrew Fielding held out his hand to Julia, who passed it to him. He squinted at the small object.

'Ah, yes . . . of course.' He looked up. 'It's a snake all right, or rather half of one.'

'*Half?*' Sinclair asked.

'A snake with two heads . . . a double-headed serpent . . . here, let me show you.' He searched his pockets and after a moment produced a pencil and an envelope, which he laid facedown on the table in front of him. 'The design is repeated, only the second snake's head is facing in the opposite direction.' He sketched busily and after a few seconds passed the envelope over to Sinclair for his inspection. The chief inspector peered at the simple drawing, frowning.

'I've marked the spot where the serpent's body has been cut in half,' Fielding explained. 'The matching piece must be on the other cuff link.'

'Yes, I see what you mean.' Sinclair nodded after a moment. 'Do you recognize the design?'

'Certainly.' Fielding seemed to have no doubts. 'The double-headed serpent was an important religious symbol to the Aztecs. This is a copy of one, but I doubt it has any religious significance. It looks more like a piece of costume jewellery to me.'

'So it's Mexican in origin?' Professor Waites had taken the cuff link from him and was examining it again.

'That seems likely,' Fielding agreed. 'The original objects were a good deal larger—several inches across—and were carved out of wood and covered with a mosaic of turquoise. They date from the fifteenth or sixteenth centuries and only a few have survived. The British Museum has one.'

'And what was their religious significance?' Sinclair asked.

Fielding hesitated. He was weighing his reply. 'Well, we know they were important,' he said. 'The word for a serpent in the Aztec language was *coatl*, which forms part of the names of a number of their gods. It's thought that the habit of snakes to shed their skin each year led the Aztecs to see them as symbolizing the idea of renewal and transformation. One finds a corresponding idea in Greek mythology.'

'Are you thinking of the *ouroboros*?' Professor Waites cocked an eye at him, and the anthropologist nodded.

'The snake devouring its tail had the same meaning, or

one very like it. It was regarded as a symbol of the universe renewing itself from itself, and on a personal level possibly also our own ability to re-create ourselves. It appears the Aztecs had similar notions.'

'How was it used?' Sinclair asked. 'I mean, what part did it play in their ceremonies?'

'We don't know that for certain.' Fielding frowned. 'But it's thought that these objects, the original ones, I mean, were worn as pectorals by Aztec priests. I don't imagine this one here was ever part of a single piece. It was more likely designed as one of a pair of women's earrings that were later turned into cuff links for some reason.'

'Didn't the Aztecs go in for human sacrifice?' Sinclair asked. He'd been a fascinated listener.

'I'm afraid so.' Andrew Fielding looked regretful. 'It was very much part of their culture.'

'And the priests played a major role in that, I suppose?'

'Indeed they did. In fact, they were almost certainly the ones who performed the bloody rite.'

'What bloody rite?' Julia's eyes lit up.

'Well, it's not really a suitable topic for the dinner table.' Andrew Fielding had come to life. He was enjoying himself. 'But they used to cut their victims' hearts out, or so we believe. While they were alive, that is.'

'Goodness!' She caught her breath. 'How awful.'

The anthropologist turned to Sinclair. 'Has any of this been of help to you?' he asked.

'I really don't know.' The chief inspector scratched his head. 'I shall have to think about it.'

'But has it helped to solve your mystery?' Ann Waites asked.

'Believe me, if I knew I'd tell you.' Sinclair gnawed at his lip.

'And does it mean you'll be staying on in Oxford?'

Once again the chief inspector had no answer. In fact, he was asking himself the same question: whether he should return home or make a last attempt to ascertain the identity of the mysterious Mr Beck.

Before sitting down at the writing-table in his room he had retrieved the leather-bound notebook from his suitcase and he spent some minutes now jotting down brief accounts of his meeting earlier that day with Alf Hutton and of the dinner he had just attended, with particular reference to Andrew Fielding's remarks about the cuff link. That done, he sat back and considered his options.

The thought of a quick visit to Chipping Norton the following morning was tempting. It was hardly likely to cause trouble for anyone. (He was thinking of his old colleagues at the Yard.) In fact, it would probably go unnoticed, and he might learn much in Meadow Close.

But there was the snow to consider. According to the forecast it was going to get worse.

Unable to come to a decision, the chief inspector went to the window and for some minutes he stood there gazing out into the night as the feathery flakes continued to fall.

8

SINCLAIR PUT A PILL in his mouth and swallowed it (meanwhile uttering a silent prayer of thanks that he'd remembered to bring the tablets with him). A few minutes earlier he'd felt a familiar tightening in his chest, and had reached instinctively for the bottle in his coat pocket. Now he sat warming his hands on the pot of tea he had ordered and considered his predicament.

He was stuck, marooned, trapped by the snow—which he could see through the plate-glass window of the tea shop was falling more heavily by the minute. There was no getting away from it. He'd made a damn fool of himself, and now he must pay the price.

But what, in practical terms, should he do?

He had taken his fateful decision to come up to Chipping Norton soon after waking. A glance out of the window of his hotel room had revealed that although it was still snowing the traffic below seemed to be circulating without difficulty. The brief conversation he had had with the clerk at the reception desk when he went downstairs for breakfast had not been discouraging either.

'There's a front moving in from the Atlantic all right,' the man had told him. 'They're predicting heavy snow all over southern England. But I've just heard on the wireless that the worst of it's not due to arrive until midafternoon, so you should be able to get up to Chipping Norton and back this morning without a problem. But I should leave right after breakfast if I were you, sir. You don't want to be caught there. The roads can become quite tricky if the snow settles, especially up in the Cotswolds, and the bus service has been suspended more than once in the past.'

The chief inspector had settled on his plans over breakfast. Once he reached Chipping Norton he would find his way to Meadow Close and discover whether number 15 was a private dwelling or a boardinghouse. In either case he would determine whether there was a man called Beck living there and if confronted by the individual would offer to return the cuff link to him, explaining that he was on a business trip to the town, something he had mentioned when he had recently hired a car from Hutton's, and that the manager of the firm, who was known to him personally, had asked him to return the object to its presumed owner as a favour. Although the explanation was somewhat specious there was no reason it should arouse Beck's suspicions, and meeting him would give the chief inspector some indication of the sort of individual he was dealing with—in short, whether he could be considered a suspicious character.

But his journey had been cursed from the outset. First the bus, which he had boarded in Oxford, had been held up while a car that had come to grief a few miles from the city was laboriously hauled by a tractor out of the ditch into which it had skidded. The operation had taken close to half an hour and by the time the bus, grinding along in low gear, arrived at its destination, a trip that should have taken no more than forty minutes had ended up consuming more than double that amount of time.

As the passengers disembarked Sinclair had cast an

anxious glance at the sky. The low grey cloud was unbroken and seemed ready to disgorge even more of the fat white flakes, which were falling in greater numbers now. He had gone into a nearby tea shop to ask the way to Meadow Close and, having been told that it would take him no more than ten minutes to walk there, had set off in reasonably good spirits unaware of the disappointment that awaited him. Thanks to the narrow pavements, now well over ankle-deep in snow, it had taken him longer to reach his goal than he'd hoped, and when he did it was only to find that his efforts had been wasted.

Meadow Close, as its name suggested, was a dead-end street. It was lined with houses, five on each side, with one at the end of the road. The numbers ran up to eleven. There was no number 15.

If there was any advantage to be drawn from what was rapidly turning into a fiasco, it lay in the fact that this man who called himself Beck had deliberately provided the car-hire firm with a false address; or so Sinclair told himself as he laboriously retraced his steps. Depending on how things turned out, it was information he could offer to the police at some later stage. It might prove valuable to them. But the satisfaction was small consolation for the pickle he presently found himself in.

On reaching the main square where the bus terminus was situated he learned to his dismay that the service had been suspended. There had been another accident on the Oxford Road just beyond the village of Enstone, which he could remember passing by on the way up to Chipping Norton. A lorry had collided with a motorcar on the now slippery road and the larger of the two vehicles had overturned, blocking the traffic in both directions.

'They've sent for a crew from Oxford to deal with it, sir, but the latest word I've had is that it won't get there until this afternoon. All traffic going beyond Enstone has been stopped and the same goes for cars coming from the other direction. There may be detours that lighter traffic can take, but I'm afraid that doesn't apply to our vehicles, which are simply too big.'

The doleful news had been imparted to Sinclair by an employee of the bus line posted at the stop to warn off hopeful passengers. He was dressed in a blue uniform and wore a military-style cap, on the peak of which the snow was collecting like icing on a wedding cake.

'What with the weather getting worse, the powers that be have decided to halt the service for the rest of the day.' He had sounded genuinely regretful. 'I'd like to be able to tell you that we'll get things going again tomorrow morning. But in all honesty it depends on the snow, and the forecast isn't promising. You may be stuck here for a while.'

There being no point in asking the man what he thought any passenger hoping to return to Oxford should do about it, the chief inspector had repaired to the same tea shop he had visited earlier to consider his options. They were depressingly few in number. All he had with him were the clothes he was wearing, but that was the least of his problems. Not knowing a soul in Chipping Norton, he'd be obliged to find a room in a hotel or boardinghouse where he could spend the night . . . or perhaps nights, since there was no certainty that the bus service would resume the following day. He would have to telephone the Randolph Hotel in Oxford and ask them to pack up his things and hold them until his return.

But these were merely inconveniences. More upsetting was the fact that the Maddens were due to return from their

Italian holiday that very evening and the chief inspector had been counting on being back in Highfield before them with an account of his escapade, suitably edited, ready to impart to his friends. This was now impossible and he was faced with the disagreeable prospect of having to ring them as soon as they returned in order to explain his absence. He could only imagine what Helen's reaction would be when she discovered what her ailing patient had been up to. He had put himself right in it and with no excuse (at least none she would be willing to entertain) that might lessen the opprobrium soon to be heaped on him.

'Excuse me, sir?'

Sinclair looked up. A man was standing by the table. Broad-shouldered, with dark hair neatly combed, he was dressed in a double-breasted black suit and tie. Though he cut an impressive enough figure, his expression was diffident and when he bent forward it was in the obliging manner of a waiter about to take an order.

'Mr Sinclair, is it?'

'That's right.'

'Mrs Lesage is wondering if she can be of help.'

'Mrs Lesage?' The chief inspector's jaw dropped.

'She's outside, sir.' The man pointed towards the shop window and Sinclair saw the smiling face of Julia Lesage through a second window—that of a large motorcar that was parked in the street outside. She waved to him.

'I'm sorry . . . I don't . . .'

'We've just learned that the bus service to Oxford has been halted.' Although affable enough, the man's manner stopped well this side of familiarity. He seemed more intent on being of service. 'Mrs Lesage thinks you might have been planning to return there, in which case you could be stranded, and if so she would like to help.' He paused for a moment. 'My name is Baxter,' he added. 'I'm Mrs Lesage's chauffeur.'

'Yes, I see . . . good heavens . . . well, I really don't know . . .' The chief inspector was at a loss. Outside in the car Julia was beckoning to him.

'I think what Mrs Lesage has in mind is that you should accompany us back to her house, sir, at least until the snow clears. She believes you mean to get back to Oxford, but as things stand there really isn't any way you can do that.'

'That's very kind of her. Her house, you say?'

'She lives the other side of Great Tew. It's not that far from here. The turnoff is at Enstone, so we can get there all right. It's only beyond Enstone that the traffic has been stopped.'

Sinclair took a deep breath. A quick decision was called for. 'Will you thank her for me,' he said, 'and tell her I accept her kind offer?' He rose to his feet.

'She'll be so pleased, sir.' Baxter's somewhat solemn features broke into a broad smile.

'And tell her I'll be with her in a moment, just as soon as I've paid.'

'My dear Mr Sinclair—thank heavens I spotted you through the window. Here, take some of this blanket. I don't want you freezing to death.'

'Please . . . I thought we agreed you would call me Angus.' The chief inspector gratefully accepted a part of the plaid blanket that was draped across her legs.

'I rembered that was your name but I hardly dared use it.' She spoke teasingly. 'Ann says you were a very distinguished detective—quite famous, in fact.'

'Then she was exaggerating.'

Sinclair removed his hat, which he'd forgotten he was still wearing, and regarded his companion with a smile. Julia Lesage was wearing a fur coat and a woollen cap that all but covered her red hair. Only a short strand of it was showing against the pale skin of her forehead. They were seated together on the spacious backseat of what he thought was a Bentley, though he'd hardly had time to take in the car before Baxter, who'd been standing by the open door when he came out of the tearoom, had gently urged him into it. The chauffeur had quickly resumed his place behind the wheel and was now steering them skilfully down a narrow street in near blinding snow.

'Baxter was driving me back from Oxford when we heard on the car radio that the snow was going to get worse. I thought we'd better come up here to Chipping Norton and do some last-minute shopping in case we got cut off. Wickham Manor is rather isolated. That's the name of my house, by the way. I'm afraid you may find yourself trapped there for a day or two.'

Though Julia herself seemed unworried at the prospect—she seemed to be enjoying the sight of the falling snow—she was plainly concerned for her passenger, and Sinclair hastened to reassure her.

'I can't think of a more welcome fate,' he told her. 'You were quite right—I've been caught out. I thought I'd have ample time to return to Oxford this morning, but I should have known better. I was trying to come to terms with my situation when you providentially appeared. I can't thank you enough.'

'What you can do, though, is tell me a little more about

this mystery you're trying to solve.' Her glance contained a challenge. 'I'd hardly finished telling Baxter about the fascinating gentleman I met at dinner last night and the cuff link he showed us when I saw you sitting there in the tearoom. Isn't that so?'

This last remark was addressed to the figure in front of them.

'Quite true, ma'am.' Baxter nodded. He kept his eyes firmly fixed on the snow-covered road ahead.

'I refuse to believe that your trip to Chipping Norton had nothing to do with it, and since you're going to be my guest, or should I say my prisoner, for at least a day or two, I'm going to insist that you tell me all about it. Fair's fair: I think you owe me an explanation.'

'I do indeed.' The chief inspector surrendered gracefully.

'But let's wait till we get home and can settle down by the fire.' She sat forward. 'What do you think, Baxter?' she asked. 'Will we make it all right?'

'Provided no one runs into us, ma'am,' he growled. 'You've got to watch it with some of these drivers. You'd think they'd never seen a bit of snow before.'

'Dear Baxter . . . I'm sure you'll keep us safe and sound. You always do. Where are we, by the way? I can't see a thing.'

'Not that far from Enstone, ma'am.' The chauffeur too was leaning forward, peering through the windshield where the wipers were working busily. 'They'll be stopping cars there, I expect, but it won't affect us. We'll be turning off. There shouldn't be too much traffic on the road after that.'

'That's just as well.' Julia turned to Sinclair. 'The roads are very narrow and the snow will be piling up by now. But there's no need to worry. Baxter can handle anything. Isn't that so?'

Her words brought an answering chuckle from the front seat.

'If you say so, ma'am.'

'So you think this man Beck may be . . . what? A *murderer*?' Julia Lesage's eyes shone with excitement.

'Oh, I wouldn't go that far—not at this point,' Sinclair responded cautiously. 'I can't say for sure that poor Mrs Hartmann's death wasn't an accident. I just feel there's something about him that doesn't add up. Why leave a false address with a car-hire firm? It's not as though he was trying to avoid paying them. He settled his bill without any dispute.'

'Because . . . because . . . what do you think, Baxter?' Julia turned to her chauffeur, who had come into the drawing-room a few minutes before and was busy laying plates and cutlery on the two small tables they were to eat off. Julia had decided they would take their lunch in front of the fire. 'Why is this Mr Beck behaving so mysteriously?'

Baxter kept silent until he had completed his task. Then he straightened up, his brow furrowed by a frown.

'Well, at a guess, ma'am, I'd say he was trying to cover his tracks for some reason.'

'That's a good answer. What do you think, Angus?'

The pair of them were seated in armchairs facing each other beside a roaring fire, which the chauffeur had started as soon as they came in, though not before he had settled his mistress—first helping her to move into the wheelchair, which she had used to get from the garage, where the car was parked, to the house, and then transferring her into a comfortable armchair in the drawing-room. It was clearly a routine they were both well used to, and Julia had smiled her thanks when it was over.

What with the snow falling as thickly as it did there'd been little chance for the chief inspector to take in the countryside as they had made their slow and slippery way from Enstone to the twin villages of Little and Great Tew. All he'd had was a blurred impression of stone walls and snow-laden trees pressing in from both sides of the narrow road. Luckily they had met no traffic coming in the opposite direction during the journey, for if they had, it had seemed unlikely— to Sinclair at least—that the two vehicles would have been able to pass one another without at least one of them sliding off the road and possibly into a ditch. Baxter, to his credit, however, had seemed unfazed by the challenge. It was only when they had finally left the scattering of houses that constituted Great Tew behind them that he had finally admitted to some misgivings.

'Now for the difficult part,' he had muttered.

The road—it was really no more than a lane—linking the village with Julia's house had wound its way through rolling woods for well over a mile and the chauffeur had had his work cut out for him keeping the large, unwieldy car on the track while at the same time preventing it from stalling. When the faint outlines of the house at last became visible ahead of them Julia had broken into a burst of spontaneous applause, clapping her hands.

'Well done, Baxter!'

Built of the same honey-coloured Jurassic limestone for which the area was famous, Wickham Manor proved to be an imposing structure—or so Sinclair judged from what he could see of it in the still driving snow—and it had come as a relief to him when they were finally safe inside the house. While he and his hostess were seated by the fire awaiting their lunch he had learned that besides her secretary, who he was yet to meet, there were two live-in maids, who had remained in residence there while their mistress was in London. Baxter, he was told, had driven her to the capital, but then spent the following week with his widowed mother, who lived in Suffolk, before returning to London in order to drive his mistress back to Oxford.

'Daisy went down to the village this morning to check on her mum,' Baxter told Julia. 'The poor lady's down with bronchitis and Daisy wants to make sure she's coping in this snow. Doris has taken over the kitchen. She'll fix your supper tonight if Mrs Dawlish hasn't got back by then.'

Mrs Dawlish, he gathered, was the cook. She had been away during Julia's absence, visiting her daughter in Bicester, and would doubtless have returned by now if it weren't for the snow.

Meanwhile, arrangements for the chief inspector's stay were already in hand.

'We'll put Mr Sinclair in the Hunt Room,' Julia said. 'It's got a fine view, not that there's much to see at present apart from falling snow. But he'll need some things—pyjamas, for instance. I wonder . . .'

'Leave it to me, ma'am,' Baxter reassured her. 'I'll see that Mr Sinclair has everything he needs. Daisy will get his room ready when she returns from the village, but I'll light a fire there now . . .'

He broke off as the door behind him opened and a woman burst in.

'Mrs Lesage . . . I'm so sorry. I had no idea you were back. I wasn't informed.' Her eyes swept the room, looking for someone to blame, it seemed to Sinclair.

'It's quite all right, Ilse. We've only just got here.' Julia's tone was placatory. 'This is Mr Sinclair.' She gestured towards the chief inspector. 'He's going to be our guest—for a few days most likely if the snow keeps falling. This is Mrs Holtz, my secretary.' She turned to Sinclair, who bowed his head in greeting.

'How do you do?'

The woman's voice was unusually harsh, her accent guttural. Thin as a rake, she had a curved nose not unlike a bird's beak and raven-black hair cut close to her head. Her dark gaze took in the chief inspector's figure.

'I'll need you after lunch, Ilse.' Julia spoke in the same soothing tone. 'I've been missing my massages. And I expect we'll have some business to deal with as well.' She turned to Sinclair again. 'Ilse keeps my affairs in order,' she said. 'I don't know what I'd do without her.'

Baxter coughed.

'If that will be all, ma'am . . .'

'Yes, thank you, Baxter.' Julia turned to him . . . with relief Sinclair felt. She was smiling again. 'Unless there's anything more you can think of, Angus, anything you need . . . ?'

'I've only one favour to ask,' the chief inspector replied. 'I really ought to have been back in Highfield some days ago. I have some friends there who've been on holiday in Italy who are due back today. They'll be more than surprised to find my cottage empty, and possibly a little worried. I wonder if I might ring them this evening; and also my hotel in Oxford.'

'Of course . . .' Julia began to speak, but was cut short by Ilse Holtz.

'I'm sorry, Mrs Lesage, but the phone isn't working. The line must be down.'

'Oh, dear.' Julia bit her lip. 'It does happen from time to time. It's probably due to the snow.'

Baxter spoke up. 'They may still be working in the village, ma'am. I'll slip down there and find out.'

'Dear Baxter . . . would you? Are you sure you can manage in this snow? And if she hasn't come back by the time you go, keep an eye out for Daisy. And don't go until you've had some lunch.'

Julia turned to her guest. 'You see how well I'm looked after. But I am sorry about the phone. I hope your friends will understand.'

The chief inspector swallowed his disappointment. He had been counting on getting word to the Maddens.

'I'm sure they will,' he said.

9

'WELL, WHERE ON EARTH IS HE?' Helen Madden demanded. 'He can't have gone for a walk, not in this weather. And anyway it's getting dark.' She turned to her husband. 'Didn't Lucy say he was supposed to have got back on Monday from Hampshire?'

'She did.'

Having returned from the Continent earlier on the cross-Channel ferry, Madden had rung their daughter from Waterloo station while he and Helen were waiting to set off on the last leg of their journey home. Alarmed by the heavy snowfall—and aware that it was expected to last for some time—they had both begun to worry about the chief inspector. He might well be trapped in his cottage, they thought, and Helen had decided it would be best if they had him to stay with them until the worst was over.

'It's not just for Angus's sake, but for ours as well,' she had pointed out. 'It'll be easier to look after him if he's under our roof.'

Accordingly, soon after they got back to the house, Madden had walked down to Sinclair's cottage expecting to see the lights on and smoke issuing from the chimney. Instead he had found the small dwelling in darkness with no sign of a footprint in the banked snow outside.

Worried now, he had hurried back to the house to find Helen—still with her coat on—anxiously awaiting his return.

'I think I'd better ring the Bennetts in Fernley,' she said after hearing what her husband had to report. 'It's possible Angus felt poorly during the weekend. He may still be with them.'

She returned to the sitting-room after only a few minutes.

'Sir Wilfred's just told me he put Angus on the train at Winchester two days ago. I asked him how Angus was feeling during the weekend and he said he appeared to be in good health. As far as he knew, Angus was heading back to Highfield.'

'As far as he *knew*?' Madden had caught the note of uncertainty in her voice.

'He said Angus had got into a state while he was staying with them. That's how he put it. Some woman living in Fernley had a fall recently while crossing a stream and died as a result. He said Angus had got it into his head that it might not have been an accident, as was assumed. "He's got a bee in his bonnet," was how Sir Wilfred put it.'

'Oh, no!' Madden clutched his head.

'You can see what's happened, can't you?' Helen's glance was meaningful. 'He's playing at being a detective again.'

'He can't be.'

'All we know is that he got on the train at Winchester. Who knows where he is now?' She hesitated. 'Do you think he might be ill?' she asked.

Madden considered the possibility. 'Why not call the hospital at Guildford?' he suggested. 'He may have been taken off the train.'

'I'll do that.'

She hurried out.

At a loss himself, all Madden could think to do was light a fire. The sitting-room was freezing. He was down on his knees on the hearth laying kindling and logs in the empty grate when Helen reappeared, her brow knit in worry.

'He's not there,' she began, but broke off when she saw the look on her husband's face. It was one she knew well.

'I've just been thinking . . .' Madden scowled. 'That was the London train Angus was travelling on. He'd have had to get off at Guildford to change trains, and since it's obvious he didn't he must have gone on.'

'To London, you mean?' Helen watched as he struck a match. 'But why would he do that? And how can we find out?'

'I'm only guessing . . .' Waiting for the fire to catch, Madden sat back on his heels. 'But the most likely explanation is because there was someone there he wanted to speak to.'

'About this business in Fernley, do you mean—about the woman who died?' Helen studied her husband's face.

Madden nodded. Dusting off his hands, he stood up.

'And if I'm right, then I've a good idea who that might have been.'

'I can't credit it . . . and after I expressly told him not to exert himself.' Helen shook her head in disbelief. 'And who is this "war criminal" he thinks he's chasing? It sounds like an old man's fantasy to me.'

Expecting her husband to say something, she waited. They were sitting side by side on the sofa now in front of a crackling fire. Madden had poured each of them a drink. When he stayed silent, she sighed.

'Didn't he give Billy any hint of where he might be going next?' she asked.

'None at all.' Madden shrugged. He had rung his former protégé at Scotland Yard and caught him as he was on the point of leaving for the day. 'Angus *said* he was returning to Highfield, and the last Billy saw of him he was going off in a cab headed for Waterloo. But he must have changed his mind again. It's obvious he went somewhere else, and if I had to bet I'd say it was probably Oxford.'

'Why there?'

'Billy got the whole story at lunch.' Madden rose to put a log on the fire. Returning to the sofa, he repeated in detail the account of it he'd been given.

'And now Angus has gone off in search of this mysterious man with the flat tyre?' Helen shut her eyes as though to block out the image she had conjured up. 'He's taken it on himself to track down the supposed murderer, who may or may not be a war criminal. And what does all this have to do with Oxford?'

'Angus told Billy the car this man was driving was hired from an Oxford firm. There was a notice to that effect pasted to the windshield. If I had to make a guess I'd say that was where he went after his lunch with Billy. He could have caught a train from Paddington.'

'It's insane.' Helen shook her head. 'Didn't he realize how upset we'd be not to find him here?'

Glancing at Madden, she saw him put his hand to a scar that marked his brow near the hairline. It was a souvenir of his time in the trenches during the First World War and touching it was something he did subconsciously when he was thinking.

'John?'

'Angus knew we were due back today.' Madden awoke from his trance. 'And he also knew just how concerned we'd be if we found him missing. So why hasn't he left a message with someone explaining his absence—with Lucy, for example . . . or Will Stackpole?'

'What are you trying to say?'

'I think he expected to be home when we arrived, or soon afterwards. Oh, he'd have some explaining to do—there's no question of that—and to you in particular. But the last thing he'd have wanted to do was worry you. I think something unexpected has happened to him—today, I mean. And I wouldn't be surprised if the snow hadn't got something to do with it.'

'Do you mean he's stranded somewhere, out of reach of a telephone?'

'It's quite possible. But I'm still hoping he might ring us this evening. He wouldn't have known what time we were getting back.'

Helen considered his words.

'And if he doesn't ring?' she said.

Once again her husband was wordless.

'My dear, I'm not exaggerating.' She turned to him. 'I only wish I were. Angus is in no condition to be behaving like this. Any sort of physical effort or stress might be dangerous for him. It could even put his life at risk. I tried to make that clear to him. But it seems I was wasting my breath.'

'I think he knows, all right.' Madden found his tongue. 'And that tells me this must be important to him. But I'm not going to sit here doing nothing. Tomorrow I'll ask Billy to see if he can get me a list of car-hire firms from the Oxford police. That way I can find the one that rented a car to this man.'

'I don't see how.'

'It'll be the one that had a car returned to them with a flat tyre. I can check whether Angus has been to see them.'

'But even if he has, that won't tell us where he is now.' Helen seemed determined to see only the difficulties.

'True. But it'll be a start.'

'Couldn't the Oxford police do that for you?'

Madden shook his head. 'It wouldn't be right to ask them. This is not a police matter—or not yet. That was Angus's problem, you see. He thinks a murder might have gone unnoticed, but he knows he doesn't have enough to start an investigation. He made that clear to Billy. What he's looking for is something he can offer them, something they'll accept as real evidence that a crime has been committed. His reputation's on his side, of course, and I'm sure the Oxford police will be helpful—but only up to a point. They can't start a search for him, not without good reason. But I can.'

Madden smiled. He took her hand in his.

'And if I get even a hint that he's in Oxford I'll go over there and track him down myself. There—will that satisfy you?'

'So long as you can persuade him to come home.' Helen was unyielding.

'What if he refuses?'

'Then do what you think fit. Clap him in irons if you think that's necessary.' She kissed him. 'But bring him back.'

10

'MR MADDEN, IS IT?' The man stepped out from under the shelter of the station awning. 'Morgan's the name.'

'Inspector!' Madden grasped the other's outthrust hand. 'It's good of you to meet me, but you shouldn't have. I'm sure you've got better things to do.'

'Nothing that can't wait.' Morgan chuckled. Lean and sinewy, his fox-like features were split by a wide grin. 'I wasn't going to pass up the chance of meeting you, not when Billy mentioned your name.' He spoke with a lilting Welsh accent. 'That Melling Lodge case is still talked about, you know. And of course you and Mr Sinclair were on it together.'

'Good lord!' Madden laughed. He allowed himself to be guided off the platform through the waiting-room. 'That's ancient history.'

'Maybe so. But if we get a moment together while you're here you might just find yourself having to answer a question or two about it. And also what Mr Sinclair's up to now. It sounds like something we should know about.'

Although the sky had cleared temporarily, the snow that had already fallen was almost knee-deep in some places, as Madden saw when they came outside onto the forecourt.

'According to this morning's forecast, it's not over yet.' Morgan had read his thoughts. 'We're expecting more tomorrow. But to business . . .'

Madden had waited most of the preceding day hoping the chief inspector would get in touch with them. But when the telephone finally rang late in the afternoon it proved to be Billy, who had found what he needed to know unexpectedly quickly.

'I've got the name of that firm in Oxford you want,' he told his old chief. 'It's Hutton. What's more, they had a visit from Mr Sinclair two days ago. He was asking about that bloke with the flat tyre and he got a name out of them and also an address apparently. The fellow you want to talk to in Oxford is an inspector called Morgan. He's by way of being a pal of mine. We worked together on the Ballard case a few years ago. If you're going over there yourself you should get in touch with him. He's expecting to hear from you.'

'Billy, I can't thank you enough. This is more than I asked for.'

Helen had come into the study while Madden was speaking and he'd given her a thumbs-up sign.

'Has Morgan any idea where he is now?'

'If he has, he didn't say so. I didn't want to push him.' Billy had chuckled.

'I know. This is hardly police business. I'll be going over to Oxford at once. I'll talk to you again when I know more.'

'I know you only asked us for a list of car-hire firms.' Morgan was scanning the road outside for a taxi. 'But I've got a couple of new recruits sitting around at headquarters doing nothing useful, so I got one of them to make the calls for you. He hit on Hutton's eventually and I talked to the chap in charge there myself. He gave Mr Sinclair the name of the bloke who hired the car and an address as well. Here—I've written them down for you.'

He handed Madden a slip of paper.

'Chipping Norton . . . that's not far, is it?'

'You can get there in half an hour by car, a bit more by bus. The road was blocked for a day by an accident earlier this week. It happened during the worst of the snow. I don't know if Mr Sinclair planned to go up there. He may still be in Oxford.'

'I'd feel guilty asking you to do anything more,' Madden said. 'This isn't a job for the police.'

'Oh, never mind that.' Morgan flashed his foxy grin. 'I don't mind doing a favour for a couple of old coppers. Who's to know? I'd like to come with you now, but there's stuff back at the station I have to attend to. My office is at St Aldates, by the way. But I expect you want to go over to Cowley and talk to the car-hire chap yourself. He's called Alf Hutton.'

'I was planning to do that,' Madden said.

'Here's a cab now.' Morgan whistled and held up a hand. 'Come round to the station when you're done. I may know by then where the chief inspector's staying here in Oxford. I've got my two greenhorns on the job now. They're calling round the hotels. Here we go . . .'

He pulled open the door of the taxi and ushered Madden inside.

'Thank you again, Inspector.'

'Tom's the name.' Morgan grinned. 'Good hunting.'

Madden looked at the slip of paper in his hand.

'Beck,' he said. 'J. H. Beck. Is that the name you gave Mr Sinclair?'

Alf Hutton nodded. 'The bloke left an address too, in Chipping Norton. Have you got it? Mr Sinclair said he was going up there. But what with the snow and all I wonder if he made it.' He looked out of the plate-glass window fronting his office. 'It's stopped now, but I heard on the wireless this morning there's more to come. You say you're worried about him, sir? He seemed quite well to me.'

'I'm glad to hear it, Mr Hutton. As it happens my wife is his doctor and she's concerned about his health.'

'And is it true he used to be a detective at Scotland Yard?'

'Quite true—a distinguished one, in fact.'

'That's a relief.' Alf Hutton beamed. 'It gave me quite a turn, I can tell you, getting a call from the police this morning. I thought for a moment he might have been up to no good, your Mr Sinclair.' He hesitated. 'But isn't he a bit . . . well . . . past it to be working as a private investigator?'

'Is that what he told you?' Madden managed to mask his surprise. 'Well, my wife would certainly agree with you. But what he's doing is quite unofficial. In fact, he's making these inquiries on behalf of a friend.' Caught himself now in the web of lies the chief inspector had spun, Madden was forced to do some inventing himself.

'The one who's owed money by this chap Beck?' Hutton frowned.

'Yes, exactly,' Madden said, after a pause. It occurred to him that Angus Sinclair might have missed his true métier as a creator of fictions in the manner of, say, Edgar Wallace, and privately resolved to proffer just such a suggestion to him when they next met. 'Did he tell you anything else?' He hardly dared to ask.

Hutton shook his head. 'Only that he was planning to go up to Chipping Norton to look for this fellow.'

'You're sure of that.'

'It's what he said.'

Madden took a moment to reflect.

'In that case, have you got a car available?' he asked.

'A car?' Alf Hutton's face brightened.

'I'd like to hire one.'

The desk sergeant looked up from his ledger.

'Mr Morgan, you say? I think he's busy at the moment, sir. Could you tell me what it's about?'

'Just give him my name, Sergeant.'

Madden went to the door. Two schoolboys, satchels strapped to their backs, were sliding along the packed snow on the pavement in front of him. But the sky above was still clear, apart from scattered cloud. There was no sign yet of the fresh snowfall that the weather forecasters were promising.

At the sound of quick footsteps behind him, he turned and saw Morgan's wiry figure descending the uncarpeted stairs.

'Ah, there you are!' The inspector hailed him. 'I don't suppose you've had any lunch, sir. Would you care to join me for a sandwich in the pub down the road? I've got some more news for you.'

'I was going to suggest it myself.' Madden smiled. He matched his long stride to the inspector's quicker steps as they set off down the road. 'News, you say? Don't tell me you've managed to locate Mr Sinclair.'

'Not quite. But we know where he was staying. It's the Randolph Hotel.' Morgan chuckled. 'There's a chief inspector's pension for you. Mind you, he's Scottish, isn't he? I expect he's been thrifty, got a nice nest egg tucked away. But the thing is he never checked out and they've been wondering what happened to him. He told the clerk at the reception desk yesterday that he was taking the bus up to Chipping Norton, but would be back by lunchtime. It seems he was planning to go back to Highfield that afternoon.'

'Just in time to welcome us home, I dare say. My wife and I returned from holiday that day. Mr Sinclair knew he would have some explaining to do. Helen wouldn't have been best pleased to hear he'd been gadding about.'

They had reached the pub, but Madden stopped outside the door.

'If he never came back to Oxford, he must have got stuck in Chipping Norton. You said there was an accident on the road. Was that the same day?'

Morgan nodded. 'The bus service was suspended. The road wasn't cleared until early evening. He must have stayed up there, got himself a hotel room. But the odd thing is he never rang the Randolph to tell them he wouldn't be back that day. What's more, he hasn't been in touch with them since.' He blew on his fingers. 'Let's get out of the cold, shall we?'

Settled in a corner of the tap room a few minutes later, with pints of beer and a plate of sandwiches in front of them, they continued to puzzle over the mystery.

'There's one answer I can think of,' Morgan said. 'Phone lines have been down all over the Cotswolds. It happens when there's heavy snow.'

'Does that include the line between Oxford and Chipping Norton?' Madden bit into a cheese sandwich.

'Not that I heard.' Morgan shrugged. 'But the same goes for the road. It's open now—the main road, I mean—but a lot of those side roads are still blocked. Some of the houses are cut off. He could be stuck in a village somewhere; perhaps he's still looking for that fellow—what's his name?'

'Beck.' Madden scowled. 'I suppose that's possible,

though the address Hutton gave us is in Chipping Norton. To tell the truth I'm baffled for the present. I can't think where he's got to.'

Morgan took a deep swallow of his beer.

'Tell you what,' he said. 'I'll give the police in Chipping Norton a call when we get back to the station and ask them to check local hotels and boardinghouses to see if Mr Sinclair is or was staying in one of them. That'll tell us something.'

Madden muttered his thanks. 'One way or another, I think I'm going to have to go up there myself this afternoon. I've got a car now, by the way. I hired one from Hutton.'

'That was a stroke of luck for him.' Morgan grinned. 'And now since we've got a moment, could you tell me a little more what this is about? Billy said the chief inspector thought there might have been foul play involved in this woman's death. But that was all.'

'I'll do my best, though only Mr Sinclair knows the full story.' Madden sampled his beer. 'But it seems to revolve around this woman—Greta Hartmann. Who she was, I mean, her past.'

'What about it?' The inspector cocked an eye at him.

'She was German . . . a refugee? She came to England before the war. Her husband died in a concentration camp. Mr Sinclair thinks that may have something to do with her death: that this man she saw might have a Nazi background . . . something of that sort. He's written to an old friend of his, a senior inspector in the Berlin police, asking him to check their records and see if they can find any mention of Mrs Hartmann's name.'

'He was thinking this man might be a war criminal, you mean?' Morgan whistled. 'I'm not sure I like the idea of him going after a bloke like that, not at his age.'

'Nor do I,' Madden said bleakly. 'That's one reason I want to find him. The other is his health. My wife's concerned about him. He shouldn't be exerting himself in this way.' He caught Morgan's eye.

The inspector set his glass down. 'In that case it might be as well to check the hospitals—here and in Chipping Norton.'

'I was thinking the same thing.' Madden felt relieved. He'd been reluctant to ask for yet more help.

'I'll see to it when we get back to the station.' Morgan swallowed the last of his beer. 'You say you're going up to Chipping Norton this afternoon? Keep an eye on the weather. They say the next lot of snow won't be coming in until tonight, but you never know; it might arrive earlier than that.'

It was after two when Madden pulled into the small market town. The drive from Oxford had taken longer than the half hour Morgan predicted. With the snow banked up on either side of the road and a lot of it still covering the tarmac surface, mostly in the form of slush, drivers were taking more care than usual and Madden had resigned himself to the slow pace forced on him.

The car he was driving—it was the same one Hutton had rented to Beck—was equipped with a radio and he had kept it turned on so as to pick up any fresh forecasts about the weather. Apart from the war in Korea, a regular topic for more than a year now, there was little to interest him. But listening to the newsreader's solemn tones, he was reminded of a decision by the BBC earlier that year that had left Helen seething: in future, news bulletins were to be read only by men, the corporation had decreed. Studies had shown that a large number of people did not like to hear news of a serious nature read by a female voice, it was asserted, though who these particular people were was never spelled out. The weather report given at the end of the news had confirmed what Morgan had already told him: it seemed they were due for more heavy snow in the coming hours and the fall would be followed by freezing weather, which would make the roads even more dangerous.

Having parked his car in the centre of town, Madden asked in a chemist's shop for directions to the address he'd been given—Meadow Close—and on learning that it wasn't far off walked the short distance along snow-covered pavements. One look at the short, dead-end street was enough to tell him he was unlikely to find a house bearing the number 15, and so it proved. Aware now that he was in all likelihood treading in Sinclair's footsteps, he returned to the main square, where earlier he had seen a bus stop with a vehicle drawn up showing Oxford as its destination ready to depart.

'Only they weren't running that afternoon, were they, Angus?' He murmured the words to himself. 'You found the service had been suspended. So what did you do next?'

Madden looked about him. He saw there was a tea shop nearby, and reasoning that the snow must have been falling heavily and his friend most likely was in search of shelter, he went into it and sat down at an empty table.

Having discovered that his quarry had left a false address with the car-hire firm, what would Sinclair's next move have been? Madden wondered. Aware that in all probability he wouldn't get back to Oxford that evening, he must have thought of finding some place to spend the night: a hotel or boardinghouse. Once installed there, too, he could have telephoned the Randolph Hotel to report his predicament, and later in the afternoon or evening, when he was sure they had returned from their holiday, his friends in Highfield. *Yes, he would have called us,* Madden thought.

But since he hadn't done either, it meant he almost certainly hadn't spent the night in Chipping Norton. He had found some other refuge, albeit one without a working telephone.

'Excuse me, sir? Can I take your order?' A middle-aged woman wearing a black dress with a white frilled apron stood by the table, pad in hand.

'A pot of tea, please, and a slice of Madeira cake.' Madden had spotted a heavily laden trolley being wheeled by. Just then he had an idea. 'Look, this is an odd question: but do you happen to remember serving an elderly gentleman with a marked Scottish accent yesterday?'

'Goodness me!' She blinked. 'I'm afraid not. We get so many customers. But if you wait a moment, I'll ask Betty. She might remember.'

Two minutes later a second, much younger waitress approached his table. She was carrying a tray.

'Here you are, sir, your tea and cake.' Dark-haired, with bright eyes and a beauty spot in the middle of her cheek, she busied herself for a moment arranging things on the table. Then her brown eyes locked on his. 'Mrs Denham says you were asking about a Scottish gentleman?'

'That's correct.'

'There was one came in yesterday, I recall.'

'Did you serve him?' Madden asked.

She nodded. 'All he wanted was a pot of tea, and I remember he put his hands on it to get them warm, so I suppose he must have been outside for a while. I thought he seemed a bit upset. The snow was really coming down. Was he a friend of yours, sir?'

'An old friend. He hasn't been too well lately and I'm trying to find him, but he seems to have disappeared.'

'Oh, dear . . .' She bit her lip.

'You say he was upset?'

'Bothered more like it.' She frowned. 'And since I'd never seen him before, I thought he wasn't from around here and may have been hoping to get back to Oxford that day, only the buses had stopped. It was the snow, you see.'

'He didn't happen to ask you about hotels or boarding-houses, did he? I was thinking he might have wanted to find somewhere to spend the night.'

'No, sir, nothing like that.' She shook her head. 'But I did notice him talking to a man who came into the shop for a moment.'

'Was it someone he knew?' Madden frowned. 'Could you tell?'

'No, I couldn't, sir. I wasn't watching. We were really busy that day, what with the snow. This other man wasn't here long, and after he went out your friend paid his bill at once. He was in a hurry to go, and the funny thing was he hadn't even drunk his tea. I saw his cup was dry. He hadn't touched it.'

'How extraordinary!'

Madden racked his brains for an explanation. The girl waited patiently for him to speak.

'And you didn't see what he did when he went outside, I suppose?'

'I'm afraid not, sir.' She sounded genuinely regretful. Then her face brightened. 'But there was one thing I noticed . . .'

'Yes?' Madden prompted her.

'This other man who came in, the one who was talking to him, I remember now he had a cap under his arm.'

'What sort of cap?'

'Well, military like, if you know what I mean?' The effort of trying to explain what she meant made her pull a face.

Madden stared at her for a long moment. Then enlightenment came to him.

'Could it have been a chauffeur's cap?' he asked.

Her face cleared at once.

'That's right, sir. That's it. Just like a chauffeur's cap.'

'I'm making a wild guess,' he told Morgan. 'I think someone picked him up at the tea shop, someone passing by in a car driven by a chauffeur, someone who knew him. But who? I can't imagine. To the best of my knowledge Angus had never set foot in Chipping Norton before and I can't believe he knows anyone who lives here. It's a mystery.'

Madden's last question to his informant in the tea shop had been to inquire where the nearest public telephone was located. She had directed him to the post office on the other side of the small market square. He had caught Morgan at his desk.

'Still, you've learned one useful thing, haven't you? It sounds like this bloke the chief inspector's after is a wrong 'un all right. People who leave false addresses behind them generally have a good reason for doing so. Mind you, that doesn't mean he's a war criminal,' he added after a moment's thought. 'What now?'

'I can't do anything more from here. Since Angus failed to call anyone we have to suppose he was taken somewhere

where the phones aren't working, and that could be in any of the villages roundabout if what you told me is true.'

Morgan grunted an acknowledgement. 'The lines are down all over the place. Are you coming back to Oxford, then?'

'Right away. I'll stop off at the Randolph. I want to know if they've heard from Angus. I can also explain what's happened. I don't want them charging him for his room if he's snowbound somewhere. And I want to find out if they can tell me about his movements.'

'Here in Oxford, you mean?'

'He was at the hotel for two nights. I wonder, did he meet anyone there? I'm looking for some connection to Chipping Norton, Tom. How did he come to bump into someone who knew him up there? Maybe the hotel can shed some light on that. I'll ring you again when I get back.'

The inspector was sitting at a table in the lounge with a drink on the table in front of him when Madden came down from his room.

'So you've booked in here too? I don't know where you fellows find the money.'

'Don't you start,' Madden said. 'I've just had my wife on the phone. She wanted to know what I was doing staying at a hotel like the Randolph. It seems she was here with her parents years ago. I tried to explain about it being the best place to wait for Angus in case he showed up. But the main thing is she had some information for me that may have solved our problem. I think I know where Mr Sinclair is.'

'And where's that?'

'I'll explain in a moment. First, I need a drink.' Madden signalled to a waiter.

Since his return from Chipping Norton an hour or so earlier he had been trying to sort out Sinclair's situation with the hotel, and fortunately his explanation for the chief inspector's absence had been well received.

'We've been worried about him, sir,' the clerk at the reception desk had told him. 'We held his room for him, of course, and I'll have to check with management, but I'm sure we won't be charging him for last night. Actually, he's not the only one of our guests caught out by the weather. There's an American couple snowbound at a village near Bicester, though they managed to get in touch with us.'

Madden had proposed a further solution to them.

'I need a room for a night or two,' he said. 'I'm trying to locate Mr Sinclair and this seems to me to be the best place to wait for him to get in touch. Why not let me have his? If he turns up suddenly we'll make other arrangements.'

His suggestion had met with approval once 'management'—which apparently resided in an office behind the reception desk—had been consulted, and shortly afterwards he'd had been shown upstairs.

'Don't worry about Mr Sinclair's things,' he had told the porter who carried his overnight bag up. 'I'll pack them into his suitcase and put it in the cupboard.'

He had done as he said, but not before he'd gone through the chief inspector's belongings and satisfied himself that his heart tablets were not among them. The fact that he had his pills with him was something Helen would want to know and Madden had put in a call to Highfield at once. She hadn't been at home when he rang, but he had left a message for her with Mary Morris, their maid of many years.

In the course of going through Sinclair's things he had noticed a leather-bound notebook and after a brief struggle

with his conscience—it was too close to prying for comfort—
he had glanced at it and seen that the chief inspector had
jotted down a brief account of the inquiries he was making.
It contained no surprises other than some cryptic notes at the
end about a cuff link, of all things.

Costume jewellery? Religious rites? Mexico??

The question marks seemed to suggest puzzlement on the
chief inspector's part, or at least curiosity, and the double
query after 'Mexico' was particularly intriguing.

On the last page he had listed some names—Waites, Lesage, Fielding—but without indicating what significance, if
any, they had for him.

Unable to solve the riddle, Madden had been on the point
of going downstairs to continue his investigations with the
desk clerk—he'd been hoping he might learn something
about Sinclair's movements during his brief stay at the
hotel—when the phone in his room had rung. It was Helen
returning his call, and once she'd done teasing him about his
choice of accommodation she had produced a piece of news
which, as he told Morgan now, had proved to be crucial.

'You remember me saying I thought Mr Sinclair had encountered someone at Chipping Norton who knew him, or
at least recognized him, and probably took him off in a car.'

Morgan nodded.

'Well, my wife had had a call earlier today from the
people Angus was staying with in Hampshire before he came
here.'

'You mean Bennett, the old A.C. at the Yard?' Morgan
grunted. 'Billy told me about them.'

'It was Sir Wilfred's wife who rang. She was worried after
we called to ask if they knew where Angus went after he left
them. Helen told her we thought now he'd probably gone to

Oxford and Lady Bennett wondered whether he might have had contact with another guest they had staying with them that weekend: someone called Ann Waites. She's a former psychiatrist and a professor now at Somerville. Angus made a note of her name. Apparently they had a long conversation in Hampshire and almost the last thing she did before she left to return here was to make him promise to get in touch with her if he ever came to Oxford.'

'Which he did only a couple of days later?' Morgan snapped his fingers. 'I can easily get her numbers for you, home and college.'

'That won't be necessary. Lady Bennett gave them to Helen. I've just been speaking to her—Professor Waites, that is. It turns out she bumped into Angus here, in this very hotel, on Tuesday and invited him to dinner at her house that same evening. One of the other guests present was a lady named Julia Lesage, who was staying with Professor Waites. I gather she's a wealthy woman. But more to the point, she travels around in a chauffeur-driven Bentley . . .'

'And you reckon it was her who picked up Mr Sinclair in Chipping Norton?'

'It seems to have been someone with a chauffeur, and all things considered I think Mrs Lesage is our most likely suspect. She probably spotted Angus sitting in that tea shop when they drove by and realized he was stranded.'

'Does she live near there?'

'She has a house in the Cotswolds near a place called Great Tew. Does that mean anything to you?'

'I've been there a couple of times. It's near another village called Little Tew.' Morgan grinned. 'They're a few miles off the main road between Oxford and Chipping Norton. Ten to one they're snowed in right now, and very likely with the

phone lines down.' He tugged at an earlobe. 'Lesage . . .
Lesage . . . would that be the lady who's stuck in a wheelchair? If so I've heard of her.'

'She was a skiing champion before the war,' Madden told
him. 'She broke her back in an accident and has never walked
again. I got all that from Professor Waites. She and Angus
seemed to have hit it off, which makes it all the more likely
she was the one who came to his aid.'

He took a swallow of his whisky.

'The only trouble is if he's stuck there with her, as I think,
I won't be able to speak to him until the phones are working
again.'

'And meanwhile your wife wants him back in Highfield?'

'She insists on it. She wants him to stop playing detective,
as she puts it. I had to tell her there was nothing I could do
for the moment. I'm not sure I could even drive up there in
the old heap Hutton gave me, especially with this fresh
snowfall we're expecting, and even if I could I wouldn't want
to risk coming back with Angus as a passenger. What if we
got stuck on the road somewhere?'

Madden stood at the window of his room looking out. His
faint hope that the snow might relent, at least for a while, had
been dashed by the sight that met his eyes now. The dense
curtain of white had reduced the buildings on the other side
of the street to little more than a blur, while the Ashmolean
Museum, only a few steps away, had disappeared altogether.

He was still taking in the scene when the bedside
phone rang.

'Hullo, sir!' Billy Styles's familiar voice sounded in his
ear. 'I'm glad to have caught you. I've just had a word with

Tom Morgan and he told me where you were staying. He also said you had a good idea where the chief inspector might be, but you could explain it better than he could.'

'I'm guessing he's stuck in a house in the Cotswolds,' Madden said. 'He went up to Chipping Norton and was caught out by the snow. But the phones are out up there so I haven't had a chance to discover if I'm right. Why do you ask?'

'I've just been speaking to a bloke who's particularly keen to know. He's that German copper Mr Sinclair wrote to: *Kriminalcommissar* Probst.' Billy chuckled. 'I think I got that right.'

'Did he call you from Berlin?' Madden was astonished.

'No, Ramsgate, as it happens. He'd just got off the Channel ferry and wanted a word with me before he caught his train. He's coming up to London tonight.'

Madden needed a moment to digest this news. 'Let me get this straight,' he said. 'Is Probst worried about Mr Sinclair's health? You told me Angus had written to him from Hampshire.'

'He didn't mention it, sir. It's Greta Hartmann's name that got them all excited.'

'Them?'

'The Berlin CID—we had one of their senior blokes on the phone yesterday. He spoke to Mr Chubb and Mr Chubb had a word with the assistant commissioner and as a result it was agreed Probst should come over right away. I've been detailed to hold his hand, and since it's known that Mr Sinclair went to Oxford on the trail of this chap he's after, that's where we'll start. Tom Morgan will handle things at the Oxford end—it's been okayed by his chief constable. We're meeting him in his office tomorrow morning. Tom said you'd be welcome to join us if you want to.'

'Oh, I'll be there. You can count on it.' Madden hesitated. 'You say it was Greta Hartmann's name . . . ?'

'That's right. It seems she was mixed up in some case over there a long time ago, just like the chief inspector thought. It was before the war. That's all I know. Probst didn't have time to say more. He had to catch his train. He just wanted to know if Mr Sinclair was all right. Is he safe and sound? That's what he said. Well, at least I can put his mind at rest on that score.'

Madden was silent.

'What is it, sir?' Billy had sensed something.

'If it's not Angus's health he's worried about, why is he so concerned about him?'

'Oh, well, that's because of the man Mr Sinclair's been chasing,' Billy said. 'Probst was afraid he might have caught up with him.'

'And why should that have worried him so much?' Madden felt the first faint prick of alarm.

'Because they know who he is, or think they do. And if they're right, he's killed before—and more than once.'

11

HANS-JOACHIM PROBST.

Madden had never forgotten the name, nor the relish with which Angus Sinclair had pronounced it years before in describing the Berlin detective who had come to London to help with a murder investigation, and he had risen that morning with the welcome prospect ahead of finally meeting the man who had left such a deep impression on his old friend.

'To look at him you might think he was a schoolmaster or some fussy bureaucrat,' Sinclair had told him. 'But don't be deceived: he's far from that.'

The chief inspector's words came back to him a short while later when he arrived at the police station. Unable to find a taxi—it was still snowing heavily—Madden had been forced to make the short journey from the hotel on foot and he found Billy and his charge already seated in Morgan's office and the meeting under way.

'Mr Madden! What a pleasure to meet you after all these years.' Probst had risen from his chair to shake his hand. His fluency in English came as no surprise: Madden had often heard Sinclair speak of it. A slight, unassuming figure, with thinning hair that receded from a high forehead, there was more than a touch of the schoolmaster about him. But although his polite bow as they shook hands only strengthened the impression of formality, Madden sensed something else behind the mild blue eyes that met his for a moment: a sadness that had no part in the present moment, but dwelt in some other realm beyond the reach of any healing touch.

'I have heard so much about you from our mutual friend.' Probst had pressed his hand for a moment. 'It's a pleasure finally to make your acquaintance.'

Their discussion had got under way before he arrived and Morgan had asked the German detective if he would mind repeating what he had just told them. Before responding, Probst had asked if the other two would bear with him for a moment while he satisfied himself on a point that was troubling him.

'I understand you have not been able to make direct contact with Angus since he wrote that letter to me?' He addressed the words to Madden, who had taken a seat beside him. 'Inspector Styles tells me you are reasonably sure of his whereabouts. All the same I'd be grateful if you could tell me exactly what you know of his movements.'

In response, Madden outlined the inquiries he had made on arriving in Oxford and the conclusion he had come to as a result of them.

'I can't be a hundred percent sure, but all the signs are that he met someone he knew by chance in Chipping Norton, a lady he had met at a dinner in Oxford the night before. Realizing that he was stranded there—the bus service had been cancelled because of the snow—she appears to have offered him a place to stay for the night and taken him home with her. But because of the snow he's been trapped there.'

'I can add something to that,' Morgan chipped in. 'I've discovered that the phone lines in that area have been down since that day. I was going to tell you this morning, sir.' He glanced at Madden. 'I was told they started to clear the roads yesterday. But now we've got this fresh fall.' He indicated the window behind him, where the thick white flakes could be seen spiralling down. 'So I can't say how long it'll be before you can get up there.'

'But the important thing is he's safe.' Probst nodded as though to reassure himself. 'This is what was worrying me.' He turned to face Madden. 'I will explain now why I have been so concerned. As you know, it was Greta Hartmann's name that caught our eye in Berlin. It is linked to a particularly brutal double murder that took place there in 1937. The victims were a widowed lady named Frau Klinger and her lawyer. The two murders took place on the same evening, but in different locations in the city and bore no similarity to one another. That is to say, Frau Klinger appeared to have been the victim of a deranged killer—she had been savagely attacked and her body badly mutilated—while the lawyer died of head injuries received in what seemed to have been a clumsy attempt to rob him in the street. Nevertheless, it was eventually accepted by the detectives investigating the cases that the two murders were connected and that the motive was the same in each case.'

'And what was that?' Morgan asked.

'By killing these two people the murderer hoped to draw the attention of the police away from a quite different crime—one of embezzlement—in which he would have been a prime suspect. The lady in question had been systematically robbed of a large sum of money over a period of time. Because of the circumstances of her death—and her lawyer's—this did not come out at once, but when it did it was assumed her lawyer had detected the fraud and paid the price, as indeed had Frau Klinger. In the event, these two murders were instrumental in giving the killer time to vanish from the scene. The case was eventually closed during the war, or at least put on ice, and has never been reopened until now.'

'And how was Mrs Hartmann involved?'

'She was a close friend of the deceased lady, who was a member of the congregation of the Lutheran church where Greta's husband, Manfred Hartmann, was pastor.' Probst frowned. 'I believe you're aware that he had spoken out against the Nazis and been imprisoned in a concentration camp as a result. At the time of the murders he had already fallen ill with typhus, from which he died soon afterwards. I mention that because of the effect it had on Frau Hartmann. She was in an extremely distressed state when she was interviewed by the police and probably not the most convincing witness, at least as far as they were concerned.'

'What was it she was trying to tell them?'

'That she had long held suspicions about a man who had somehow worked his way into Frau Klinger's confidence and who the police eventually realized—though unfortunately too late—was almost certainly the murderer they were seeking. He was called Klaus Franck, though the name is unimportant. It was later learned that this same person had used a number of aliases in the past. In fact, determining his true identity proved difficult and delayed the progress of the investigation for some time.'

'I take it you weren't involved in the case yourself?' Madden had needed a moment to absorb what he had just been told before putting the question.

'I played no part whatever in the investigation. In fact, I was no longer with the police.' Probst shrugged. 'I resigned in 1933 shortly after the Nazis came to power. I had no wish to serve under such a regime in any capacity.'

'But you returned to the force later?'

'After the war ended I was offered my job back, though I did not accept immediately.' A shadow crossed his face. 'However, I decided in the end to take up my old profession again and at the same time I wrote to tell Angus, with whom I had lost contact during the war, only to find that he had retired in the meantime. We have continued to correspond since.'

Probst glanced at Morgan, who cleared his throat.

'That's as far as we'd got,' he told Madden. He turned to their visitor. 'Yet you seem to know a lot about this case, sir.'

'You're quite right, Inspector . . . but only in a sense.' Probst sighed. 'When I returned to my old job one of my first tasks was to review what I think you call cold cases— investigations that had been shelved for one reason or another. Needless to say this double murder was among them and I found it to be so extraordinary that I studied it in detail—without, I should add, coming to any conclusion as to how it might have been handled differently by the detectives at the time. It's fair to say they were led by the nose—is that the correct expression?' He paused to cast an inquiring glance at Morgan, who nodded after a moment. 'But I was forced to wonder whether I would have done any better. It was clear that the killer was a criminal of a most unusual kind.' He shook his head in seeming disbelief. 'We are all familiar with confidence tricksters. We know how they seek out gullible victims and prey on their weaknesses. But in general they are thieves and nothing more. This man was different. Oh, a thief certainly—there was no question of that—but a cold-blooded murderer as well: a man who reacted with complete coolness when he realized his fraud was found out; who in the course of a day or two was able to plan and execute two murders, one of them excessively cruel and bloody, while maintaining a front of innocence that the police, for a while at least, found perfectly convincing. Have any of you ever come across a criminal of this kind?'

In the silence that followed, it was Madden who spoke.

'You said this man had had various aliases in the past. So you know something of his background?'

'A good deal, as it happens.' Probst turned to him. 'But most of it was learned much too late to be of any use. To begin with he was born in Argentina, of English parents . . .'

'Good God!' Morgan couldn't contain his surprise.

'Yes, that must come as a shock.' Probst was apologetic. 'But until now his connection with this country seems to have been nonexistent. His father was an engineer employed in the construction of railways, named Arthur Butler, who travelled to South America with his bride around the turn of the century. But after only three years, when they already had two children, a boy and a girl, he was killed in an accident in the Andes and a year later his widow married a German rancher who had also emigrated to Argentina, called Karl Voss. The two children subsequently took his name, so for purposes of clarity I will refer to the boy from now on as Heinrich Voss, since at some point, perhaps at his stepfather's behest, he changed the name he was born with, which was Henry. The two children were raised speaking English and German as well as Spanish and this polylingual background was to come in handy for young Voss later in life. During the time he spent in Berlin he was taken for what he professed to be—a German brought up in South America, though he claimed Chile as his place of birth rather than Argentina for reasons that will become clear. I might add that what I am telling you comes from a variety of police sources not only in Argentina but also Peru and Mexico. Needless to say it took many months to gather it and by the time all the facts about Voss were assembled war broke out and the investigation was put aside.'

Probst broke off to drink from a glass of water that had been placed on the desk in front of him. Morgan watched him, frowning.

'If I could interrupt for a moment,' he said, 'there's something I'd like to clear up. As I understand it, the assumption is Mrs Hartmann may have recognized him when he stopped in . . . where was it again?' He glanced at Madden.

'Fernley. It's a village in Hampshire.'

'Let's suppose it *was* this Voss character, and let's suppose also that he knew he'd been spotted. Would he really have killed her as Mr Sinclair thinks? Wouldn't that have been an extreme reaction?' The Oxford inspector spread his hands. 'All she could have had was a glimpse of him. Even if their eyes met it was hardly enough for a positive identification, particularly given the number of years that had passed since she'd last seen him. Is it likely he would have taken the risk of killing her in the open like that? What if he'd been seen?'

Probst put his glass down. He looked thoughtful.

'To deal with your last point first, I think we may take it for granted that he would have made sure they were not observed,' he began. 'This is a very cool assassin we are dealing with, Inspector, a man of ice. But the really interesting question is, always supposing he did kill her, *why* should he have chosen to do so?'

'*Why?*' Billy broke in. Apart from greeting Madden when he'd arrived, it was the first time he'd spoken.

'I mean, even if he knew or guessed that Mrs Hartmann

had possibly recognized him, what could have prompted him to take such a risky course?'

'The fear that she might report seeing him to the police, I suppose.' To Billy the point seemed obvious.

'Of course. But would even that have alarmed him enough to take violent action?' Probst seemed to struggle with the question. 'What sort of story would she have to tell? That she had seen a man who she thought might be someone she believed guilty of a murder committed in another country many years before. Even if the police took what she said seriously would they really have started a search for him on such flimsy evidence? All things considered I think this same coolheaded man, who was only passing through the village, who had no connection with Hampshire as far as we know, would simply have gone on his way, leaving her to her suspicions.'

'Well, then why *did* he kill her . . . *if* he did?' Billy felt he'd painted himself into a corner.

'To answer that, I shall have to tell you a little more about Heinrich Voss.' Probst acknowledged the problem with a nod. 'In order to discover his real identity the Berlin CID had recourse to the International Police Commission, which was based at that time in Vienna. Although there was no mention of a Klaus Franck in their records they were in possession of information regarding three unsolved crimes that seemed related to the murders that had taken place in Berlin. Requests had been received from the police in both Peru and Mexico for any information regarding a criminal with a very particular modus operandi: a man who preyed on women, first robbing them and then killing them as a means of either hiding his crime or at least muddying the waters so that he had time to make his escape. Since this was almost a copy-book example of what had happened to the unfortunate Frau

Klinger and her lawyer, we were naturally interested to know more and it was by contacting the police in both Lima and Mexico City that we finally began to piece together the past of this dangerous man. I say "we", though of course I played no part in these inquiries. But the detectives who handled the investigation were well known to me.'

Probst paused to take another sip of water.

'One of two murders he committed in Mexico bore similarities to an unresolved killing that had occurred in Argentina some years previously. The Mexican police were aware of this as it had been something of a cause célèbre at the time, at least in Latin America. In both instances the bodies of the victims had been savaged with a knife; in the case under investigation in Mexico—it involved the murder of a young woman—the victim's heart had actually been cut out and placed on her forehead.'

'Good God!' Morgan couldn't stop himself.

'And that wasn't all. There were two servants in the house at the time—a cook and a maid—and both were butchered along with their mistress. It seemed like the work of a madman, as was no doubt the intention of the man who performed the act. Right from the start he sought to point the police in the wrong direction and away from the real motive of the crime. However, the brutality of the killings was reminiscent of the murder that had taken place in Argentina and the Mexican police got in touch with the Buenos Aires CID. In this way a tentative connection was made between the two crimes: a link that had now been communicated to us.'

'So this Voss character had also murdered someone in Argentina? Have I got that right?' Morgan was trying to keep up with the complicated story.

'It would seem so.' Probst shrugged. 'But once again there

was no positive evidence on which to charge him. The case I'm about to describe for you occurred in the late twenties when he was still at university in Buenos Aires. A fellow student of his, a young man from the provinces, was found murdered in his room. There was no apparent motive for the crime, other than possibly a sadistic one: the body had multiple stab wounds, none of them on its own fatal, but cumulatively enough to kill him. He was gagged and seemed to have taken a long time to die. This boy was one of a group of students with a proclaimed belief in a nihilistic creed, fashionable at the time, that rejected all religious and moral principles, and not surprisingly they all came under suspicion, though none of them in the end could be tied to the murder. Voss was one of the group, and interestingly, in hindsight at least, had the solidest alibi of all: on the night in question when this luckless boy met his end he was with his sister. Or so she said.'

'His *sister*?' This time it was Billy Styles who was the first to react.

'Alicia . . . or Alice, as she had been named at birth; she was a year younger than her brother. At this point she was a student at the conservatory in Buenos Aires, studying the piano. They were very close—so close in fact that shortly after the affair of the murdered student she was sent by her stepfather to live with a brother of his who had settled in Córdoba, several hundred miles away . . .' He paused deliberately.

'Are we to assume the two facts were related?' Madden asked the question.

Probst seemed unsure how to reply. He pursed his lips.

'We are in the dark where that is concerned. But reading the reports we received from the police in Buenos Aires—and this was many years afterwards—I formed a strong impression that the detectives who investigated the murder of the student believed that in spite of his alibi Voss was in fact the culprit and that his sister had lied on his behalf. Both were questioned rigorously, but neither cracked under pressure. The police further believed, though they could offer no proof of this, that Karl Voss had deliberately separated the pair as soon as the investigation was concluded. It seems there was a suspicion among those who knew them that their relationship was . . . unhealthy.'

'Do you mean incestuous?' Madden asked.

Probst could only shrug in response.

'What became of Heinrich?'

'Soon after this affair, and without graduating from university—he was studying to become an architect—he left Argentina, never to return. The police had reason to believe that his stepfather cut him off from the family. He was known to have given him some money, enough to live on for a while, and was heard by servants at the ranch to have told his stepson that he never wanted to see him again. I should have mentioned that by this time Karl Voss was a widower. His English wife, and the mother of the two children, had died three years earlier. And one further point: when Karl Voss was asked some time later to provide photographs of both children he replied that he had destroyed every picture he had of them, an answer that speaks volumes, do you not think?'

Madden rubbed his chin. 'It certainly sounds as though he believed his stepson was guilty of the murder.'

'Indeed. And since he was not in Buenos Aires himself at the time it can only have meant that he based his judgement on what he already knew of the boy's character—a disturbing thought.' Probst's face showed pain. 'However, that was the sum of what the Argentine police were able to tell us about Heinrich Voss, and together with what we learned from the police in Lima and Mexico City we were able to form a rough picture of the career of this man of many aliases. In brief, he had managed to form relationships of a sort with women in both those cities and, having extracted considerable sums of money from them by fraudulent means, had disposed of them, though in the case of Mexico City, the death of the second of his victims, a wealthy spinster, was not initially treated as a case of murder—she drowned in her own swimming pool. But a subsequent examination of her financial dealings, in which Voss played a significant part, led the police later to regard it too as a likely case of murder.'

'I take it he kept changing his name during those years.' Billy spoke again.

Probst nodded. 'We had a list of his aliases and just prior to the outbreak of war we also acquired photographs of him from the Argentine police. From these we were able to confirm from people who had encountered Klaus Franck in Berlin that it was the same man. However, I regret to have to tell you these photos were lost during the war. Because the case had been put to one side, they were stored with other evidence not involved in ongoing investigations in a warehouse that was destroyed in a bombing raid. Until I received Mr Sinclair's letter a few days ago we had not thought to ask the Argentine police to send us copies. Despite the inquiries we had made via the international commission, there had been no reported sightings of Voss anywhere in Europe following his disappearance; nor had the investigation been advanced in any way during the war; to all intents and purposes it had been closed. That mistake has now been remedied. Requests have already been cabled to Buenos Aires asking for fresh copics of the photographs to be wired to Berlin. They will be forwarded to London as soon as possible. However, we can't be sure how good the quality will be, given that the pictures were taken a long time ago and they'll be radio photographs.'

Probst drank from his glass again.

Madden shifted in his chair. Watching him, Billy saw his old chief put a hand to the scar on his forehead.

'I was wondering what happened to Voss's sister,' Madden said. Looking up, he found that Probst's gaze was on him. The German detective had a wry smile on his face.

'You must be a mind reader, Mr Madden. I was about to return to that very subject. To answer your question, Alicia Voss remained with her uncle in Córdoba until she came of age a little over a year later and then promptly quit his household and without even making contact with her stepfather disappeared. Did she rejoin her brother, who was in Peru? I cannot say. All I can tell you is that the police in both Lima and Mexico City had no record of her being there. Of course, she could easily have changed her name too, and may have done so at her brother's direction.'

'Is it thought he was controlling her?' Madden asked.

'Again, I can't be sure. The simple truth is she disappeared—at least for some years. But the story doesn't end there. When detectives began investigating the murder of Frau Klinger they naturally interviewed the man she had been seeing so much of, Klaus Franck, though not as a possible suspect at that stage, simply as a source of information. However, after Frau Hartmann had communicated her suspicions to them they questioned him again, in particular about his movements on the evening in question. He told them he had spent the night with a woman friend at the Adlon Hotel. She was a divorced woman who lived in Munich, he said; they had been in a relationship for more than a year. His story was confirmed both by the lady herself when she was contacted by the Munich police and by the Adlon, which is to say that they had both certainly checked into the hotel that evening.'

'Though he could easily have slipped out.' Madden nodded to himself. 'And the lady from Munich . . . ?'

'Resigned from her job with a travel agency quite soon afterwards and was not seen or heard from again. Eventually the Berlin police came to the conclusion that in all likelihood she was Voss's sister, Alicia. There was no proof of that, of course, but it was hard to imagine who else she might be. A description of how he behaved with Frau Klinger when he appeared in Berlin, which we obtained from acquaintances of hers, painted a picture of a polite, rather diffident man who seemed genuinely fond of her while never overstepping the bounds of propriety; who seemed anxious only to help with the practical problems faced by a woman, recently widowed, who suddenly had to cope with the sort of difficulties her late husband had always dealt with.'

'I assume they were of a financial nature?' Madden framed the remark as a question.

'Exclusively so. He managed to persuade her to invest a large sum in several South American companies which eventually proved to exist only on paper. It was this scheme that her lawyer uncovered after she had grown suspicious and turned to him for help. If only she had gone directly to the police she would at least have emerged from the debacle with her life, if not the money she had parted with. But she chose to give Voss a chance to explain himself, a decision that proved fatal to her—and her lawyer. It seems she had come to trust him utterly and probably couldn't believe that he might have betrayed her. This at least will show you how persuasive a confidence man he was. None of her friends could credit what had happened either; they thought the person they knew as Klaus Franck was incapable of committing the crimes he was suspected of.'

'Except Greta Hartmann . . . and now she's dead too.' Madden scowled.

Billy stirred uneasily in his chair. 'Excuse me, sir, but what I don't understand is how he managed to fool all these women. And how could he have known they were the kind of people who would fall for his line?'

'That's a fair question.' Probst nodded. 'And the short answer is, because he was willing to take the time to ensure they would. He was prepared to be helpful and understanding, always agreeable; to help them in every way he could with favours great and small; and above all to be endlessly patient. His first such victim was the widow of a Peruvian businessman, and it took him all of two years before he was ready to strike. Having convinced her that the financial advisers she had turned to after the death of her late husband were taking advantage of her, he had persuaded her to invest a substantial sum of money in what were purported to be government bonds. Needless to say this always helpful man handled the details of the purchase for her. The scheme would not have stood up to any sort of scrutiny beyond the first issue of interest, which was due six months after the purchase date, but by then the lady was already dead. She had an accident in her motorcar, which went off the road and tumbled into a ravine, where it burst into flames. It was only much later, and after exhaustive medical tests, that it was determined she had died prior to the accident. By that time Voss had made good his escape and later it became clear that he had gone to Mexico.'

Probst stretched to ease a stiff muscle. Billy glanced at his watch. They had been listening to their visitor for the best part of an hour, though the time seemed to have passed more quickly than that.

'I have told you about this Peruvian incident in some detail so as to give you an idea of how this man operates. He was to follow much the same pattern in the crimes that followed. The important thing to notice is the time he was prepared to spend lulling whatever doubts his victims might have had about him before moving on to his prime purpose—and something else too.'

The Berlin policeman hesitated. A frown creased his brow.

'What I say now is pure speculation, an idea I have formed about this man. It seems to me there is something almost sensuous about this lengthy period of near seduction he engages in, the many months he has been prepared to spend hiding his true nature, which is savage and pitiless, behind a mask of pretended benevolence. Did he gain some satisfaction from it? I ask myself. Was the prospect of what he would eventually do to these poor women enough to compensate him for what must have seemed many wearisome hours? In this regard we should not forget his first murder in Buenos Aires. He stood to gain nothing by the boy's death. There was only the pleasure he took in killing him as he did, in prolonging the death agony over many hours. To say he is very likely a sadist is just to touch on the mystery that such a mentality presents. Or, to put it another way, is it the final act, the murder or murders he knows he will eventually commit, that mean the most to him—more even than the money he has extracted from his victims.'

Probst paused, weighing his next words. 'Of course the irony is, had he waited a little longer, had he kept a curb on his appetites, he would have found himself living under a regime where his worst instincts might have been given free rein; protected by a black uniform with a death's-head badge he would not have had to look far to satisfy his urges. But his life took another course and he has left a trail behind him that he must be aware of. This is the point I wish to get over to you.'

'I'm not sure I understand . . .' Morgan began, but he was cut off by Madden.

'Yes, I see. That's why he killed Greta Hartmann.'

'Now you've lost me, sir.' Billy shook his head.

'He didn't want the authorities alerted in any way,' Madden explained. 'While the police might not take anything Mrs Hartmann said to them seriously, they would remember it later if they had reason to and get in touch with the Berlin CID. The hunt for Heinrich Voss would be on again.'

'If they had *reason* to?' Billy still didn't understand.

'If a crime of the same sort took place again—only this time in England—and if they had been warned about this man in advance.'

'This is what I fear.' Probst broke in. 'It's why I persuaded my superiors to let me come here to lend any help I can to you. I was afraid too that Angus might actually confront this man without knowing how dangerous he was.'

'Sir, I still don't see . . .' Morgan interrupted.

'If Voss was the man Frau Hartmann saw, then we have no idea how long he has been in this country.' Probst turned to him. 'But if his past record is anything to go by, he may well have found a fresh victim by now, and if so, we have no way of knowing who she is or how long she has to live.'

12

'I FEEL LIKE ONE of Chekhov's heroines,' Julia Lesage said, 'stuck in the country miles from Moscow with the snow coming down. Mind you, it is rather beautiful, isn't it? I love the way the snowflakes spin round and round and land like tiny flying saucers.'

The chief inspector stayed silent. He had no opinion on either topic just then. Despite the pessimistic weather forecast he had been hoping the snow might finally relent, but the morning had brought a continuation of the previous day's fall, with the slight but dispiriting difference that it was even heavier than what had gone before. There was no escape from the mess he'd got himself into: he was stranded with a vengeance.

'It reminds me of when I was in Switzerland before I hurt myself. I used to ski off piste with friends up on the glaciers. I knew it was dangerous, but the thrill it gave us was something you couldn't find anywhere else. There's something to be said for living on the edge, Angus.' She glanced up at him. 'It's like having extra oxygen in your lungs or . . . or wildfire in your veins.'

Her green eyes were alive with remembered pleasure and Sinclair met her eager gaze with a smile. They were in the drawing-room in front of a large picture window that looked out onto a snow-covered terrace and beyond to what might in another season have been a long descending lawn divided by flower beds and hedges and marked with an ornamental pond, which alone among all the features dimly glimpsed now was not cloaked in a mantle of white.

'I remember when I had my fall. For those seconds when I was in the air I felt I was flying. It was as if I had wings.' She held his gaze. 'I can see what you're thinking—well, she's certainly paid for her foolishness.'

'I'm thinking no such thing.' It wasn't enough, and the chief inspector knew it. 'The truth is I've never known what you experienced in the mountains, or anything close to it, though I wish I had, and I envy you more than I can say.'

He laid a hand on her shoulder. She pressed it with hers.

'That's quite enough of maudlin reminiscence. I must get back to work. Ilse and I have still got a load of paperwork to go through. After Andre died I made up my mind that, whatever else, I wasn't going to decline into a useless cabbage. I was going to learn how to handle all the business he used to deal with. But it's been a hard road and I don't think I could have managed without Ilse's help. So I must leave you to your own devices for a while.'

With a smile she spun her wheelchair around and set off at speed. She had already given the chief inspector cause to admire the dexterity with which she handled her unwieldy vehicle, swerving around corners, spinning on the spot, and, when necessary, coming to a sudden halt with the help of the two small handbrakes attached to the wheels. He watched now as she went shooting through an open door at the far end of the room, which, he knew from the tour she had given him the day before, led to her study, and where no doubt Ilse Holtz was sitting now at one of the two desks placed facing each other that he had noted earlier when Julia had led him through the room.

'We won't disturb you, Ilse,' she had said as they went by, interrupting for a moment the rattle of typewriter keys. Her secretary had been hard at work on the instrument. 'I'm just going to show the chief inspector the library.'

Mrs Holtz had looked up for a moment, but once again Sinclair had been aware of the probing glance she had sent his way. Her dark eyes were unreadable. Nor had he got any clearer impression of her at dinner that evening, when she had said little, and then only in reply to remarks that were addressed to her.

'I'm sorry, Angus, Ilse can be heavy going at times.' Julia had apologized for her secretary when she and her guest took their coffee in front of the fire in the drawing-room. 'But she's very loyal. I'm not blessed with a head for business and I need someone who can read a balance sheet and keep track of things. Andre was the dearest man, but he left me far too much money and I spend half my time thinking of ways to get rid of it—good ways, I hasten to say. I'm always on the lookout for deserving charities.'

They had both gone to bed early, but the chief inspector had lain awake for some time considering his predicament. Twice during the night he had got up to look out of the window, only to find that the snow was still falling steadily.

It had come as little surprise to him to learn from his hostess at breakfast that the phone was still out of order. Baxter had ploughed his way down to Great Tew once again and returned with the discouraging news that there too the telephone line was down.

'I'm so sorry, Angus,' Julia had told him. 'I know you were hoping to ring your friends in Highfield.'

The chief inspector had half hoped he might be offered a lift in her car at least as far as Enstone, where he could have hoped to catch a bus back to Oxford (provided the service was operating). But the fresh fall of snow had put paid to that hope. Word from the village, which arrived in the shape of the baker's boy, who had appeared while they were having breakfast with a basket of fresh bread for the household, was that the road was closed for the time being, not simply because of the depth of snow covering it but because a lorry that had attempted the passage the previous day had got stuck two miles outside of Little Tew and all efforts to shift it thus far had failed.

'It'll take Mr Emsley's tractor to pull it out of the ditch,' the lad had predicted confidently after Julia had had him brought in from the kitchen so that she could question him. 'And he'll have to come over from Enstone first.'

There was nothing left to do but to make the best of things, the chief inspector decided as he dutifully swallowed his morning tablet, and in that respect he could hardly have landed in kinder hands. Julia had been determined that he should be entertained in one way or another and directly after breakfast the day before she had taken him on an extended tour of the house, leading the way from room to room in her wheelchair. They had started in the kitchen, where they came on Baxter, who was sitting at the long oak table finishing his breakfast in the company of the two maids, Doris and Daisy, the first a woman in her forties, or so Sinclair judged, who had little to say but exuded a sense of calm dependability, in contrast to the second, who seemed barely out of her teens and sported a headful of blonde curls that were tied with a red ribbon.

Julia had consulted her chauffeur on the likelihood of the road to Enstone being cleared by the end of the day. Baxter had not been optimistic.

'All this fresh snow's not going to make things any easier, ma'am. Even if they move that lorry I wouldn't want to risk driving you anywhere just for the moment. We could easily get stranded.'

'I was thinking of Mr Sinclair,' Julia had said. 'He really needs to get back to Oxford.'

Baxter had examined the question, sipping his cup of tea.

'It might be best if we wait for news from Enstone,' he said finally. 'We'd need to know if the main road to Oxford is open. I could walk over there myself and find out. It would take a few hours, but I could manage it.'

'Dear Baxter! No, I don't think that will be necessary.' She had glanced at the chief inspector, who had nodded his agreement. 'Let's wait and see. Who knows? The phones may start working again at any moment and then we can find out what the situation is.'

They had continued with their tour, passing through the flagged entrance hall, where a wide stone staircase led to the floor above. Julia had paused at the foot of it to direct her guest's attention to the electric-powered mobile seat that was attached to a metal rail fixed to the bannisters.

'You'll have noticed that, I'm sure,' she said. 'But you haven't seen it in operation. I'll give you a demonstration.'

She had wheeled briskly to the steps then and, leaning over to grip the arms with which the contraption was equipped, had lifted herself up and spun round in a single movement, coming to rest on the seat. Next her questing fingers had found the switch behind her and the contraption had begun to move upwards to the accompaniment of a low hum.

Sinclair had followed her at a measured pace and when he got to the top of the stairs she allowed him to assist her into a second wheelchair that was standing ready there. The swift tour she gave him of the upper floor had ended at her bedroom, which was at the far end of the long corridor. A spacious room decorated with landscape paintings, most of them depicting lakes and snow-covered peaks, its two sash windows looked out over the garden and a stretch of rolling countryside beyond it.

A long table covered with a cloth stood a little apart from the bed.

'That's where I get my massages,' Julia told him. 'I'm not sure I could do without them. Ilse has wonderful hands.'

It was on their quitting the room, however, that the most dramatic moment of the tour had occurred. Julia had paused in her wheelchair and directed the chief inspector to continue along the passage to the stairs.

'Wait there for me,' she said with a smile, 'but keep out of the way. I'm not really allowed to do this. My staff would have a fit if they saw me.'

Sinclair had done as he was told. When he got to the stairs he had turned round and watched as she set her chair in motion, employing short, powerful thrusts of her forearms and leaning forward in her chair as she must once have done when speeding down a mountain slope on skis. He was amazed to see how quickly she gathered speed and had stepped aside to give her room, expecting her to go racing past him down the corridor. Instead, when she was only a few feet away, the chair swerved suddenly to the right and before Sinclair had a chance to move, or even cry out a warning, it came to a sudden halt inches away from the top of the stairs. Expecting to see his hostess thrown forward and possibly out of the chair by the impetus, he saw instead that she was gripping the arms of the chair tightly and bracing her feet against the footrest.

'*Madam!*'

Looking down, Sinclair saw Baxter in the hall below. The chauffeur was carrying a basketful of logs. He was staring up at them, aghast.

'Oh, dear! I've been spotted.'

Anything but contrite, Julia's cheeks were flushed with excitement. Her eyes shone.

'Now, don't be upset, Baxter,' she called out to him. 'I was just providing our guest with some entertainment. I promise to be good in future.' She spoke with feigned meekness.

'That's what you always say, ma'am.' The chauffeur looked distressed. 'It's just asking for trouble. What if you didn't stop in time and fell?'

'Then I should probably end up with a good few bruises,' she said, 'but it hasn't happened yet and with any luck it never will. Besides, I had Mr Sinclair here standing by in case of emergencies, so there was no need for you to worry.'

Baxter's muttered reply was inaudible. But his reaction was clear from the glance he sent the chief inspector's way. It seemed to question just how much help such a demonstrably senior citizen could offer in the event of an accident occurring.

'Dear Baxter—he means well,' Julia murmured as they watched the chauffeur continue on his way towards the drawing-room. 'They all do. But sometimes I feel I'm surrounded by nannies.'

In the short time they had been together the chief inspector had happily fallen victim to his hostess's charm and he found it hard to believe that her vibrant personality together with her striking looks had not attracted a flock of admirers before now. Could it be that she had dwelt in a sort of self-imposed purdah following the untimely death of a husband who had meant so much to her? It was something to ponder, and if his curiosity was still left unsatisfied by a conversation they had later that day, it at least left him with further food for thought.

'I'm sorry Philip's not here,' she had said, without preamble, after they had settled down by the fire in the drawing-room after lunch. 'Philip Gonzales—he's a dear friend of mine and I'm sure you two would get on.'

'Were you expecting him?' Sinclair asked. He had thought it best not to reveal that he already knew something of the gentleman in question.

'I wouldn't go that far.' Julia had laughed. 'In fact, to tell the truth I'm never quite sure when he's going to appear. He was staying here as my guest a few weeks ago and I was expecting to see him again when I went up to London. But he has a tendency to vanish, usually on some mysterious errand, and I'm never quite sure when he'll turn up again.'

She had spoken in a light tone, smiling as she did so, but the chief inspector had not been deceived. He felt there was more behind her words than she had revealed: that her feelings for Mr Gonzales might be stronger than her manner implied and that she felt let down by his nonappearance. After all, if Ann Waites was to be believed, the man had asked her to marry him.

'But I know how Philip feels,' she went on. 'I was just the same when I was young. I hated being pinned down. I liked the thought that one could just pick up and go . . . anywhere. I lost both my parents early. Father was killed in the First War and Mummy fell ill and died when I'd just turned twenty-one. It was discovered too late she had a weak heart. So there was no one to stop me.'

Her gaze had gone to a painting hanging over the fireplace while she was speaking. It depicted a couple who the chief inspector assumed must be her parents. The woman, seated in a chair, had the same red hair as Julia's, while her husband, who was standing behind her and a little to one side, bore an even more striking resemblance to his offspring. Julia's high cheekbones matched her father's and both were gifted with the same direct, piercing gaze.

'That was when I got really interested in skiing; obsessed with it, you might say. Philip claims he saw me competing in one of the championships—it was before the war—but we only met years later after I'd returned home.'

She had said no more, and although Sinclair would dearly have liked to question her further he remained silent. But not long afterwards, when Julia had left him to join Mrs Holtz in the study, he was given a further insight into her relationship with those around her. He had wandered next door into the library, an attractive room furnished with a large circular table covered with books and two armchairs strategically placed on either side of the fireplace and was contentedly making his slow way around the handsome teak bookshelves, pausing now and then to pull out a volume and glance at it, when he heard the door open behind him and turned to see Baxter's figure framed in the doorway.

'I don't mean to disturb you, sir, but I thought you might like a fire in here.' He was carrying a fresh armful of logs.

'Thank you, Baxter.' The chief inspector welcomed him with a smile. 'I was thinking of settling down with a book.'

The chauffeur had shed his habitual black jacket and with his shirtsleeves rolled up now to his elbows he set about laying the fire, placing the logs in a careful pattern that hinted at long experience in the art.

'How long have you worked for Mrs Lesage?' Sinclair asked him.

'Let's see now . . .' Baxter paused in his task, frowning. 'It'll be two years come next March.'

'Was that when she returned home from Switzerland?'

'No, Madam had been back a while by then and she'd brought a chauffeur with her.' Baxter positioned the last few logs. 'I never knew him . . . he was Swiss. But he had an accident, poor chap.'

'While he was driving Mrs Lesage?'

Baxter struck a match to the kindling and sat back on his heels to observe the result. He shook his head.

'No, it happened in Oxford. He was knocked down by a van while crossing a road.'

'How did you come to work for Mrs Lesage?'

'It was by chance. I heard through the grapevine she was looking for a chauffeur. I'd been driving for an American couple who came over to London after the war. They were working for a refugee agency, but they had plenty of money and they'd taken a house in the country as well. I used to drive them back and forth. Anyway, they went home after a couple of years and it was about that time that I heard Mrs Lesage was looking for a chauffeur, so I wrote her a letter applying for the job.' He grinned. 'So did a few others. We all had to come down here to meet her and take her for a drive before she made up her mind. I was the lucky one who got the job.'

'Lucky?' Sinclair smiled.

'It was for me.' Baxter turned from the fire, which was burning brightly now. His face seemed lit from within. 'She's a very special lady. But I expect you know that already, sir. It's not like a job, this . . . it's more like . . .' He struggled to find the words he wanted. '. . . like something I was meant to do. Mrs Holtz feels the same. She's said as much to me.' He broke off, red-faced with embarrassment.

Sinclair regarded him in silence for a moment.

'I would say you'd both found your calling,' he said gently.

'Oh, I wouldn't go that far, sir.' Baxter flushed a deeper red. 'It's more like . . .'

He was interrupted by a voice behind him.

'Ah, there you are, Baxter.' Ilse Holtz stood framed in the doorway. 'Mrs Lesage wants you to walk down to the village again before it gets dark. You must find out if the phones are working and also if the road to Enstone is open yet.'

As though unable to help herself she spoke in the harsh tone of a general issuing orders, or so it seemed to Sinclair. Yet Baxter appeared unruffled.

'Yes, of course, Mrs Holtz,' he said as he dusted off his hands. 'I'll go right away.'

'And could you see if there's any post for us? There's been no delivery for the past few days. I expect the postman couldn't drive his van up here. But he might have left some letters with Mr Greaves. Could you check? I'm also expecting a package from the chemist in Chipping Norton with some liniment for Mrs Lesage. I can't do my massages properly without it. Mr Greaves is quite likely to have put it somewhere and forgotten about it.'

'Now, don't you worry.' Baxter rose. His tone was soothing. 'I'll see to it. I'll have a word with Bob.'

'Thank you, Mr Baxter.' Her face softened and for a moment it seemed she might smile. Instead she turned around and disappeared into the hall behind her.

'She gets worried if anything goes wrong.' Baxter seemed to feel some explanation of Mrs Holtz's abrupt manner was called for. 'With Mrs Lesage, I mean. It upsets her to see Madam put out in any way, and I can understand why.'

Possibly because they were two of a kind, the chief inspector thought. And perhaps they were both trying too hard. He was remembering Julia's remark to him earlier.

'I'm surrounded by nannies.'

She was like a bird in a cage, he thought, a wild bird that once had flown free in the mountains and now was forced to accept the care of others who might well be devoted to her in their own way, but who, all unknowing, were filling the role of warders in the prison her life had become.

'I was about to send out a search party for you, Angus,' Julia said. 'But unfortunately Baxter hasn't got back from the village yet. Ilse went upstairs to knock on your door but said you weren't there and I tried the library myself.'

'I slipped outside for a few minutes,' Sinclair confessed. 'The snow stopped for a moment and there was just enough light for a quick constitutional. But I quickly decided the snow was too deep. I only had my ordinary shoes on.'

'I shall lend you a pair of wellingtons,' Julia said. 'See to it, would you, Ilse? There should be some in the gun room.'

On returning from his abortive stroll, the chief inspector had found his hostess settled by the fire in the drawing-room overseeing the arrangement of some flowers that had been brought from the conservatory by Mrs Holtz. Dressed in a black velvet gown, long-sleeved and buttoned at the throat, and with her red hair drawn back to display her pale skin and slender neck, she cut a striking figure.

'I've rung for tea,' she said. 'It'll be here in a moment. But in the meantime I'm going to go on cross-questioning you. I don't feel we've got to the bottom of your mysterious mission. I was telling Ilse about it earlier. I explained why you went to Chipping Norton to try and find that man. But what neither of us understands is, if he left a false address with the car-hire firm, as he seems to have done, how will you be able to find him now?'

'That's easily answered.' The chief inspector grinned. 'I can't. I simply haven't the means. And I might as well admit to you now that I shouldn't have got involved in this business in the first place. I should have stayed at home and cultivated my garden, as Candide advised. Unfortunately it's covered with snow at the moment, which made that option impractical. Still, I've no excuse and will be roundly ticked off by my doctor when I finally get home to Highfield.'

'Your doctor?' Julia pounced on the word. 'Are you unwell, Angus?'

'Not at all,' he assured her breezily. 'Helen tends to be overcautious. She and John are old friends of mine and Helen thinks I shouldn't exert myself.'

'They're the Maddens, are they? Ann told me about them when I was staying with her. John Madden is the man you

worked with at Scotland Yard, is he not?' When Sinclair nodded, she went on: 'Ann told me you were both involved in a
famous murder case years ago.'

'That's true, and it was how we met Helen. The murders
took place in Highfield, where she was the village doctor.
John quit the force after that. He retired to the country and
became a farmer.'

'Did you miss him—as a partner, I mean?'

'I should say so.' The chief inspector laughed. 'In fact, I
was inclined to blame Helen for luring him away. They got
married soon afterwards. But I realized later that John was
doing what he'd always wanted to do. He grew up on a farm.
It was in his blood.'

Julia sighed. 'I should love to meet them.'

'And so you shall. Highfield's not that far away. Baxter
would have no trouble finding his way there. I wish I could
offer to put you up, but I'm afraid my cottage is too small
for that. But don't imagine that something else couldn't
be arranged. Would you at least consider coming over to
see us?'

'I don't need to consider.' She bathed him in her smile.
'It's already decided.' She hesitated a moment. 'But to go back
to what you were saying before, is your investigation at an
end, then?'

'I fear so.' Sinclair looked wry. 'I shall simply tell the police what I've found out about this man, which is little
enough. It will be up to them to take any further action, but
the chances are the matter will be dropped. There simply isn't
enough evidence to interest them. It's quite possible Mr Beck
is nothing more than a small-time fraudster.'

'And there I was hoping your little grey cells had been
hard at work.'

'You're confusing me with that Belgian gentleman again.' The chief inspector chuckled.

Mrs Holtz cleared her throat. She'd been occupied arranging flowers in a vase on a table by the picture window on the other side of the room, but staying so silent—she had not uttered a word since he came in—that Sinclair had forgotten her presence.

'Will there be anything else, Mrs Lesage?' she asked.

'Not now, Ilse, but you might see if Daisy has got the tea trolley moving yet. I fear her mind isn't on the job at present; it's on young George Griggs, the butcher's son. Mind you, he is rather dishy. But that's no excuse for trifling with her affections, which I strongly suspect him of doing. No, wait! Not another word . . .' She put a finger to her lips. 'There she is now.'

The sound of rolling wheels reached their ears and after a moment the younger of the two maids materialised in the doorway, pushing the tea trolley ahead of her.

'I'm sorry for the delay, ma'am,' she said. 'The kettle broke down and we had to ask Baxter if we could borrow his.'

'He's back from the village, is he?'

'Just now.' Daisy propelled the vehicle across the room to where Julia was sitting. 'He says the phones are still out there.'

'So Baxter has a kettle of his own!' Julia had waited until the maid had settled the trolley beside her before speaking. 'Who would have guessed it?'

'He says he likes to have a cuppa last thing before he goes to bed.' Daisy seemed pleased to be in possession of this piece of arcane information. 'He doesn't want to have to come all the way downstairs to the kitchen.'

'Did you hear that, Mr Sinclair?' Julia laughed. 'I have a

chauffeur of infinite resource. Would you make a note, Ilse dear?' she called to her secretary. 'We ought to take the kettle into Chipping Norton next time we go and have it repaired; or better still, buy a new one. Oh, and while I think of it . . .'

But she failed to finish the sentence. Just then the sound of men's voices came from the hall outside. One of them was Baxter's, the other new to Sinclair.

'You walked all the way from Enstone, sir?'

The chauffeur's words were clearly audible; the reply, uttered in a lower tone, less so, but Sinclair saw Julia's face light up at the sound.

'Philip!' she called out. 'Is that you?'

'Julia!'

Now it was the sound of hurried footsteps that came from the flag-stoned hall and in a moment the figure of a man wearing an overcoat sprinkled with snow appeared in the doorway. He paused there for a second, as though to take in the scene, and then strode across the room to where Julia was seated. With a flourish he bent to kiss her hand—and then the cheek that she offered him.

'What a wonderful surprise!' Her face lit up. 'Have you really walked all the way from Enstone?'

'There was no other way to get here.' He removed his coat and tossed it onto the sofa.

'Angus, this is Philip Gonzales. I told you I was expecting him, but I never thought he'd get here in this snow. Philip— this is a new friend of mine, Angus Sinclair. Chief Inspector Sinclair, I should say.' It was plain she was enjoying herself.

'Former chief inspector, please; retired; emeritus.'

Sinclair was happy to play along with his hostess, whose spirits seemed to be soaring. But he didn't fail to notice the startled glance that Philip Gonzales sent his way. Free of the heavy overcoat he'd just shed, he was revealed to be wearing a well-cut tweed suit given a dash of colour by the red silk handkerchief that spilled out of his lapel pocket. Though not especially good-looking—his carefully barbered black hair and regular features were of the anonymous type to be glimpsed in cigarette advertisements and the like, or so the chief inspector thought—he had the relaxed manner of someone at ease in whatever company he found himself and the warmth with which he regarded Julia seemed genuine enough. As for his age, it was difficult to guess. Late forties perhaps, Sinclair guessed. He watched as Gonzales drew up a chair close to where Julia was sitting, but before he could speak, Mrs Holtz cleared her throat for a second time.

'If you'll excuse me, Mrs Lesage, I'll tell Baxter to light a fire in Mr Gonzales's room,' she said.

At the sound of her voice Gonzales looked up. He had not registered her presence, Sinclair realized. Julia's secretary had remained where she was, beside the vase of flowers she'd been arranging, half-hidden in the shadows at the far end of the room.

'Yes, would you please, Ilse?' Julia replied after a moment. 'And tell Daisy to get it ready. Oh, and could you take Mr Gonzales's coat with you and hang it up?' She turned to her newest guest. 'Where on earth have you been these past couple of weeks, Philip? I was expecting to see you in London.'

'Switzerland,' he replied. He watched as Mrs Holtz crossed the room to where they were gathered around the fireplace and collected his coat.

'Good lord! That's my old stamping ground. What were you doing there?'

'Oh, this and that . . .' Sinclair saw Gonzales's dark eyes

meet Ilse Holtz's, and in that instant the chief sensed what might have been a current of hostility passing between them. But if so, it lasted for only a second and then the woman turned and headed for the door, the coat over her arm.

Julia laughed. 'You'll have to do better than that,' she said. 'I want to know all about it.'

'And so you shall.' He turned back to face her, taking her hand in his. 'I've a lot to tell you.'

13

'Who is this lady exactly?' Billy Styles sipped his whisky.

'Her name's Ann Waites,' Madden told him. 'She's a neurologist or a psychiatrist, or perhaps both, and also a professor at a college here. The chief inspector had dinner with her the night before he went up to Chipping Norton and disappeared. Professor Waites thinks he was probably rescued by another one of her guests that evening, named Julia Lesage, when she realized he was stranded by the snow. Mrs Lesage has a house in the Cotswolds not far from Chipping Norton. But I haven't been able to call her number to see if Angus is there because the phones are down.'

Billy had come to the Randolph Hotel to join his old chief for dinner and found him waiting at a table in the lounge with a drink in front of him.

'She also told me they had a very interesting conversation at dinner,' Madden explained. 'She thinks it had to do with whatever brought Mr Sinclair to Oxford, though he wouldn't let on what that was. It's fair to assume it was linked to this man he's searching for and it occurred to me you might want to know why she found the conversation so interesting.'

'You mean it could have a bearing on the Voss case.' Billy understood. 'Let's hope it does. As things stand we haven't got much to go on.'

The news he had brought with him was of the largely frustrating day which he and Morgan had spent. Although, with the help of the telephone directory and by checking local hotels and boardinghouses, the Oxford inspector had identified a number of men called Beck living in the area, all had proved to be respectable citizens with no connection to the individual who had hired a car from Alf Hutton.

'About the only good news I've got is that Charlie is sending me some reinforcements,' he told Madden. He was referring to his superior, who in his earlier days had been dubbed with the nickname Cheerful Charlie. 'He wants this bloke Beck found, and tomorrow won't be soon enough. Lily Poole is coming down from London to join me.'

'That would be Detective Sergeant Poole?' Madden said, and Billy nodded with a grin.

'Lil finally got her promotion,' he said, 'and about time too. Mind you, it's put a few backs up in London, I can tell you. But what am I going to do with her when she arrives, is what I'm wondering. Where do we start? It's not even a case of looking for a needle in a haystack. I mean, where's the haystack, never mind the needle?'

Madden nodded in sympathy.

'About this conversation they had at that dinner,' Billy said, 'did Professor Waites give you any hint what it was about?'

Madden shook his head. 'I tried to get it out of her, but she was too cagey. She made it clear she wanted to talk to me in person. She told me she had engineered Angus's invitation to Hampshire just so she could meet him. She's one of those people still fascinated by the Melling Lodge murders and she knew I was involved in that case. In the end I decided the easiest way of learning what we want to know was to invite her to join us this evening.'

'I'm glad you did, sir.' Billy smiled. 'Although it was the *Kriminalkommissar* I was expecting to meet.' He seemed to enjoy saying the word. 'Mr Probst is staying at the hotel, isn't he?'

Madden nodded. 'But we both decided it might be best if he remained in the background for the time being. I've a feeling Professor Waites would be more than interested to discover that a German detective had turned up in Oxford and it's likely she'd relay the information to others. She already knows all I'm trying to do is locate Angus and get him back to Highfield and I can quite truthfully introduce you as an old friend and colleague who's here on police business.' He scowled at Billy. 'And, incidentally, one who I've told more than once to stop calling me "sir".'

Billy chuckled. He hadn't yet managed to bring himself to address his old mentor by his first name. 'I'm working on it,' he said, 'sir.'

Madden shook his head in mock despair.

'To be serious for a moment, it could be that whatever Professor Waites has to tell us may be of use to you and Tom Morgan. In that case you'll have to decide how frank you want to be with her: whether you'll let on that the police are taking an active interest this affair.'

Sober now, Billy nodded. 'I won't decide till I hear what she has to say.'

'That might be best. And you won't have long to wait.'

Madden had just caught sight of a woman, dressed in a skirt and blouse topped by a jacket, who was threading her way between the tables towards them.

'If I'm not mistaken, there she is now.'

———

'Tell me about this cuff link,' Madden said. 'Was it your impression that Mr Sinclair felt it was important?'

'On the whole I'd say yes.' She spoke at last. 'But I should add that only became obvious at the end.'

'The end . . . ?'

'. . . of the discussion we'd been having. It was quite light-hearted and began when I teased Mr Sinclair about being on some mysterious mission.' She smiled. 'As I told you, I'd seen him a few days earlier in Hampshire and I remembered him saying he was going straight home to Highfield from there. Instead I happened on him by chance. He rather deftly avoided our questions at dinner by producing the cuff link and saying here was a mystery if we wanted one. He wondered if any of us knew what the design signified.'

'Describe it again, would you?'

Madden caught Billy's eye. It was not until they finished their meal and were drinking the last of the wine that they'd finally got onto the subject of the dinner conversation and what bearing it might have had on the chief inspector's visit to Oxford. Instead Madden had been obliged to recount the part he had played in a murder investigation now nearly three decades old and, more generally, to share with the professor his thoughts about the dangerous psychopath he and Sinclair had finally tracked down. Ann Waites had been surprised—and delighted—to discover that his other guest had also been involved in the case, something she hadn't been aware of, but her attempts to provoke a reaction from Billy had got nowhere.

'Oh, I was just Mr Madden's dogsbody,' he told her cheerfully.

'Come now, Billy, that's not true,' Madden chided him.

'Fetching and carrying. That was my job. I was as green as they come.' Billy laughed. 'But I'll say this for myself: I grew up quickly.'

'And what brings you to Oxford now, Inspector?' Professor Waites asked. 'Don't tell me you've also come in search of Mr Sinclair.'

'Lord, no.' Billy brushed the notion aside. 'I'm here on ordinary police business. But it came as a nice surprise to run into Mr Madden. We've always kept in touch and I was interested to hear that Mr Sinclair had gone missing, if I can put it that way. I worked under him for years. But we're not looking for him. He'll turn up.'

Whether the professor had swallowed Billy's attempt to pull the wool over her eyes was open to question, or so Madden felt. As a former psychiatrist she had probably been told more than her share of tall stories and knew flannel when she heard it. But she had allowed Billy's explanation of his presence in Oxford to go unchallenged and after they went into dinner and Madden raised the issue he was interested in, she had proved more than ready to satisfy his curiosity.

'The snake on the cuff link was what fascinated us,' she said now, 'but it wasn't until another of my guests explained what it meant that Mr Sinclair began to show real interest. He's a curator at the Pitt Rivers Museum called Andrew Fielding. He recognized the design as being Aztec in origin. The snake was part of a double-headed serpent, he said, and the missing half must be on the other cuff link. The original objects were bigger and worn by Aztec priests; the cuff link was probably a piece of costume jewellery, or part of it. He thought the piece when it was whole might have been a pendant worn by a woman, or perhaps, if it was already cut into two pieces, a pair of earrings. Why it should have been made into cuff links, though, was anyone's guess.'

'Aztec, you say?' Madden was frowning. 'So it could have been made in Mexico?' He was remembering the cryptic jottings he had read in Sinclair's notebook.

'That was suggested,' Professor Waites agreed.

'And was it at that point that Angus began to take the matter seriously?'

The professor regarded him, head cocked to one side.

'Yes, now that you mention it, I think it was,' she replied after a longish moment. 'But I don't see how that will help you find him. Unless there's more to this than meets the eye.'

'More to this?' Madden did his best to look baffled. 'No, it's simply that I find the whole business of the cuff link fascinating . . . just as you did.' He signalled to a nearby waiter to fill their wineglasses. 'Angus left some notes in his room here. They included a reference to Mexico and I wondered what that meant.'

Swirling her wine about in her glass Professor Waites appeared to weigh his words.

'Let me put the question another way, then,' she said. 'What exactly is your friend Mr Sinclair up to? What brought him hotfoot to Oxford?'

'Why do you ask that?'

'Because he half admitted that he was on the trail of something, only he wouldn't tell us what it involved. He said it was confidential. After Andrew Fielding had explained about the origin of the cuff link design I asked Mr Sinclair if it had solved his mystery for him. "Believe me, if I knew I'd tell you." That was his answer. So you see, the mystery, whatever it was, remained unsolved.'

She took a sip of her wine.

'I wish I could help you.' Madden spread his hands. 'I've no doubt he came here for a reason, but since Helen and I were away when he went to stay with the Bennetts, I haven't had a chance to speak to him. As I told you when we talked before, my wife is his doctor and she's concerned for his health. What I want to do is track him down and take him back to Highfield—in irons, if necessary, was how Helen put it.'

Professor Waites laughed lightly.

'That was a masterly piece of misdirection, Mr Madden,' she said. 'I've seldom heard a subject changed so skilfully, and believe me I've dealt with some artful patients in my time.' Her smile seemed to suggest no offence had been taken. 'But to bring you up to date, I should tell you I've sent a message of sorts to Julia Lesage via an intermediary. It was to ask her if Mr Sinclair was staying with her and if so to let him know that you're here in Oxford trying to discover his whereabouts.'

'How on earth did you do that?' Still coming to terms with what she had said a moment before, Madden was startled anew. 'I know the phone line is still down. I tried myself to ring her this evening, and so far as I'm aware the road to the village where she lives is still blocked.'

'A gentleman by the name of Philip Gonzales came down from London by train this morning. He rang me to ask if I had any news of Julia and when I told him she was cut off by the snow he announced his intention of going up to Great Tew immediately. He said he would take the bus as far as Enstone and then walk the rest of the way. I was somewhat taken aback. Granted, he's an ardent admirer of hers—in fact, he's asked her to marry him—but all the same I thought he might have waited a day or two until the road was cleared.

But it was obvious he was determined to get there as quickly as possible and I wondered why.' She shrugged. 'Anyway, he was the bearer of my message and if it truly is love that's spurring him on I'm sure he'll have got there somehow.'

Madden had been studying her face as she spoke.

'I get the impression you don't entirely approve of him,' he said.

'You policemen!' She laughed. 'That was exactly what Mr Sinclair said when I told him about Philip.' She hesitated, choosing her words. 'My concern has to do with Julia,' she said finally. 'I don't want to see her hurt. Mr Gonzales's intentions towards her are no clearer to me than his background, which is . . . well, shall we say murky?'

'In what way?' Madden was intrigued.

'He appears to have lived a wandering life and has many amusing stories to tell of his experiences in far-flung places. But he never quite comes into focus, if you know what I mean.' Professor Waites frowned. 'I'm not even sure where he was born, and if he has any family I'm not aware of it. None of which seems to bother Julia, I might add.' She shook her head.

'But enough of that.' She gathered herself. 'Would it be very rude of me if I left you two to finish your wine? I've got an early start tomorrow and I ought to get home. I promise to let you know if I hear anything from Julia.' She addressed these last words to Madden. 'And thank you for a very enjoyable evening.'

The two men rose to bid her goodnight.

Billy waited until their guest was out of earshot.

'I reckon she read us,' he said.

'Like a book,' Madden agreed.

'What she told us about the cuff link was interesting,

though.' Billy sipped his wine. 'The connection with Mexico, I mean. It seems to tie in with what Mr Probst was saying about Voss's background. No wonder Mr Sinclair was puzzled by it. He'd got it into his head that this bloke he was after might be a war criminal.'

Madden's grunt seemed to signal his agreement. But it was plain his thoughts were elsewhere. Billy studied his old chief's face. Something was bothering him.

'This Julia Lesage person, with her house in the Cotswolds and her chauffeur-driven Bentley—does she sound like a wealthy woman to you?'

'I'd say so,' Billy responded cautiously.

'Do you think it's worth checking on this fellow Gonzales?'

Billy's eyes opened wide in surprise.

'You mean, could he be the same bloke we're after? Could he be Voss? That would be some kind of coincidence.'

Madden said nothing.

'Do you really think it's possible, sir?'

'No, I think it's highly unlikely.' Madden laughed. 'But you were saying something earlier about needles and haystacks and the thought came to mind.'

'With the chief inspector just *happening* to be a guest there?'

'You're right. It wasn't a serious suggestion. You'd best forget it.'

'No, no . . . you've got me interested now.' Billy finished his wine. 'Tell you what—I'll give the Yard a call tomorrow and see if we've got anything on record about him. You never know. *Philip* Gonzales—that was the name she gave us, wasn't it?'

14

'I'M AFRAID IT'S NOT WORKING YET, sir. The telephone, I mean. I've just got back from the village.'

Red-cheeked from the cold, Baxter stamped the snow off his boots. Sinclair had put his head outside to check on the weather and found the chauffeur about to mount the shallow steps to the front door.

'I thought I'd save the baker's boy another trip and find out about the phone at the same time.' Baxter indicated the pair of loaves wrapped in brown paper he had under his arm. 'Bob Greaves told me the phone line was down between the village and Enstone. The trouble is the repair crew's having trouble getting there because of the road being blocked. It's not just that lorry we heard about. Bob said there were a couple of cars that had also got stuck after the drivers tried to get through. The lord knows how long it'll be before they clear it.'

'That's a pity.'

The chief inspector did his best to hide his disappointment. His abortive sortie into Oxfordshire in search of the mysterious Mr Beck was becoming a serious embarrassment to him. The previous evening he had learned from Philip Gonzales's lips that none other than John Madden had come to Oxford, presumably with the intention of laying him by the heels and hauling him ignominiously back to Highfield and the reproaches he knew were awaiting him there. He had gone to bed hoping that the line would be restored by morning so that he could at least ring his old friend and explain how he had got into what must seem to both Madden and Helen like an absurd situation.

'Well, I'd better tell Mrs Lesage,' Baxter said. 'Do you know if she's come down yet?'

'I had breakfast with her and Mr Gonzales twenty minutes ago,' Sinclair told him. 'Then they disappeared into the study, just the two of them. I wouldn't disturb them if I were you. They seem to be having some kind of conference.'

He spoke lightly, but saw Baxter's eyes widen.

'Without Mrs Holtz, you mean?' He took a second or two to absorb what Sinclair had said. Then, as though remembering himself, his face broke into a smile. 'Oh, well, I'd better leave them to it, then.'

He started to go past the chief inspector, but stopped. 'If you're thinking of going outside, sir, you'd better put on that pair of wellingtons I left out for you in the gun room. The snow came up to my knees in some places. I'll go and get them for you if you like.'

'No, don't bother, Baxter. I know where that is.'

The chief inspector was indeed preparing to venture out. Like a long-distance runner pausing to catch its breath, the overnight snow had diminished to a mere scattering of flakes. But the forecast Sinclair had heard on the wireless less than an hour before had warned that renewed heavy falls could be expected in the next few hours.

'As you wish, sir.'

The chauffeur disappeared inside. Sinclair surveyed the white expanse before him. The line of footprints leading across the forecourt to the driveway lent force to the cautionary advice Baxter had just given him. Each step had left a deep imprint in the snow. Nevertheless the chief inspector was not discouraged. He felt the urgent need for some fresh air. He was starting to feel what he had once heard an American acquaintance of his describe as 'cabin fever'.

A subtle change had occurred in the atmosphere of the household—Baxter's reaction a moment ago was just another symptom of it—and while it undoubtedly dated from the moment Philip Gonzales had arrived the night before, the chief inspector had so far been unable to put his finger on what precisely that change involved. Observing the new arrival at dinner, it had been clear to him on the one hand that the man was a practiced charmer. If indeed Gonzales was playing the part of a devoted admirer, as Ann Waites seemed to suspect, his performance could hardly have been better, while his account of his trudge through the snow from Enstone was related with the sort of self-deprecating humour that had robbed it of any heroic aspect. Yet withal the chief inspector thought he detected a real fondness in Philip Gonzales's manner towards their hostess, and it seemed to him too that the feeling was reciprocated.

But quite separate from all that, there had been a certain tension in the air during the meal which had seemed to emanate from Ilse Holtz, whose customary silence had taken on what the chief inspector could only characterize as a watchful edge as Gonzales had laughingly fended off Julia's attempts to get him to reveal what he'd been doing in Switzerland this past fortnight.

'This isn't the moment to go into all that,' he had said, dismissing the notion with a graceful gesture. 'Why don't we sit down together tomorrow morning, just the two of us, and I'll tell you all about it. I promise you won't be bored.'

As he spoke the words he had turned his head in Mrs Holtz's direction and the chief inspector had seen her glance harden. Thinking about it later he surmised that she had taken what he'd said as a not so subtle hint; she was being told, if she hadn't grasped it already, that she would not be included in the meeting.

Reflecting on the scene later, it had occurred to him that there was something of the hothouse about Wickham Manor—something artificial in the atmosphere, and beyond that, something of the precious bloom requiring careful tending about its attractive owner, who had surrounded herself, not necessarily by design, with a retinue of devoted followers among whom feelings of jealousy and possessiveness seemed to thrive.

Unless, of course, he was imagining the whole thing, the chief inspector thought with a rueful grin as he donned the pair of wellington boots he found sitting on a table in the middle of the gun room a few minutes later. No longer used for its original purpose—blood sports had been one of her father's passions, Julia had told him when they toured the house the first morning—it had become a depository of odds and ends, and apart from the sporting prints that still hung from the walls, most of them depicting dead game, the sole reminder of its former status was an old shotgun that rested on a pair of brackets fixed to the wall.

'That's to frighten away the rooks that congregate in the elms behind the stable yard,' Julia told him. 'Baxter likes to take it out now and again to bang away at them with birdshot. I'm not sure he's ever managed to bring one down.'

Outside once more, clad in his overcoat, with a scarf wrapped around his neck and wearing his borrowed boots, Sinclair found that the forecast had not lied: a biting cold had set in and already the top of the snow was developing an icy crust. He had intended walking around the house to the terrace in front, but on viewing the expanse of snow covering the forecourt, no doubt more than knee-deep, he changed his mind and decided instead to restrict himself to an inspection of the garage and stable yard, which lay at the other end of the house. He was taking his tablets as prescribed and had been gratified to discover that his breathing—and presumably his pulse as well—remained regular. But despite the slow pace at which he set off now, making sure that one foot at least was secure before he moved the other, he found the effort was placing a greater physical strain on him than he'd foreseen and he was relieved when he found the garage doors open and could slip inside and pause in the relative warmth to catch his breath.

Other than the Bentley, which occupied half the garage, the space was taken up by a pair of lawnmowers and a large wooden chest, half-filled with an assortment of tools and bric-a-brac, which stood open with its lid pushed back. Nearby, leaning against the wall, was a pair of skis—sad reminders of the past for their owner, Sinclair thought; he wondered why she had kept them—and further along a toboggan was stood on its end.

There was a door at the back of the garage and when he opened it the chief inspector found it gave onto a small yard adjoining the house where the snow had been trampled into a dangerously slick surface. Reasoning that the lighted window he could see must be that of the kitchen, he was about to tempt fate by crossing what looked like an ice rink in front of him when the door next to the window opened and the burly figure of Baxter appeared.

'Ah! There you are, sir.' He hailed Sinclair. 'I was afraid

you might have gone outside. I should have warned you. It's getting dangerous with all this ice about.'

'Too late now,' the chief inspector responded cheerfully.

'Just hang on a moment and I'll give you a hand.' The chauffeur's concern was plain. 'This yard's particularly dangerous. I nearly came a cropper myself this morning.'

He stepped cautiously onto the icy surface and began to cross it, half sliding and half walking. Sinclair waited until he was close by and then, taking his proffered arm, accompanied him back to the open door and into the comforting warmth of the kitchen, where he found the older of the two maids, Doris, standing with a spoon in her hand beside a steaming pot that was resting on top of a massive iron stove.

'Come in, sir, come in.' Somewhat flustered by his unexpected appearance, she put down the spoon she was holding and drew him towards a chair by the kitchen table. 'Can I make you a cup of tea?'

'There's nothing I'd like more,' the chief inspector confessed. 'But could I have a glass of water first?'

During his slow passage across the icy yard he had felt a familiar stab of pain in his chest—it was like a bolt tightening—and following his doctor's instructions he took the bottle of pills from his pocket and tipped one of them into his free hand.

'Are you all right, sir?' Baxter was regarding him anxiously, as was Doris.

'Perfectly well, thank you,' Sinclair reassured them. 'It's a simple precaution, nothing to worry about.'

Swallowing his pill without fuss he saw that Doris's eye was still on him.

'What do you say to a freshly baked scone with your tea?' she asked.

'I wondered what that delicious smell was.'

Although somewhat reserved in manner, she seemed friendly enough now and as the chief inspector doffed his hat and unwound the scarf from around his neck he reflected on the changes that had come about among domestic staff in the course of his lifetime. During his youth a house like this would have been filled with soft-footed maids taught to know their place, moving about with downcast eyes. Listening to Doris as she prattled on to Baxter, he thought how congenial the change was and wondered if it was due, at least in part, to the open nature of their mistress. It was hard to picture Julia Lesage ruling her household with anything resembling a rod of iron.

'I see you're still filling in for the cook,' he said to her.

'Poor Mrs Dawlish.' Doris switched on the electric kettle. 'She must have been trying to get back. I just hope she's still with her daughter in Bicester and not stuck somewhere. I know Mr Baxter's worried about *his* mother.' She nodded to the chauffeur, who'd taken a seat facing Sinclair and was still rubbing his hands together to get the warmth back into them.

'Didn't Mrs Lesage tell me she lives in Suffolk?' Sinclair wondered.

'That's right.' Baxter nodded. 'She and my dad retired there, but he died during the war. She's got some good neighbours, but I do worry about her. They say the snow's been bad all over. I just wish the phones would come back. Mum hasn't got one of her own, but there's a family just down the lane that I can ring. They tell me how she is.'

'I know how you feel.' The chief inspector sighed ruefully. 'I have friends I want to call. They must be wondering what's become of me. Ah! Those look wonderful.'

Doris had just deposited a plate of golden-topped scones

together with a dish of butter and a jar of strawberry jam on the table between the two men, together with a plate and knife for each of them. As she turned to attend to the boiling kettle, the sound of hurried footsteps reached them. It was coming from the passage outside. The next moment Daisy burst in. Flushed and out of breath, she came to an abrupt halt as her gaze fell on Sinclair.

'What is it?' Baxter looked up from buttering his scone. Then, when the girl remained silent: 'What's the matter, Daisy? Cat got your tongue?'

Daisy's eyes went to Doris. Her glance was pleading.

'What is it, girl?' Doris repeated the question, but more urgently this time. She went over to Daisy and put her arm around her. 'Has something happened?'

The girl's gaze stayed fixed on Sinclair. The chief inspector spread his hands.

'I've a feeling I'm in the way,' he said jokingly. 'Is it something you'd rather I didn't hear?'

'Now, we'll have none of that.' Baxter broke in before the girl had time to answer. 'Just tell us what it is—right now.' He struck the table with the palm of his hand. 'Spit it out.'

Still flushed, Daisy stood by the table, fists clenched. It seemed she was plucking up her courage to speak.

'Something's happened.' She gasped out the words. 'It's Mr Gonzales and Mrs Holtz—they're having a go at each other.'

'What did you say?' Baxter shot to his feet. When the girl failed to answer he barked at her. 'What do you mean— *having a go*?'

'They were shouting . . . I could hear them outside.'

'Outside where?'

'The study . . .'

'Have you been eavesdropping, girl?' Baxter scowled.

'No, it wasn't like that,' Daisy protested. 'I was walking down the corridor to the library when I heard the door to the study open behind me. I looked round and saw Mr Gonzales come out. He went the other way towards the hall and I heard him calling to Mrs Holtz. She must have been up in her room. "Mrs Holtz . . . Mrs Holtz," I heard him calling out. And then he said, "Would you come down here right away? Mrs Lesage wants to speak to you."'

'And . . . ?' Baxter's expression had changed. Now it seemed he couldn't hide his curiosity.

'After a minute or two I heard her coming down the stairs, so I popped into the library.' Daisy's flushed cheeks grew redder. 'I thought it would be better if they didn't see me. But I heard them come back into the study next door where Mrs Lesage was and that's when they started arguing.'

'Do you mean Mr Gonzales and Mrs Holtz?' Baxter's eyes had narrowed.

Daisy nodded.

'What about Madam?'

'She wasn't saying anything. It was just them two and they were shouting at each other. Mr Gonzales was the loudest, but I could hear Mrs Holtz answering back. She was really angry, I could tell.'

'So what was it all about?' Baxter glanced at Sinclair. He seemed to realize that he had stumbled into a questionable area: eavesdropping at second hand. 'No, don't tell me that.' He checked himself. 'I don't want to know.'

'It's all right, Mr Baxter.' Daisy sought to reassure him. 'I couldn't hear anyway. I don't know what it was they were arguing about. And I didn't hang about in the library to find out. I came straight here.'

'So they're still at it.' Doris seemed the least impressed of any of them. 'I thought that Mrs Holtz would run into trouble one of these days, her with her airs.'

She appeared to have forgotten Sinclair's presence, but her words brought a scowl to Baxter's face.

'Now, that's enough of that.' He spoke sharply, and Sinclair noted that his assumption of the senior position seemed to be accepted by the other two. 'I won't hear any talk against Mrs Holtz. I know she's not easy, but she's always stood by Madam.'

The two maids shared a quick glance. Then Doris clapped her hands together.

'Right. Let's get on with things, then. I've got lunch to prepare, but I could do with some help. Daisy—those potatoes need peeling. Get busy.'

15

'So you really haven't made any progress at all,' Helen said. The fact that her voice carried no hint of criticism somehow made the reproach harder to bear. 'I'm sure it must be very frustrating, my dear.'

'If I could just find out for sure that Angus is stranded in that house it would make a world of difference.' Madden tried not to sound as though he was justifying his lack of success so far. 'I rang the Chipping Norton police myself earlier this morning to see if they had any news of him, but they couldn't help. But I managed to get the number of the Enstone bobby off them and I rang him too. He confirmed that the road to Great Tew was still unusable. Several people had tried it in their cars and come to grief in one way or another. He also told me there was a telephone pole down, which is why the phones aren't working. But he was expecting a repair crew from Oxford to get there sometime today, which was good news.'

Helen's silence at the other end of the line was unnerving.

'I also asked him if he'd had any news from Great Tew, particularly anything to do with Mrs Lesage. He said he hadn't but that he'd seen her car passing through Enstone three days ago on its way home.'

'Was Angus with her?' Helen came to life.

'He doesn't know. He was aware that she'd been away for

a while and of course he hadn't seen the car during that time. But he happened to be out on the road when it passed through and he waved to her chauffeur, who waved back. He spotted Mrs Lesage because she was on his side of the car. But he didn't notice whether there was anyone in the back with her.'

Even as he recounted what he had learned Madden was aware there were things he wasn't telling his wife; the disturbing thought that their old friend might all unknowing be on the trail of a dangerous killer lay unspoken at the back of his mind, but it would do no good to tell Helen that. It would only upset her.

'And you couldn't possibly drive up there yourself?' Helen spoke after a pause, breaking into his thoughts.

'My darling, I've just been explaining about the roads.' Madden was growing desperate. 'I don't know how things are in Highfield, but it's freezing in Oxford. The pavements are covered with ice. They haven't been able to clear the road to Great Tew yet so all the snow that was on it must be frozen by now. I'm quite ready to try driving up there if you think it's a good idea, though I'll probably end up in a ditch myself. And if I get stranded and it turns out Angus isn't at Mrs Lesage's house after all but somewhere else, I won't be in a position to do anything about it.'

Helen said nothing.

'If I could just satisfy myself that he really is with her, then at least we'd know he was safe and sound.'

Madden paused again, hoping for some word of encouragement from his wife. Women were adept at this tactic, he thought bitterly. They knew how to let simple silence suggest there was something more that ought to be done—usually by some hapless male—even if they weren't prepared to say what it was.

'So for the time being I'm going to keep ringing her number in the hope that sooner or later it will answer. Until the road has been cleared there really is nothing else I can do.'

'Of course not, dear.' Helen's tone was soothing. 'I quite understand.'

Did she mean it, though? Madden knew there was no point in asking. He was going to have some stern words with Angus Sinclair when he finally caught up with him.

'Are things as bad in Highfield?' he asked tentatively. 'Weather-wise, I mean?'

'We've had lots of snow, and it's starting to ice up. I'm not sure I'll be able to make my rounds this afternoon, not to all of the farms.' She hesitated. 'Oh, and I've just remembered: Lucy's threatening to come down to join you.'

'She's what?' Madden was stunned. 'Threatening . . . and what do you mean, *join* me?'

'She says if necessary she'll take a few days off from work. She's very worried about Angus, you know. We both are. She said she was going to call you. Unless you find him soon she'll probably turn up.'

It occurred to Madden that his women were ganging up on him.

'Can't you stop her?' he pleaded.

'My darling, we're speaking about our daughter.' Helen laughed. 'When have we ever been able to stop her doing anything once she's set her mind on it? I'll have another word with her, but I doubt it will help.'

There being nothing more he could do for the moment other than call Julia Lesage's number again—he found the line was still dead—Madden went downstairs to the lobby, where he came on Hans Probst in the process of shedding his overcoat and gloves prior to handing them over to the cloakroom attendant. The Berlin detective told him he'd just returned from a briefing at St Aldates police station called by Tom Morgan.

'He had nothing to report as yet,' he said after they had settled down in the lounge and ordered coffee. 'But that is hardly surprising. He is still in the process of organizing a search for Voss. I think it was arranged mainly for the benefit of a detective who came down from London earlier today to join in the hunt: a young woman named Detective Sergeant Poole. I believe you know her.'

'Billy Styles told me she was coming.'

'She brought copies of those old photographs of Voss taken when he was detained by the Buenos Aires police twenty years ago.' Probst frowned. 'They were sent by radio teletype overnight via New York and I'm afraid the images are blurred. I wonder if anyone would recognize him now. I brought one of them to show you.'

He handed the print to Madden. A standard police snapshot, it bore the grainy image of a shaggy-haired young man who stared back at the camera without expression. Due to the lack of definition, his eyes appeared simply as two dark holes, lending a somewhat eerie impression to the otherwise blank visage.

'Morgan is to have copies of this circulated to police stations in the area together with the name Beck. But it's hard to imagine what else he can do at this stage. I don't envy him his task.'

He put a hand to his head and massaged his temples. To Madden, his face seemed paler than before.

'Are you feeling all right?' he asked.

'Oh, yes, thank you.' The Berlin detective smiled wanly. 'I didn't sleep very well last night, but that's nothing new. As one grows older, the memories come crowding back. It can make for a long night.'

Madden hesitated. He wasn't sure what to say.

'I was plagued by them myself when I came back from the First War,' he said, after a pause. 'Haunted, I should say. I tried to keep them out of my mind, but they kept returning in dreams. I was in a bad way. It was Helen who showed me how to deal with them. She told me not to try to block them. "We have to remember before we can forget," she said, and she was right.' He glanced at the other man. 'Are you married?' he asked.

'I was. Margarethe died during the war.' Probst lowered his eyes. 'After I resigned from the police we went to live in Hamburg, which was where she was from. I had difficulty finding a job. I was no friend of the Nazis, as you know, and in the end I was reduced to giving private lessons. I taught English, of all things, to those who wished to learn the language, a choice of profession that in the end proved to be ironic, if that's the right word.'

He sat with eyes downcast.

'What are you telling me?' Madden felt a chill.

'In July of 1943 the British and Americans bombed Hamburg for seven days and nights. They created what is now called a firestorm. Forty-two thousand people were killed. I was away from the city at the time. When I returned I found that not only my wife but my daughter, Elise, too had been killed. She was sixteen at the time. I never found their bodies.'

Madden stared at him.

'Hans, I'm so sorry.' It was the first time he had used the other's given name.

'What I cannot forgive myself is not being there when they needed me most. I had gone to Berlin to attend to some business; it was a small matter of no great importance. But I wanted a break, you see, and the chance to look up some old friends. If I'd been at home where I ought to have been I might have reacted a little quicker when the sirens went off; I might have got them to safety somehow. Nothing can ever change that.'

Madden searched his mind for something to say.

'Was Elise your only child?' he asked.

'No, we had a son called Ulrich. He was conscripted of course. There was no escaping that. He died on the Russian front, like so many others.'

He looked up to meet Madden's gaze.

'I don't know how much you know about that campaign. Our troops behaved atrociously. Millions died, and I'm speaking of the civilian population as a whole, not just Jews. I only heard the full story later from those who came back and then I had to wonder what part my son might have played in the killing. He was raised to be a decent human being, but war does terrible things to even the best people.'

Lost for words, Madden could only keep silent.

'So the memories keep returning,' Probst said, 'and although your wife was very wise to say what she did, I must tell you that there are some things one cannot forget, pain that even time cannot heal, and if they return to us at night in the shape of dreams perhaps we should be grateful. To think of them in the light of day, to see the lost faces again, is near to unbearable.'

He put a hand to his brow.

'But enough of that. Let us speak of other things. Have you any news of Angus? Do we know yet where he is?'

Madden repeated what he had told Helen a short time before.

'I'll keep ringing this lady in the hopes that the line will have been repaired and I'm also hoping that if Angus is there he might call me. By now he may know that I'm here in Oxford. A message to that effect has been given to a friend of Mrs Lesage's who was set on reaching the house on foot. Due to the state of the road I may not be able to rescue Angus right away, but it would set my mind at rest to know he's there. What are your plans for the rest of the day?'

Probst ran his hands through his thinning hair.

'I was thinking of paying a visit to the Ashmolean Museum. It's just across the road, I am told.'

'Well, for heaven's sake watch your footing if you do,' Madden cautioned him. 'I had a look outside earlier. The pavements are a death trap. I hope you didn't walk back from St Aldates.'

'Inspector Morgan kindly provided me with a car and a driver. But I shall take your advice about the pavements.' Probst hesitated. 'Would you care to accompany me?' he asked, with a trace of his earlier formality.

'I'd like to, but unfortunately I'm chained to the hotel at the moment. Quite apart from wanting to be here if Angus rings, it seems my daughter is thinking of coming down from London to help in the search. I'm expecting a call from her and I have to try and put her off. There's really nothing she can do to help. She and Angus are very close. They're as thick as thieves.'

'I'm sorry?' Probst's brow furrowed.

'It's a saying.' Madden smiled.

'Thick as thieves . . .' The Berlin detective tested the words. 'It has an agreeable ring to it.'

'The trouble is I don't know what I'm going to say to her. I don't want to tell her about this man Angus was after who may turn out to be Voss. It'll only upset her, and she's bound to tell her mother. I was hoping to keep it from both of them until we know he's safe.'

'Surely your daughter will do as you say,' Probst said solemnly and was taken aback when Madden burst out laughing.

'I'm sorry,' he said. 'I couldn't help myself.'

The Berlin detective cocked an eye at him. 'Would I be intruding if I asked you to tell me a little more about her?'

'Oh, no . . . not at all. She's . . .'

Madden was struck by a sudden pang as he recalled what the other had just told him about his loss. He wished now he hadn't brought up the subject.

'It's all right, John.' Probst laid a gentle hand on his arm. It seemed he had read Madden's mind and by using his first name seemed to confirm the sense of intimacy that had sprung up quickly between them. 'Describe her, if you would. I should like to see her through a father's eyes.'

Madden took a deep breath.

'Then I would have to say she's beautiful, and that's not just a father speaking.' He had needed a second to compose himself. 'But also quite unpredictable, and utterly unmanageable.'

'Ah!'

'In fact, I might as well admit that I never know what she's going to do next. I can only hold my breath and hope.'

'Yes, of course . . . I understand.' Probst's gaze had grown misty. 'And naturally you adore her.'

Madden's laugh came as a relief to them both.

'Is it that obvious?' he said.

16

SINCLAIR STOOD AT THE WINDOW gazing out at the snow-covered landscape. His hostess had referred to his room as 'the Hunt Room', doubtless because of the prints decorating it, most of which featured red-and-black-jacketed riders and packs of multicoloured hounds galloping across green fields crisscrossed by hedges and other obstacles. Out of curiosity he had examined them closely for any sign of a fox and found only one instance where their prey appeared, hurrying across a field with the hunt in full cry behind it. The autumn colours of the trees and hedges spoke of another season far removed from the stark, bone-white expanse of countryside he was looking at now.

The chief inspector shivered. The fresh fall of snow promised on the wireless that morning was yet to arrive, but it was deathly cold outside and in spite of the fire burning in his grate he felt a chill. His earlier impression that something was amiss in the household had only increased with time, but he was yet to put his finger on it. He had come up to his room to rest before lunch and lying on his bed he had gone over in his mind what Daisy had told them in the kitchen. Were Gonzales and Ilse Holtz enemies of a sort—perhaps competing for Julia's favour—or was there more to their verbal clash than that?

Earlier, it had struck him as strange that the man should

have chosen to walk the four or five miles from Enstone to Great Tew in a heavy snowfall rather than wait for better weather, but he had put it down initially to the apparent attraction that Julia had for her admirer. Now he was inclined to put a different interpretation on events. For one thing, it was possible Gonzales had undertaken the difficult journey to Wickham Manor because he had something important to communicate to its mistress. Casting his mind back, Sinclair recalled the look that had passed between him and Mrs Holtz after Gonzales had revealed to Julia that he'd recently been in Switzerland. The chief inspector had been unable to read it, but he remembered now that Ilse Holtz herself was Swiss. Were these facts somehow linked?

And then there were the other currents swirling about in the household. Although Baxter had given no outward indication of his feelings, Sinclair sensed a certain reserve in his manner towards Gonzales. Once again the image of a hothouse came to him, with its corollary of overheated emotions and reactions. Much of his working life had been spent trying to make sense of just such puzzles and he wished now that John Madden was with him. His old partner had a gift for making sense out of seemingly unconnected facts—a talent for joining up the dots, as more than one of his colleagues at the Yard had noted. The knowledge that he was close by— no further away than Oxford—but still out of touch only added to the chief inspector's sense of frustration.

To put it in a nutshell, then, was there something going on beneath the surface at Wickham Manor that he ought to be concerned about? Or was he just an old man trying to recreate an image of his former life out of the tensions that so often arose in small, tightly knit—one might even say claustrophobic—communities?

The chief inspector couldn't decide, and whatever the answer was he doubted it would reveal itself in the short time remaining to him as Julia Lesage's guest. He would simply have to hope that his fears were misplaced and leave the occupants of the house to get on with their lives.

He glanced at his watch. It was nearly one o'clock. Lunch would be served soon, though not by Daisy. The previous afternoon, a further disruption to the household had presented itself in the shape of George Griggs, the butcher's son, who had walked up from the village with troubling news.

Sinclair himself had not been present when the young man arrived, but he heard about it soon afterwards when he came upon Julia in the drawing-room. Her meeting with Gonzales, and later with Mrs Holtz as well, having apparently concluded, she had been sitting on her own by the fire and it was clear from the way she was staring into the fire that she had something on her mind.

'Angus!' She had looked up when he entered. 'You're just the person I want to speak to,' she began, but got no further. At that moment the sound of hurried footsteps in the hall outside had caused her to break off and a moment later Baxter had entered in haste.

'Sorry to disturb you, ma'am, but Daisy has just had some worrying news. It seems her mother is quite poorly. I told you she was down with bronchitis, didn't I? Young George Griggs has come up from the village to tell us and to say that Dr Ferguson thinks that if you could spare Daisy it would be best if she could be with her mum, at least until the weather clears and they can get her into hospital, which is where she belongs, he thinks.'

'But of course.' Julia had cut him off. 'She must go down

at once and she's to stay with her mother as long as necessary. Is there anything we can do to help?'

'I don't think so, ma'am. It's just that Daisy's mum's cottage is a bit isolated and there ought to be someone with her. Don't worry about things here in the house. Doris and I can manage on our own. And Mrs Dawlish might turn up at any moment.'

'Not in this weather, she won't,' Julia had predicted with a wry smile. 'If she's got any sense she'll stay where she is in Bicester until the snow clears.'

At all events she had appeared untroubled by this new development, possibly because it was merely an inconvenience compared with what she had on her mind, and which she had not yet shared with him. Or so the chief inspector surmised as he left his room now to go down to lunch.

As he went out of his room into the passage he saw Julia in her wheelchair emerge from her bedroom at the other end of the long corridor. Ilse Holtz was already standing at the head of the stairs waiting to help her. As Julia approached she began to pick up speed, working the wheels of her chair with the same sharp downward thrusts he remembered from before. Realizing that at the right moment she would swerve and bring the chair to an abrupt halt, he waited for her to make the same sharp turn he had witnessed before. Instead, just as she reached the stairs the chair gave a sudden lurch, slewing around in a half circle and then tipping over, flinging its occupant out of her seat and headlong down the stairs.

Stunned by the sight, Sinclair stood rooted to the spot. It was Ilse Holtz's scream that brought him to his senses. Calling out Julia's name, he hurried to the top of the stairs and saw her body lying sprawled on the steps below. Ilse Holtz was already there, crouched by her employer's side, and at the same moment Baxter appeared. He was running across the hall from the direction of the kitchen. The chief inspector saw that Julia's face was covered in blood.

'Julia! . . . Julia!'

The shout came from behind him and when Sinclair looked back he saw that Gonzales had burst out of his bedroom, which was opposite his own. Brushing past the chief inspector, he raced down the stairs.

'Stand back, both of you. Leave her to me.'

The order came from Baxter, who had already climbed the steps, and the other two drew back as he collected Julia's body in his arms. About to carry her up to her room, he was checked by her voice.

'Will you stop making such a fuss, all of you?'

Sinclair saw that her eyes were open. Blood was flowing freely from a cut on her forehead.

'Do you think I'm made of glass? I've had worse falls, I can tell you. Baxter, take me down to the drawing-room. Ilse, get a basin of warm water and a cloth of some kind and come and clean me up. I appear to be bleeding. Philip—you can keep me company. Don't just stand there, all of you.'

At that moment she caught sight of the chief inspector; Sinclair hadn't moved from his place at the top of the stairs.

'You see, Angus?' Her bloodstained face broke into a smile. 'I told you I'd provide you with some entertainment. Join us in the drawing-room, would you?'

'Ma'am, I've told you before not to do that.' Baxter found his tongue. Obeying her command, he carried her carefully down the stairs, followed by Gonzales. Ilse Holtz watched them go and then turned and hurried up to the landing. Her face was pale as she went past Sinclair.

Left on his own, the chief inspector's gaze went to the wheelchair. It lay on its side, almost at his feet, two steps down. Righting it, he dragged it up to the landing and then peered closely at it. It took him only a minute to find what he was looking for. He saw that the chair was equipped with a pair of brakes—rubber pads perhaps three inches long—that were designed to clamp on the wheels. The handles for each were placed conveniently just below and outside the arms of the chair. The left-hand brake was in working order, but the one on the right had come loose. The nut holding it tight was missing and he found he was able to pull the brake pad off the bolt it was attached to.

Why hadn't Julia realized it was malfunctioning? He recalled the moment when he had seen her emerge from her room and turn into the passage.

Shouldn't she have been alerted to the flaw in her brake at that point?

Not necessarily, he decided. Since the chair was controlled manually by the push rims projecting from the wheels, she wouldn't normally have needed to use the brakes. It was only when she approached the head of the stairs at high speed—when she gave herself the kind of thrill she had once enjoyed in the mountains—that she would have had to employ them. In the event, when she'd tried to bring the chair to a sudden halt, the right-hand brake hadn't worked and the chair had slewed round, flinging her out of her seat and down the steps. She was lucky to have escaped with only a cut on her head, unless she had some other injuries not yet diagnosed. The chief inspector had got down on his knees to make his examination and after a minute or two he became aware that Gonzales was coming up the stairs to join him.

'Was something wrong with it?' he asked. Once again

Sinclair found his dark eyes unreadable. He explained about the missing nut.

'It must be either in the passage or in Mrs Lesage's room,' he said.

Gonzales stared at him, and Sinclair felt for a moment he was about to say something more. But then his gaze shifted and the chief inspector saw that Ilse Holtz was approaching down the passage from the direction of Julia's room with a bowl in her hands. She passed them with only a glance and then continued down the stairs. Gonzales followed her and they went into the drawing-room together. A few seconds later Baxter appeared.

'That shouldn't have happened, sir.' He too came up the stairs to join Sinclair. 'I've told Madam time and again not to do that. It only takes a small mistake.'

'This was no mistake,' the chief inspector told him. He explained about the missing nut.

Seemingly appalled by what he had heard, Baxter listened to him in silence.

'Those brakes are only meant for parking the chair, sir. They're not supposed to be used in any other way. If you want to stop, you use those things outside the wheels.'

'The push rims?'

The chauffeur nodded. 'It's dangerous using the brakes. Madam knows that.' He struck his forehead. 'It's my fault.'

'Hardly,' Sinclair said.

'It's my job to look after those chairs. I check them every week. How could I have missed that?'

'Have you inspected them since you got back?'

Baxter shook his head. 'I haven't had time. But that's no excuse.'

'Don't blame yourself. These things happen.'

'If only Madam wouldn't take these risks.'

'Ah, but she can't help herself, you see.' Sinclair sighed.

'What do you mean, sir?'

'She told me the other day that when she was a skier she loved living on the edge of danger because it made her feel more alive. That's something she can never get back.'

Julia ran her fingers over the piece of sticking plaster covering the cut on her forehead. She studied her reflection in the hall mirror.

'Well, I certainly don't look like one of Chekhov's heroines anymore,' she said, 'but if you gave me a rifle and a flag I might pass for a Communard. What do you think, Angus?'

Already the brief disruption of household routines brought about by her accident seemed all but forgotten. The crisis, if crisis it was, had been summarily dealt with.

'No, I don't require further examination,' she had informed the circle of anxious attendants that had gathered about her in the drawing-room after Ilse Holtz had finished her ministrations. 'And don't tell me I might have broken a rib. I've done that a couple of times in the past and believe me I know just how it feels. As for getting poor Dr Ferguson up here to examine me, I absolutely forbid it. The effort might very well prove fatal for the old boy. In fact, the subject of my general health and fitness can now be considered closed. I did something stupid and if I feel sore for the next few days, I've only myself to blame.'

Her continuing high spirits had got them through a difficult lunch, one which Mrs Holtz had not attended, pleading a migraine headache, and at which Philip Gonzales had been only a shadow of his previously agreeable and entertaining self. Whether shaken up by Julia's accident or for some other reason, he had offered little in the way of conversation and once or twice Sinclair had caught him gazing out of the window lost in thought, causing the chief inspector to wonder just what had transpired at his meeting with Julia in her study. Indeed, it had seemed to Sinclair that even their hostess was making an effort to keep up appearances, an impression that only gained strength when at the conclusion of the meal she abruptly asked Gonzales if he would walk down to the village to make further inquiries on her behalf.

'See if you can find out what's happening with the phone,' she had said. 'And bring back any news you can about the road to Enstone. I hate being cut off like this. Baxter's already been down once this morning and I don't like to ask him to do it again.'

If Gonzales was surprised by her sudden request he gave no sign of it—it seemed to Sinclair he was even eager to go— and he'd gone upstairs at once to change into more suitable footwear. Julia had led the way across the hall to the spot where they were standing now.

'Angus, we were interrupted before, but I need to consult you about something.' She spoke in a low tone. 'But I'm going to wait until Philip has gone. It's a serious matter and I'd prefer to talk to you alone.'

With no choice but to be patient, the chief inspector kept his curiosity in check and before long Gonzales returned wearing a pair of boots into which he had tucked the bottoms of his trousers. As he went to collect his coat from the clothes tree by the front door, Baxter appeared on the landing above.

'I've found it, ma'am.' He was holding up something in his fingers. 'It's the nut that was supposed to hold your brake in place. It was lying on the carpet just outside your room. I'll screw it back on now.'

'Well done, Baxter,' Julia called out to him. Glancing round, she saw that Gonzales had paused at the front door and was listening to them. 'Take care, Philip,' she said. 'It can be dangerous walking on ice. I know from experience.'

Caught off guard—or so it appeared to the chief inspector—he stared at her for a long moment. Then he collected himself.

'Have no fear, dear lady.' With a return to his earlier flamboyance, he swept her a low bow. 'I'll be back before you know it.'

Julia waited until the door had shut behind him. Then she turned to Sinclair.

'Let's go to my study,' she said. 'There's something I want to show you.'

He followed her down the corridor and, having waited until she had settled herself behind her desk, drew up a chair beside her.

'First, I'd like you to read this letter.'

She handed him a single sheet of paper, which he saw was a typed letter from a company of estate agents with an address in Lausanne. It was dated a fortnight earlier.

Dear Mme Lesage (it read),

I must apologize to you for a slight delay that has arisen in the matter of the sale of your property. While the purchaser, M. Martineau, has every intention of completing the contract as agreed, he has asked if you would allow him a little more time before the settlement is finalized. As you know, we anticipated receiving a cheque from him for the full

*amount this week. He has assured us that the only
reason for the delay is that it is taking him longer
than he anticipated to liquidate certain investments
in order to realize the necessary funds and has asked
for a postponement of a fortnight, after which he
assures us the sum owing will be paid. He trusts that
this will not put you to any inconvenience.*

*May I add that before advising you to agree to this
sale we made discreet but searching inquiries into the
financial status of the prospective buyer and were
satisfied that he was fully able to meet the financial
requirements of the purchase. Accordingly it is our
recommendation that you agree to the short delay he
has requested, while joining him in expressing our
deep regret for any inconvenience it may cause you.*

We look forward to hearing from you.

Beneath the scrawled signature there was a typed name:
Maurice Jansen.

Sinclair looked up. 'Yes?'

'The property M. Jansen refers to is the home I shared
with my late husband.' Julia moved her wheelchair around to
face him. 'It's a villa not far from Lausanne overlooking Lake
Geneva. I couldn't bear to part with it when I left Switzerland. It meant so much to both Andre and me. But after I'd
made one trip back—that was a little over a year ago—I realized I couldn't do it again. The house held too many memories for me and finally I decided to sell it and it went on
the market a few months ago. There was no shortage of
offers—it's a lovely villa—and the one I accepted was made
by the gentleman mentioned in the letter. He was willing to
pay the asking price, which was well over a million Swiss

francs, and in due course we exchanged contracts and the deal was completed. However, I received this letter just before I went to London a fortnight or so ago.'

'Were you concerned about it?' Sinclair asked.

'Not in the least,' she replied without hesitation. 'It's not uncommon for there to be delays when it comes to raising funds for a costly transaction. I learned that from Andre. The buyer naturally wants to make sure he's getting the best price for whatever securities he needs to sell. I mentioned it to Philip just before we left—me to London and him to Switzerland, though I didn't know that at the time. In fact, I made a joke about it. I said the rich were never in a hurry to pay their bills, and M. Martineau is beyond question a wealthy man.'

She paused to collect her thoughts. Sinclair waited. He was sure there was more to come.

'You'll recall that when Philip turned up unexpectedly the other night he promised to tell me what he'd been up to in Switzerland. Well, it all came out the following day when we had our meeting and it's left me in a state of shock. It seems that letter you've just been reading wasn't written by M. Jansen; he knows nothing about it. At least that's what I've been told.'

Sinclair didn't hide his surprise.

'But how did Mr Gonzales . . . ?'

'. . . discover that?' Julia's expression hardened. 'By doing something he had no right to do—if indeed he did it, if this isn't some story he's cooked up. I'll tell you what he told me and you can make your own judgement. Philip claims he's had his suspicions about Ilse Holtz for some time; he feels I've allowed her too big a hand in dealing with my business affairs and he thinks she may have taken advantage of it. I should say at once I've absolutely no evidence of that, nor has Philip produced anything to support his assertion.'

'But what made him go to Switzerland—what reason did he have to approach these estate agents of yours?' The chief inspector was still at sea.

'That's what I want to know, and I still haven't got a sensible answer out of him. He simply said there was something about this letter that didn't seem right to him and he decided to take the bull by the horns and go and speak to the man who had been personally responsible for handling the transaction.'

'That doesn't sound very convincing.'

'I said as much to him.' Julia frowned. 'But be that as it may, he apparently took himself off to Lausanne while I was in London and managed to meet Maurice Jansen in person. Introducing himself as a close friend of mine, he had the gall to say I was concerned about the delay in the sale going through and could M. Jansen assure him that all was in order. According to Philip the man didn't know what he was talking about—the sale had gone ahead as planned, he said, and the money had been paid and he was awaiting my instructions as to where to deposit it. M. Jansen said he had posted a letter to that effect to me more than a week before. I have to say I have not received it. Mind you, I could have been in London when it arrived, but it should have been waiting for me here when I got back, and it wasn't. I could have sorted this out already if the telephone was working. I could have called M. Jansen in Lausanne. As it is, I've been left up in the air.'

She looked pleadingly at him.

'I'm so sorry to land this on you, Angus, but I don't know

who to believe. Does Philip's story sound fishy to you? Or
do you think there might be something in what he's told me?'

At a loss himself, the chief inspector hardly knew how to
answer.

'Has there been any ill feeling between them—I mean Mr
Gonzales and Mrs Holtz?' he asked.

'Not to my knowledge,' Julia replied. 'But as I think I told
you, Ilse's a difficult person. Baxter seems to know how to
handle her, but I couldn't say the same for the rest of the staff.
But she's always been loyal to me. In fact, I don't know what
I'd do without her, and to have Philip come out with these . . .
well, they're not exactly accusations, they're more like insin
uations, is just too much.'

Sinclair hesitated.

'Look, I'm going to have to question you like a detective
now, Julia.' He tried to keep his tone light. 'How is your post
delivered?'

'In the normal way.' She shrugged. 'The postman brings
it in his van. We've had the same one for years and he always
drops it off in the kitchen because he knows he'll get a cup of
tea there. Eventually it finds its way to my study, where Ilse
deals with it. And before you ask whether she might have
tampered with it, I should tell you I happened to be at my
desk when this particular letter arrived and I saw her open it.
She passed it over to me at once and said something like,
"You'd better read this."'

'And was Mr Gonzales staying here at the time?'

'He was. It was just before I went up to London, as I said,
and I told him about it. But I made it quite clear that I wasn't
bothered by the delay M. Martineau had requested. It was
just something I mentioned casually.'

She looked expectantly at Sinclair, who could only shrug.

'The trouble with this is that I can't see how sending you a letter with incorrect information could possibly benefit anyone.' The chief inspector found his tongue. 'The moment the phones are working again—and that could be any minute now—you'll be able to clear this whole matter up. A single call to Lausanne will suffice. I'm tempted to wonder if this isn't someone's idea of a joke. But if so, it's in poor taste. And I can't understand what Mr Gonzales is on about. I ought to tell you that I'm aware there was some kind of altercation between him and Mrs Holtz. It was overheard by Daisy, quite innocently, I assure you. But I understand feelings ran high.'

'It was horrible.' Julia shivered. 'Philip asked her if she was up to something, or words to that effect, and poor Ilse was terribly upset. She said she didn't know what he was talking about and she accused him of trying to stir up trouble between us.'

Again the chief inspector hesitated; he knew he was about to step onto shaky ground.

'It's not my business, Julia, but how well do you know him?'

'Well enough, I would say.' Her tone sharpened. 'No, better than that—I might as well tell you he's asked me to marry him, and I'm considering his proposal.' She paused. 'Does that surprise you?' Her voice was edged.

'Not in the least. He's an attractive man and from what little I've seen I would say he's genuinely attached to you.'

'Genuinely?' She tested the word. 'What exactly do you mean by that?'

Now Sinclair knew for certain he'd stepped into a mine-field. But it was too late to retreat.

'You're a rich woman, Julia, and as such a tempting target for a certain kind of man.'

'Do you think I don't know that?' She flared up. 'I might add it's something several of my friends have been only too willing to point out. They seem to think I'm a lovesick ninny. Is that your opinion of me?'

'Certainly not.'

'Then why bring it up?'

'Because, as I said, nothing about this makes sense.' The chief inspector stuck to his guns. 'Because, if he has genuine doubts about Mrs Holtz, why hasn't he been more explicit? What's holding him back? And finally, why didn't he tell you he was going to Lausanne to look into this business? There's something going on here I don't understand. That letter must have been sent to you for a reason, but I can't see what that is. *Cui bono?* Who benefits from it? I'm damned if I can see.'

He shook his head in exasperation. Julia too seemed lost for words. But she reached for his hand.

'Forgive me, Angus,' she said. 'I shouldn't have snapped at you. I asked for your help and you only said what had to be said. I'm fully aware what people think of Philip and they may be right. All I know about him really is what he's told me. I know he's been all over the world doing this and that and it may be he's what my friends think he is: no better than an adventurer. But he lightens my heart. I don't know any other way to put it. I just feel better when he's with me and, whatever you think, I know he has feelings for me, even if I can't prove it. That's why I hate what's happened.'

She shook her head angrily.

'Oh, God! How much longer do we have to wait for that bloody telephone to start working?'

'Excuse me, sir. Could I trouble you for a moment?'

The note of urgency in Baxter's voice roused the chief inspector from his reverie. He had been sitting on his own in the drawing-room for the past twenty minutes, staring into the fire, trying to make sense of the conversation he had had with Julia Lesage a short while before. Their discussion having reached no conclusion, she had decided to go upstairs and rest for an hour—she had finally admitted to feeling not quite herself following her fall on the stairs.

He looked up.

'What is it, Baxter?'

'Could you come to the kitchen, sir?' Baxter's face was a picture of worry. 'Doris has something to tell you.'

Mystified, Sinclair followed the chauffeur across the hall and down the long corridor to the kitchen, where he found the older of the two maids pacing about nervously. Doris's plump cheeks seemed paler than usual; she appeared agitated.

'Tell Mr Sinclair what you've told me.' Baxter looked hard at her. His tone brooked no refusal.

The maid swallowed.

'It was while I was doing Mr Gonzales's room, sir.' She had turned her gaze on the chief inspector. 'With Daisy gone, I had to put off doing it until after lunch. But once I'd seen Madam settled I went to his room and it was while I was making his bed that I saw it.'

'Saw what?'

'What Madam told Mr Baxter about when they were coming back from Oxford. I mean that cuff link with the snake's head on it. Mr Baxter told us about that and how he'd heard you say you were looking for the man who owned it.'

'And you're telling me you found it in Mr Gonzales's room?'

Doris nodded.

Without a word the chief inspector reached into his pocket and brought out the broken link, which he'd been carrying on him since his meeting with Alf Hutton.

'Was it like this one?' He showed it to the maid.

'Just like that, sir.' She nodded vigorously. 'It was lying there in a bowl on the dressing-table. It was with some other stuff, a set of keys and loose change . . .'

Sinclair could feel his heartbeat increasing. He took a moment to calm himself.

'What did you do with it?' he asked.

'Nothing, sir. I just left it where it was and came downstairs and told Mr Baxter.'

She broke off to glance up at the chauffeur, whose face too had paled, or so it seemed to the chief inspector. They looked at each other. Baxter's broad brow was grooved by a frown.

'What are you going to do about it, sir?' he asked.

Sinclair had already asked himself the same question. 'Go upstairs and have a look at the thing myself,' he said.

'And then?' The chauffeur waited for a moment, and when no immediate response was forthcoming, he added: 'What are you going to say to Mr Gonzales, sir?'

'I'm not sure.' Sinclair bit his lip. 'But he must be given a chance to explain how it came into his possession. Shouldn't he be back by now?'

'You'd think so.' Baxter's face had darkened further. 'He's been gone more than an hour. But what about Madam— shouldn't she be told?'

'Of course, and I'll do that as soon as she comes down from her room. I don't want to disturb her now.' The chief inspector knew he was prevaricating. In truth he was so shocked by what hc'd heard he hardly knew what to say. 'I suggest you all carry on as usual, at least for the time being.' It was the best he could manage.

'I'm sorry, sir, but from what you told Mrs Lesage before about this cuff link, Mr Gonzales might be some kind of criminal.' Baxter's jaw was set. 'I have to know; we have to think about Madam. Could he be dangerous?'

'I don't believe so.' Sinclair knew he'd replied too quickly. But he could see no advantage to sowing panic among the staff, not when they were still effectively cut off from outside help. 'It's important we keep this to ourselves for the time being.' He looked at them both. 'And I want to be informed the moment Mr Gonzales returns from the village.'

Baxter nodded his agreement. 'I'll tell you what I'll do,' he said after a moment's thought. 'I'll lock the front door. That way he'll have to come round by the kitchen and I'll be sure to spot him.'

17

Madden peered through the windshield through narrowed eyes. Though cleared for traffic, the road to Chipping Norton was still pocked with icy patches, some of them hidden beneath freshly fallen snow and impossible to spot until you were on them, when the temptation to brake had to be fought as it was likely to send the car slewing from side to side or even spinning in a circle. He had witnessed just such an event only a few minutes earlier when a light van coming towards him had struck one of the patches and turned on its axis in slow motion before coming to rest facing the wrong direction. As he went by, the driver, a young lad, had waved gaily to him.

After three days of inaction—and heartened by the knowledge that the road, as far as Great Tew at least, was open again—he had seized the opportunity to make contact with Sinclair. The news had been brought to the hotel by Lily Poole, who had appeared just as Madden and Hans Probst were sitting down to breakfast.

'The bobby at Enstone says you can get through if you take it carefully.' At Madden's invitation she had joined them at the table. 'Mr Morgan spoke to him on the phone this morning. He doesn't know about the road up to Wickham Manor, though. But he said if you decide to go, you'd better do it right away. According to the weather forecast there'll be more snow tonight along with high winds. In fact, they're predicting a blizzard. But that'll be the end of it. There'll be no more snow after that; it'll have blown itself out.'

She had paused for a moment to order a cup of coffee and some toast and marmalade from the waitress who was hovering beside her. It was the first chance Madden had had to speak to the young policewoman since her arrival in Oxford, but they were well acquainted. A protégée of Angus Sinclair's—the chief inspector had been instrumental in securing her transfer from the uniform branch to the CID at the end of the war—Lily had shown her worth by earning no fewer than four commendations for her work as a detective and, having passed the sergeant's exam with distinction, had recently been promoted to her present rank of detective sergeant (though not without ruffling some feathers along the way, particularly among the longer-serving DCs who believed they should have been given precedence over a mere woman).

Quite separate from that—and against all the odds—she had also become a friend of Lucy's, the pair having met by chance when Madden had been staying with his daughter in London a year or so earlier attending to some family business. No two young women could have been less alike both in background and interests, or so Madden thought, but they had nevertheless struck up an instant friendship, with the result that Lily was now a frequent weekend guest at the Maddens' home in Highfield. Indeed one of the fruits of their friendship was evident that morning in the garments Lily was wearing. Formerly a somewhat dowdy dresser, she now presented an appearance bordering on the elegant and Madden fancied he could detect his daughter's hand in the well-cut blue skirt and silk blouse topped by a jacket of the same shade that the young detective sergeant was sporting.

'Mr Styles asked me to drop in here on my way to the station and give you the news about the road,' Lily told him. 'He and Inspector Morgan are driving up to Banbury this morning.'

'Why there?' Madden knew that the town lay beyond Chipping Norton.

'It's because of a report we had late yesterday from the Banbury police.' Lily sipped her coffee. 'They'd had a woman in for questioning yesterday, or rather to give a statement about a man who she said had broken into her house the night before. She lives in a village some way out of the town and said she'd been woken by a noise in the middle of the night and found a man prowling about her cottage. Luckily her husband returned just then—he's a travelling salesman— and the man ran off. But she was scared by what happened, or so she said, and when they went into Banbury the next day she made a complaint to the police. While she was doing that she caught sight of that photograph of Voss that was stuck up on the wall and said it was him.'

'He was the man who broke in?' Madden was astonished.

'That's what she said. She swore it was him. Apparently she'd got a good look at the bloke. Anyway, Mr Morgan thought they ought to drive up there and have a word with her.'

Probst, who had been silent throughout Lily's recital, awoke at that point as though from a trance. (Noting the telltale signs of sleeplessness in the dark circles beneath his eyes, Madden had wondered where his thoughts were.) 'This is a strange story,' he said. 'It doesn't sound like something Heinrich Voss would do.'

'That's what Mr Styles thought.' Lily nodded. 'But the weather may have played a part in it.'

'The weather?' Madden was nonplussed.

'We don't know where Voss is based, but we think he might be somewhere in the general area. Perhaps his car broke down or he got stuck in the snow. Perhaps he was just looking for shelter. It's been freezing cold at night.' She saw the expression on the faces of her two listeners and grinned.

'I know. It doesn't sound very likely. But we've had nothing to go on up till now, not so much as a whisper. I'm not counting the people who've claimed to have seen someone who they say looked a bit like him. There've been a few of those. This is the first positive sighting we've had and Mr Morgan thought it ought to be checked. He also felt it'd be a good idea to show the plod up there that we're taking this business seriously.'

'And what will you do in the meantime, Lily?'

'Nothing really, just wait.' The young woman shrugged. 'I did ask Mr Styles if I could drive you up to Great Tew in our car—he doesn't need it today, he's with Mr Morgan—but he said we weren't here to rescue retired chief inspectors who should have stayed home and not got themselves stranded in the snow, and anyway it was something you could do perfectly well on your own.'

Madden chuckled. He was glad to hear that his erstwhile protégé was prepared to speak his mind. 'Well, he was right there.'

'But at least he didn't suggest I go with them to Banbury.'

'You didn't fancy a drive in the country?'

'Not when it's a wild-goose chase, sir.' Lily grinned.

'Ah, yes . . . the wild goose!' Probst brightened. 'I have heard of this bird.'

'And that reminds me, sir . . .' Lily turned to Madden. 'I almost forgot. Mr Styles also asked me to tell you he'd heard back from the Yard. We've got nothing on that Gonzales bloke you were wondering about. He's not in our records.'

'Gonzales?' Fully alert now, Probst intervened. 'This is a name I have *not* heard before.'

'He's the man I told you about yesterday,' Madden explained. 'The friend of Mrs Lesage's who was determined to get to her house, even if he had to walk part of the way.'

'You have been making inquiries about him?' The Berlin detective's tone had sharpened.

'Apparently he's an admirer of hers. In fact, he's asked her to marry him. I got that from another friend of hers, a lady academic who lives here in Oxford. She has doubts about Gonzales's intentions towards Mrs Lesage. He seems to be a somewhat mysterious figure. She implied that his background was obscure.'

Probst looked thoughtful.

'Mrs Lesage is a wealthy woman, is she not?'

Madden nodded.

'And so you thought it might be worthwhile to make some inquiries about this man?'

'I wouldn't put it as strongly as that.' Madden frowned. 'In fact, I wasn't entirely serious when I mentioned it to Billy. I certainly didn't suggest that he might be Voss. That would be too much of a coincidence. But Billy decided to check with the Yard just in case they had something on him.'

'He was right to do so.' Probst gave an approving nod. 'I should have done the same. One cannot be too careful. Wild goose or not, I think I will telephone my colleagues in Berlin this morning and ask them to check our records as well.'

'About four miles, you say?' Madden asked.

'Closer to five,' Sam Butterworth, the Enstone bobby, replied. 'It's a pity you weren't here earlier, sir. You could have gone over to Great Tew with me and Bert Emsley. Bert took me in his tractor and we had no problem with the road. Some of the cottages in the area have been cut off by all this snow and I wanted to be sure none of the residents was in any difficulty.'

'I'm hoping to manage in my car,' Madden said. 'I want to bring Mr Sinclair back with me if he's there.'

'Well, I've got some news for you on that front, sir.' Butterworth's face lit up. 'I had a word with Bob Greaves. He runs the village store and he said Mrs Lesage's chauffeur has come down from the house a couple of times on foot to pick up supplies and told him they had a Scottish gentleman staying with them.'

'That sounds like the chief inspector all right.' Madden was relieved to learn his journey was not in vain.

'And you know about the phone working again, do you, sir, between here and Great Tew anyway?'

'No, by God, I did not.' Madden was startled by the news.

'Mind you, it only happened this morning. We had a repair crew come from Oxford. They found a telegraph pole down and managed to fix it.'

'But only as far as Great Tew, you say?'

'I'm afraid so, sir. I tried calling the manor. I know they must be wondering what's going on. But it was no go. There must be another break in the line. We'll have to get the crew out again. Will you tell Mrs Lesage that when you see her?'

'I'll do that.' Madden nodded.

'As for the road itself, it's not too bad, as I say, not as far as the village anyway. But keep to the tracks Bert made with his tractor if you can. He's cut a path through the ice. It's still very slippery either side of them and you should try and get back before dark. They say there's more snow on the way tonight and high winds too. It could turn nasty.'

'I'll bear that in mind.' Madden smiled his thanks. 'But what about the road from Great Tew to Wickham Manor? Is that manageable?'

Butterworth shook his head. 'I shouldn't think so, sir,' he said. 'It's just a narrow lane and I'm not sure anyone's tried to clear it yet. As far as I know, it hasn't been used since Mrs Lesage got back. It might be best if you walked up to the house from the village.'

It was not something Madden had wanted to hear. He knew that over flat ground his old friend would have no difficulty walking a mile or two. But whether the same applied to a slippery lane covered with snow and ice was another matter. He had rung Helen in Highfield just before he'd left Oxford and received her warm approval for his projected expedition. How she would feel about it now he was less certain. But it was too late for a change in plans. And since he had already received confirmation from Butterworth that the phone to Wickham Manor was still down, there was no way he could consult Sinclair on the matter. Having come this far, all he could do now was proceed.

'Thank you, Constable. I'll be on my way.'

'Oh, he's Scottish all right, no question of that.' Bob Greaves spoke with assurance. 'In fact, I think Mr Baxter said something about him once having been a chief inspector, or something of the sort.'

Bent over the counter in his shop attending to some paperwork when Madden had entered by a swing door, causing the small bell attached to it to emit a faint tinkle, the proprietor of Great Tew's only grocery store had greeted his visitor with raised eyebrows.

'I'm sorry, sir, but we're shut, it being Sunday.' Short and stout, he wore a long white apron tied about his waist that seemed only to emphasise the extent of his girth. 'I was just doing my accounts for the week. I'm afraid I can't sell you anything, not without breaking the law.'

Madden had explained his mission.

'I would have driven up from Oxford earlier if the snow hadn't been so bad,' he said. 'I want to collect my friend if I can and take him home. Do you happen to know if the road up to Wickham Manor is usable?'

'Offhand I'd say it's not, sir, and I don't know of anyone who's tried.' Greaves seemed in no doubt. 'I can tell you Mrs Lesage's car hasn't been seen in the village since she arrived back a few days ago, and although Mr Baxter has been in once or twice I know for a fact that he came down on foot. But the turnoff to the lane that goes up to the manor is just at the end of the street.' He pointed. 'You can have a look at it and decide for yourself.'

Madden received the news in silence. He had a sinking feeling he might have made a mistake in hurrying over at the first opportunity. On the point of quitting the store, he paused.

'Do you happen to know a Mr Gonzales?' he asked.

'Oh, yes, sir. He's a friend of Mrs Lesage's. But I haven't seen him for a while.'

'He didn't come through the village the other day?' Madden was surprised. 'I was told he walked all the way from Enstone to get here.'

'Did he? My word!' Greaves was impressed. 'Well, I didn't see him myself and I've not heard that anyone else did. Mind you, if it was dark when he passed through I doubt he would have been spotted. Most people have been staying indoors.'

His words were born out a few minutes later when Madden walked up the short, snow-covered street to where he had parked his car by the village church. Although lights were on in one or two windows there wasn't a soul to be seen outside. He looked at his watch. His trip that day had been plagued by delays, the first of which had been the failure of his car to start. The old Hillman he had hired from Alf Hutton had been standing in the hotel car park for two days in freezing weather, and he had to get the hotel to summon a mechanic from a nearby garage and have a new battery installed.

His troubles were far from over, however. Not surprisingly, with the road declared open, it was now being used again and twice he had met cars coming in the opposite direction, encounters which had required agonizingly slow manoeuvres on the part of both drivers as the vehicles squeezed past one another on the narrow lane. But no such desperate measure had been possible when he'd met a heavy farm lorry only a mile or so short of Little Tew. Both drivers had drawn to a halt and the two vehicles had faced one another, like bulls in a pasture, Madden thought, but with one so much outweighing the other that he had had no choice but to back up until he'd found an empty space by a gate where he was able to edge off the road and watch as his tormentor went by (without so much as a wave of acknowledgement on the part of its driver).

An agonizing five minutes had followed while Madden had repeatedly tried to shift his car out of the deep snow into which he'd been forced, wrestling with the steering wheel as he tried to gain traction, only to fail time and again, until he reached a stage where he'd been all but resigned to leaving his car where it was and walking the remainder of the distance to Great Tew. At that point, however—and quite miraculously—his tyres had suddenly gained a grip and with a surge he had shot back onto the road and thereafter managed to complete his journey without further mishap.

However, he had planned to reach the village before one o'clock, but he saw it was now well after three, and whatever faint hopes he might have had of driving his car up to Wickham Manor were dashed when he reached the turnoff to which Greaves had directed him. One glance was enough to show him that the narrow lane would almost surely have to be cleared of snow before it could be safely navigated.

Having no intention of getting stuck again, he returned to where he had parked the car by the village church, but only to retrieve his hat and a scarf that he'd left on the front seat and a torch that he'd had the foresight to bring with him. All he could do now was walk up to the manor, make his presence known, and hope that Julia Lesage was every bit as helpful and understanding as she appeared to be. He was sure that together with Sinclair they could devise some means of extricating the chief inspector from his predicament.

Of more concern to him, though, was the strengthening wind. Already it was starting to blow in sudden gusts and he realized that if the promised blizzard arrived earlier than expected he might well have to spend the night at Wickham Manor.

As he set off along the lane he saw that a path of some sort had been trodden in the snow—no doubt by the chauffeur and any others among the staff who might have walked down to the village—and he followed the tracks, placing his feet in the holes that had already been made in the snow. The shoes he was wearing were good stout country brogues, but with the snow knee-deep in some places he wished he'd thought of bringing a pair of boots with him to Oxford. The wind was growing stronger—it forced him to clutch at his hat to stop it blowing off—but before long the lane entered a wood, which gave some shelter, but also allowed showers of snow to drop down on him from the drooping branches overhead.

Trudging on, head bowed, he had covered what he thought was more than a mile—it was hard to judge the distance moving at such a sluggish pace—when he saw ahead of him in the fading light a pair of wrought-iron gates standing open and deduced that he had reached the start of the drive that must lead up to the manor. As he passed through the gates, still walking with bowed head against the wind that burst on him as he left the shelter of the trees, he caught sight of something lying on the snow in front of him, an object he didn't recognize.

Stooping to pick it up, he found it was a leather glove of good quality, lined with fur. Puzzled, he stood for a few moments turning it over in his hands. While it was quite possible to imagine someone dropping it by mistake, it was hard to picture whoever it was continuing on his or her way without being aware of its loss. Not when it was as cold as it was.

Stuffing the object into his coat pocket, he continued on his way. In the last few seconds the wind had picked up even further, and as he plodded around a bend in the drive, which was bordered by hedges, he saw the house ahead of him, a dark shadow in the gathering dusk showing only a single light above the front door. At the same moment a tremendous gust of wind set him rocking on his heels, almost bowling him over, and all at once he was enveloped in a whirling cloud of icy snow.

Hardly able to breathe, he stood for second or two, blinded by the stinging particles, unsure for a moment where he was in relation to the house, which direction to take. He peered at his watch. It was after four; darkness was falling and it appeared the promised blizzard had arrived with full force.

18

AS HE MADE HIS WAY back to the hall, Sinclair was only too aware that the calm front he'd presented to Baxter and Doris in the kitchen was far from reflecting his true state of mind. If Gonzales was the man who had killed Greta Hartmann— always supposing she had been murdered—then he was danger personified and the chief inspector was only too aware that with the phone still not working both he and the whole household were in peril.

True, he could send Baxter down to the village to seek help, but without his presence they would be even more at risk. And what if he encountered Gonzales on the way? Would he be able to hide his suspicions, and if not, what might result? If Gonzales had already killed once—if he had murdered Greta Hartmann—there would be nothing to stop him doing so again. And why had he been absent for so long? What was he planning?

The chief inspector's head was in a whirl. There'd been a time when he could have stood back from all this and considered it coolly. But those days were past; he was no longer the man he'd been and his present confusion was merely a symptom of the decline in his faculties brought about by age. Or so he told himself as he paused at the foot of the stairs to consider his next move.

He had no doubt now that the strange letter Julia had

shown him was somehow connected to Gonzales, and the fact that her admirer had done his best to shift suspicion away from himself and onto Ilse Holtz was reason enough to persuade Sinclair that he ought to speak to Julia's secretary. He didn't as yet know what her reaction to the letter was. She had not been feeling well that morning according to her employer and hadn't emerged from her room for some time.

Meanwhile, there was something else he had to do, and having climbed the stairs he walked to the end of the corridor where Gonzales's room was located—it was opposite his—and went in. The bowl Doris had mentioned was sitting on the dresser at the foot of the bed and when he went over he spotted the cuff link at once. Unlike the broken one, which he took from his pocket, it was intact and lying on top of a bunch of keys. Placed side by side on top of the dresser the heads of the two snakes faced in opposite directions. Had the ends of their coils been joined they would have made what he had heard Andrew Fielding describe at the dinner they had attended in Oxford: a double-headed serpent.

The discovery, though expected, still came as a shock, and the chief inspector felt the need to steady his nerves as he replaced the second link in the bowl just as he had found it.

Would Gonzales really have been so careless as to leave it there in plain sight? he wondered, and almost at once he realized that the question was an idle one. Unless he was aware of the quest that had brought Sinclair to Oxfordshire he would have had no reason to conceal the object, and so far as the chief inspector knew Julia had not found an occasion to explain his presence in the house other than to say that she and Baxter had come across him snowbound in Chipping Norton and 'rescued' him.

Although he would dearly have liked to search the room,

the knowledge that he was only a guest in the house was sufficient to keep the impulse in check and, having left things as he had found them, he crossed the passage to his own room. His need at that moment was to take one of his pills and lie down. His breathing had grown short in the last few minutes, no doubt the result of the growing tension he felt. But when he reached into his pocket for his tablets he got a shock. The bottle wasn't there. Even more disturbing was the discovery a few seconds later that the pills weren't on his bedside table either. Obviously he had left them somewhere else in the house, but where?

Troubled as he was by this new turn of events, the chief inspector knew he had to remain calm. Although he wanted to go in search of the tablets—he felt exposed without them— he knew that a wiser course would be for him to rest for a few minutes. Stretched out on his bed, he waited for his breathing to resume its normal rhythm, and while he did so he retraced his movements during the last few hours, trying to isolate the moment when he was most likely to have mislaid the bottle.

He had swallowed a pill the previous morning at breakfast, which he had taken with Julia and Philip Gonzales, but he knew for a fact that he had still had the bottle with him when he'd encountered Baxter in the yard outside the kitchen, because he had taken a further pill then to counter the effects of the effort it had cost him to cross the deep snow in front of the house. He recalled Doris giving him a glass of water to wash it down, but thereafter his memories of the moment were overlaid by the dramatic irruption of Daisy into the kitchen and her tale about the argument between Gonzales and Ilse Holtz, which she had overheard.

Had he left the bottle on the kitchen table? It was quite possible. He couldn't remember putting it in his pocket, but if he had forgotten it Doris would certainly have noticed it lying there after his departure and put it aside for him. Not knowing that they were missing, he hadn't raised the question with her when they had been together in the kitchen only a few minutes before and neither had she. But that was hardly surprising, given what had just come to light. The only other place it might be was in Julia's study, where he had spent some time with her after lunch. But he had not taken another pill while he was there and as far as he could remember hadn't even put his hand into his pocket, let alone brought the bottle out. So the kitchen seemed to be the most likely place to go in search of it and he resolved to rouse himself as soon as he felt better and go downstairs.

Glancing at his wristwatch he saw it was nearly four o'clock; already the light outside was dying as the clouds, harbingers of the coming storm, gathered in a grey mass overhead. The product of a strict Presbyterian upbringing, it was not in his nature to indulge in fanciful thoughts, but it occurred to him just then that his earlier feeling that there was something amiss at Wickham Manor had proved all too prescient. Nor was he alone in his fears. He had every reason to believe they were shared by Baxter. The chauffeur had made no secret of his concern at the sudden appearance of the cuff link and its possible implications.

Increasingly troubled by the line of reasoning he had embarked on, Sinclair rose from his bed and went to the window. It had begun to snow again, only this time the flakes weren't falling in slow spirals as before but were being driven by a wind that seemed to be gaining in strength by the minute. It wouldn't be long before the storm was on them and the realization only added to the chief inspector's feeling of helplessness. Cut off from the outside world, the occupants of Wickham Manor were at the mercy of the elements.

First things first, however, he told himself. Before he did anything else he must find his pills.

Quitting his room, he went downstairs to the hall and set off in the direction of the passage that led to the kitchen. But he'd hardly taken two steps when he heard a knock on the front door.

Gonzales! It had to be.

Rooted to the spot he saw the handle of the door turn and braced himself for an encounter he would much rather have avoided. But the door remained shut. Baxter had been as good as his word. He had promised to lock it.

Now he need only get to the kitchen, where the chauffeur would be waiting. Having failed to enter by the front door, Gonzales was certain to make his way there and the two of them could confront him together. But on reaching his destination—it was at the far end of the corridor—the chief inspector found a fresh shock awaiting him. The room was deserted. There was no sign of either Doris or Baxter. It was possible the maid had gone upstairs to rest, he thought; she would be down later to get tea ready. But where had Baxter disappeared to?

Although the kitchen was in half-darkness he checked his impulse to switch on the light. He didn't want to be seen from outside. Instead he went to the window above the sink and peered out into the yard.

'Good lord!'

In the few minutes it had taken him to come downstairs the beginnings of the blizzard he had glimpsed from his window had turned into a maelstrom of swirling snow and ice, which the savage wind flung against the window like a thousand tiny daggers, while the yard itself had been all but swallowed up in the whirling cloud of white particles. As he stood there, transfixed by the scene, he heard what sounded like a door being slammed and saw that a man who was not Baxter had appeared outside. Head bowed, he was coming from the direction of the garage, crossing the icy ground towards the kitchen door and lighting his way with a torch.

Instinctively Sinclair stepped back out of sight, and then moved further away to the end of the room, putting the kitchen table between him and the back door. His heartbeat had quickened, but there was little he could do about it except wait and watch as the handle turned. After a second the door was pushed open and the figure of a man appeared. Little more than a silhouette in the doorway, his entry was accompanied by a sudden rise in the gusting wind's pitch along with a cloud of ice and snow that blew into the kitchen and settled where his torch was pointing at the floor in front of him.

'*Gonzales?*' The chief inspector spoke more harshly than he meant to.

At the sound of his voice the torch shifted. It turned upwards and when Sinclair saw the face that appeared in the bright beam a flood of relief the like of which he had never experienced before washed through him.

'John!' he exclaimed. 'Thank God it's you.'

19

'I DON'T KNOW what I'd have done if you hadn't turned up. I was near the end of my tether.'

It was the first chance Sinclair had to unburden himself. He had hardly got over his astonishment at Madden's unexpected appearance when the outer door of the kitchen had opened again and Baxter had stumbled in carrying an armful of logs. At any other time his surprise at seeing the new arrival might have seemed comical. The chauffeur's jaw had dropped, quite literally.

'Mr Madden is a friend of mine,' Sinclair had been quick to explain. 'He had lost track of me and heard I might be staying here with Mrs Lesage.'

'I was hoping to take Mr Sinclair back to Oxford with me.' Madden had added his explanations to the chief inspector's.

'Well, I doubt you'll be able to do that now, sir.' Baxter had had time to collect himself. 'You've seen what it's like outside. I'll have to have a word with Mrs Lesage, but I'm sure we can put you up for the night.'

He told them he'd gone outside for a minute to collect some wood for the fire in the drawing-room.

'We keep a store of logs in one of the stalls in the stable yard,' he said. 'I must have missed you by seconds, sir.'

These last words had been addressed to Madden as the

three of them made their way to the drawing-room, where Baxter busied himself attending to the fire while the other two, forced to hold their peace for the moment, waited for him to finish.

'Madam will be down soon,' the chauffeur said. 'She rang the bell in the kitchen a few minutes ago and Doris went up to help her. Mrs Holtz must still be unwell.'

Mention of the maid's name had jogged Sinclair's memory.

'Before you go, Baxter, I seem to have mislaid those pills of mine. I think I may have left them in the kitchen. Could you have a look there, please? Ask Doris if you can't find them. She may have put them somewhere.'

'I'll do that, sir.' The chauffeur rose to his feet. 'There's still no sign of Mr Gonzales,' he added, with a glance at Sinclair. 'You haven't had a chance to talk to Madam yet, have you, sir?'

The chief inspector shook his head. 'Not yet. But I will.'

'So you've lost your pills, Angus?' Madden had kept his peace while the chauffeur was still with them, but Sinclair's drawn look and shallow breathing hadn't escaped his friend's sharp eye and Madden's scowl was accusing. 'Helen won't be happy to hear that. She couldn't believe you'd taken it into your head to go off chasing after some supposed war criminal. Yes, I heard all about that from Billy. And I know about the lady in Fernley you think was murdered. You won't believe what I have to tell you about *that*. But first, what's this about Gonzales? Has he disappeared?'

'So you know the name?' Sinclair was astonished.

'I had dinner with your friend Ann Waites in Oxford. She had a good deal to say about the gentleman. She seemed to think he was after Mrs Lesage's money.'

'If only that was all!'

'Did she tell you about the cuff link?' Sinclair asked.

'The one you showed them all the night you had dinner with her?' Madden nodded. 'I wondered about that.'

'I think it belonged to the man who killed Greta Hartmann. He lost it by mistake. It's one of a pair, and the other one has turned up here.'

'In *this* house?'

'It's sitting in Philip Gonzales's room . . .' Sinclair was stopped short by the expression on the other man's face. 'My God, John, what is it?'

Before Madden could answer, the chief inspector heard a sound that made him check his old partner's reply with a gesture. It was the low hum of the mobile seat descending the stairway.

'It'll have to keep,' he said. 'There's Julia now.'

'You say he's *disappeared*? But that's ridiculous.' Julia Lesage's pale face was flushed. 'He went down to the village two hours ago. He *must* have come back by now.'

'Well, he hasn't, ma'am, and that's the truth.' Baxter caught Sinclair's eye. He seemed to be hoping he would say something. But the chief inspector stayed mute.

'The reason I asked Mr Gonzales to go down was to find out if the phones there are working, and now Mr Madden here tells me the line has been repaired. I can't believe Philip wouldn't have hurried back to let me know.'

'All I can tell you, ma'am, is that I went up to his room just a few minutes ago in case he'd returned without our knowing it, but he wasn't there.'

'What about the rest of the house? Have you looked in the library and the morning-room, and what about the study?'

'I'll do that now, ma'am, but I don't think he's here.' Baxter's face wore a stubborn look.

Lost for words, his mistress shook her head in disbelief. Clad in a black velvet gown, long-sleeved and buttoned at the throat, and with her red hair drawn back to display her pale skin and slender neck, she cut a striking figure, one marred only by the strip of sticking plaster still attached to her forehead. She had wheeled herself into the drawing-room escorted not only by Doris but also by Baxter, who it appeared had been waiting at the bottom of the stairs to receive her. Although he could only have had her ear for a minute he had managed to advise her of Madden's unexpected arrival so that when she entered the drawing-room it was with a smile and words of welcome ready on her lips.

'I know exactly who you are, Mr Madden. Angus and I were talking about you only yesterday. No, please don't apologize . . .' She cut him off as he began to explain himself. 'I could say I'm sorry you're going to be trapped here for a bit, but the truth is I'm not sorry at all.' She smiled. 'I'm delighted to meet you. Could you bear to spend the night with us? I really don't think you can spirit Angus away in this weather. It'll be best for everyone if you wait out the storm.'

It was then that she had asked where Gonzales was and it had been left to Baxter to break the news of his disappearance to her.

'Have *you* any explanation for this, Angus?' She turned to the chief inspector now. 'Can you think of any reason why he hasn't returned? Could he have had an accident on the way to the village? The lane must be deep in ice and snow.'

'If he had, I'm sure Mr Madden would have come across

him when he walked up.' It was Baxter who supplied an answer to her question.

'Mr Madden?' She turned to him. 'I take it you saw nothing amiss?'

Madden shook his head. 'I asked in the village if anyone had seen Mr Gonzales, but it seemed no one had.'

His words seemed to come as a surprise to her. At all events she paused to give what he had just said some thought and when she eventually spoke it was in a different tone.

'And why should you have done that?' she asked.

'I'm sorry?' Madden began, but was cut off.

'You're not even acquainted with Mr Gonzales, are you?'

Sinclair winced. He realized too late he should have warned his friend in advance about their hostess: Julia Lesage missed nothing.

'No, but I knew his name.' Madden sought to cover his slip of the tongue. 'I had dinner with a friend of yours in Oxford, Professor Waites. It was she who told me that Mr Gonzales was going to make his way somehow to Wickham Manor, even if he had to walk, and that she had asked him to tell Angus if he was here that I was in Oxford searching for him. What I didn't know was whether Mr Gonzales had managed to get here.'

'And that was why you inquired after him in the village.' Julia Lesage nodded as though she accepted the explanation. She turned to the two servants, who were standing a little way off, near the door. 'Doris, could you bring our tea now, please; and Baxter, get a room ready for Mr Madden, would you? He'll be staying the night.'

She waited until they had left the room. Then she turned back to the two men.

'I hope you won't take offence, Mr Madden, but I don't

believe you're telling me the truth, or not the whole truth. I've had a bad feeling all day—Angus can vouch for that—and a lot of it revolves around Mr Gonzales. Don't ask me to explain why—call it a woman's intuition if you like—but I know things are being kept from me. So do me the courtesy of taking me into your confidence, please. I mean *both* of you.' She shot a sharp glance at Sinclair. 'If you know anything about Philip Gonzales, anything at all, you're not to keep it to yourself. I insist on knowing the truth.'

'I don't care what you say. I refuse to believe it.'

Julia Lesage turned her stricken face to the fire. She had been sitting in her wheelchair, silent for the most part, listening as Sinclair went briefly through the chain of events that had led him to Oxford and explained how he had discovered the existence of the broken cuff link left in the car the supposed killer had hired from Alf Hutton.

'It was clear that the last person who drove the car must have lost it. It had fallen out of his cuff and was obviously one of a pair.'

'Does that matter?' Julia's tone had been icy. 'And what has it got to do with Mr Gonzales?' Although she had said little thus far, the chief inspector had been left in no doubt as to the effect his tale was having on her.

'I'm afraid it does matter.' Sinclair met her angry gaze. 'If you remember, I told you how I'd found out that this man I was following had left a false address in Chipping Norton. It was when you'd rescued me from the tea shop and we were driving back here.'

'I remember very well. You agreed with Baxter that he was probably trying to hide his tracks.'

'At that point, I didn't think any more about it,' Sinclair went on. 'I felt I'd already gone further than I ought to in pursuing the inquiry. I'm not a policeman any longer. But then a few hours ago I got a shock when Doris told me she'd seen the other cuff link, the mate of this one, in Mr Gonzales's room.' He drew the broken link out of his pocket and held it up for her inspection. 'She knew what it was because Baxter had told the two maids about your conversation with him. I subsequently went up to Mr Gonzales's room and examined it for myself. It was lying in a bowl on his dresser. There's no doubt the links are a match.'

'Wouldn't it be rather foolish of Mr Gonzales to have left it in plain view?' Julia had turned pale.

'Not necessarily. He could have had no idea of its significance to me.'

'And based only on that you think Philip was the man who was driving through the village in Hampshire where you were staying, and by extension the man who killed that poor woman there?'

'I wouldn't go that far, not without more evidence.'

Sinclair could see that his hostess was barely managing to control her feelings. Her face was flushed and her eyes, brighter than usual, were flashing warning signals. He had managed to retain his composure, though only just, and as he spoke he shot a glance at Madden, who had been standing silent all this time.

'But I believe there's more to this story,' he went on. 'Just before you came downstairs Mr Madden was about to tell me something.'

Before either of them could continue, however, they had been interrupted by the sound of rolling wheels and Baxter had appeared pushing the tea trolley ahead of him. In the silence that followed the chauffeur had kept busy handing around the cups of tea which his mistress poured with unseeing eyes. Her thoughts were so plainly elsewhere that he became visibly concerned, and sensing that something grave must have occurred in his absence he had remained by her side when his duties were over, hoping perhaps that she wouldn't notice his presence. But after a moment she had looked up.

'Thank you, Baxter. That will be all.'

Sinclair stirred uneasily on the sofa. Along with their tea the chauffeur had brought him some unwelcome news. His pills were nowhere to be found. Doris had searched for them high and low in the kitchen, opening every drawer.

'Are you sure you left them there, sir?'

Baxter's words had woken Julia momentarily from her trance.

'What's this about your pills, Angus?'

'I seem to have mislaid them. Don't worry, it's nothing. I'm sure they'll turn up. I'm feeling quite well at the moment.'

'You don't look it.' Her glance had been penetrating and for a moment it seemed she might pursue the question. But in the end she simply shook her head.

'Have a look around the house, Baxter. See if you can find them.'

Now she tore her eyes away from the flickering flames.

'I believe you have something to say to me, Mr Madden?' She turned her gaze on him.

Madden seated himself in an armchair facing her and spoke now for the first time.

'First, let me say I've no idea whether Mr Gonzales is involved in this business. Most of what Mr Sinclair told you was news to me. My only purpose in coming here was to collect him and take him back to Highfield. My wife, who is his doctor, is concerned for his health and I very much hope these pills of his, which are meant to control his blood pressure, can be found because they're important to his well-being. I'm sorry, Angus . . .' He turned to the chief inspector. 'But that had to be said.'

'I understand.' Julia nodded. 'But I don't believe that's all you have to tell me.'

'No, it's not.' Madden returned her gaze. 'I happen to be in possession of other information which until a few minutes ago I had no reason to believe was connected to anyone here at Wickham Manor. I'll explain how I came across it in a moment, but I should warn you now that you'll find it unsettling, to say the least.'

'I'm unsettled enough already, thank you.' Her green eyes glittered. 'Could you be more precise?'

'This will come as a surprise to you too, Angus.' Madden cast a glance at the chief inspector, who grimaced.

'I had a feeling it might.'

'The lady Angus believes was murdered was German—her name was Greta Hartmann—and as a result of what he suspected he sent a letter to an old friend of his, a Berlin detective called Hans Probst, asking if the police there had any knowledge of her. He suspected she might have been a witness to some crime committed in the past and that the man she saw that day in the village was somehow connected to it. Frau Hartmann's husband was a pastor. He'd been strongly opposed to the Nazis and died in a concentration camp. Angus wondered if the man Frau Hartmann saw in the village that day might in fact be a war criminal, someone she had come in contact with and whose face she remembered.'

'And was I right?' Sinclair asked.

'No, as guesses go yours was well wide of the mark, Angus.' Madden's smile flickered for a moment. 'But you've turned up something far worse. That letter of yours set off all kinds of alarm bells in Berlin and they're still ringing. The man you've been chasing has been sought by the police in several countries, including Germany, over the past twenty years and he's thought to have murdered a number of people, most of them women . . . rich women . . . after he'd defrauded them.'

He stopped. He had caught a look in Julia Lesage's eye.

'And now you're about to say this man could be Philip and he has me in his sights,' she said. 'Is that it?' Her face was ashen.

'No, I'm simply telling you what I know.' Madden was careful in his reply. 'I came by this information because I got in touch with the Oxford police when I arrived in case they had any knowledge of Angus's whereabouts. It was then that I learned what effect this letter of his had had and I was allowed to sit in at a conference where Probst revealed what the German police had in their records.'

'Is Hans here—in *Oxford*?' Sinclair was astounded.

'I haven't had a chance to tell you, Angus. He came over at once with the blessing of his superiors and our commissioner. That will give you some idea of how seriously they take this matter.'

He directed these last words at Julia, who'd gone silent. Clearly she was struggling to come to terms with what he had just said.

'This man the police are seeking has used a lot of names in his time. Could Gonzales be one of them? I have no idea, Mrs Lesage, and, until I heard what Angus had to tell us, no reason to believe he had anything to do with this business.

But the presence of this cuff link puts a different complexion on things. Where is he exactly? How can he have disappeared?'

'How indeed?' Her distress was plain. Sinclair hesitated. 'Can I speak frankly, Julia?' he said.

'I wish you would.'

'For the past day or so I've felt there was something wrong in the house, something I couldn't put my finger on. It seemed to start around the time Philip Gonzales turned up, though I'm not saying he was the cause of it. With your permission I'd like to tell John about the letter you received regarding the sale of your house in Switzerland and what that brought in its wake. I'd also like you to send for Ilse Holtz. I know she's been feeling unwell, but it's important we talk to her. Would you do that?'

'If you insist . . .' She reached for a bell push on the table beside her and pressed it.

'Let's wait until she comes,' Sinclair said.

In short order the sound of footsteps in the hall outside reached them and Baxter reappeared.

'Would you go upstairs and knock on Ilse's door?' Julia said to him. 'Tell her if she's well enough I'd like her to come down and join us.'

As the chauffeur left the room Madden rose and went to the windows overlooking the terrace. It was too dark to see anything outside, but the howl of the wind remained constant and the windows continued to rattle.

'It's still blowing like the devil,' he remarked.

His words brought no response from his listeners. Lost in her thoughts, Julia was staring into the fire, while the chief inspector for his part was trying to gather his strength for what he foresaw would be another difficult passage as they sought to untangle the mystery they were all caught up in now.

Again footsteps sounded, but not measured like before. They were hurried, and when Baxter came through the doorway it was in a rush.

'Ma'am, she's not there.' He stood panting.

'What did you say?' Julia came to herself with a start.

'Mrs Holtz's room is empty.' Baxter stared at her, stunned. 'She's disappeared.'

20

SOMETIMES THE PICTURES came in dreams; sometimes in memories.

The night of July 27 had been the worst. A force of several hundred RAF bombers had attacked the city with block-busters and incendiaries, creating a blaze of unimaginable proportions, a tornado of fire that had reached a height of three hundred metres—or so they said—and in which winds of more than two hundred kilometres an hour had been re-corded. Twenty square kilometres of the city had been incin-erated. The asphalt covering the streets had caught fire and oil from damaged ships and tankers in the port had spilled into the canals with which Hamburg was laced, setting them ablaze. Later the American bombers had followed.

They were not scenes that Hans Probst had witnessed; he had been absent from the city when the raids took place. But he had learned about them from survivors and they had taken shape in his imagination and his dreams along with the resulting devastation he had seen for himself when he re-turned. Such was the degree of damage inflicted by the raids that the city he remembered had all but vanished; only the rubble remained, the rubble and the fires that continued to burn for days after the last bomber had left despite the efforts of the firemen, who were unable to reach them because what had once been streets were now so choked with debris that they could not pass through them with their machines.

For a time the collapse of all normal life in the city had given him hope. Unable to discover what had become of his wife and daughter—the house where they had lived and the houses around it had quite simply ceased to exist as recognizable human structures—he could still hope that they were alive and had found sanctuary elsewhere. But as hope faded he had come to believe that they must have been among the thousands who had sought safety in bomb shelters and cellars and perished from carbon monoxide poisoning when the oxygen in the air above them was consumed by fire.

Still, their bodies at least might have been preserved, he thought; he could at least bury them. But his dreadful search for their remains had proved fruitless. They were not among the dead who had been identified. Later he had heard stories of people trying to flee the bombing who had been sucked into the flames, snatched up like leaves into the raging inferno, never to be seen again. Later still—and this was long after the war had ended—he had read that according to a study made by the American air force the effects of the fires that night had been worse than those caused by the dropping of the atomic bomb on Nagasaki. There had never been anything like it before or since.

Present in his dreams too were the faces of his wife and daughter: usually it was Margarethe who came, wearing her familiar frown of worry, but occasionally, as now, it was Elise who appeared, bending over him, with her hand resting lightly on his shoulder as though she wished to waken him.

'Excuse me, sir . . .'

'What . . . ? I'm sorry . . . who . . . ?'

Hans Probst woke with a start. He had been drowsing in

an armchair in the hotel lounge, only half conscious. When he opened his eyes he saw there was a young woman in a white blouse standing before him. He recalled seeing her face behind the reception desk. She had touched him on the shoulder.

'I'm sorry to wake you, sir, but there's a phone call for you.'

'A phone call?' Probst dragged himself back to the present.

'It's from Berlin. You can take it in the lobby if you like.'

'I've only been told the outline of the story, the bare bones, as you might say. It had all the makings of a classic fraud.'

Probst looked up from the pencilled notes he had laid on the table in front of him. He saw that Lily was listening intently. She had returned to the hotel from St Aldates a short while before in response to a phone call from the Berlin detective, who had told her he had new information about Philip Gonzales that he wished to share with her.

'He used a German name—Josef Schulz—but he claimed Havana as his birthplace and told anyone who was interested that he had a German father and a Cuban mother. This was in Madrid three years ago and it's worth noting that although he arrived in the city without any introductions it wasn't long before he gained entry into the upper levels of society. It seems he had the gift of making himself agreeable to all.'

'So who did he get his hooks into?' Lily scowled. It was the first chance she'd had to talk to the *Kriminalkommissar* one-on-one. All she really knew about him was that he'd come to London years before to help Scotland Yard with a case that had a German connection and that he and the chief inspector had hit it off. According to Billy Styles, who was

the source of her information, they had struck up a friendship which even the war hadn't affected. Sinclair considered
Hans Probst to be one of the best detectives he'd ever worked
with, Billy said.

'And a good bloke too. He wouldn't have anything to do
with the Nazis. He resigned from the police as soon as they
came into power. Things can't have been easy for him.'

Nor could they, Lily thought. She could tell that just by
looking at him. Behind the mild blue eyes and gentle manner
there was pain—she sensed it—some burden weighing on
him that couldn't be shifted, like it was a part of him and he
had to live with it. Yet she had warmed to him from the first.
When they'd been introduced the previous day he had taken
her hand in his and for a moment Lily had thought he was
going to kiss it. Instead he had bowed over it politely and
thereafter behaved to her with the kind of old-world courtesy that had gone out of fashion in England.

'His hooks . . . ?' Baffled for a moment, Probst blinked.
Then he nodded. 'Yes, of course . . . his hooks.' He chuckled.
'His chosen victim was a widowed lady still in mourning for
her husband, a military man who had died fighting in the
civil war. What he proposed was that she set up a charity in
his name to aid the widows of men who had fallen fighting
for the Nationalist forces under Franco. The idea must have
appealed to her because she agreed at once and arrangements
for setting it up were well advanced when her son returned
from a diplomatic posting abroad and put a stop to it. A subsequent investigation of the scheme showed it to be fraudulent and a police investigation was launched, at which point
Señor Schulz disappeared. Later it was found that he had
been using a false name.'

Probst tugged thoughtfully at an earlobe.

'Now, since no fraud had actually been committed—the widow hadn't parted with any money as yet—the police were tempted to let the matter drop. But the son objected strongly. He felt his mother had been humiliated, and thanks to the pressure he was able to exert the police eventually identified the forger who had supplied Schulz with his false papers. Although he had no idea of the man's current whereabouts, he was able to provide them with one crucial detail: his name; I mean the name he was using when they met.'

Probst eyed his listener meaningfully.

'It was Gonzales: Philip Gonzales.'

Lily pursed her lips in a silent whistle.

'That information was passed on to the International Police Commission in Saint-Cloud, as I discovered this morning. When I asked my people in Berlin to see if we had any record of Gonzales's name I suggested they check with the commission since fraud is one of the crimes they keep a close eye on, given that it frequently crosses borders. The name Gonzales was in their files under the heading of suspected fraudsters and confidence men.'

'That still doesn't mean it's his real name, does it?'

Probst shook his head. 'It could be merely the one he's been living under, and he's not been charged with anything up till now—under that name at least—as far as we know.'

Lily was silent. She was thinking over what she'd been told. She had a shrewd idea now of what was in Hans Probst's mind and knew that in the next few minutes she was going to be asked to make a decision and it would not be an easy one.

'But there's no evidence to suggest he's Voss, is there?'

'Not as such, no. But all the same, I think we should take what precautions we can in the event that it proves to be the case. We must alert Mr Sinclair and Mr Madden to the

possible danger they're facing, not to mention Mrs Lesage.'
Probst's mild blue eyes had taken on a steely glint. He waited
for Lily's reaction.

'But the phone to Wickham Manor is still down. I tried
calling the number from the station less than an hour ago. I
wanted to see if Mr Madden had arrived safely.'

'I wasn't thinking of the telephone.'

Lily had guessed as much.

'Did you not say you had a car at your disposal today?'
Probst's tone was deceptively mild.

She took a deep breath. 'It's a police car, sir, the one Mr
Styles drove you down from London in, and I can't just go
off in it without his say-so. I could try calling him if you like.
I might catch him at the Banbury police station. But I'd need
to explain to him why you think it's necessary for us to drive
up to Wickham Manor. He'll want to know why it can't wait
until he gets back. Even supposing Gonzales is Voss, what
makes you think he's . . .' She couldn't quite finish what she
meant to say, and it was her companion who voiced the
thought that was in her mind.

'. . . ready to complete the charade he's been engaged in up
till now—to kill her and move on?' Probst grimaced. 'I must
tell you I have good reason to fear something of the sort
might happen, and soon. Let me explain.'

To Lily's surprise he fell silent then. But as he busied himself collecting his notes and stacking the pages neatly in front
of him, she saw it was because he was considering his next
words carefully.

'There is an aspect of this matter you are perhaps not familiar with, Sergeant.' Probst looked up. 'Are you aware that
when the road to Great Tew was closed to traffic this man

walked for several miles through the snow in order to reach Mrs Lesage's house?'

'I was told that, sir. But I don't see what bearing it has,' Lily responded cautiously.

'What was so urgent about his mission? Why was it so important that he couldn't wait for a day or two when it would have been possible to make the journey by car? The lady who passed on this piece of information to Mr Madden said jokingly that perhaps it was love that had spurred him on. Apparently he has asked Mrs Lesage to marry him. But I am not persuaded by this line of reasoning, particularly now that we know a little more about Mr Gonzales. Confidence men don't marry their victims as a rule, though they may offer to do so. We have no idea what Voss may have promised the women he defrauded, but one thing is certain. When he was done with them he killed them.'

'Yes, but I still don't understand why you think he's ready to move *now*.'

'It's because I can't believe he would have chosen to walk miles through the snow in bitter weather unless he had a pressing reason for doing so: unless he *had* to be at Wickham Manor.' Probst paused. He saw that he still had not convinced his listener. 'If we look carefully at Voss's record we can see that in all but one instance he carried out his frauds with an eye to the moment when he was in danger of being unmasked, at which point he terminated the exercise, if I can put it that way. It was only in Frau Klinger's case that he was taken by surprise when she became suspicious and consulted her lawyer. His response, as we know, was both savage and immediate. He murdered them both in the course of a single evening.'

He went silent again for a moment, glancing down at his hands, which were folded on the table in front of him.

'Voss was lucky to escape arrest then.' He looked up. 'Perhaps he had let things run on for too long, grown greedy. If so, the lesson will not have been lost on him, this cold killer. He won't make the same mistake twice. If, as I say, he chose to walk through the snow in order to reach his victim on that particular day, it may be because whatever scheme he's been engaged in was about to be discovered. This is only a guess, I admit, but if I'm right it follows that he may well be on the point of bringing the business to an end, with fatal results not only for Mrs Lesage, but also for our friends who are quite unaware of the danger they're in.'

'Would he really be prepared to take both Mr Madden and Mr Sinclair on?' Lily wasn't convinced. 'And there must be staff at the manor, maids and so on.'

Probst shrugged. 'In the past Voss showed a gift for creating a mise-en-scène designed to deceive the police. In one of his two murders in Mexico he killed not only his victim but the two maids who worked for her, with the result that the police were persuaded a crazed killer had broken into the house. He did something similar with Frau Klinger—he butchered her with a knife—but then killed her lawyer in a quite different way. He made it seem like a clumsy assault, a robbery gone wrong. He can't have bargained for the presence of two strangers at Wickham Manor, one of them a retired senior detective, but he can hardly afford to let them live. And bear in mind he will have the advantage of surprise. He can pick his moment. Who can tell what he might be planning? The snow has been both his friend and enemy. On the one hand it has kept Wickham Manor isolated, which is to his advantage. On the other it has made his escape that much more difficult. How he means to resolve this problem I can't say, but I think it's of the utmost importance that we get there as soon as possible. I fear for our friends, Sergeant. If anything happened to them and we did nothing I could never forgive myself.'

Probst sat back. He had said his piece. Lily saw it as up to her now.

'I'll make one attempt to call Mr Styles in Banbury. If he and Mr Morgan are there they might get to the manor quicker than us.'

'And if you can't get hold of him?'

She swallowed. 'Then we'll go ourselves.'

21

'LET ME SEE if I have this right,' Madden said. 'The letter arrived just before you left for London?'

'It came with the post that day.' Julia nodded. 'There was nothing to be done about it. Baxter was driving me up to London that afternoon. But as I explained to Angus, I wasn't in the least bothered. It's quite common for there to be delays in transactions of this kind. I said as much to Philip.'

'He was here then when the letter arrived?'

'He'd been staying with me for a few weeks.'

'But he didn't accompany you to London. He went to Switzerland instead. Have I got that right?'

Julia nodded. 'Apparently he went to see the estate agents in Lausanne, on my behalf he said, though he had no right to do that, not without consulting me.'

She shivered involuntarily, though not from the cold, Sinclair thought. It was warm in the drawing-room—the fire was blazing. It might have been in response to the wind outside, though, which had dropped a little in the past half hour but could still be heard beating against the windowpanes. Or was it a reaction to the word that Baxter had brought them only a few minutes before? Acting on his mistress's orders he had scoured the house from top to bottom, searching every room, he said, but finding no trace of Ilse Holtz.

'Her overcoat's missing, though, ma'am. She usually hangs it on the rack by the front door. It's not there.'

'One moment . . .' Madden had cut in. Rising from his chair he'd crossed the room to where his own coat was lying where he had dropped it on a chaise longue by the window. Feeling about in one of the pockets, he had fished out a leather glove and brought it over to Julia.

'Does this belong to her?' he asked. 'I found it lying on the ground when I walked up the drive. I'd clean forgotten about it.'

'I'm not sure . . .' She had examined the object, turning it over in her hands. 'Baxter?' She held it out to the chauffeur, who took it from her.

'Yes, ma'am.' His response was immediate. 'I think it is. I've seen her wearing gloves like this one.'

'On the drive, you say?' Julia looked at Madden. 'But if she went down to the village you would have run into her, wouldn't you?'

'I would have thought so.' Madden scowled.

'And why would she go down there anyway without telling me?'

The question had gone unanswered. Then Baxter had spoken again.

'Perhaps she lost it earlier, ma'am . . . I mean not today. What with this wind she could have dropped it outside the house. It could have blown there.'

'Yes . . . yes, I suppose so.' Julia bit her lip. 'But that doesn't tell me where she is. Go and have a look outside, would you, Baxter? And check the stables too while you're at it. I just don't know what to think . . .'

Madden waited until they were alone. He had resumed

his seat by the fire, facing Julia. 'Tell me about this letter,' he said.

In reply she'd explained the sequence of events to him, and now Madden wanted to be sure he had the story clear in his mind.

'So Mr Gonzales returned from Switzerland in a hurry— a great hurry—and told you this letter you received from the estate agent was a fraud. So, far from there being a delay, the agent said, the sale of the house had gone through, at least according to Mr Gonzales.'

'He said M. Jansen had already written to me asking what my instructions were about the money—where it should be deposited. When I told him I'd received no such letter he began to question what part Mrs Holtz played in managing my affairs. Unfortunately I let him call her down from her room to join us and they had an awful row. I wish now I hadn't let him do it. She was terribly upset.' She shook her head.

'Could I see that letter, do you think,' Madden asked, 'the one Mr Gonzales said was false?'

'If you must, but it seems perfectly straightforward to me. There's been a delay in the sale going through, that's all.' She turned to Sinclair. 'Would you, Angus? It's in that folder on top of my desk.'

The chief inspector was back in a minute with the missive in question. He'd returned to find Madden down on his knees in front of the fire adding a fresh log to the blaze.

'When exactly did it arrive?' Madden looked up.

'On the day I went up to London, as I said,' Julia explained. 'The post was late that day, I remember. It didn't arrive until after lunch when I was packed and ready to go. There was no rush about replying to it, as far as I was concerned, but I took a moment to dictate a brief note to Ilse telling Jansen there was no problem about the delay.'

'And Mrs Holtz would have typed the letter for you?'

'Naturally . . .'

'And how are your letters posted? Are they taken down to the village?'

'No, they're given to the postman, who comes up here in his van. He takes them to the nearest post office at Enstone.'

'So it would have been Mrs Holtz's responsibility to see that the letter you wrote to the estate agents was dispatched in the proper way.'

There was a pause. When Julia eventually replied her voice had grown tense. 'Forgive me, Mr Madden, but you seem to be suggesting Ilse might be behind this. That was just what Philip was trying to imply when we had our falling-out . . . that she had somehow been up to no good. You can't imagine how upsetting this is to me.'

'I'm sorry. I understand.' He looked down. 'But there's something else I have to tell you and I'm afraid it will only upset you further. It has to do with this man the police are looking for. From as far back as they can trace him he seems to have had an accomplice, his sister. She has twice given him alibis that enabled him to escape arrest. From all accounts they seem to have had . . . an unusual relationship.'

'Dear God!' Julia had turned white again. 'Now you're trying to tell me Ilse might be this woman—that she could be Philip's sister.'

'It's something we have to consider.' Madden kept his voice calm. 'Especially since, like him, she seems to have disappeared.'

'Even though with my own ears I heard Philip practically accuse her of being behind this business of the false letter?'

'Even so. You see, it could have been an act they were putting on.'

'An *act*?' Julia shook her head in disgust. 'No, I can't listen to this any longer. I really can't. Angus, would you help me, please?'

She indicated her wheelchair, which was standing beside the armchair where she was seated. As Sinclair rose to help her move into it, she pressed the bell push on the table beside her.

'I'm going to go upstairs and lie down,' she said. 'I have a headache. And I'm sure you two would prefer to be on your own to discuss whatever it is you think has been going on in my house. But let me make one thing clear. I'm not about to swallow any theory you might have, particularly if it involves someone I truly care about and who has done nothing but help and support me these past few years—at least not without some evidence to back it up. No, Angus, I won't need you.' She had seen the chief inspector start towards the door. 'Doris will help me upstairs.'

Spinning her wheelchair around, she rolled across the room and disappeared into the hall.

With a sigh, Sinclair resumed his seat.

'What do you think, John?' He looked at his old partner. 'Does any of this make sense to you?'

'Sense?'

'Do you really think Gonzales is this Voss person and Mrs Holtz is his sister?'

'I wish I could doubt it.' Madden shrugged. 'But that cuff link is a damning piece of evidence. There's no getting around it.'

'So Gonzales must be the man Mrs Hartmann saw in Fernley.' Sinclair gnawed at his lip. 'But why have they both suddenly disappeared? Could it be because they know their plans have gone awry and it was time to cut their losses?'

'If they're simply a pair of fraudsters, then very likely so; but if they're Voss and his sister, then I wouldn't count on it. They've invested too much time in this scheme. There's nothing in their record to make me think they'd give up so easily.'

'But where could they be?'

'I wish I knew.' He caught Sinclair's eye. 'Tell me, Angus—how much do you really know about them?'

'Only what Professor Waites told me. Julia met Gonzales a year ago. He introduced himself to her at some party in London and told her he'd seen her competing in a skiing championship before the war and never forgotten it. I get the impression that he set out to make himself indispensable to her and she seems to have grown fond of him.'

In the silence that followed they heard the sound of muted voices in the hall; and then a low humming sound as the mobile seat ascended the stairway.

'What about Mrs Holtz?'

'She's Swiss, or says she is. They met after Julia's husband was killed in a motor accident. I don't know how exactly, but Mrs Holtz was already working for her when she decided to leave Switzerland and return to England.'

'And how would you describe her? What sort of person is she?'

'Opaque.' The chief inspector frowned. 'Reserved to the point that I wouldn't even hazard a guess as to what was passing through her mind. Julia went so far as to apologize for her, saying she was a "difficult person" but someone who had always been loyal to her.'

'All of which tells us nothing, really.' Madden stroked his chin.

'One thing I did glean—though again it came from Julia—was that Mrs Holtz managed all her business affairs. Indeed she said she couldn't have coped without her after her husband died.'

'Now, that *is* interesting. So presumably she knew all about the sale of the house.'

Sinclair sighed heavily.

'You'll have to help me here, John. This business with the false letter—what do you think they were up to? How was the fraud going to work?'

Instead of replying Madden rose to his feet and began to pace about the floor, moving away from the hearth at first as though to give himself room, but then returning to stand in front of the fire, hands in pockets. The sight brought a faint smile to the chief inspector's lips. It struck a familiar chord. His old colleague had always claimed he thought better on his feet.

'I'll tell you what I think, Angus.' Madden spoke at last. 'It's got some rough edges and it's mainly guesswork, but it seems to fit the facts. Assuming Gonzales and Ilse Holtz are behind this—I'll call them that for now—I think their plan has been long in the hatching. They were waiting for an opportunity and it came when Mrs Lesage decided to sell her house. At least one thing Gonzales told her was true, though why he should have done so is a mystery to me. I'm sure the agent wrote telling her the sale had gone through and asking where she would like the money deposited. That letter was intercepted, most likely by Mrs Holtz, and unfortunately for the two of them it arrived just as Mrs Lesage was about to leave for London. All they could do on the spur of the moment—it must have happened on the same day—was to provide her with a substitute, one that Mrs Holtz could have typed and signed.'

'You mean the one saying the sale had been delayed?'

Madden nodded. 'And though Mrs Lesage found time to dictate a reply, it didn't matter since her letter was never posted. Mrs Holtz would have seen to that. The important thing was that it gave them a breathing space and they used it to send a letter at once to the estate agent in Mrs Lesage's name instructing him to deposit the money from the sale in an account they had already set up in Switzerland, probably in the name of a company. It wouldn't have aroused the agent's suspicion. He must know Mrs Lesage is a wealthy woman with various business interests inherited from her late husband. Of course, whether *his* letter acknowledging receipt of *hers* has arrived yet we don't know, but if it has it would also have been intercepted again by Mrs Holtz.'

Sinclair interrupted. 'But wait a minute. That false letter about the sale being delayed—it was opened by Mrs Holtz in Julia's presence. I happen to know that.'

'That doesn't surprise me. It had to look like a normal letter arriving in the normal way. And since it was Mrs Holtz who opened it, all she had to do was hand the letter to Mrs Lesage.'

Sinclair scowled. 'That's all well and good, but I can't see what they hoped to gain from it. All Julia had to do when she returned was get in touch with the estate agent and she'd have discovered the truth. In fact, if it wasn't for the weather their whole scheme would have fallen to pieces by now.'

'Would it?' Madden cocked an eye at his old partner.

'What are you suggesting?' Sinclair felt a cold hand on his heart.

'We're back with the same question, aren't we? Are Gonzales and Mrs Holtz Voss and his sister?' Madden mused. 'If so, then the weather would simply have been an inconvenience. In fact, in some ways it worked to their advantage. This house has been cut off for days.'

'I don't follow, John . . .'

'We'd have to look at their past behaviour. These two are killers: never forget it. By the time Mrs Lesage returned from London they would have been ready to bring matters to a head, most likely through an accident or something that looked like one . . .'

He broke off. He had seen the change of expression on Sinclair's face.

'What is it, Angus?'

'Did you notice that bit of plaster on Julia's forehead?' Sinclair had just remembered. 'She took a tumble down the stairs in her wheelchair this morning. One of the brakes failed. A nut came loose.'

'Imagine that . . . were either Gonzales or Mrs Holtz in the vicinity?'

'Both as it happens.'

'But so were you.' Madden's sudden smile took the chief inspector by surprise. 'That probably made the difference, Angus. One way or another you've played a notable role in all this.'

'I've done nothing of the sort.' Sinclair scoffed at the notion. 'I've been played for a fool along with poor Julia.'

'No, don't you see—it was your unexpected arrival here that spoiled their game? You must be the last person in the world they wanted to see turn up unexpectedly: a former Scotland Yard detective, a chief inspector no less. I doubt your hostess would have survived that fall if you hadn't been close at hand.'

He saw Sinclair's eyes widen as the realization struck him.

'Yes, that's right, Angus. If they are Voss and his sister then it's only thanks to you that Julia Lesage is still alive.'

22

LILY WATCHED AS HANS Probst got up from his chair and went to the window. It was the third time he'd done so. From where she was sitting on the other side of the room she could hear the rattle of ice crystals as they were flung against the glass panes by the blizzard raging outside.

'I'm sorry, sir, but we can't go on yet.'

Lily could see that her companion was growing increasingly frustrated by the delay, but there was nothing she could do about it. Having failed to make contact with Billy Styles—he and Inspector Morgan were still out of touch, the Banbury police told her—they had set out from Oxford in the knowledge that the promised blizzard was expected to arrive sooner than anticipated, or so the clerk at the reception desk had told them when they left. He'd been listening to the radio. In the event the storm had broken just as they'd reached the turnoff to Enstone and with the road ahead of them suddenly all but invisible she'd had no option but to stop in the village and wait for it to subside.

While sitting in their car at the side of the road Lily had spotted a man making his slow way along the pavement towards them, head bowed against the driving snow, and got out of the car to intercept him. Intending to ask if he could tell them where they might find the local bobby, she had discovered he was the village baker and had been with the constable, Sam Butterworth, only minutes earlier.

'Sam got me to open the shop for a moment so that he could pick up a loaf of bread for an old lady who's been stuck in her cottage for the past couple of days,' the man had told her. 'He said he wanted to check on her to see if she was all right. I doubt he'll be home, but you can try his house. It's two doors along and you're sure to find Nora there. She's his missus.'

His words had been confirmed shortly afterwards by Nora Butterworth herself when Lily knocked on her door.

'It's Granny Murdoch he's gone to see. She's been all on her own, poor dear. Sam said he'd stay and chat with her for a while.'

A small, neat-featured woman, Mrs Butterworth's horn-rimmed spectacles gave her the appearance of a benevolent owl. She had shown no surprise at the impromptu arrival of her visitors and barely glanced at the warrant card Lily showed her before urging them to come in out of the storm. But her reaction on being introduced to the *Kriminalkommissar* had given Lily a moment to treasure and she had needed all her resources to keep a straight face. It was clear that Nora Butterworth had never met a Jerry in her life (and probably never expected to), let alone find one sitting in her front parlour. But she had rallied well, and after only a moment's jaw-dropping surprise had got them both settled in the room, where a fire was burning, and then brought them each a cup of tea.

'It won't be long now, sir,' Lily said as the Berlin detective resumed his seat. 'It'll blow itself out, you'll see. It said so on the wireless.'

'Forgive me.' Probst sighed. 'I'm being impatient. One cannot hurry nature. Tell me, Sergeant, if it's not an impertinent question, how old are you?'

'Twenty-seven, sir. And please call me Lil. Everyone does.'

A smile came to his lips. 'May I call you Lily rather?' he asked. 'It's such a beautiful name.' His glance took her in. 'Twenty-seven, and already a sergeant: that is most impressive. My daughter, Elise, was a little younger than you: she would have been twenty-four.'

He nodded, as though to assure himself of the fact, and then sat silent. Lily waited. *Would have?*

'She was a remarkable child in many ways. Gentle, always truthful, and much loved by her friends. But as war approached everything changed. Suddenly the voices around us were filled with hatred and we came to learn, slowly at first, but in time with certainty, that terrible things no one spoke of were being done to a whole people, some of them friends and formerly neighbours of ours. Yet somehow she remained herself. I often ask myself what she would have done with the rest of her life. I have a feeling she might have become a teacher.'

Lily knew she had to say something.

'Did she . . . was she . . . ?'

'. . . killed in the war? Yes, I fear so. She and her mother together: they both perished in an air raid. But I did not, as you see, for the simple reason that I wasn't there.'

'There?'

'At home with them, in Hamburg: I was in Berlin, on business, or so I told myself, but in truth I had felt the need of a break from the routines of daily life, which in wartime take on a grimmer aspect; like iron bars they lock us in the prison of our lives and we look in vain for relief. So a few days in Berlin and a chance to see old friends seemed like a good idea. I would return refreshed, I told myself, altogether a better person, more agreeable to live with. How easily we persuade ourselves of our good intentions.'

His expression had changed while he was speaking and Lily saw that he was suffering now, in the grip of some strong emotion.

'I had intended to be away for only three days, but at the last moment, just before I was due to catch my train, I was invited to attend a dinner where some of my closest colleagues from the past, men I respected, would be present. The temptation was too great to resist. I postponed my return to Hamburg by a day.'

Although the room was not unduly warm—the fire was a small one—Lily could see the drops of sweat on his brow.

'The first bombers came to Hamburg that same night. They arrived with little warning, but all the same the sirens would have sounded and if I'd been there, as I'd planned, I might have reacted a little quicker than my wife and daughter. I might have found some place of safety for us all; or, failing that, I would have died with them.'

Lily watched in horror as he covered his eyes with his hands, and they sat like that, in silence, for minutes on end it seemed.

'I was too late, you see . . .' Probst looked up. 'That was all I meant to tell you, and I can never forgive myself. If I had returned a day earlier as I'd meant to . . .' He shrugged hopelessly. 'As for the rest, forgive me, please, I did not mean to burden you with it.'

'No, don't say that,' Lily burst out. She could feel the tears running down her cheeks.

Probst looked at her in amazement. His blue eyes, like hers, were overflowing.

'What you were telling me,' she said, 'what you meant to

say was that you want to get where we're going as quickly as possible. Is that right?'

'You guessed that?' He looked at her in wonder. 'You understood me? Dear Lily, you remind me so much of my Elise. And yes, you are right.'

He bowed his head in affirmation.

'I can't help it. I fear for our friends. We must go on as soon as we can. I cannot be late a second time.'

23

'CRIKEY, SIR—YOU'RE RIGHT. Look at that!'

Baxter pointed his torch at a spot on the wall beneath the study window. Madden followed the direction of the beam and saw that the dark strand of telephone cable picked out by the light had been cut. They had been tracking the wire from the corner of the house, brushing away the snow that was banked up against the wall. The worst of the blizzard had passed, but there was still a strong wind blowing from the east and the snow they'd been clearing away was crusted with ice.

'Who'd do a thing like that?' Baxter bent lower to peer at the severed line. He glanced at Madden. 'You were expecting something of the sort, weren't you, sir? Tell me the truth: could it have been Mr Gonzales?'

'. . . who cut the line? It's possible. Whoever did it wanted to be sure there'd be no contact between the manor and the outside world.'

Baxter brooded on his words in silence.

'What's going on, sir?' he pleaded, frosty plumes of breath issuing from his lips as he spoke. 'Can't you tell me? Is this all to do with Madam? I know things aren't right. First Mr Gonzales goes off without a word, and now Mrs Holtz has disappeared too.'

Madden sighed. 'It's a long story, Baxter, and I haven't got all the answers. Also I'll have to consult with Mrs Lesage before I can speak freely about it. But I've a feeling she'll want you to be fully briefed. You'll just have to be patient.'

He slapped his gloved hands together. It was bitterly cold standing there in the wind, but he paused for a moment longer to look about him. Although night had fallen he could see that the sky was clear of clouds at last. Stars glittered faintly in the distance and the moon cast enough light to illuminate the snow-covered garden that stretched away beneath the terrace where they stood and the fields beyond it.

Suspecting that the line had been cut—the absence of any link with the world outside, despite the fact that the phones were working in Great Tew, seemed too much of a coincidence—he had first gone in search of Baxter and found him busy chopping wood in one of the stables. A strapping figure in the dim light shed by a paraffin lamp—he had dispensed with his jacket in spite of the cold—the chauffeur was plying his axe with the skill of a lumberjack, but stopped his work at once when he heard what Madden had in mind.

'I've got a feeling the phone line might have been cut. Can you show me where it is?'

Together they had circled the manor, and having located the spot where the cable from the telegraph pole linked up with the house had traced its course down to the bottom of the wall and then around to the front of the house, past a flight of steps leading from some French doors to a point beneath the study window where they stood now, and where the line finally vanished inside via a hole drilled in the wall.

Not wanting Sinclair burdened with the physical effort of plodding through the snow, Madden had left his former colleague facing the almost equally testing challenge of having to explain to Julia Lesage why they both feared for her safety.

'She won't want to believe that of Gonzales,' the chief inspector had predicted. 'If all you say is true she might well ask why he told her the sale had gone through when they had their row about the false letter.'

Madden had nodded his agreement. 'That's one of the rough edges I mentioned. I can only think it was intended to muddy the waters . . . to create confusion. But if so, it tends to strengthen the probability that it's Voss we're dealing with. He has always left a puzzle behind him, something that would complicate and delay police inquiries, giving him and his sister time to vanish.'

'But where could they have gone now, and in this weather?' Sinclair had not been persuaded. 'They've no transport.'

'Can we be sure of that?' Madden shrugged. 'Gonzales told everyone he walked here from Enstone. But did he? If he had a car parked somewhere in or near the village they could be well away by now. And if past experience is anything to go by, they'll have other identities already prepared for them to move into. But I'm only guessing, Angus. Who knows what they have in mind?'

'And the devil of it is we can't even alert the police in Oxford. The bloody telephone still isn't working.' Sinclair had been unable to contain himself.

It was at that point Madden had decided to settle at least one question by going outside to inspect the line. Turning his back on the house now he scanned the white expanse of moonlit garden below the terrace. Nothing moved there. All was deathly still.

'This cold gets into your bones, doesn't it, sir?' Baxter stamped his feet. 'Enough to freeze the balls off a brass monkey, if you'll pardon the expression.'

'I couldn't agree more,' Madden said. 'Let's go back inside.'

'What's your advice, then, Mr Madden? What should I do? Angus here has just finished telling me what you think Philip and Ilse were up to, if that's who they really are, and I've been rather short with him. Can they really have been putting on an act all this time? It's so hard to believe, hard and *hurtful*. But now you tell me the phone line has been deliberately cut. What am I to think?'

Julia looked at him.

'What am I to *do*?'

Madden had returned to find that their hostess had returned to the drawing-room in his absence and was occupying the same chair she had sat in earlier, while the chief inspector had moved from the sofa and was seated opposite her, on the other side of the hearth. From the look on his old friend's face he divined that their conversation had not been an easy one.

'It's plain that whoever cut the phone line wants to prevent you from having any contact with the outside.' Madden warmed his frozen hands at the fire. 'But instead of trying to guess who's behind it, or why Mr Gonzales and Mrs Holtz have both disappeared, I suggest we focus on practical matters and leave the rest until later.'

'At last some sensible advice.'

'We need to alert the police, even if it proves that everything Angus and I have been telling you is wrong, simply as a precaution. And you need to speak urgently to your estate agent in Lausanne. I don't know whether that can be done tonight, but even if you don't have his home telephone number it's possible the international operators can track him down. All of which means we must find a way of getting you—in fact, all of us, including Baxter and your maid—down to Great Tew, where we know the phone is working.'

'I couldn't agree more.' Her face lit up. 'How do you propose we do that?'

'I wanted to check with you first, but I think we should make a stab at driving down to the village in your car. I realize the road is choked with snow, but it might be possible. And even if it's not . . .'

'Yes?'

'Even if we get stuck, there's a way of getting around that.'

'I can't wait to hear it.'

'When I arrived earlier I noticed there was a sledge in the garage . . .'

'My *toboggan*!' Julia's cry was one of delight. 'Why didn't I think of that? Father bought it for me when I was a child. I think that's when I first fell in love with the snow. What a wonderful idea, Mr Madden. Do we even need to bother with the car? I think I could manage without it.'

'At night . . . are you sure?' Madden was dubious. 'It's freezing out. I think the car's a better idea, even if we only get part of the way.'

'Then why not wait till morning?' She looked to Sinclair for support. He glanced at Madden.

'What do you think, John?'

'I'd rather not.'

Something in his old partner's tone caused the chief inspector to look at him sharply.

'Surely it makes more sense,' Julia began, but Madden cut in.

'Not to me,' he said firmly. 'I feel the sooner you're out of this house, the better.'

'Oh, for heaven's sake!' She threw up her hands. 'I've just had Angus telling me my life might be in danger and now you are implying the same thing. I'm sorry, Mr Madden, but I simply won't accept that. I might just be persuaded to believe that Philip has concocted some devious scheme to defraud me. He knows how to charm, I'm well aware of that. But I won't accept that he's a murderer, either actual or potential. I know the man. It's not in him.'

'I'd like to believe you're right.' Madden spoke in a calm voice. 'But I'm forced to remind you that Heinrich Voss was credited with a similar talent for lulling any doubts his victims might have had. I'm afraid the signs point to him and Mr Gonzales being one and the same man and if that's the case I have to believe you're still in danger.'

'I can't see how. For one thing, I have plenty of protection at present.' She smiled. 'Your arrival here has been fortuitous, Mr Madden. Not only do I have you and Angus at my side, I've also got Baxter in reserve. And quite apart from that, if what you say is true, surely the fraud has been uncovered now and the miscreants have fled.'

'Again, I'd like to think so. But let's stop for a moment and consider the facts. Both Mr Gonzales and Mrs Holtz disappeared before I arrived, so it's odds on they don't know I'm here. If they haven't made a run for it—if they're still somewhere in the vicinity—they probably think you only have Angus with you, Angus and Baxter.'

Madden paused. He glanced at Sinclair.

'I've a good idea those pills of yours didn't disappear by accident, Angus. Did either Gonzales or Mrs Holtz know you were taking them regularly?'

'Both, I suspect.' The chief inspector pulled a face. 'Gonzales certainly saw me take one at breakfast. And Mrs Holtz knew about them. I might tell you, though, that I feel quite well at the moment.'

'But you haven't exerted yourself for a while, have you?' Madden turned to their hostess. 'I don't expect Angus has mentioned it, but it's important he takes these pills regularly.'

'Oh, Angus . . . you should have said.' Julia sent an accusing glance his way.

'But what I'm trying to say is that if this man who says his name is Gonzales is really Voss you might still be at risk,' Madden continued. 'I didn't want to tell you this, but in the case of one of his victims, a Mexican lady, he not only butchered her but also killed her servants, a maid and a cook, in the same manner, leading the police to think it was the work of a maniac. As a result it was some time before they discovered the true motive for the crimes.'

'So what you're saying is we might all be in danger?' Julia had turned pale. 'Though I can't help feeling you would have this man's measure.'

'I'm flattered you think so.' Madden smiled bleakly. 'But frankly it's something I'd prefer not to have to find out. And for all we know he may be armed. Our best move is to get you out of harm's way. I don't know where he is now—perhaps not far off. But when he realizes his prime victim has escaped he'll think only of saving his own skin, and with any luck it will be too late by then. Once Angus and I have got in touch with the police he and his sister will be caught in a trap, one from which there'll be no escape.'

'His prime victim!' Julia raised an eyebrow. 'You have a way with words, Mr Madden, but I take your point. And I'll follow your advice.' She reached for the bell push beside her. 'We'll set out for Great Tew at once, all of us. But first I must get changed.'

———

Madden, with Baxter at his elbow, scanned the empty stable yard. Sheltered from the wind, the ice-covered cobbles glinted in the moonlight.

'You checked all the stables, did you?' he asked.

'Each and every one, sir. It was when Madam told me to go outside to look for Mrs Holtz. They were all empty. There was no sign of her.'

'Is there anywhere else near the house where the two of them might have sought shelter: some place where they wouldn't freeze to death?'

'None I can think of. We've already looked upstairs.'

It was Julia who'd suggested the servants' quarters as a possible hiding place. Only three of the rooms on the top-most floor of the manor were presently occupied—by Baxter and the two maids. There were three more, two of them empty and the third assigned to Mrs Dawlish, the cook, who was yet to make her return from Bicester, where she had gone to visit her daughter. Shown the way by Baxter, who had thought to arm himself with a golf club taken from a bag in the gun room—'just to be on the safe side, sir'—Madden had satisfied himself that none of the rooms, Daisy's and Mrs Dawlish's included, harboured the vanished pair.

'If you ask me, they legged it to the village,' Baxter said. 'Gawd only know where they are now. We'd better get ready. The sooner we're off, the better.'

Having heard Madden out, Julia had summoned both Baxter and Doris from the kitchen and advised them of her decision to go down to the village.

'There isn't time to explain,' she had told them, 'but there's a telephone call I must make—it can't wait—and Mr Madden and Mr Sinclair need to speak to the police urgently.'

'The *police*—?' Unable to restrain himself, Baxter burst out. 'What's going on, madam?' he had pleaded with his mistress. 'I know there's trouble in the air—the phone being cut and those two disappearing. Just tell me. Are you in any danger?'

'Not at this moment.' Julia had been touched by his concern. 'I have all of you to look after me. But both Mr Madden and Mr Sinclair think it would be wisest if we left the manor and went somewhere safe. None of us is sure exactly what's going on, but I find this whole business unnerving. I don't need to point out to you that this house is quite isolated and the thought makes me uneasy.'

Then, not giving them the chance to question her further, and having suggested to Madden that he and Baxter search the servants' quarters, she had directed Doris to accompany her upstairs so that she could change into warmer clothes. Silent all this time, Sinclair had listened to them with a long face.

'I'm nothing but a burden to you,' he'd complained to Madden. 'Do you really think Gonzales pocketed those damn pills of mine?'

'Either he or Mrs Holtz,' Madden replied. 'Did you leave them in your room?'

'To tell the truth I can't remember.' The chief inspector scowled. 'But since I didn't have them on me I must have left the bottle on the bedside table.'

'Where either one of them could have spotted it. They must have guessed by then that you needed them. Still, you're looking much better now for having rested.' Madden sought to encourage his friend. 'And I mean to keep you that way; otherwise, Helen will have my hide.'

Leaving Baxter to make his own preparations for departure, Madden returned inside to find that Julia, now in a pair of warm trousers and a heavy sweater, was back in the drawing-room with Sinclair. He learned that in his absence the chief inspector had gone upstairs to collect his things and also to pay a brief visit to Gonzales's room.

'I thought I might as well keep this as a souvenir.'

He handed the single cuff link together with the broken one to Madden, who took the pair over to one of the lamps to examine them.

'Angus showed them to me,' Julia said. 'They're just the same. I don't know what to think any longer. I thought I knew Philip. I was quite wrong.' She turned her gaze to the fire, now reduced to a few smouldering embers.

'Madam?'

Clad in her coat, Doris stood in the doorway.

'What is it?' Julia looked up.

'We're ready to leave.' The maid's eyes were bright. She seemed caught up in the excitement of the moment. 'I've locked the kitchen doors and turned out all the lights except the ones in the hall. We can leave by the front door: Mr Baxter's cleared a path from there to the garage so you can get there in your chair. He says there'll be room for it in the boot once it's folded.'

'Dear Baxter. He thinks of everything. Right, then— we're on our way.'

Julia set off across the drawing-room in her wheelchair with Sinclair and Madden at her heels. Pausing only to switch out the lights in the room, Doris followed them.

They waited while Sinclair donned his coat and then

Doris opened the front door and they filed out one by one. She locked it behind them.

'What a lovely night!' Julia looked up at the starry sky. 'But I don't care for this wind one bit.' She pulled the hood of her coat up so as to cover her ears.

Assisted by Madden she descended the shallow steps of the portico in her chair and then allowed him to wheel her across the rough path that had been cleared through the snow towards the garage, where the doors were open and the lights switched on.

'Baxter, are you there?' Julia called out, but there was no response.

'He said he was going to the stables to get something,' Doris murmured at her elbow.

When they reached the garage, she and Madden helped Julia from her chair and into the back of the big car. The boot was standing open and again with Doris's help Madden folded the wheelchair and put it in on top of the toboggan, which was already lying there.

'Where's Baxter got to?' Julia sounded impatient. 'Why don't you back the car out, John? When he hears the engine start he'll come running.'

With a nod of assent Madden settled behind the wheel. He waited until Sinclair and Doris had climbed into the back and then pressed the starter button.

There was no response.

He tried a second time, but with the same result.

'Please God it's not the battery.'

He got out and went to the front of the car to release the catch on the bonnet.

'Perhaps it's just cold,' Julia called from the back.

Madden peered into the engine.

'Oh, no!'

Sinclair struggled out of the backseat to join his old colleague.

'What is it?' he asked.

'Look . . .' Madden pointed. 'It's the distributor cap. It's missing.'

The space where the cap should have fitted was empty. The spark plug wires that should have fed into it were hanging loose.

'What is it, sir? What's wrong?'

Looking round, Madden saw the burly figure of Baxter. The chauffeur was standing in the doorway to the yard.

'Someone's taken the distributor cap,' he said. And then: 'What's that you've got there?'

'This?' Baxter looked down at the axe he was holding in his hand. 'I thought I'd better bring it with me, sir. I wasn't going to be caught without anything if we run into trouble. Did you say the distributor cap, sir?' Laying the axe aside, he joined them at the front of the car and stared down in dismay at the trailing wires. 'We can't go anywhere without that,' he muttered. 'Who did this?'

'I don't know.' Madden shrugged.

'Was it Mr Gonzales?'

Madden simply shook his head. He turned to Sinclair.

'We're stymied, Angus. We'll have to go back into the house.' To Baxter he said, 'Tell Mrs Lesage, would you? And you'd better get her chair out.'

The chauffeur was still staring at the loose spark plug wires. Shaking his head, he went to the back of the car and opened the door on Julia's side.

'Madam, I'm sorry. Someone's been messing with the car; it won't start.'

'That's all right, Baxter. Don't fret. It's not your fault.' Her voice was calm. 'Just bring my chair around here, would you?'

Sinclair and Madden stayed where they were, watching. Doris had remained inside the car to help her mistress out. For the moment they were on their own.

'Enemy action, would you say?' The chief inspector glanced at his companion.

'Without doubt.' Madden looked grim. 'He wants to keep us trapped in the house—or Mrs Lesage, at any rate. But what's he up to? What's his plan?'

He went to the door at the back of the garage, the one Baxter had come through, and scanned the yard outside. It was deserted. When he returned he found that Sinclair was staring at the floor beside him.

'What is it, Angus?'

'That chest . . .' The chief inspector pointed at the long wooden container that lay pushed up against the wall alongside the car.

'What about it?'

'It was open before.'

'Before when?'

'Yesterday, when I walked through here: there were tools inside. It was standing open, but now it's locked.' He indicated the heavy padlock that was fixed to the metal latch. 'I wonder why.'

'What is it?' The call came from Julia. Seated in her chair again, she had wheeled herself around the back of the car and was looking at them. Baxter stood at her elbow.

'It's this chest,' Sinclair replied. 'It was open yesterday, but today it's shut and locked.'

'Did you do that, Baxter?' Julia looked up at him.

'No, ma'am, I did not.' The chauffeur left her and came

over to where the two men were standing. He peered down at the chest. 'I never touched it. And that padlock lives on the shelf up there.' He indicated a wooden ledge fixed to the wall above. 'There should be a key to it. Hang on . . .' He ran his fingers along the surface. 'Yes, here it is!'

With the key in his hand he crouched down to open the lock. Tugging the latch free, he lifted the lid of the chest and pushed it back against the wall.

'Jesus Christ!'

Madden, with Sinclair at his side, peered into the chest. Stretched out on top of the tools was the body of a woman.

'That's Ilse Holtz.' The chief inspector caught his breath.

'*Oh, no!*'

The cry came from Julia. Thrusting her chair forward, she steered a path between the car and the wall until she'd reached the spot where they were standing.

'Oh, Ilse, my poor dear . . .' She stared in horror at the body.

Madden, meanwhile, had gone down on one knee to examine the corpse. The woman was lying on her back with her head twisted around at an unnatural angle. Out of old habit he touched her throat, feeling for a pulse he already knew would not be there.

'I'm so sorry, Julia.' He met her anguished glance. 'I'm afraid her neck's broken.'

24

LILY LOOKED UP. She could see a sprinkling of lights in the distance.

'It's not far,' she panted. 'We'll soon be there.'

Hans Probst's only response was a grunt. The Berlin detective had lost none of his sense of urgency—he was leading the way, setting a stiff pace—and though Lily was with him in spirit it was all she could do to keep up. Her shoes were the problem. The smart court shoes she was wearing had not been designed for tramping through the snow.

Stifling a groan, she looked about her. Although the blizzard had passed and the moon had risen, she wasn't able to make out much of the countryside around: only flat snow-covered fields and the dim outlines of trees, their long shadows marked like ink stains on the white surface beneath. It had still been light when they'd left Enstone, but the early winter darkness had set in quickly and before long Lily had found herself having to drive with extra care and keep a sharp eye out for patches of ice that showed up as flat, grey-ish circles in the beams of her headlights and to which she'd reacted by lifting her foot off the accelerator and resisting an impulse to put the same foot on the brake so that they could freewheel across them. She had recently taken an advanced course in driving—one of several ways that she'd sought to distinguish herself, reasoning that it was necessary, being a woman, to keep at least one or two steps ahead of her male colleagues at the Yard if she wanted to progress in the force, a strategy that so far had yielded dividends—but she had never encountered anything quite like the conditions she was faced with that evening.

Yet somehow she had coped, and they had passed through the hamlet of Little Tew without incident and were well on their way towards the larger of the two villages when disaster had struck.

And all on account of a blooming fox!

Breasting a slight rise, she had come on the animal standing in the middle of the road with its pointed ears pricked and its eyes shining bright in the headlights. It had taken Lily all of a second to realize what it was and another second to react automatically by swerving to one side. Even as she did so, the animal had leaped off the road and disappeared, but by then it was too late. When she sought to correct her mistake and bring the car back on course it had simply continued in the same direction, sliding on a patch of ice she hadn't seen at the side of the narrow lane they were following and then straight down the slippery slope into a bank of snow. Although no damage had been done to the car—they'd been going at a moderate speed, less than twenty miles an hour—Lily had found it impossible to reverse. Try as she might, she had only managed to cover a few feet before her spinning wheels lost their grip and the vehicle settled back in its original position buried nose-deep in the drift.

Forced to accept defeat finally, she and her passenger had climbed out of the car and studied the situation. Probst had been the first to accept the obvious.

'It seems we will have to walk the rest of the way,' he had said.

Tempted to express her frustration in somewhat stronger terms, Lily had managed to keep control of her tongue.

'You're right, sir. We'll have to leg it.'

What she hadn't realized, though, was how cold it would be out in the fields, exposed to the elements. Although the blizzard had spent itself—or at least moved on—there was still a frigid wind blowing and the air was full of flying snow and bits of ice that stung when they struck the exposed flesh of her cheeks. Lily had a coat equipped with a hood, which she had pulled up over her head, while Probst was sporting a fur-lined cap with flaps that came down over his ears. But somehow the wind found its way to the bits of her left unprotected, her nose in particular, and she was forced to plod forward with her head bent, keeping her eyes on the heels of her companion, who, lucky man, was wearing what looked like a stout pair of boots well suited to the conditions.

To add to Lily's woes there was the car to think about. It was the same police Ford Billy Styles had used to drive down from London in—she herself had come later by train—and, good bloke though he was, one of the few who had helped to advance her career in the male-dominated world of Scotland Yard, he would not be best pleased to learn what had happened to his transport; nor that, unable to locate him, Lily had taken it on herself to commandeer the vehicle for what was coming to look more and more like a harebrained mission.

Her only excuse—that she'd been talked into it by Hans Probst, a senior police officer to be sure, but unfortunately one who hailed from Germany—was unlikely to weigh much when her punishment was eventually decided by some disciplinary board, manned solely by men, which Lily was tolerably sure she would be summoned to appear before at some stage. Up to now her career had followed a charmed path; she had four commendations to her name, something almost unheard of at her age, never mind her sex, but that flawless record would soon be marred by a formal reprimand at the very least and might even lead to her losing her sergeant's stripes. It had happened before.

And as if that weren't enough, she was becoming increasingly concerned about their expedition, whether it even made sense.

'I'm just not sure how we're going to do this.' She had raised the question during their drive from Enstone. 'As I see it you want to get Mrs Lesage out of possible harm's way, and the same applies to Mr Sinclair and Mr Madden. But how can we do that without alerting this Gonzales bloke, who may or may not be Heinrich Voss? I mean, if he senses we've got his number, if he thinks he's in danger, there's no telling what he might do.'

'I'm aware of that.' Probst had nodded calmly. 'We must tread carefully. And before anything else we must determine whether in fact he is there, at the house.'

'Yes, but we can't just turn up, can we?' This was what was really bothering Lily. 'What's Mrs Lesage going to think? We've got to have a reason for calling on her.'

'That would certainly be of help.' Her words had brought another judicious nod from her passenger. 'I shall be more than content to go along with anything you can think of, Lily.' He had smiled at her.

And thank you very much, Lily said to herself. The ball was back in her court and there it had stayed and she had no idea what to do with it.

All she could do was to keep walking.

25

MADDEN STOOD IN THE OPEN DOORWAY of the garage and watched as Baxter, with his heavy overcoat buttoned up and a woollen cap pulled down over his ears, started down the drive. He was carrying a torch in one gloved hand and his trusty golf club in the other.

'Just in case I run into him on the way,' he'd confided to Madden. 'I know Madam doesn't want to say so, but I reckon that Mr Gonzales has got some explaining to do. What did he think he was doing running off this way, and just when Madam needs him?' He shook his club to add emphasis to what he'd just said. 'I might as well tell you there've been some funny things going on in this house these past few days, sir, and it's clear now who was behind them. If you ask me he's scarpered.'

'You may be right, but we'd better not jump to conclusions.' Struck by Baxter's haggard expression—it seemed the sturdy chauffeur was finally starting to wilt under the shock and strain of the past few hours—Madden seized the opportunity to cut him short. 'The important thing now is that you get down to the village as quickly as possible. We have to report Mrs Holtz's death to the police. You're sure you have it all straight in your mind?'

'I think so, sir.'

'Let's go through it once more. As soon as you get there

you're to ring the Oxford police. I've given you the number.
Try and get hold of the station commander. He's a superintendent called Maxwell. If he's not there, then ask for the
senior officer on duty. Tell him there's been a murder here.
Explain who Mrs Holtz is and then say you're calling on
behalf of Chief Inspector Sinclair. It's important you mention his name. Tell him Mr Sinclair believes there's a dangerous man at large in the vicinity and he's concerned for Mrs
Lesage's safety.'

'Madam's *safety*, sir? You never said that.'

'That's because I'm not sure it's true.' Madden had done
his best to calm him. 'But I want them to know how seriously we regard this business. You must tell them Mr Sinclair
thinks it's vital they get some police officers here as soon as
possible and to get in touch with Inspector Morgan and Inspector Styles. You've written those names down?'

'I have, sir. Morgan and Styles.'

'They're either at the Banbury police station or on their
way back to Oxford. I don't know whether they're in a radio
car, but every effort should be made to intercept them and
direct them here. It's possible the bobby at Enstone can help.
He should certainly be alerted to what's happened here. And
there's one further thing I haven't mentioned yet. In some
ways it's the most important.'

Madden had paused to lend extra weight to his words.

'They are to be told that it may concern a man called
Voss.'

'I beg your pardon, sir.' Baxter's eyebrows had shot up in
astonishment. 'Who did you say?'

'Voss is the name.' Madden had spelled it out. 'You don't
need to write it down. You'll remember it. But it's vital they
pass that on to Mr Morgan and Mr Styles.'

'Voss, you say?' Baxter repeated the name. 'Very well, sir, but can you tell me who he is?'

'Not now. There isn't time. In fact, we're wasting precious minutes. You must hurry up and get down there and then come back as quickly as you can. You're needed here.'

'Don't you worry, sir, I won't waste a moment.'

He had set off at once and Madden stood in the doorway of the garage waiting until his swiftly striding figure had disappeared into the darkness.

The decision to send for the police had been taken earlier at Sinclair's prompting when the whole party had returned indoors from the garage.

'It's not just Mrs Holtz's death that has to be reported: it's also clear that an attempt is being made to isolate this house and the people in it.' The chief inspector had sent a meaningful glance Julia's way. 'We can't have that. Someone must go down to the village at once and alert the authorities.'

Baxter had been quick to volunteer, but Sinclair had wondered whether he was the right man for the job.

'Wouldn't it be better if you went, John?' he had suggested. 'No offence, Baxter, but Mr Madden was a policeman himself once. He can explain better than you what's going on here.'

'No, let Baxter go.' To the chief inspector's surprise his old colleague had disagreed. 'And he must ring the police in Oxford.' He had turned to the chauffeur. 'We'll give you the number and tell you what to say. But you'd better go and get ready now. There's no time to waste.'

'Ma'am . . . ?' Baxter had looked at Julia for confirmation and she had nodded.

'Yes, do that. And, Doris, will you bring us something to eat . . . sandwiches, I think, and a pot of tea.'

Julia had waited until the two servants were out of earshot.

'Is it possible?' She had looked at them both. 'Could Philip really have done this, murdered poor Ilse and then stolen . . . what is it again . . . the distributor cap? I must tell you I find it all but impossible to believe.'

'You have to think of him as someone else.' Sinclair had tried first to explain. 'Not as the person you thought you knew, but as someone quite different.'

'Could he truly have deceived me that way?'

'If he's Voss, as we fear, then he's had long practice at it.' Now it was Madden who took up the task. 'But there's nothing to be gained by trying to understand it. You'll only torment yourself. All we can do for the moment is to wait until Baxter gets back. I'll go and give him instructions now. With any luck it won't be too long before the police are here. Then we'll all breathe easier.'

In no hurry to rejoin the others, Madden remained in the garage after Baxter had gone. He wanted a few minutes to himself while he wrestled with the puzzle confronting them. Earlier he had thought that Gonzales and Ilse Holtz were working together, even that they might be Voss and his sister, Alicia, though this last had seemed unlikely. The presence of the murderous pair at Wickham Manor at the same time Angus Sinclair happened to be there had seemed to stretch the bounds of probability past breaking point. He had thought it more likely they were simply a pair of confidence tricksters whose attempt to defraud Julia Lesage had come unstuck, prompting them to flee.

Now, with the murder of Ilse Holtz, he was forced to

accept the possibility that Gonzales and Voss were one and the same man. Mrs Holtz's role had been no more than that of a faithful employee. Her decision to slip out of the house without anyone knowing and make her way to the village had presumably been prompted by a need to get in touch with Julia's estate agent, Maurice Jansen. She had wanted to test Gonzales's story about their supposed meeting in Lausanne: whether indeed they had met and whether Jansen had denied writing the letter received by Mrs Lesage reporting a delay in the sale. Their argument the previous day suggested she thought Gonzales was lying. Whatever her reason for quitting the manor, however, it had resulted in her death. Gonzales himself had apparently gone down to the village at Julia's request to inquire about the telephone. But Madden knew from talking to the storekeeper in Great Tew that he'd not been seen there. It seemed likely now that he had lingered somewhere near the house, perhaps in the garage or in one of the stalls in the stable yard, uncertain what to do next until he caught sight of Mrs Holtz heading for the village and taken immediate steps to stop her reaching it, after which he'd had no choice but to hide her body.

Baxter's bluntly expressed view—that Julia's supposed admirer had simply 'scarpered'—might in essence be correct. Gonzales's scheme, whatever it was, had come unstuck and he'd been forced to cut his losses. Sabotaging the car's engine by removing the distributor cap had simply been a way of giving himself more time to escape. Madden had earlier suggested that he might have a car of his own somewhere nearby, perhaps in the village, and this now seemed even more likely.

But the crucial question remained, and Madden knew he had not yet found the answer to it. Was Philip Gonzales simply a confidence man who had got in over his head and committed a crime he would never have contemplated in advance and to which he'd been driven by the fear of exposure? In that case he would more than likely have fled. But if he was Voss then the murder of Ilse Holtz would of itself be no reason to abandon his plans and there was every chance that he would have stayed in the vicinity of Wickham Manor to complete what he'd set out to do.

But in that case why hadn't he gone ahead then with his presumed plan to bring matters to a bloody close? Why hadn't he returned to the house at once and dispatched the occupants? It seemed to Madden that if his earlier reading of the situation was correct—if Voss had managed to divert the money paid Julia Lesage for her house to an account he controlled, the only way he could be certain of securing it was to ensure that the person to whom it was owed was no longer in a position to reveal the fraud: in other words, dead. It was his modus operandi; it was how he had acted in the past.

Possibly the presence of Baxter, a formidable opponent and one devoted to his mistress, had deterred him, Madden thought, while his own unexpected arrival at the house not long afterwards—most likely observed—might have been enough to tip the balance and persuade the would-be killer that his scheme had gone irretrievably wrong, that he must abandon it and depart. But that was no more than a guess—and a hope.

As for Voss's sister, Alicia, it seemed she had played no part in the charade. But then more than a decade had passed since the two of them were known to have collaborated in a crime: the murder of Frau Klinger and her lawyer in Germany. Much could have happened since then. It was possible they were no longer together; it was possible she was dead. There had been a war in the intervening years, a conflict in which uncounted millions, most of them civilians, had lost their lives. Had she been one of its casualties?

These were questions to which he had no answers, but thinking of Ilse Holtz and the role he and Sinclair had wrongly ascribed to her reminded him of something they had not done earlier when the discovery of the unfortunate woman's corpse had prompted them to return Julia Lesage to the warmth of the house as quickly as possible so that she would not have to look at the body of her friend any longer. Now that he had the opportunity he opened the chest and made a quick search of the murdered woman's clothes; it yielded nothing beyond an empty used envelope addressed to Mrs Lesage and bearing Swiss postage stamps, which he found in one of her coat pockets. Not wishing to waste any time examining it—the light in the garage was dim—he slipped it into his pocket and, having closed the chest again, went out into the yard. As he crossed the icy surface he caught sight of Doris through the lighted kitchen window and when she saw him approaching she went to the kitchen door and opened it.

'I've been keeping it locked,' she told Madden as he came inside. 'I can't stop thinking about poor Mrs Holtz.'

She was clearly on edge, biting her lip as she turned away to collect a plate of sandwiches from the counter where she'd been working and lay it on the table with the cups and saucers and other tea things that stood ready there.

'Are those for us?' he asked.

She nodded. 'Madam wants to have supper in the drawing-room. Just sandwiches, she said. Now, where's that kettle?' She looked about her distractedly.

Madden indicated the silvery object he saw standing on a sideboard, but Doris shook her head.

'Not that one, sir, it doesn't work. We had to borrow Mr Baxter's . . . there it is.'

She fished the kettle she was looking for out of the sink and began to fill it with water from the tap.

'Do we really have to worry, sir?' She turned to look at him while the kettle was filling. Her eyes were wide and bright. 'And is Madam in any danger? If so, then Mr Baxter ought to be told.'

Madden made no response. He had fallen momentarily into a trance and he watched with empty eyes as she took the kettle out of the sink and plugged it in.

'Sir?' She awaited his answer.

'What?' Madden came to himself with a start.

'Ought we to be worried, sir?' She looked at him.

'No . . . no, I'm sure we'll be all right. You mustn't be concerned.' His mind was a blank.

'Could you tell Madam supper will be ready in a few minutes?' Doris turned back to the kettle.

'Yes . . . yes, of course.'

Still shaken—for a moment he had lost his bearings—Madden walked down the long corridor to the hall. He tried to tell himself that the thought that had struck him a moment before was nothing more than a fanciful notion brought on by an association of ideas with no basis in fact. Where had it come from? he wondered and then realized he knew only too well.

When he reached the hall he stopped near one of the tall standing lamps positioned about the cavernous room. Taking the envelope he'd retrieved from Ilse Holtz's body, he held it under the light. He had already noted that it was addressed to Julia and bore Swiss stamps: now, on closer examination, he saw that the sender's name, Maurice Jansen, together with the name and address of his company, ABC Immobilier, was printed in the top left-hand corner. The date stamp was November 25, some three weeks earlier, and Madden calculated that it must be the envelope that held the letter Julia had received on the same day she went up to London, the one that had informed her about the delay in the sale of her house.

Why hadn't Mrs Holtz thrown it away? he wondered. Why had she chosen to preserve it?

With a sickening sense that he already knew the answer, he turned the envelope over to look at the other side.

'God Almighty!' Unable to stop himself, he spoke the words out loud. It was just as he'd feared.

26

'ALL SET, THEN.'

Lily slapped her gloved hands together and stamped her feet. The pair of wellingtons she had on weren't a perfect fit—she could feel her feet still sliding about in them—but they were an improvement on the shoes she'd been wearing, which would never have coped with the deep snow they were going to have to plough through on their way up to Wickham Manor.

'I'm ready when you are, sir.'

She was doing her best to sound cheerful, though the more she thought about what they were bent on—she and Hans Probst—the less she liked it. The way Lily saw it they would either turn up at the manor only to find that all was well and this Mr Gonzales a perfectly kosher bloke—as far as con men went anyway—and would then have to throw themselves on Mrs Lesage's mercy since there was no way they could get back to Oxford that night, not with their car stuck in a snow drift.

That was the 'either'. The 'or' was much worse. Gonzales would turn out to be just what Commissar Probst feared—Heinrich Voss in disguise—at which point almost anything could happen, none of it good. Even if he was Voss he might have been biding his time and their arrival, together with the suspicions Probst harboured about him, could easily have the effect of setting him off and triggering an act of violence. It didn't seem to have occurred to her companion that the bloke might well be armed, and with something more than the knife that he'd presumably used on his other victims. All Probst seemed set on doing was reaching their objective as quickly as possible and to the devil with the consequences. Lily was ready to answer the call of duty if she had to, but she just thought they might have done better to wait until some reinforcements were on hand. As it was she'd left a message for Billy Styles with the Banbury police telling him where she and Probst had gone, and could only hope that he and Inspector Morgan would decide to join them there, preferably that evening.

The rubber boots she was wearing had come to her courtesy of the owner of the village store, a chap called Greaves, who they had encountered in the pub, the only establishment open when they'd finally reached Great Tew cold and footsore. Lily had taken it on herself to ask him if he knew whether a Mr Gonzales was up at the manor, and Greaves had replied that she was the second person who had asked him that—Lily assumed the first had been Madden—and that he still didn't know the answer to that particular question. As far as he knew, no one had come down from the manor that day. He had asked Lily if she and the gentleman she was with were planning to walk up there and when Lily said they were he had volunteered the opinion that the shoes she was wearing weren't up to the job.

'You'll need something more in the boot line, miss,' he had told her—he seemed to have taken a shine to Lily. 'Tell you what—I've got a pair of secondhand wellies in the shop next door. They're up for sale, but I'll lend them to you if you like. You can leave those shoes you're wearing behind as security.' He'd pointed at her footwear, grinning as he spoke. 'What do you say, miss?'

Lily had said yes, and she and Probst had trooped out of the pub after Greaves and waited until he had unlocked the door to his shop and switched on the lights inside, revealing an emporium that, far from being a mere grocery, seemed to stock all manner of articles along with the trays of fruit and vegetables on display and the shelves stocked with tinned goods. Probst's eye had quickly lighted on a pair of torches standing on their ends, but his offer to buy them had initially been refused by Greaves on the grounds that Sunday was not a day he was permitted to engage in trade.

'But I could make out the receipt for tomorrow,' he had added, with a wink, 'if you're prepared to overlook it.'

Assured that this deceit would remain a secret between them he'd been further encouraged to sell a pair of thick socks to Lily, which had gone some way towards alleviating the problem of the overlarge wellingtons.

Finally, equipped now for their trudge up to Wickham Manor, they had gone outside with the proprietor, who had pointed up the road and told them if they walked a bit further on they would find a sign directing them to their destination.

'There've been enough people up and down these past couple of days to leave a good set of tracks. Follow those and you can't go far wrong.'

Waving goodbye, he had disappeared back into the pub and Lily had proclaimed her readiness.

'All set, then.'

27

MADDEN STARED AT THE ENVELOPE. The evidence was plain, the implications chilling, and for a moment he felt paralysed. It took the sound of squeaking wheels to break the spell.

'Is something the matter, sir?'

Preceded by the tea trolley she was pushing, Doris had emerged from the corridor that led to the kitchen.

'You look like you've seen a ghost.'

It was all Madden could do to answer her. 'It's nothing.'

He took note of the inquisitive glance she sent his way as she went by. She had spotted the envelope in his hands.

'Would you ask Mr Sinclair to join me?' he said.

'Yes, of course, sir.'

He watched as she disappeared into the drawing-room and presently he heard voices, Julia's and the maid's, and then, after another few seconds, a murmur of assent from Sinclair.

'John?' The chief inspector had appeared in the doorway. 'What is it?'

Madden put a finger to his lips. He beckoned. Frowning, Sinclair crossed the paved floor to join him.

'Have a look at this.' Madden kept his voice low.

The chief inspector took the envelope from his hands. He held it under the light. 'I see it's addressed to Julia,' he said in the same muted tone, 'and from her estate agent by the look of it.'

'Look at the date stamp,' Madden said.

Sinclair squinted at the rectangle of paper. 'Posted three weeks ago: it must have been the letter she received just before she went up to London. Where did you find it?'

'In Ilse Holtz's pocket.'

'And?' Sinclair waited to be enlightened.

'How do you imagine it was opened?' Madden said.

The chief inspector studied the envelope again. 'In the normal way . . . with a letter opener I would say.'

'Now look at the back.'

Sinclair did as he was told. He saw that the flap had come loose from the paper beneath it and was barely attached to the body of the envelope.

'I see what you mean. It looks as though it's been tampered with, opened before it ever reached Julia.'

'And the letters switched.' Madden nodded. 'The one saying the sale had gone through was destroyed while another saying it had been delayed was put in its place and the envelope sealed up again, but not very securely.'

'Yes . . . yes, that would make sense.' The chief inspector weighed the envelope in his hand. He played with the loose flap. 'Steamed open, would you say?'

'Unquestionably.'

'By Gonzales?'

'I doubt it.'

Sinclair froze. 'What do you mean, John?'

'I think it was opened by someone in this house who has a kettle of his own.'

The chief inspector turned pale.

'My God, John! Do you know what you're saying? I happen to know Baxter has one. You can't mean him.'

'Think about it, Angus.' Madden's voice was deathly cold. 'It has to be one or the other of them, and while it's true Gonzales was here when this particular letter arrived, that was only by chance. Baxter lives here. He was in a position to open Julia's letters whenever he chose. The post is delivered in the kitchen and taken from there to Mrs Holtz in the study. I've a feeling you'll find it's he who assumed that responsibility. He more or less runs this place, after all.'

The chief inspector shook his head. He couldn't hide his dismay.

'But we still don't know where Gonzales is. It's quite possible he made a run for it.'

'After killing Mrs Holtz, you mean?' Madden's gaze offered no comfort; it was bleak as his tone. 'I have to tell you I find that hard to believe, Angus. In fact, if you want my opinion Philip Gonzales is no longer with us. He's gone the way of Mrs Holtz.'

Sinclair put a hand to his head. 'Dear God . . . poor Julia . . .' He cast an anguished glance behind him at the drawing-room door. 'You'd better tell me what you think.'

'I'll make it quick.' Madden kept his voice muted. 'It all has to do with the phone. If either Gonzales or Mrs Holtz had got down to the village and discovered it was working, the killer's plan would be scuppered. He couldn't afford to let them live.'

'You mean Baxter?'

'I mean Baxter. I'm not sure he wouldn't have murdered us all by now if the car hadn't been sabotaged. Do you remember he brought an axe with him into the garage when we thought we were leaving earlier? I couldn't think why. But if I'm right, once he grasped the situation he had to stop and think. If he'd killed us then and there he'd have been left with only a few corpses for company and no means of escape.'

'Succinctly put.' The chief inspector winced. 'So you don't believe it was he who took the distributor cap?'

Madden shook his head. 'I think it was Gonzales. He had already smelled a rat, but he thought it was Ilse Holtz who was trying to defraud her mistress. I think he removed the cap as a way of trapping her at the manor until he'd discovered the truth. If he'd found the phone working in the village he would have tried to call Julia's estate agent in Lausanne, probably to find out who the money for the house had been paid to. But he never got there: I know that for a fact.'

He paused, biting his lip.

'Assuming Baxter is Voss he must be close to cracking. Everything's gone wrong for him—his plan is a shambles. He's as much trapped as we are. By now he must have realized the cap was removed by either Gonzales or Ilse Holtz. For all we know he may already have searched Mrs Holtz's body.' Madden hesitated. 'Were you present when Gonzales left the house?' he asked. 'Did you see him go?'

'Julia and I were both here in the hall. We were talking.'

'Where was Baxter?'

'At the top of the stairs. He'd just found the nut that came off Julia's wheelchair when she fell—or said he had.'

'So he couldn't have followed Gonzales at once. He'd have had to catch him up on the road to the village. That's probably where he's gone now: to search the body, wherever it is; in the woods most likely.'

'Rather than call the police in Oxford as he was supposed to do.' The chief inspector nodded. 'And if he finds it, the distributor cap—what then?'

Madden shrugged. 'I wouldn't give much for our chances. We're dealing with a desperate man, Angus, and a hardened killer to boot. Don't let's deceive ourselves we're anything like a match for him. But Julia's the one he wants dead the most. We must get her out of the house and Doris too.'

'How do we do that?'

'Well, we can't leave until he returns; otherwise, we risk being spotted by him.' Madden pondered. 'Tell me, are there any other doors to the outside other than the hall and the kitchen?'

Sinclair thought. 'There's one at the end of the house off the gun room. It's as far from the kitchen as you can get, if that's any help.'

'It is.' Madden grunted. 'I'm going to meet Baxter when he gets back. I expect he'll tell me he's called the Oxford police and help is on the way.'

'Which may in fact be true,' Sinclair observed. 'You could be wrong about him, John.'

'In that case I'll feel like a damn fool.' Madden smiled for the first time. 'But that's a small price to pay.'

'What do you plan to do? You're not thinking of taking him on, are you?' The chief inspector was alarmed at the thought.

'Not for a moment.' Madden grimaced. 'He's got twenty years on me; and he must be as wary as a cat at this point. I can't surprise him. But I want to try and divert him. We need time to get away. Your job will be to persuade Julia she has to get out of this house. Tell her as little as possible and don't mention Baxter's name unless you have to. Just say we believe she's in imminent danger and we want to take her down to the village at once.'

'She's bound to ask how we mean to do that without a car.'

'I'm sure she will. But I've thought of something that might appeal to her.'

'What's that?'

'Tell her she'll be going by toboggan.'

Leaving Sinclair to attend to the thankless task he'd set him, Madden returned to the kitchen. Finding the room empty and the yard deserted, he was on the point of going to fetch Julia's sledge from the car when he saw the garage door open and the burly figure of Baxter appear. At the same moment the chauffeur caught a glimpse of him through the lighted window and raised his hand in a salute. With no choice but to respond, Madden unlocked the kitchen door.

'That was quick,' he said as the chauffeur came in.

'I was in luck, sir.' Breathing hard, as though he'd been walking fast, Baxter laid the golf club he was carrying on the kitchen table. 'I found Bob Greaves in the pub and we were able to go next door to his shop, where I made the call.'

'You spoke to the Oxford police, then?'

'I did, sir.' His cheeks reddened by the cold, Baxter held his hands close to the stove to warm them. 'The station commander had gone home, but I managed to get hold of the officer in charge. I didn't catch his name, but he recognized Mr Sinclair's all right and said he'd try to get hold of those two detectives.'

'Morgan and Styles?'

'That's right. But he didn't seem to have heard of the other fellow you mentioned.'

'You mean Voss?'

Baxter nodded. 'Who is he, sir? You didn't have time to tell me.'

Madden hesitated. Thus far he'd seen nothing in the chauffeur's manner to suggest he had anything to hide. Baxter's brown eyes were devoid of guile. But that meant nothing. If it was Voss he was talking to, the man had been at this game all his life, hiding his true nature, presenting a bland face to the world. He would need to probe a little deeper.

'He's a dangerous criminal, I'm afraid.' Madden watched for any change of expression on the other's face. 'I heard about him when I was in Oxford. He's thought to be living under a false name and there's been a report he might be somewhere in the area.'

'Is it the same chap Mr Sinclair was after?' The chauffeur's eyes had narrowed. 'He told us he was looking for someone.'

'It could be.'

'What's his game, then?'

'He defrauds women. They're his chosen victims. He steals money from them and then disappears.'

'Like Mr Gonzales, you mean?'

'That's what I'm not sure about.' Madden kept his tone neutral. 'You see, he usually kills his victims before he vanishes.'

Baxter pursed his lips in a silent whistle.

'But what about Mrs Holtz?' he asked. 'She was murdered, wasn't she?'

Madden was silent. Just then he had caught the first faint

hint of something new in the other's face; there was a different look in his eyes.

'Is that why *you* came here, sir, because of this man?'

His glance was cooler, more detached, almost calculating, Madden felt, and he silently cursed himself for prolonging their conversation.

'No, I was looking for Mr Sinclair.' He tried to sound natural. 'But I heard about Voss in Oxford and when I was told about Mr Gonzales disappearing in that way I began to wonder if there was some connection.'

It was a poor answer and he knew it. The feeling of tension between them was real now, almost palpable, and he felt a chill as he saw Baxter reach idly for the golf club that lay on the table beside him. Weighing it in his hands, he began to swing it to and fro. There was no overt menace in the action, but Madden knew he was in danger and that the threat was growing by the second.

'Actually there's something you could do for us,' he said quickly.

'What's that, sir?'

'We need more wood in the drawing-room. It'll be some time before the police arrive. Could you cut some and bring it in?'

Baxter's response was slow in coming; as the seconds passed in silence, to Madden they seemed to stretch into an eternity. He needed no one to tell him that the instincts of a man like Heinrich Voss would be razor-sharp. Had he detected something in their exchange that didn't ring true? For an instant the scales seemed to tilt that way and as he watched the golf club swinging to and fro in the chauffeur's hand, steady as a metronome, he got ready to defend himself . . . though how . . . and with *what*?

'Some wood, sir? Yes, of course.'

With a slight nod—suddenly once more the obliging servant—Baxter laid the club down and headed for the door.

'I'll tell Mrs Lesage what you've told me.' Madden found he was sweating. 'She'll want to talk to you herself, I'm sure.'

As the door shut behind the chauffeur's broad back he expelled his breath in a long, heartfelt sigh. Peering out through the window he saw Baxter's dark form disappear through the gate into the stable yard. If he himself slipped out now and crossed the inner yard to the garage it would be the work of minutes to retrieve Julia's toboggan from the boot of the car and bring it inside. But if the other man heard his footsteps on the crusty ice—and with an axe in his hand—all might be lost.

Abandoning the idea, Madden hurried back to the hall. He could hear the sound of voices coming from the drawing-room (Julia's louder than any: 'If you could just tell me *why*, Angus . . .') but didn't pause to listen further. Instead he went to the front door and opened it. The garage away to his left lay in darkness. But with the sky clearing and the moon up, he could see that the double doors were slightly ajar. Not wasting a second he crossed the snow-covered forecourt and slipped through the narrow opening.

The boot of the car was only a few steps away and without pausing he opened it and lifted the toboggan out. He barely had time to close it before the door at the other end of the garage opened and a bulky figure appeared. At almost the same moment the light in the garage came on. Clutching the toboggan under one arm, Madden ducked down. He heard the shuffle of footsteps, then a creaking sound that prompted him to lift his head for a second to peer through the Bentley's rear window. The hood at the other end of the car had been raised. For a moment at least he was hidden from Baxter's view, and seizing his chance he slipped out of the garage into the cold night outside.

Although every second was precious now, Madden stayed where he was for the moment. There was something he had to know, and, having laid his burden down softly in the snow, he risked a quick glance through the narrow aperture between the doors. He was rewarded by a glimpse of the chauffeur as he appeared from behind the raised bonnet with an axe in one hand and something else in the other, a small object not much bigger than a cricket ball, which Madden couldn't identify but which he deduced must be the missing distributor cap.

As he watched, ready to draw back if Baxter looked his way, he saw him lean the axe against the wall and then bend down to peer into the innards of the engine.

It was all he needed to see: the final proof.

Picking up the sledge he quickly retraced his steps to the front door, and, having shut it behind him, he turned the key in the lock. Only then did he notice that his hands were shaking.

'My God, you're serious, aren't you? You've got my to-boggan.'

Madden had barely set foot in the drawing-room when Julia Lesage turned her furious gaze on him. He caught Sinclair's eye. The chief inspector shrugged.

'First it was Philip and poor Ilse, now it's Baxter. I tell you I don't believe a word of it. Neither does Doris.' She glanced at the maid, who was sitting on the sofa, shaking her head in distress.

'Please . . . there isn't time to explain,' Madden pleaded with her. 'We must leave at once.'

'Where is he? Where's Baxter?' She ignored his words. 'I want to speak to him.'

'Busy.' Madden met her angry gaze. 'I've just seen him replacing the distributor cap in your car. It was removed by Philip Gonzales before he set off for the village. He thought you were being cheated, defrauded, over your house in Switzerland and wanted to stop the guilty person from escaping. He was right about the fraud, but wrong about the person. It wasn't Mrs Holtz, as he thought. It was Baxter.'

'Who is busy at this moment trying to get my car working?'

'With the distributor cap, yes, which he took from Gonzales's body.'

She tried to speak, but no words came. She had turned pale.

'Baxter had to stop him getting to the village and using the phone there. It was the same with Mrs Holtz. She also realized you were being robbed and wanted to discover the truth. I wish I didn't have to tell you this, Julia. If it's any consolation I believe they were both loyal to you.'

Somehow he had to put an end to their conversation. The seconds were ticking by. He had to find some way of persuading her to quit the house and for a moment it seemed his last words had had an effect. Though her gaze was still angry, the furrowing of her brow hinted at uncertainty.

'You're asking me to believe that Baxter killed them *both*?'

'You have to stop thinking of him as Baxter.' Unconsciously Madden echoed the same words Sinclair had used earlier that day, though with a different man in mind. 'His real name is Heinrich Voss. He's quite ruthless, a murderer several times over, and the only assurance I can give you is that if you don't let us take you away now, this very minute, you won't leave this house alive.'

She gasped then. His words had finally struck home.

'I don't know what to say.' She shut her eyes. 'How can I argue with you?' She opened them. 'You speak as though you know all the facts. I'm forced to follow your advice. But don't imagine for a moment that I'm convinced by what you've just said. I shall want proof. What do you want us to do?'

'We must leave by the side door, the one off the gun room. Baxter is busy in the garage, as I said. When he's done there he'll come looking for us. Doris, help your mistress into the wheelchair.' He turned to the maid, who seemed stunned by what she was hearing, incapable of movement. 'Now,' he said sharply.

With a start she jumped to her feet and hurried over to Julia.

'Is the gun room door locked?' Madden asked.

'Probably.' Julia had collected herself quickly. But her green eyes still held an angry glint. 'But the key should be in the door.'

'Angus, would you go down there and make sure?' Madden turned to his old partner. 'We'll join you shortly. And don't hurry. There's no rush.'

The chief inspector couldn't help but smile as he rose from his armchair to obey. 'Forgive me if I take that with a grain of salt,' he said as he went out. But although he was able to mask his anxiety, he couldn't fool his body and as he crossed the hall and started down the long corridor that went past Julia's study and the library beyond it to the end of the house he felt a stab of pain in his chest and immediately slowed his pace. 'Get a grip, Angus Sinclair,' he muttered to himself through gritted teeth. 'This is no time for a bloody heart attack.'

Julia meanwhile had donned her coat and was ready in her wheelchair. She'd been wearing a woollen shawl draped about her shoulders as she sat by the fire and she pressed the garment on Doris, who was dressed only in her maid's uniform with a sweater on top. 'It'll be cold outside,' she said.

Madden picked up the toboggan from the floor where he'd laid it. The sight brought a derisive smile to his hostess's lips.

'So . . . my carriage awaits.'

At his urging they left the room and crossed the flagged hall silently with Doris leading the way and Julia following close behind, propelling herself forward in her chair with hands and arms.

'It's a good thing I told Baxter to oil these wheels,' she remarked.

Bringing up the rear and carrying the toboggan—he was straining to catch any sound that might be coming from the direction of the kitchen—Madden drew what comfort he could, if not from her words, then from the cool tone in which they were uttered. There was no hint of a tremor in her voice and he reminded himself this was a woman who had sped down many a snow-clad mountain slope heedless of danger to life and limb, who must have nerves of steel.

Light was showing at the end of the dark corridor and when they got there they found Sinclair in the gun room awaiting their arrival. He had already unlocked the outer door, which stood open, and was engaged in donning the pair of wellingtons that Julia earlier had put at his disposal. As he rose to his feet Madden saw to his astonishment that his old friend was holding a shotgun in his hand.

'I thought we'd better take this with us,' the chief inspector said. He indicated the now empty gun rack on the wall.

'That won't do you much good.' Julia was scornful. 'We only have birdshot.'

Sinclair thrust two cartridges, which he'd dug from his pocket, into the twin barrels.

'Still better than nothing,' he muttered.

Hefting the toboggan, Madden led the way out and down a short flight of steps onto the snow-covered path below. It was the same one he and Baxter had used when they went to see if the telephone line had been cut and he knew it went round to the front of the house, where the chauffeur, if he was still in the garage, might very well spot them. For the same reason it would be too dangerous to take the road down to the village. It was the first place their pursuer would look for them once he realized they were no longer in the house.

'Is there a way we can take through the woods?' he asked Julia as he returned to the top of the steps to help her out of her chair and carry her down.

'Father and I marked out a trail years ago when I was a girl,' she replied. 'We had to cut down some bushes and sap-lings. It must still be there.' She weighed next to nothing in his arms and when he smelled the jasmine scent she wore he realized it was the same as Helen's.

The toboggan was one made for lying on full length and

before bringing Julia down Madden had taken off his coat and laid it on top of the wooden slats.

'You're being very gallant, Mr Madden,' she murmured as he lowered her gently onto the sledge. 'But you do realize that if you're wrong about this and poor Baxter has been maligned I'll skin you alive.'

28

LILY PEERED INTO THE DARKNESS ahead of them, though there wasn't that much to see: just the bone-white surface of the narrow lane they were plodding along, which showed the tracks left by earlier walkers who had made the journey to and from Wickham Manor earlier in the day, Mr Madden among them, or so she assumed. He had turned up in Great Tew that afternoon, according to Bob Greaves, the chap who had lent her the wellington boots that were proving to be such a godsend.

Quite apart from the challenge this Gonzales fellow they were after might pose for them, there was another matter troubling Lily just then, one she wanted to consult both Madden and ex–chief inspector Sinclair on. It had come to light a short while ago when she and Hans Probst had taken their leave of Greaves and were on the point of setting off from the village. At that point the German policeman had put his hand into his coat pocket and pulled out a pistol, a Luger of all things, at least as far as Lily could judge from the brief glimpse she had of it.

Before her astonished gaze—she'd been struck dumb by the sight—he had checked the weapon's mechanism, pulling the breech back with an oiled click, making sure that it was in order, before replacing it in his pocket.

'What's that you got there?' Lily had found her tongue.

'You can't go waving one of those around, not in this country.' And then, as though her words needed further explanation: 'We're not allowed to carry arms, you know, the police I mean, not unless it's authorised, and that doesn't happen very often.'

'I'm aware of that, Lily,' Probst had replied in a soothing tone. 'But we German police operate under different rules, and I thought it as well to bring my pistol along in case it's needed.'

'But . . . but you're breaking the law . . .' It was all Lily could think of to say. She knew that by rights she ought to arrest him, but she couldn't do that. It would turn what was already a dicey enough expedition into something resembling a farce, and she could see herself ending up not simply getting her knuckles rapped for misuse of a police car but actually on a charge, though for what she wasn't sure exactly, which was why she wanted urgently to seek the advice of two old coppers who, even if they were retired, were still held in high regard at the Yard and might come up with an answer to her dilemma.

'Yes, yes, I quite understand and you can be sure I will throw myself on the mercy of the authorities when the time comes.' He had patted her consolingly on the arm. 'But we may find ourselves facing an extremely dangerous man and having dragged you into this business I would never forgive myself if I let you come to any harm. And now let us be going. There is no time to waste.'

Flummoxed—short of actually putting the cuffs on her companion there was nothing more she could think of doing, or saying—Lily had swallowed her objections, which in any case were too numerous to list, and followed him as he set off. But she hadn't let the subject drop entirely.

'Have you ever actually shot anyone?' she asked as she trudged along in his footsteps.

'Not to my knowledge.' The reply was spoken breathlessly over his shoulder. The deep snow made for heavy going.

'To your knowledge?'

'I was a soldier in the war, Lily—not this one, the one before. We all had our rifles and we fired at the enemy and they fired at us. Who can say what we hit, if anything? In my case I hoped it was no one, and luckily for me, before I had time to turn into a battle-hardened veteran I was wounded, then captured, and finally spent the last two years of the war in a British prisoner-of-war camp.'

'Did you really, sir?' Lily was intrigued in spite of herself. 'Where was that?'

'Near the city of Carlisle—do you know it?'

'Can't say I do. That's to say, I've never been there. What was it like? How did you spend the time?'

'I learned English, since you ask, something I've never regretted. The language has been a great comfort to me over the years.'

Probst came to a halt. Lily stopped with him.

'What is it, sir?'

'I was wondering how much farther we had to go. That man we spoke to in the village said he thought the house was a mile away, did he not?'

'A little more than that, closer to a mile and a half, he reckoned.'

'Would you say we'd covered about a mile?' Probst's panting breaths were visible in the frosty air, as were Lily's.

'It's hard to say, sir. It feels like more, but that's because of the snow. It slows you down.' Lily herself was glad of the chance to pause and catch her breath. The road they were following went up and down like a switchback, but mostly up, so that each time they got to the top of a rise they saw another rise ahead of them, just a bit higher. She'd kept hoping they would see the lights of the manor ahead, but thus far the darkness around them had been unbroken, apart from the moonlight, which was a help as far as it went.

'We must keep going,' Probst said.

Lily followed. They were at the bottom of yet another rise and as they reached the top Probst halted again.

'What was that? Did you see it?'

Lily had caught a glimpse of the same flash of light some way ahead. One moment it had been there, the next gone.

'It can't be the house,' she said.

They stood in silence gazing ahead. After a few moments the light flashed again, but only for a second or two and then vanished.

'Could it be a car?' Probst said. 'If so, it seems to be coming our way.'

29

'Look! He's coming.'

Sinclair pointed a gloved finger. Turning, Madden saw there was a wash of light edging down the road from the gates of Wickham Manor. He switched off his torch. The car was travelling on a route parallel to the path they were on, but moving slowly as though the driver was keeping an eye on the narrow lane ahead of him, which must surely be buried in deep snow.

'Stop, everyone.'

He bent to check the forward movement of the toboggan he was towing. Sinclair, who was behind the sledge, halted at once, but Doris was not so quick. Taken by surprise she bumped into the chief inspector and then stumbled and fell to the ground with a sharp cry.

'Keep still.' Madden spoke sharply.

The maid got to her feet, whimpering. The events of the last hour—in particular the unmasking of Baxter—had been too much for her and she'd trailed along behind Sinclair sobbing quietly.

Following the directions Julia gave them—somewhat reluctantly, it seemed—they had taken a roundabout route so as to avoid showing themselves at the front of the manor, heading first towards the back and then turning off it through a gap in a low box hedge, which took them into a small ornamental garden cloaked in snow, where Madden had had to manoeuvre the toboggan along narrow paths decorated with statuary until they reached the far side where an expanse of open ground, possibly a lawn or a meadow, but like everything else covered with a blanket of white, met their eyes. There they had paused for a few moments while she got her bearings.

'Over there.' She had pointed to a small shed on the far side of the meadow. 'The path we cut starts in the woods just behind it. I haven't been down it for years. It may be overgrown by now.' She hesitated. 'I might as well admit I'm having second thoughts about this, Mr Madden. I should have known better than to let you talk me into it. You say you saw Baxter replacing the distributor cap; but you didn't ask him where he found it.'

'That was the last thing I would have done, seeing as he had his axe with him.'

'His axe?' She stared at him for a long moment. Then she shook her head. 'Well, we've come this far. We can't stop now.'

Before setting off Madden had picked up a short length of rope he'd seen lying in a corner of the gun room along with other odds and ends and tied it to the toboggan, whose runners at the front, curling back like ram's horns, were connected by a wooden bar. Using the rope as a tow he had pulled Julia along behind him and with Sinclair and Doris in their wake they had crossed the field to the shed, on the other side of which was a high brick wall with a gate in it.

'The path starts where the woods begin on the other side of the wall,' she had told them.

Before going through the gate Madden had glanced back at the house. Although the shed blocked his view of the front door he could see the garage and noted that the double doors had now been opened to their full extent.

'It looks like he's getting ready to leave,' he had murmured to Sinclair, who was standing beside him. 'But if I'm right he'll have business to take care of first. I'm hoping he'll spend some time searching the house before he realizes we've all gone.'

Safely out of sight on the other side of the wall they had halted again while Julia raised herself up on her elbows to study the line of trees in front of them, searching for the path she and her father had made.

'That way, I think . . .' She had gestured to their right and Madden had towed her across the snow for a short distance until she checked him. 'There it is.' She pointed to a passage between the trees that was clear of undergrowth and one by one they had entered the dark tunnel it presented.

Still dragging the sledge behind him—but without the aid of the moonlight now—Madden had taken out his torch and, holding it in his free hand, lit the way ahead in response to the directions that Julia gave him. Although the bushes had encroached in some areas the path was still navigable and as Julia's initial uncertainty over their route faded she had persuaded Madden to let her travel on her own on the short downhill stretches, using her weight deftly to steer the toboggan around any obstacles that appeared in front of her.

Madden had done his best to keep up, stumbling through the deep snow in her wake, until, remembering their companions, he had stopped to look round and saw Sinclair standing some way behind them with Doris at his side. The chief inspector had handed the shotgun he was carrying to the maid. He was clutching his chest and Madden could see he was breathing with difficulty.

'Angus, forgive me . . .' Madden was distraught. 'I should have realized.'

Calling to Julia to wait for them, he had hurried back.

'Look, if I need to stop, you must go on . . .' Sinclair gasped out the words. 'I'll catch up. The important thing is to see Julia safe.'

'I'm not leaving you behind, Angus.' Madden had waited until his old friend's breathing settled into a more regular rhythm. 'And that's final.'

'Those damned pills of mine . . . if only I'd taken proper care of them. I'll never hear the end of this from Helen.'

As Madden prepared to press on, the chief inspector pointed.

'Look. He's coming.'

Madden had watched as the headlights made their slow advance down the lane. The car was still some way behind them, but it would not be long before it caught up and drew level. Given that the moon was now shining brightly out of a clear sky, would they be visible through the trees?

'He's looking for us,' he said.

'Of course he is.' Julia had heard them. 'Has it occurred to you he might be puzzled by our disappearance?' she inquired.

Madden made no reply. Instead he had turned to Sinclair.

'Angus?'

'I'm feeling better. We must keep moving.'

The chief inspector's tone allowed no argument and they rejoined Julia at the bottom of the shallow slope, where Madden took hold of the tow rope again. Pausing for a last look back, he saw that the car had stopped: the headlights were still.

'What now?' As Sinclair spoke, the figure of a man appeared in the lights illuminating the road in front of the car. Although he was only intermittently visible through the trees, Madden saw him stop after a few steps and bend down to look at the snow.

'He's worked it out,' he said. 'He's realized you must be travelling on your toboggan.' He addressed the words to Julia. 'He's looking to see if there are any tracks in the snow other than the ones left earlier.'

'Then he must know by now there aren't any fresh ones.' She had raised herself on her elbows and was peering through the trees.

As they both watched, Madden saw the man straighten and turn to face the woods.

'He knows we're here. Keep still, everyone.'

He waited as the man walked back towards the car. As he moved out of the bright beam in front of the car he vanished. Next moment the headlights went out.

'He's coming after us,' Madden said. 'We must hurry.'

30

LILY WATCHED AS THE LIGHTS ahead of them flashed on and off. Probst had guessed right. There was a car coming their way, its headlights disappearing from time to time as it followed the switchback course of the narrow lane.

'We can talk to whoever's driving it,' she said. 'At least we'll find out what's going on up at the house.'

Hans Probst's grunt was noncommittal. 'This road is hardly usable,' he said. They were standing almost knee-deep in snow. 'I wonder what is so urgent that someone has to risk driving on it.'

Lily shivered. They hadn't seen a soul since they'd left the village and entered the woods, not that she'd expected to. And it hadn't been too bad while they were moving—the effort of trudging through the snow was enough to keep anyone warm—but now that they were standing still she felt the wind keenly.

'Let's go on and meet whoever it is,' she said.

Her words brought another grunt from the Berlin policeman. He seemed disinclined to move.

'I think the car has stopped,' he said.

It was true. The headlights had vanished a few seconds earlier and hadn't reappeared.

They walked on, following the tracks in front of them,

planting their feet in the footsteps already cut in the snow. But after only a few minutes Probst halted again.

'What's that?' He cupped a hand to his ear.

Lily had heard it too. 'It's the car,' she said. From the low hum of the engine it seemed to be running in low gear. 'It's getting nearer.'

Probst made a noise in his throat; it sounded like a growl. 'I don't like it,' he said.

'Neither do I,' Lily admitted. 'He's running without headlights.'

As she spoke a dark form took shape on the lane up ahead of them. It was still some distance off but coming closer.

'It might be best if we got off the road,' Probst said. 'At least until we see who is driving it.'

He got no argument from Lily. Although she could think of no reason, innocent or otherwise, why anyone should drive down an almost impassable snow-choked road with his headlights turned off, what she did sense was something menacing about the slow approach of the vehicle.

'Do you think he's looking for someone,' she asked, 'someone or something?'

With one accord they moved off the road and, having retreated a little way into the trees, they waited as the car drew nearer. They could see it was sliding from side to side in the deep snow, its wheels spinning, and as it passed by they saw there was a man behind the wheel. But Lily could make nothing of his appearance in the few seconds his dark silhouette was visible to them and soon they could only watch as the back of the car receded down the narrow lane, continuing at the same slow crawl until it came to a bend further on, where it stopped.

The door on the driver's side opened and a man climbed

out. Heavy-shouldered, his figure was made larger by the coat he was wearing and although it was too dark for Lily to see his face in any detail she knew from his size and general appearance that it wasn't either John Madden or the chief inspector she was looking at.

'Do you think it's Gonzales?' she whispered to her companion. Probst could only shrug.

As they watched, the man walked around to the other side of the car and opened the door there. He leaned in for a moment then came out with something in his hands. At first Lily couldn't make out what it was. But as he turned to stride off into the trees, he hoisted the object onto his shoulder and she saw what it was.

'He's got an axe with him,' she said. 'What's he want with that?' And then: 'I don't reckon he's here to chop wood.'

Probst made the same growling noise in his throat as before.

'It would be best if I followed him. Wait here, Lily. I will deal with him.'

'*Deal* with him?' Lily didn't like the sound of it. 'What does that mean, sir?'

By way of a reply, the Berlin policeman took his pistol out of his pocket and showed it to her.

'With this, if necessary,' he said. His voice was steady, and Lily could find no reason to argue with him, not any longer. The bloke in the woods had an axe. That more or less settled matters, for her at least.

'Is he following us?' Julia asked. She had raised herself up on her elbows so that she could keep an eye on the path ahead.

'I think so. I'm not sure. He seems to have left the car on the road, but where he is now I couldn't say.'

Madden spoke between panting breaths. It was hard enough pulling the sledge along the snow-cloaked path. It would be even harder if they had to leave it and strike out into the woods where the ground was uneven and the undergrowth dense in places. He was toying with the idea of making a sudden change of direction and heading for the road. If Baxter had picked up their trail it might deceive him long enough for them to cover the last half mile or so to the village without being caught. Thinking that the chauffeur would have a torch with him, Madden had refrained from using his own for some time and at his urging Sinclair had been keeping a close watch for any sign of Baxter. As yet he'd not seen so much as a flicker of light, but Madden didn't believe for a moment that their pursuer had given up hope of catching them and he feared for his old partner, whose laboured breathing and tortured look belied his repeated assurances that he was bearing up under the strain of their desperate flight.

With the rope looped over his shoulder, he pushed on as quickly as he could; he'd been hoping for some time to catch sight of the village lights, and when he came to a long rise, one which Julia was sure to want to slide down on the other side, he paused at the crest to survey the route ahead. At the foot of the slope he saw that the path was partially blocked by a holly bush that had spread its branches to the point where they brushed against a gnarled oak tree facing it. Finding a way for the sledge through its prickly branches would be difficult and time-consuming and he looked for a way around the obstacle. Behind the tree the ground fell away steeply, making it all but impossible to manoeuvre the

toboggan that way. But the other side looked more promising. The ground there was flatter and beyond it he could see
a clearing that prompted him to wonder again if it mightn't
be wiser for them to head for the road. As he stood there,
undecided, something else caught his eye. It was lying in
the middle of the clearing, half-hidden by the surrounding
tree trunks and dark against the white of the snow. In the
shape of a cross, it had seemed to him at first to be part of a
fallen tree, the trunk lying flat on the snow with a pair of
branches projecting on either side like outstretched limbs.

Looking at it, he felt a chill.

'Wait here,' he said.

Quitting the path, he struggled through the banked-up
snow, sinking almost to his thighs as he stumbled into a hidden gully just short of the clearing, and then having to clam-
ber up the other side to reach what he had already guessed
was the body of a man. It was lying faceup with the eyes
open and staring and the lips drawn back in a rictus of agony.

Though he had no doubt who it was, he paused long
enough to unbutton the man's overcoat and slip his hand into
the jacket pocket, where he found a wallet containing several
visiting cards with the name Philip Gonzales printed on
them. The small clearing was open to the sky and in the cold
light of the moon he could see there was a dark stain the size
of a dinner plate spread across the man's shirt front.

Apart from brushing the staring eyes shut, there was
nothing he could do and he wasted no time in rejoining the
others. When Sinclair sent a questioning glance his way Madden simply nodded. His old colleague would understand. It
was Julia who spoke.

'It's a body, isn't it?' she said.

He handed her one of the visiting cards and shone his torch on it for a moment. 'I'm so sorry, Julia.'

'How was he killed?' Her voice was calm.

'Stabbed, I believe. There wasn't time to examine the body.'

Twisting around on the sledge, she cast a lingering glance behind them.

'How could I have been so deceived?'

'I can't answer that question. I don't know anyone who can. We must keep moving.'

'Is he following us?'

'I think so. I'm not sure. He seems to have left the car on the road. But I've no idea where he is now. If we could just get to the village . . .'

His words had no effect. She continued to stare back down the path.

'Well, I'll tell you one thing, he won't get the better of me,' she said, and he heard the steel in her voice.

'How are you, Angus?' he called to Sinclair.

'Well enough.' The chief inspector's haggard face and ragged breathing belied his words.

'Doris?'

There was no answer from the maid beyond a smothered sound that might have meant anything. Huddled in the shawl her mistress had given her, she was standing behind Sinclair, who had retrieved the shotgun from her and was cradling it in the crook of his arm.

'You'd better stay here with Julia,' Madden said as the chief inspector came forward with halting steps to join him. 'There's a bush blocking the path ahead. I'm going down to see if I can find a way through it. Keep that shotgun handy.'

Without waiting for a response he set off down the slope.

It was steeper as well as longer than the others they had encountered and twice he stumbled and almost lost his footing on the slippery surface. When he got to the bottom he paused to take stock of the challenge before him. The branches of the holly had spread more thickly than he'd realized and it took him more than a few seconds to pick a way through them with his gloved hands. He was still caught in the bush, the prickly leaves clinging to his tweed jacket, but able to peer through them now, when he saw something that caused him to freeze where he was.

There was a man standing in the path not twenty yards away. Though only a dim figure in the semidarkness, Madden could see he had an axe in his hand, the head resting on the snow as he bent down to study the ground. Without warning he looked up suddenly, and the moonlight fell on his face.

It was Baxter.

Trying desperately to pierce the darkness ahead of her—she was in a section of the wood planted with pines, where the moonlight hardly penetrated—Lily ploughed her way through the deep snow. She was still kicking herself for having listened to Hans Probst; she had let him go off, pistol in hand, on the trail of whoever it was who had that axe and might very well be Gonzales, leaving her behind—to do what? The Berlin detective had spoken with such authority that Lily hadn't thought to question the order. What irked her now was that she'd let him get away with it. He had left her behind in relative safety while he took the risk of going in search of a cold-blooded murderer who wouldn't hesitate to add another name to his list of victims.

She was a copper, wasn't she? She had a job which she'd always known might one day put her in harm's way. Plus the bloke who'd given her the order was (a) not even British, and (b) carrying a firearm, which he shouldn't ought to be doing. Her place was at his side, or even better in front of him so she could assess the situation and decide what to do next.

Her mind made up, Lily walked as quickly as she could down the lane to where the car was parked and, having picked up the tracks left by Probst and his quarry, had set out to follow them into the woods. But despite the bright moonlight, somewhere along the way she had lost the trail and after spending precious minutes trying to pick it up again had settled for walking in what she thought was the general direction that Probst and the other bloke had taken—away from the road—in the hope that she would catch sight of one or the other of them at some point.

Coming out of the stand of pines and back in an area that was better lit, she cast about for any sign of the pair she was pursuing, but she could see nothing stirring. After only a few more paces, however, something caught her eye. She had just stepped over a fallen log and had her gaze fixed on the ground in case there was another one waiting to trip her up, when she saw some marks in the snow that brought her to a halt.

Two parallel lines were showing in the white surface right at her feet, and beside and between them there were footmarks. She saw at once that the lines must have been made by a sledge, or something of the kind. They ran in both directions, but the footmarks were definitely headed downhill, towards the village. She remembered that the lady of the manor, Julia Lesage, was in a wheelchair and, knowing that, it wasn't hard to put two and two together. She had had to leave her house in a hurry, or so it seemed, and she had company, which Lily could only hope included John Madden and the chief inspector.

And the man driving the car, the man with the axe, seemed to be tracking them . . .

The sound of a gunshot brought Lily's train of thought to a sudden halt. It appeared to come from close by, and without hesitating for even a moment she set off down the path, following the sledge tracks, running as fast as the clumsy wellingtons would permit and praying she would get there in time . . . though in time for what?

Afraid he might have been spotted, Madden held his breath, but the chauffeur showed no reaction to his presence and it was clear after a moment that he hadn't spotted him through the dense foliage. Watching him as he examined the path for any sign of footprints—or perhaps tracks left by the toboggan—Madden understood he'd misread the man's intentions. Baxter hadn't left the car on the road behind him. Instead he had driven on with his headlights switched off until he was sure he had overtaken the party, then come across through the woods to cut them off.

As the grim realization took shape in his mind, Madden started to move backwards, carefully extracting himself from the clinging branches of holly, trusting to the dim light to hide any movement that might catch the chauffeur's eye. Free at last he turned and struggled up the long slope behind him to where he could see the outline of Sinclair's figure standing beside the sledge.

'He's down there . . . he's coming our way.'

Gasping out the words he drew the chief inspector back a few steps so that he couldn't be seen from below. 'You'd better let me have that.' He took the shotgun from him.

'Can I do anything?' Calm as ever, Julia looked up at him.

Anguished at the thought that he had no sure way of protecting her from the threat that was drawing closer with every second—they couldn't flee and they couldn't turn back—Madden was lost for words.

'I assume that's a no.' She seemed amused.

'No, wait—take this.' He thrust the shotgun into her hands. 'I know it's only birdshot, but if he comes anywhere near you, aim at his face.'

'A capital suggestion . . . I shall bear it in mind.' Weighing the weapon in her hands, she considered the possibilities coolly and, having made up her mind, raised herself up on her elbows and rested the barrel of the gun on the bar linking the two runners at the front of the toboggan.

Madden cast about for a fallen branch, any sort of weapon, but the snow-covered ground about them was pristine, bare of any object, wood or rock, that might be of use.

'Listen . . .' Sinclair put a finger to his lips.

The sound of someone climbing the slope on the other side broke the silence that had fallen on them. Madden could hear heavy breathing.

'Doris!' Julia spoke in a low hiss. 'Go back. Find another way down to the village. This doesn't concern you.'

'Ma'am?' The maid came to life.

'Do as I say . . . hurry.'

'You too, Angus,' Madden said. He was down on one knee now beside the sledge, keeping as low as he could. 'Get off the path. Find a tree to hide behind . . . anything.'

'Thank you, John, but I prefer to remain.'

Sinclair's breath came in ragged gasps. With an effort he copied what Madden had done, lowering himself painfully onto the ground. Glancing behind him, he saw Doris making her stumbling way back up the path. Head bent, she looked round for a moment, but then went on and after a moment disappeared into the darkness.

The sound of breathing was closer now. As he waited Madden's mind went back in a sudden lurch to his time in the trenches, to the moments when he and the men he was with had waited—on the very edge of eternity, it seemed—for the whistle that would send them up the ladders and over the top into the murderous fire of the enemy's machine guns, moments that had seemed to last a lifetime . . .

It was the chauffeur's head that appeared first, his features barely visible in the half-light. Then the top half of him came into view. He was looking down, watching his footing as he struggled up the last few steps of the slope. When he glanced up, the first thing he saw was Madden's face and he raised his axe at once, lifting it with both hands, and at the same moment Madden threw himself forward, driving his shoulder into the chauffeur's chest.

Baxter's roar of fury was lost in the blast of the shotgun. Carried forward by his impetus, Madden knocked his assailant off his feet and the two of them tumbled down the slope, rolling over and over.

'Did I hit him . . . did you see? Angus, give me another cartridge . . .'

Sinclair crawled forward until he was able to peer over the top of the hill.

'They're both down. There's what looks like blood on the snow. John is moving, but he's hurt . . . it's his head, I think.' The gasped words cost him a huge effort.

'Can you push me?' Julia said. 'Just to the top so I can see.'

The chief inspector crawled back through the snow until he was behind the toboggan. Still on his knees he leaned his weight into it and felt the sledge budge a few inches.

'That's right . . .' Julia urged him on.

He went on pushing, a few inches at a time. The pain in his chest was like a vise; it seemed to tighten with every breath.

'That's good . . . I'm there.'

The sledge was at the top of the crest and he stopped pushing. But then, as though in a dream—his eyesight starting to blur—he saw Julia catch hold of a root projecting out of the snow at the side of the path and pull herself forward another few inches. As he watched she hauled herself over the crest on her sledge and vanished down the other side.

Stunned, Madden struggled to regain his senses. During their slide down the hill when he and Baxter had been locked together he had hit his head on some hard object, a rock perhaps, hidden by the snow, and he could feel the blood trickling down from his temple. He had lost consciousness for several seconds, and when he came to, he had found the chauffeur lying in the snow only a few feet away. Stark in the moonlight he could see the pool of blood spread like a black stain about his head. Baxter had put a hand to his eye, and when he took it away Madden saw there was only a dark hole where it had been. Julia's aim had been deadly.

Just then the chauffeur stirred. He raised his head and fixed his single eye on Madden. Grimacing, he began to climb to his feet. Madden did the same, and as he regained his footing and stood swaying, still not sure of his balance, he saw the axe lying close to where they were at the foot of the slope. Baxter had seen it too, and before Madden could move he hobbled over to it with limping strides and picked it up.

'Put that down, Voss. It's over.'

Madden could see that the man's injured eye was a welter of blood. It dripped down his cheeks and into his mouth.

'Over for you.' Baxter's bloodied face wore the hideous leer of a circus clown. Resting the axe on his shoulder he began to hobble towards Madden.

'There's no point any longer. You've failed. Don't you see?'

Madden circled away from him, keeping his distance. The chauffeur's actions were slow and faltering. Out of the corner of his eye he saw something move at the top of the slope. He hoped it wasn't Sinclair. He might be able to protect himself, he thought, at least keep out of Baxter's reach while the chief inspector dragged Julia to safety, if he had the strength. But he feared his old friend might be coming down to help him and he prayed that wasn't the case. Then he saw, with alarm, that Baxter was recovering. He was moving more surely now, feinting this way and that, trying to catch his opponent off guard.

Driven slowly back, Madden felt the touch of thorny leaves on his neck. He would have slipped through the holly bush if he could, but he knew he'd be tangled up in the branches, offering his attacker an easy target. Dimly in the darkness he saw there was something moving down the slope.

'God, no!'

The words were involuntary, but they stopped his attacker in his tracks: for a split second Baxter stood still, head thrust forward, eyes narrowed as though trying to read Madden's expression, to deduce what his sudden cry meant.

It was the hiss of the runners on the snow, the low whistling note they produced, that alerted him finally—though by then it was too late. As he looked back, the bar at the front of Julia's toboggan caught him squarely on the calves of his legs and he collapsed with a howl of pain.

Madden sprang forward. Driving his heel onto the sprawled man's wrist, he wrenched the axe from his hand.

'Julia, are you hurt?'

He had only caught sight of her at the last moment as she sped down the slope, hands gripping the runners on either side, steering the sledge unerringly like an arrow straight at her target. The collision had flung her off it and she was lying facedown on the snow. But after a second she raised her head.

'Not in the least.' She wore a smile of triumph. 'I've never felt better.'

She turned her head then to look at Baxter. The chauffeur was reaching down with one hand to feel his leg.

'Is the beast tamed?' she asked.

On hearing her words he glanced her way and she took in his blood-streaked countenance and ruined eye.

'My word, Baxter, you don't look at all well.'

Madden looked down at the wounded man.

'Don't move.'

He showed him the axe and then went to where the sledge was lying upside down in the snow. Righting it, he began to pull it towards Julia, but stopped when he saw what was happening. In the few seconds his back was turned the chauffeur had got onto his hands and knees and was crawling to where she lay. Madden dropped the rope he was holding, but before he could move from the spot Baxter lunged forward. Pinning the struggling woman to the ground, he reached into his coat and drew out a knife.

'Stay where you are,' he snarled at Madden. The long-bladed weapon was pressed to Julia's throat.

'Don't listen to him, John,' she called out.

'Shut your mouth . . . madam.' Baxter drew the sharp point across her throat. A dark line appeared on her skin, marking its track.

'Do you think I'm afraid of you?' She laughed in his face. 'Bowing and scraping all this time just so you could get a chance to rob me. Go on. Cut my throat if you dare. If he does, John, crack his skull in two. Then throw his body into my compost pit. That's all he's fit for . . .'

She was silenced abruptly as Baxter clamped his hand to her mouth. Rolling over, he sat up, keeping a hold of her and then gripping her head tightly against his chest with one hand while he kept the knife pressed to her throat with the other.

Madden, not daring to move, could only watch.

'Listen to me, Baxter.' He spoke in the kind of voice he might have used to quiet a savage dog. 'That eye of yours . . . you need to see a doctor. I'll get you to one as quickly as I can, I promise.'

'Too kind . . .' Baxter coughed up blood. 'But I'd rather stay where I am.' He caressed the white throat with the edge of his knife. 'And you're quite right. All good things come to an end. But one can still take whatever pleasures life offers, even in one's last moments. Don't move—!'

He had seen Madden edging forward.

'I'll tell you when I'm finished. Or rather, you'll know . . .'

It was the way he said it as much as the words that warned Madden. And even if Baxter hadn't spoken he would have seen it in the man's face as he pulled Julia's head back with a sharp jerk so that her white throat was fully exposed.

'*No—!*'

Madden's cry was drowned by the sound of a shot. Not a shotgun blast, though—it was the crack of a pistol, and he saw the top of Baxter's head explode in a mess of blood and brains and watched as he toppled over backwards into the snow, lifeless.

As Julia freed herself from his grasp, a man wearing a fur cap appeared from the shadows beside the path. When he moved forward into the patch of moonlight illuminating the scene, Madden saw it was Hans Probst. The Berlin policeman held a pistol in his shaking hand.

'I lost my way in the woods,' he gasped. 'Then I heard a shot and I feared I was too late.'

Lily was on her knees when she heard the gun go off. It wasn't like the one earlier; it sounded more like a pistol.

'Don't worry about me.' Sinclair gasped out the words.

Lily had been trying to get him to his feet. Running down the path, she had come on the chief inspector lying on his side in the snow, breathing in short gasps. He had told her to leave him there.

'I just need to rest. Go on, go on . . .' He had pointed to the top of the small hill they were on. 'Madden's in trouble . . . they both are.'

She ran to the top of the hill and looked down the other side. There were two bodies there at the foot of the slope— she could see that much in the moonlight—but who they were she had no idea. It was only when she was hurrying down the slippery incline that she spotted—with huge relief—Madden's tall figure. He was standing in the shadows holding something in his hands, and when he moved into the moonlight a second later she saw it was an axe. There was a shorter, fur-capped figure beside him that she knew must be Hans Probst.

And yes—the *Kommissar* had that bleeding pistol in his hand and there were two people lying in the snow. Now it was just a question of which one of them he had plugged and how she, Lily, was going to explain it to her superiors.

Neither of the two men had noticed her impending arrival. Tossing the axe aside, Madden walked over to what Lily saw was a sledge lying in the snow. There was a rope attached to it and he pulled it closer to the two bodies. As one of them moved, Lily heard a woman's voice and realized it must be Mrs Lesage. Well, thank heavens for that, she thought as she started down the slope.

But then something happened that drove all else from her mind.

A second woman, who must have been hidden from her sight by the trees at the side of the track, suddenly appeared. She was wearing a housemaid's black dress and had a shawl draped over her shoulders. Madden had pulled the sledge over to where Mrs Lesage was lying and was helping her into it with Probst's assistance. Neither of the men had noticed the figure walking, or rather stumbling, towards them.

Later Lily would say there was something off about the scene, something not quite right, and instinctively she quickened her pace and hurried down the slope. She was still a dozen or so paces back when she saw the woman bend down and pick up something from the snow. It was only when she lifted it onto her shoulder that Lily saw it was the axe, and only when she broke into a shambling run and headed straight for the group clustered about the sledge that Lily realized what was about to happen. The woman had the axe raised above her head now and was bent on braining someone.

She sprang into action. Though hampered by the boots she was wearing she managed to gain on the woman, whose uncertain steps were even slower than hers, and at the same time let out a yell warning the two men, who looked up in time to see who was bearing down on them—and to see Lily, too, launch herself forward in a dive, clipping the heels of their attacker so that she tripped and fell facedown with the head of her axe buried in the snow only inches from Mrs Lesage's head.

Scrambling to her feet, Lily planted herself on top of the woman, who lay sobbing. Plucking the set of handcuffs she had attached to her belt, she fixed them to her captive's wrists.

'I don't know who you are, darling,' she panted, 'but you're nicked.'

31

'But how did Mr Gonzales know it was a fraud—that's what I don't understand.' Lily Poole chewed thoughtfully on her cheese sandwich. 'I read that letter you showed me from the estate agent in Switzerland, and I still can't see how he guessed.'

'I've wondered the same thing.' Julia gazed sadly into the fire. 'Poor Philip—I was so unkind to him after he accused Ilse.' She turned to Madden. 'What do you think, John?'

'We may never know.' Madden shrugged. 'But if I had to guess I'd say it was some sort of sixth sense that alerted him.'

They had gathered in Julia Lesage's drawing-room on their return from the village: Madden and Lily and Probst, and Angus Sinclair as well. The chief inspector was lying on the sofa in front of the fire wrapped in a blanket, drowsing for the most part, only half awake, but feeling better, or so he'd assured them, after swallowing two of his pills, the bottle that contained them having been discovered tucked under Doris's mattress.

Although he'd done his best to disguise the fact, he'd been in considerable pain earlier, breathing with difficulty, and his memory of the past hour or two was confined to a series of fragmented images as he'd tried to piece together what had occurred from the time he'd collapsed in the snow after seeing Julia disappear down the slope in her toboggan.

He remembered being loaded onto the sledge sometime after that and had wondered what had become of her, a mystery that was resolved when he'd awoken from a daze to find that Madden was carrying their hostess in his arms while he himself was being pulled along in the sledge by Hans Probst. It was only when they had reached the village that he had realized Lily was one of the party too and was bringing up the rear with her prisoner. And it was she who had filled in the missing parts of the story when she had come into the drawing-room before the others appeared, lugging a basket full of chopped wood to put on the fire. The chief inspector had been struggling to recall something he thought he remembered, but might have only imagined, and had turned to her for help.

'Am I right in thinking I heard Billy Styles's voice at some point?' he asked her. 'Is he here?'

'We ran into him and Inspector Morgan in the village,' Lily told him. 'You were asleep. I'd left a message for them with the Banbury police. Then soon afterwards some more coppers arrived from Oxford and after one of them had driven Mrs Lesage's car down so as to clear the road and a local farmer had used his tractor to cut a path for us, we all came up to the manor. Don't you remember, sir?'

'Only bits of it. I was drifting.'

She had sat down beside him for a few minutes. 'They'd gone up there to talk to some lady who'd told the police that a man who looked just like Voss's picture had broken into her house the other night. But after Mr Morgan grilled her she admitted it was really her fancy man who was there paying her a visit and who had legged it when her husband turned up unexpectedly.'

Lily shook with laughter.

'Anyway, as I say, they got my message and came straight over and joined us. Mr Styles found your pills when he went upstairs to search Doris's room. She hadn't said much up to that point, nor has she since, as far as I know. According to Mr Probst she's in what he called a catatonic state, whatever that might mean.' Lily shrugged. 'But she admitted she was Voss's sister and her real name's Alicia and she came over all queer at the sight of his body. Do you remember hearing her howl?'

'Howl?'

'Like a wolf. I've never heard anything like it.' Lily shivered. 'We had to drag her away.'

'But Julia's all right, is she? Mrs Lesage?'

'Right as rain.' Lily grinned. 'Baxter was threatening to cut her throat and she just laughed in his face, or so Mr Madden said.' She shook her head in wonder. 'She's upstairs now resting, but she'll be down later.'

'And where are Styles and Morgan?'

'They came up here with us to collect the body in the garage. What was the lady's name again?'

'Ilse Holtz.' Sinclair supplied the answer.

'Then they went back to the village to see to the other two bodies—the ones up in the woods—and take Doris to Oxford and put her in the cells. But they'll return tomorrow to get statements and so forth. Mrs Lesage has invited the rest of us to stay the night. She says she'd appreciate the company.' Lily blew out a sigh. 'I'm going to have some explaining to do myself,' she said.

'What do you mean?'

'Well, I knew Mr Probst had a pistol with him when he

shouldn't have had and then he went and shot Voss. Do you reckon I'm in hot water, sir?' She had looked anxiously at the chief inspector.

'Not necessarily.' Sinclair had given a few moments' thought to the question. 'The circumstances were exceptional, to say the least, and if you need any support Mr Madden and I will be pleased to speak on your behalf.'

'Thank you, sir, I appreciate that.' But Lily still needed to be reassured. 'Then there's the matter of Mr Styles's car. I ran it into a snowbank. It's still there, as far as I know.'

'Ah . . . now that's a serious matter.' He saw the expression on her face and smiled. 'I'm only joking, Lily. I doubt you've any need to worry. You're the one who collared Doris after all.' He yawned. 'Where's Mr Madden at the moment?'

'Outside in the yard chopping wood. He managed to find a spare axe.'

'Spare?'

'The other one's been impounded as evidence. Doris tried to brain him with it.' She rose to add another few logs to the fire and then brushed off her hands. 'I've got to get along to the kitchen myself and see if I can make us all something to eat. We're a bit short of servants as you know.' She grinned.

With her departure, the chief inspector had drifted off to sleep and only awakened when the others had joined him in the drawing-room for a belated supper.

'A sixth sense?' Julia asked.

Madden explained. 'I'm afraid Philip Gonzales was known to the Spanish and German police as a confidence man, by name at any rate. Hans learned it from his people in Berlin.' He glanced at the Berlin detective. 'I think when Gonzales read that supposed letter you got from the agent telling you there had been a delay in the sale, he sensed a fraud was in the offing and thought Mrs Holtz must be the guilty party. After all, she handled most of your business affairs.'

Julia reflected on his words. 'So what you're saying, in a nutshell, is that it takes one to know one.' She shook her head. 'What a fool I've been. I never suspected he might be after my money. I was totally taken in by him.'

'No, you're wrong, Julia.' To the surprise of all, it was Sinclair who spoke up. He'd been lying silent for so long they had thought him asleep. 'I truly believe he only wanted to protect you. That's why he went to Switzerland to talk to your agent. He knew something was wrong. I saw you two together, how he behaved with you, and whatever his original intentions might have been when he made your acquaintance, I think they changed. He became devoted to you. He would never have harmed you in any way.'

She turned to him. Her smile was tinged with sadness.

'That's very sweet of you, Angus. Thank you. And I shall always think of Philip that way. But as for Hieronymus Baxter! How could I have had that monster living under my roof for two years, together with his sister of all people? The joke is I've always thought of myself as a good judge of people.'

'Most of us do, if that's any consolation.' Madden smiled. 'And some of us live to regret it. But he probably traded on that. It was just a matter of never giving you any reason to suspect him, something he'd had plenty of practice at if his record is anything to go by.'

Sinclair stirred again.

'What John is saying, Julia dear, is that if you have a fault, and I'm sure you don't, then perhaps you're too trusting.'

She threw back her head and laughed, her green eyes

shining. 'On the strength of that, I think I'll have another glass of wine.'

Probst got to his feet at once, bottle in hand. In the absence of servants, it was Lily who had made the cheese sandwiches, Madden who had brought in a supply of wood for the fire, and Hans Probst who had opened two bottles of wine, retrieved from the cellar at their hostess's direction.

'Dear Herr Probst, I haven't properly thanked you.' Julia held out her glass. 'If it weren't for you I would be quite dead.'

The Berlin policeman received her words with a bow. 'Honesty obliges me to admit it was a lucky shot, dear lady.' He shook his head ruefully. 'I am nowhere near a good enough marksman to have risked aiming at his head when it was so close to yours. I intended to send a bullet past his ear, but close enough so that he could hear it whistle by. I remember from the war how the sound used to terrify me and I hoped it would cause him to let go of you. But I was out of breath from running and my hand was shaking.'

Julia couldn't contain herself. 'Are you telling me you only hit him by mistake?' She burst out laughing.

'I fear so.' Probst hung his head.

'Isn't that marvellous? And it only proves what I've always said about life. That it's just a question of luck. Let's drink to that, shall we? Good luck to us all.' She raised her glass, and the others followed suit.

Listening to his hostess, the chief inspector recalled something Madden had said to him earlier on their way back to the manor. 'She launched herself down the hill on her sledge without a second thought. She knew exactly what she was doing, the risk she was taking, but she didn't hesitate for a moment.'

She was one of those blessed with no fear of death, the

chief inspector saw, and he realized too that he did not share her cool courage. He had always thought he would be ready when the moment came, but lying in the freezing snow, gasping for breath, and with the pain in his chest growing sharper by the second, he had found himself clinging to life, no matter if it was only to be counted in minutes, and knew he was condemned to live with the memory from now on. It was there, waiting for him, the void . . . just a heartbeat away.

'Stop pretending, Angus. You're not dead. I can tell. You're breathing.'

Sinclair opened his eyes with a shocked start. He'd been in the middle of a dream populated by dark figures in an ice-clad forest.

'Good God!' he exclaimed.

'No such luck.' Lucy Madden's smile was serpentine. 'He's otherwise occupied. Open your mouth.'

'What—?'

She popped a pill in.

'No, wait . . . I've already had two.'

'Another one won't hurt.' Raising his head, she held a glass of water to his lips.

'Stop it . . . I don't want to . . .' His protests went unheeded; the pill slipped down his throat. 'But listen . . . you here . . . why?' He half choked on the words.

'I'm surprised you have the gall to ask.' Her smile vanished. 'You're supposed to be resting, so we won't prolong this conversation. But I'd better tell you now you've a lot of explaining to do. Honestly, I turn my back for five minutes and what do you do? Go off on the trail of some fiendish murderer. Don't try to deny it. Lily's told me the whole story.'

He wilted under her fierce gaze.

'And as for this last episode, which, if I understand right, ended with you lying in the snow unconscious—well, I simply don't know what to say. But Mother will, you can depend on it.'

The chief inspector shut his eyes. 'On reflection I think I'd prefer to be dead,' he said. 'Where's everyone?' He'd woken to find himself alone in the drawing-room.

'Mrs Lesage has gone to bed. We've been upstairs getting the rooms ready.'

The voice was Lily's. She had come in from the hall while they were talking.

'You and I are going to have to share,' she said to Lucy, who rubbed her hands together in glee.

'Oh, goody.'

'And there'll be no talking after lights-out.' Madden came in from the hall. 'Angus, we're going to take you upstairs to your bedroom,' he said. 'That mobile seat of Julia's is just the ticket. We'll put you on it.'

'You'll do no such thing.' The chief inspector bridled.

'Do you see what I mean, Daddy?' Lucy turned to her father. 'He's quite impossible.'

Footsteps sounded in the flagged hall outside. This time it was Hans Probst who came in. He was carrying a plate and a glass.

'I found a cold leg of chicken in the fridge, Miss Madden. And I brought you a glass of wine as well. Will that be enough?'

'More than enough . . . you are sweet.' She favoured him with her mother's smile. 'And Lucy, please, that's my name. It's such a pleasure to meet you. I've heard so much about you from Angus.'

'The pleasure is mine, I assure you.' He bowed gravely to her. 'I had no idea I would be so fortunate as to meet two lovely young ladies in such a short space of time: first Lily, and now you.'

'Oh, for heaven's sake!' Sinclair threw up his hands.

Lucy lifted an eyebrow. But she was too busy with the chicken leg to speak.

'Let's get moving, shall we?' Madden suggested. 'Why don't you get that seat down, Lily. You'll find the switch at the bottom of the stairs. Are you ready, Angus?'

The chief inspector glowered.

'Before that,' he said, 'would you mind just explaining to me what your daughter is doing here?'

'Oh, you'll have to ask her that. It's a mystery to me.' Madden chuckled. 'Let's get things ready, then.' He turned to go out into the hall.

'I'm here to lend a hand.' Lucy put her plate down. 'Isn't it obvious?'

'Not to me,' Sinclair growled. 'How did you get here?'

'I borrowed a car from a friend, if you must know, and drove down from London. It wasn't easy finding you. First I went to your hotel, but they didn't know where either you or Daddy were. In the end I had to telephone the police. They weren't happy about handing out information over the phone, so I had to go to the station in person and persuade them I was who I said I was. All in all, you've cost me a great deal of trouble, Angus.' She finished her wine.

'Yes, but to go back, you borrowed a car from a friend, you say?' The chief inspector smiled sweetly. 'A male one, I dare say.'

'Just what do you mean by that?' Lucy flushed.

'One of your swains, was he?'

'My *swains*?'

'One of the four or five husbands you're planning to have?'

'What?' Madden stuck his head through the doorway. 'What did you say? Four or five husbands?'

'It's all right, Daddy, it's nothing, pay no attention.' Lucy made a soothing gesture. 'Angus's mind is wandering. I'll give him another pill.'

EPILOGUE

'WHAT A MONSTER.' Helen shivered. 'If anyone had told me such a man existed, I wouldn't have believed it. What could have been going through his mind all those years?'

'Yes, and when does a man like that come to understand his true nature, at what stage? That's something I'd like to know. I wish Franz were here. I'd ask him.' Angus Sinclair scowled. He was thinking of the Viennese psychiatrist whose name he had mentioned to Ann Waites and remembering what Weiss had once said to him about the darkness of the soul. 'When did he first know who he was and what he was capable of? What do you think, John?'

With a gesture so familiar to the chief inspector from their years together that he might have predicted it, Madden put a hand to the scar on his brow. His thoughts had been running along similar lines. He had not forgotten the anguished moments he had spent facing Heinrich Voss in the woods below Wickham Manor, nor the knife that his assailant had wielded.

'It's only a guess, but when he murdered that student in Buenos Aires, I would say, and took all night over it.' Madden had his answer ready; it was something he had given some thought to. 'He used a long-bladed knife—the kind carried by the gauchos in Argentina, apparently. It's called a *facon*. Hans told me that. He said it was similar to the weapon

Voss threatened Julia with; in fact, he wondered if it wasn't the same one. Isn't that so, Billy?'

He turned to the younger man, who had come down to Highfield from London that afternoon at Madden's invitation so that he could give his former colleagues an account of the lengthy and complicated investigations which he and Hans Probst had overseen in their respective countries and which were now deemed to be complete.

'That's right.' Billy Styles nodded. 'He sent the police in Buenos Aires a photo of the knife and they confirmed it was the kind of weapon gauchos carry.'

'If Hans is right, then—if Voss kept it all these years—it must have meant something to him.'

Silence followed these words and Madden rose to poke the fire and put another log on it. Close on two months had passed since he and Sinclair had taken their leave of Julia Lesage, but they had kept in touch with her and she had recently accepted an invitation from Helen to spend a week in Highfield as the Maddens' guest when the weather improved.

'She said in her letter that she had engaged a new chauffeur,' Helen told her husband, 'but he was nowhere near as entertaining as the last one. I must say I can't wait to meet her.'

She got to her feet and filled their glasses from the wine bottle that was standing on the low table beside her.

'Tell us more, Billy,' she said as she sat down again. 'How did this Baxter or Voss, or whatever his name is, and his sister come to be hired by her?'

Billy frowned. 'It's hard to believe, but we reckon she caught his eye while she was still living in Switzerland. That's where Voss and Alicia spent the war, incidentally, living as man and wife. It's where they went after that business in

Berlin. The German police only learned recently that he'd acquired residence there some time before he murdered Mrs Klinger, the lady in Berlin, and her lawyer. It was how he'd always worked: carefully, planning everything in advance—and always having a bolt-hole to escape to. He had the same sort of setup arranged for after he'd done Mrs Lesage. I'll tell you about that in a moment.'

He took a sip of his wine.

'Voss had an apartment in Zurich. He told Mrs Klinger he had to travel a lot in his business—he claimed to be a financial consultant—but actually he just used to go back to Switzerland and stay there for a while.'

'Creating an identity, you mean?' Sinclair grunted. 'One that wouldn't be questioned later after he and his sister left Germany.'

'As far as Mrs Lesage was concerned, he probably spotted her as a likely victim after her husband was killed in a motor accident. It made quite a splash in the Swiss newspapers: rich businessman leaves crippled wife, famous skier in her day and so on. He couldn't very well move against her in Switzerland, where she was well established and had friends around her. But once she decided to return to England she became a potential victim. And her going back there fitted nicely into his plans.'

'How was that?'

'The identity Voss chose for himself and his sister when they settled in Zurich was British. People who knew them there said they always spoke English together, and that suggested to Hans and me that Voss was planning to go to England when the opportunity presented itself. They couldn't go back to Germany, and South America was out of the question too. There was always the chance the law would catch up with them. Given their background, England must have seemed their best bet, and of course they spoke the language. It would just have been a matter of working on their accents, I suppose. How did they sound to you, sir?' Billy glanced at the chief inspector.

'I really couldn't say.' Sinclair scratched his head. 'Like anyone else—I mean, there are so many different accents in England you'd have had to be an expert to place them. Now that I think about it, Baxter's did sound a touch artificial at times, but then he was playing the part of a man who thought of himself as a cut above the servant class, so that fitted easily into the impression he wanted to give. To go back to what you were saying about Julia returning to England, though, it's my understanding Voss didn't try to approach her for some time. She'd been living in Oxfordshire for nearly three years before she hired him, or so I was told.'

'That's right,' Billy agreed. 'We don't know exactly what Voss and his sister were doing at that stage, but it's likely they were busy setting up the false identity they were going to need later. They could afford to take their time; they weren't short of cash. Voss had an account with a Zurich bank in the name he'd used there with close to thirty thousand francs in it when he died.'

'So it wasn't only for the money.' Madden's voice carried a bitter note. To Sinclair, who was observing him closely, it was as though a truth he hadn't wanted to believe had finally been forced on his friend. 'It was at least as much for the satisfaction it gave him. I know Hans believes that. First gaining his victims' trust, then killing them. Was that what happened with the young man in Buenos Aires? They were part of a group, Hans told us. They might even have been friends. It's seems that hatred of his fellow man—or perhaps one should say woman—was rooted in his very being, and no one was safe from it. Except his sister, I suppose'—Madden shrugged—'or was she simply his creature, someone he could use?'

'What about his sister, though?' Helen spoke after a pause. 'Where does she fit in?'

'Hard to say, except it's clear she was under his thumb.' Billy answered the question. 'She still hasn't got over his death. The psychiatrist we got to examine her says she probably never will. And she's told us next to nothing. Apparently even her lawyer is having a hard time getting through to her. The trial's set for next month. I don't know what kind of defence he'll put up, but she'll be charged as an accessory to murder.'

'Will she hang, do you think?'

'I really couldn't say.' Billy tugged at an earlobe. 'As far as we know, she never actively took part in the killings. She might get away with life.'

'How did they both come to be working for Mrs Lesage?'

'Well, as far as Doris is concerned—I'll call her Doris—it was all quite aboveboard. Sometime after Mrs Lesage settled down at Wickham Manor one of the maids she'd hired quit, and not long after that she received a letter from Doris saying she had heard Mrs Lesage was looking for a maid and applying for the position.'

'How did she know that?'

'From her brother.' Billy's grin was mirthless. 'He was already working there. Voss had got his job as Mrs Lesage's chauffeur a few months earlier. Doris being hired as well was just a stroke of luck for him. It wasn't part of his plan, as far as we know. He probably thought he could carry his scheme off on his own. But it helped having her on hand.'

'Especially when it came to the letters,' Sinclair put in.

'The letters?' Helen asked.

'The post was always delivered to the kitchen and Voss would take it from there to Julia's study. He would have known that she was selling her house in Lausanne. She talked very freely to him—it's her way with everyone—and he probably spotted early on that the sale would give him his best chance to rob her. But he had to keep an eye on the post, in particular for any letters that came from her estate agent. Doris would have been a help there. I expect she gave them to him so he could steam them open. Thank heavens for that kettle! If John hadn't realized its significance . . .' He shook his head. 'But we've told you about that.'

'Yes, but how did *Voss* get hired?' Helen asked. 'That's what I want to know.'

Billy scratched his nose. 'Look, we don't know for sure, and it's a question that'll never be answered, but what we do know is that in the past he'd always played the part of a man ready to help widowed or otherwise helpless ladies with their business dealings and that wouldn't have worked with Mrs Lesage. She handled her own affairs with Ilse Holtz's help. What she did need, though—and always would—was a chauffeur, but unfortunately she already had one, a Swiss man called Pierre Bertrand who came to England with her. Both Mr Probst and I think Voss arranged for the position to fall vacant.'

'Arranged?' Sinclair scowled. 'According to Baxter he was run over by a van in Oxford.'

'So he was.' Billy smiled bleakly. 'It was a hit-and-run. The driver has never been found.'

'Good grief!' Helen was shocked. 'Do you mean . . . yes, you do!' She stared at him in horror.

'The simple truth is Voss needed to get close to Mrs Lesage, and being her chauffeur may have seemed his only option.' Billy spread his hands. 'Of course, he still had to persuade her that he was the right choice as a replacement, but as we know he was something of a charmer.'

He glanced inquiringly at the chief inspector, who nodded.

'Julia thought the world of him, and I could see why. I rather took to him myself. You'd think after thirty years as a detective I might have seen through him, but I didn't, and that's the truth. But then neither did Gonzales and he was a crook himself. He sensed something was wrong, but he never suspected Baxter was behind it.'

Helen rubbed her brow. She appeared shaken by what she had heard.

'I must get us all some supper,' she said, 'but before I do that, tell me how Voss planned to escape after he'd done the deed, Billy: where was this bolt-hole of his?'

'In the New Forest, in Hampshire: he bought it at some stage after he and his sister left Switzerland and moved to England. It's in a small village called Burnt Elm and the pair were known as George and Ada Bancroft. They didn't live there. As far as the villagers knew, they had a flat in Manchester, where George had a job in insurance. But they came from the south of England, or so they said, and planned to retire to their cottage one day. They paid one of the locals to keep an eye on the place and would turn up, sometimes together, sometimes only one of them, and make a point of looking in at the village pub, just to remind people who they were, I suppose.' Billy nodded to himself. 'Incidentally when we showed the villagers a photograph of Voss taken after death they weren't sure it was their George Bancroft, and it was the same with Ada, so they must have changed their appearance when they went there, at least enough to put people off the scent. It was probably something they were used to doing.'

'And so when Voss passed through Fernley and was spotted by Greta Hartmann, he was coming back from a visit to their cottage?' Sinclair put the question.

'Possibly,' Billy said, 'but he also paid a visit to Southampton just about that time. It was when Mrs Lesage went up to London. Voss drove her there and then went back to Wickham Manor to return the car. But he only stayed a day and then went to Oxford and hired another one from Alf Hutton, leaving a false name and address with him. He was on a holiday break and as far as anyone knew he was visiting his old mum in Suffolk, who didn't exist but was a useful excuse for when he needed to get away. But, like I say, he actually drove to Southampton and booked passage for himself and his sister on a liner to New York. They were due to sail at the end of January.'

'That meant he was getting ready to wind things up at Wickham Manor.' Sinclair nodded. 'No wonder he reacted the way he did when he ran into Greta Hartmann. He couldn't risk her telling anyone she had seen him.'

'That's what we thought, Mr Probst and me. That's why he killed her. And he must have been all set to do the same to Mrs Lesage as soon as she got back from London. The letter from the agent in Lausanne telling her the sale of her house had gone through and asking where she wanted the money paid came on the very day she was leaving. Voss must have opened it and realized he had to act fast. He destroyed the letter and wrote a substitute—we found a typewriter in his room—telling Mrs Lesage there'd been a brief delay in the sale going through and put it in the same envelope, the one with the agent's address and Swiss postage stamps on it.'

'And then wrote a second letter to the agent instructing him where to send the money? Is that how it worked? John thought so.'

'It was paid into a company account that Voss had set up with a bank in Bern,' Billy continued. 'More than a million francs—it's been recovered. Of course once Voss had done that he couldn't turn back. It would only be a matter of days before the fraud was discovered. He had to kill Mrs Lesage as soon as she returned from London.'

'But then fate intervened in the shape of one Angus Sinclair.' Madden came to life with a smile. He'd been sitting silent, lost in thought, it seemed.

'Will you stop that, John?' Sinclair scowled. 'You know very well I never suspected a thing. I was only there by chance.'

'And against doctor's orders,' Helen reminded him. 'It seems fate knew better than I did. But bear in mind, you very nearly came to a sticky end.'

'True enough,' the chief inspector admitted. 'But then if I had minded my own business at Fernley and come straight home, it would be Julia who'd be dead now.'

Sinclair allowed the silence that followed his words to linger for a few seconds. Then he spoke again.

'That fall she had on the stairs, though, you think that was Voss's doing?'

Billy nodded. 'I had a good look at both her wheelchairs. The nuts that held the brakes were tightly screwed on. I couldn't see how one of them would have come loose by itself.'

'She used to race around the house at speed.' The chief

inspector recalled the memory with a smile. 'She likes to take risks. It's in her blood. That played into Voss's hands. But he was overtaken by events. Yes, all right, my arrival certainly upset his plans. But then Gonzales appeared soon after, followed by you, John. And don't forget the snow: it may have seemed a blessing to him at first—it meant the house was cut off—but he soon realized it was equally a trap, one he could only get out of by using Julia's car. And when he discovered the distributor cap was missing, he must have been as close to panicking as he ever came.'

He reflected on what he'd said.

'Still, he reacted quickly enough. He'd already cut the telephone line, and he couldn't allow anyone from the house to reach the village, where the phones were working. That's why poor Mrs Holtz and Gonzales came to grief. They were both trying to find out whether that letter from the agent was genuine, both trying to serve Julia.'

Helen rose from her seat on the sofa. She ran her fingers through her hair.

'One final question: how was he planning to finish things, given that his scheme to fake an accident and kill Julia that way had come unstuck?' She hesitated. 'Though I've a feeling it's probably something I don't want to hear.'

Billy glanced at Madden.

'I know what you think, sir.'

Madden stirred in his chair. He'd stayed silent for the most part, content to let others hold the floor. But the chief inspector could see from his face that the memories called up by Billy's account of his investigation had left their mark on his old colleague.

'Well, as Angus said, his only way of escape was to take Julia's car. I'm sure he was planning to go off in it with Doris and then ditch it somewhere and make tracks for Burnt Elm. I was interested to hear that he booked passage for the end of January, six weeks ahead. He was cool that way. He knew the police would be checking all ports and airfields and he was careful never to look like a fugitive. It's one of the reasons he wasn't caught earlier.'

'Do you think he might have abandoned his plan to defraud Julia?' Helen asked her husband.

'Oh, no.' Madden didn't hesitate with his reply. 'He wanted the money all right, but that was only part of it. He'd had two years and more to think about what he was going to do and he wasn't going to be cheated of that. There was a moment when I was talking to him in the kitchen, when I already knew it was him and he all but sensed it. For just a second or two I saw it in his eyes: what he was going to do.'

He met his wife's questioning gaze.

'He meant to kill us all.'

They had a light supper in the kitchen together, and when the others retired to the drawing-room for a nightcap before going to bed, Sinclair excused himself. He had been staying with the Maddens at Helen's insistence since his return from Oxfordshire and he expected to remain there until the weather improved.

'I'm not going to go traipsing down to your cottage to see how you are on these cold winter nights,' she had told him firmly. 'I want you here under my eye.'

'Do you know, you sound just like your daughter,' the chief inspector had replied.

But he'd been more than happy with the arrangement and the room he went up to after bidding the others goodnight was the same one he had always slept in before acquiring his cottage when staying with them. It overlooked the garden that ran down from the front of the house to a stream at the bottom of the valley and he stood there at the window for some minutes gazing out over the moonlit lawn to the dark woods on the far side of the stream that in summer rose like a green wave from the valley floor. Several miles in length, it was called Upton Hanger, and for no rational reason he had come to love it, just as he loved this room and this house and the people it was home to.

The dark mood that had come over him at Wickham Manor, when he had been lying on the sofa in front of the fire and had fancied he felt death's cold hand on him, had passed. He no longer shrank from the thought of his end: it would come in its own good time. And meanwhile there was the summer to look forward to, when Hans Probst had promised to come over to England again and Lucy Madden was busily planning for the three of them plus Lily Poole to hire a car and play the part of tourists.

'He's such a sweet man,' she had told Sinclair, 'and it's so sad about his family. We must try and cheer him up.'

There was a knock on the door. Sinclair looked round and saw Helen standing there.

'I was just thinking about your daughter,' he told her, 'and what a good heart she has.'

'I must try and remember that the next time she does something that gives me grey hairs.' It was Lucy's smile he saw on her lips. 'Is everything all right, Angus? You left us in rather a hurry.'

'No, I'm fine, truly. I feel quite well. But there's a letter I need to write.'

'Can't it wait till tomorrow?'

'It could. But it's something I ought to have done already, something I promised to do, and after hearing what Billy had to tell us this evening I feel I can't put it off any longer.'

'Who is it to?' Helen was curious.

'A rather fierce lady I met in Fernley.' The chief inspector smiled. 'Her name is Vera Cruickshank.'

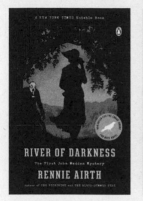 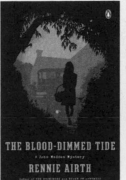